NANCY DREW DIARIES®

#7 "Doggone Town" and "Sleight of Dan"

Based on the series by
CAROLYN KEENE
STEFAN PETRUCHA & SARAH KINNEY • Writers
SHO MURASE • Artist
with 3D CG elements and color by CARLOS JOSE GUZMAN

PAPERCUTZ™
New York

KT-458-231

Nancy Drew Diaries
#7

"Doggone Town" and "Sleight of Dan"
STEFAN PETRUCHA & SARAH KINNEY – Writers
SHO MURASE – Artist
with 3D CG elements and color by CARLOS JOSE GUZMAN
BRYAN SENKA – Letterer
JEFF WHITMAN – Production Coordinator
BETHANY BRYAN –Editor
JIM SALICRUP
Editor-in-Chief

ISBN: 978-1-62991-462-6

Copyright © 2007, 2008, 2016 by Simon & Schuster, Inc.
Published by arrangement with Aladdin Paperbacks,
an imprint of Simon & Schuster Children's Publishing Division.

Printed in China
May 2016 by Everbest Printing Co. Ltd.
Nansha, China

Distributed by Macmillian
First Printing

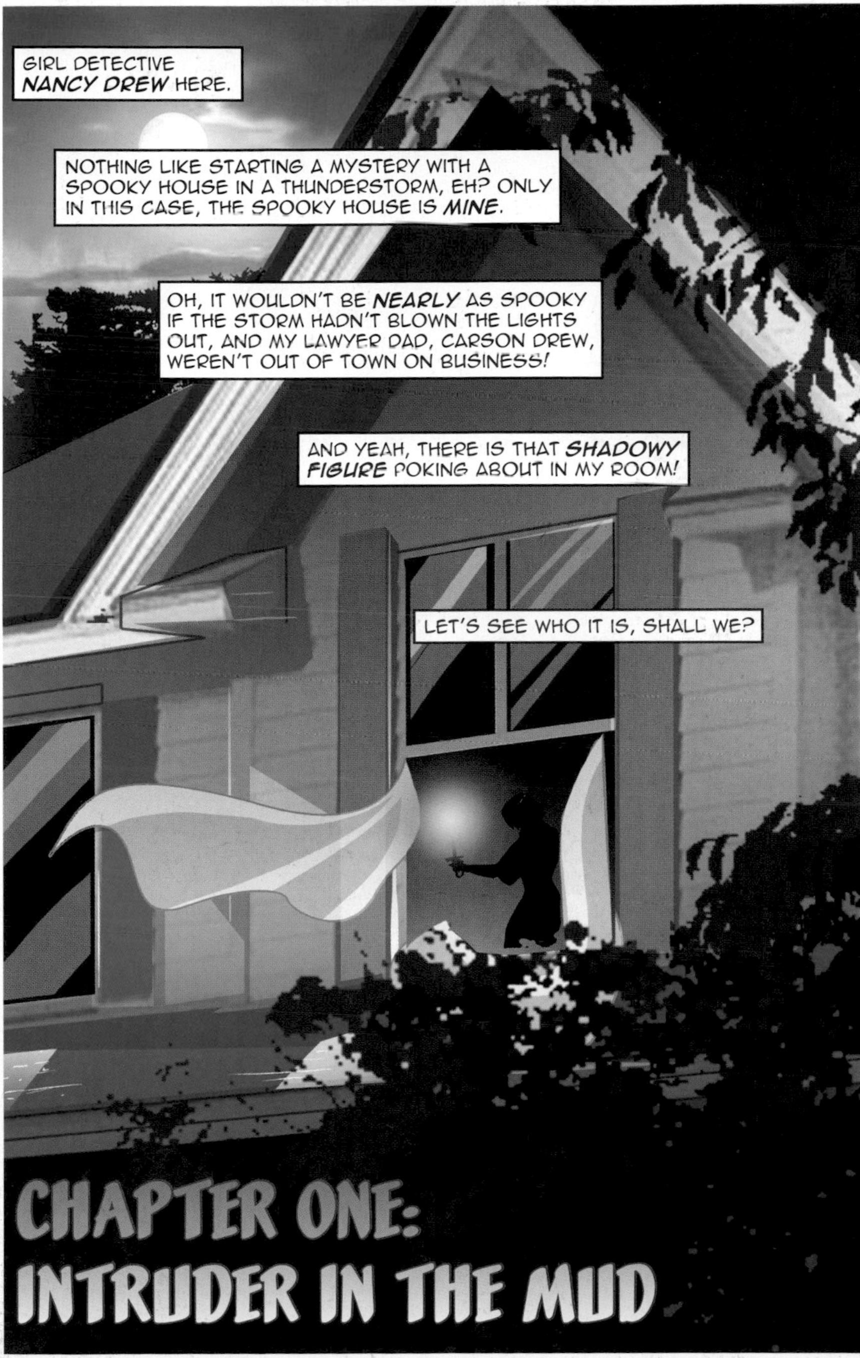
GIRL DETECTIVE NANCY DREW HERE.
NOTHING LIKE STARTING A MYSTERY WITH A SPOOKY HOUSE IN A THUNDERSTORM, EH? ONLY IN THIS CASE, THE SPOOKY HOUSE IS MINE.
OH, IT WOULDN'T BE NEARLY AS SPOOKY IF THE STORM HADN'T BLOWN THE LIGHTS OUT, AND MY LAWYER DAD, CARSON DREW, WEREN'T OUT OF TOWN ON BUSINESS!
AND YEAH, THERE IS THAT SHADOWY FIGURE POKING ABOUT IN MY ROOM!
LET'S SEE WHO IT IS, SHALL WE?
CHAPTER ONE:
INTRUDER IN THE MUD

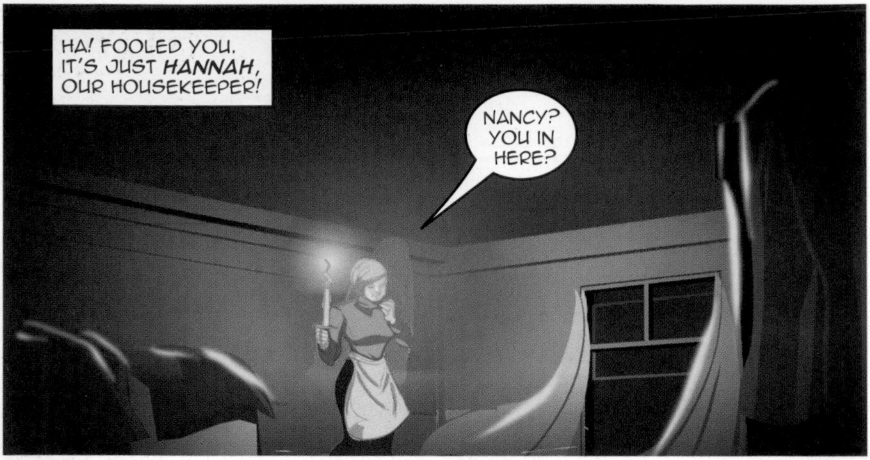
HA! FOOLED YOU. IT'S JUST **HANNAH**, OUR HOUSEKEEPER!
NANCY? YOU IN HERE?

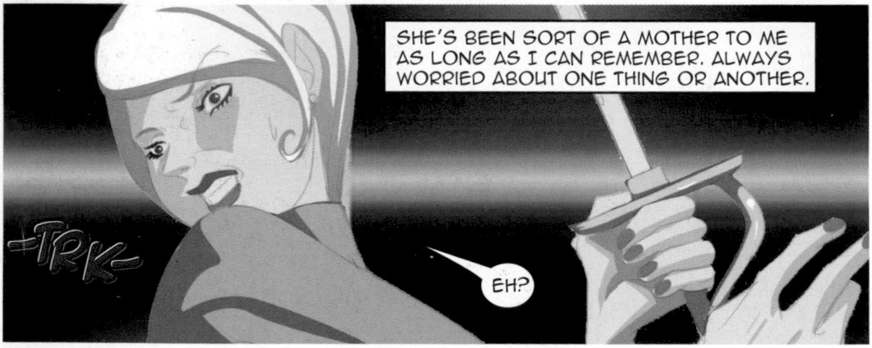
SHE'S BEEN SORT OF A MOTHER TO ME AS LONG AS I CAN REMEMBER. ALWAYS WORRIED ABOUT ONE THING OR ANOTHER.
-TRK-
EH?

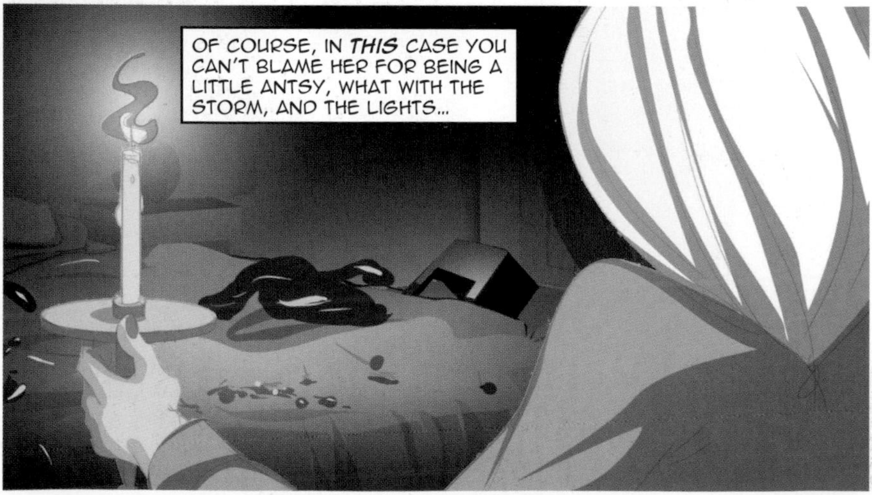
OF COURSE, IN **THIS** CASE YOU CAN'T BLAME HER FOR BEING A LITTLE ANTSY, WHAT WITH THE STORM, AND THE LIGHTS...

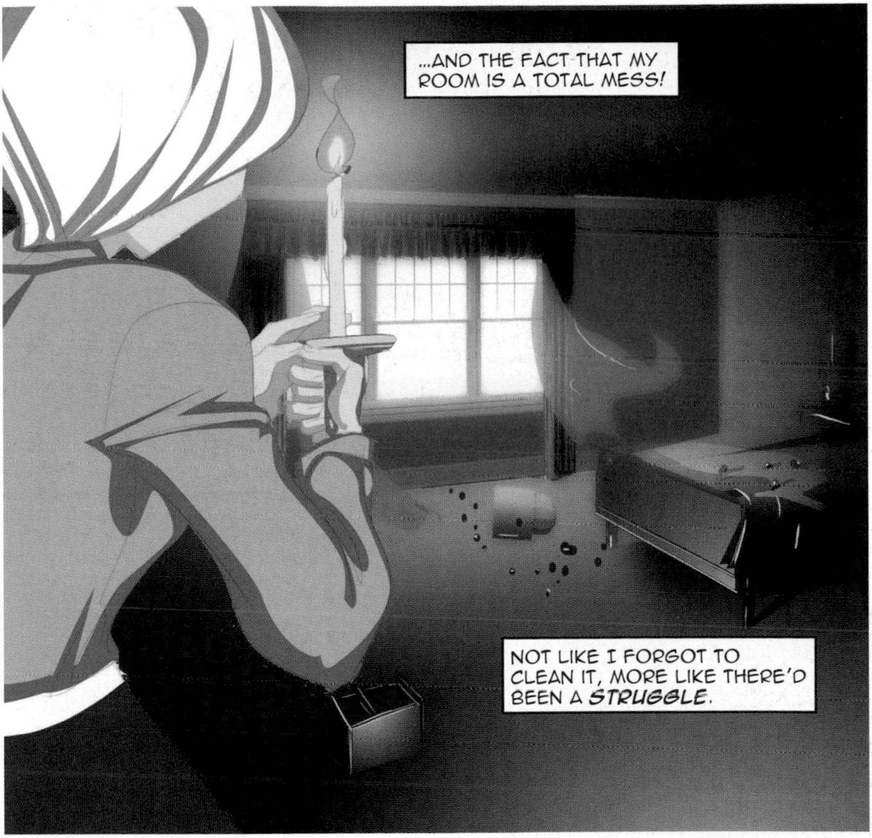
...AND THE FACT THAT MY ROOM IS A TOTAL MESS!
NOT LIKE I FORGOT TO CLEAN IT, MORE LIKE THERE'D BEEN A STRUGGLE.

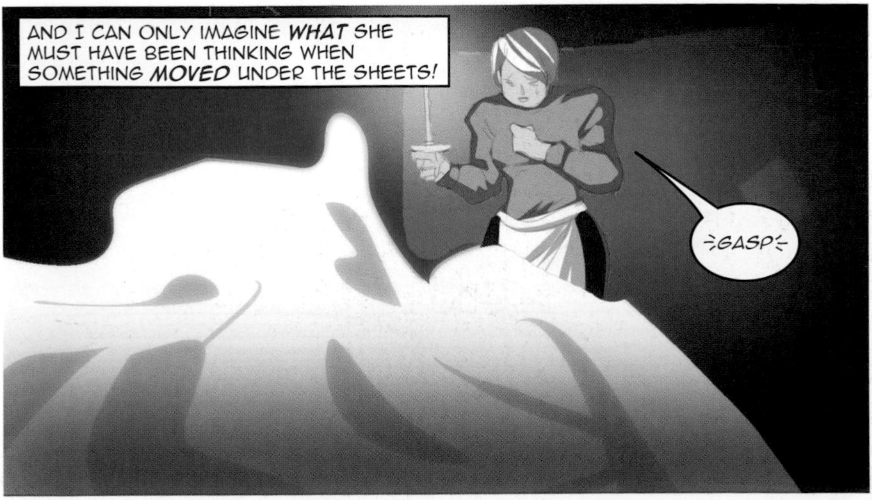
AND I CAN ONLY IMAGINE WHAT SHE MUST HAVE BEEN THINKING WHEN SOMETHING MOVED UNDER THE SHEETS!
GASP

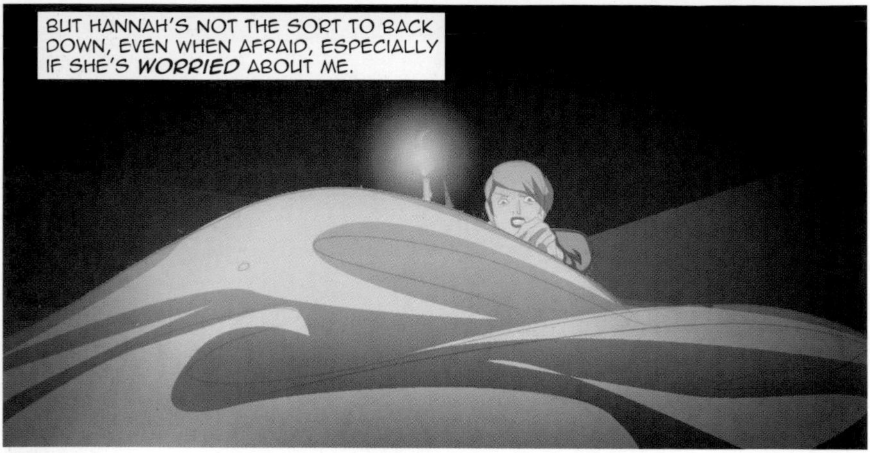
BUT HANNAH'S NOT THE SORT TO BACK DOWN, EVEN WHEN AFRAID, ESPECIALLY IF SHE'S *WORRIED* ABOUT ME.

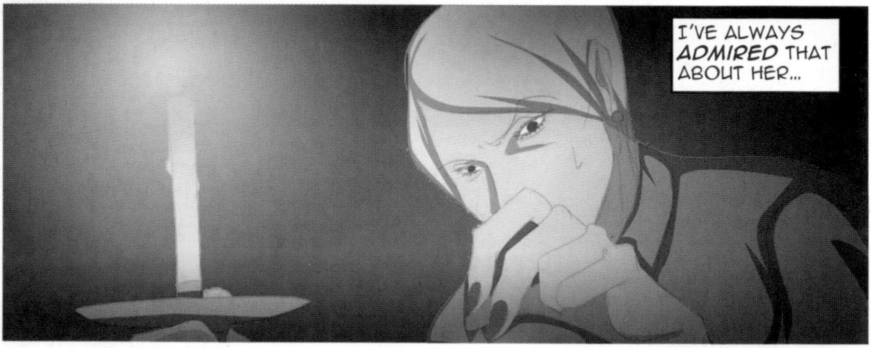
I'VE ALWAYS *ADMIRED* THAT ABOUT HER...

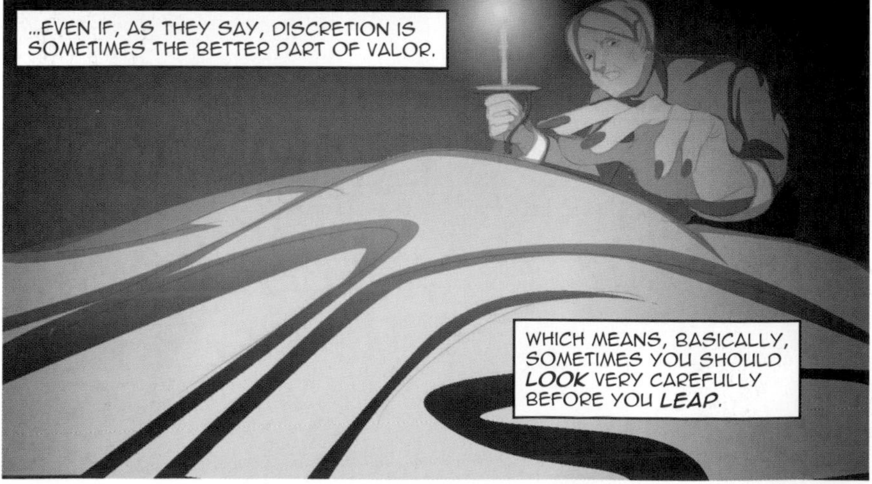
...EVEN IF, AS THEY SAY, DISCRETION IS SOMETIMES THE BETTER PART OF VALOR.
WHICH MEANS, BASICALLY, SOMETIMES YOU SHOULD *LOOK* VERY CAREFULLY BEFORE YOU *LEAP*.

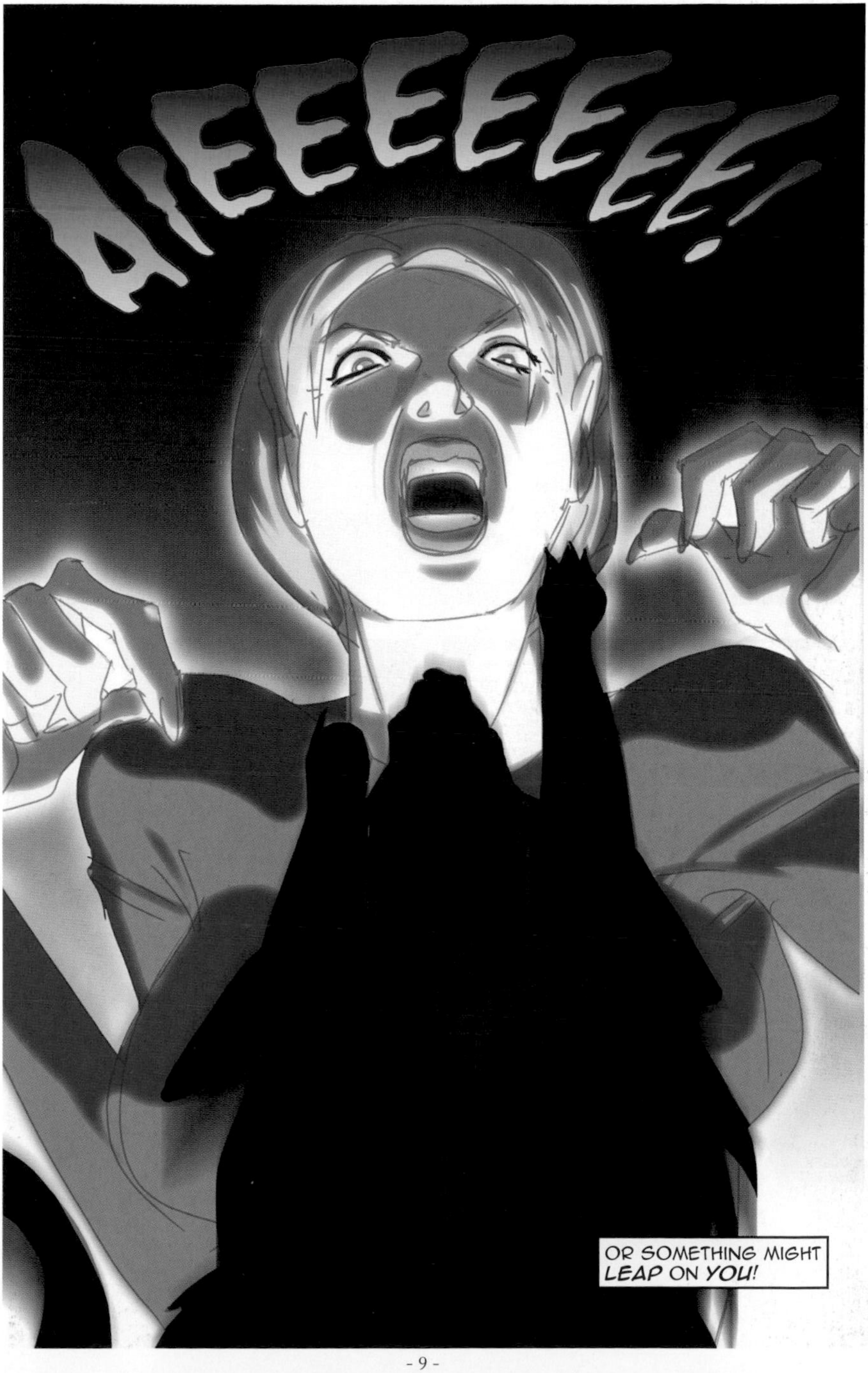
AIEEEEEEE!
OR SOMETHING MIGHT LEAP ON YOU!

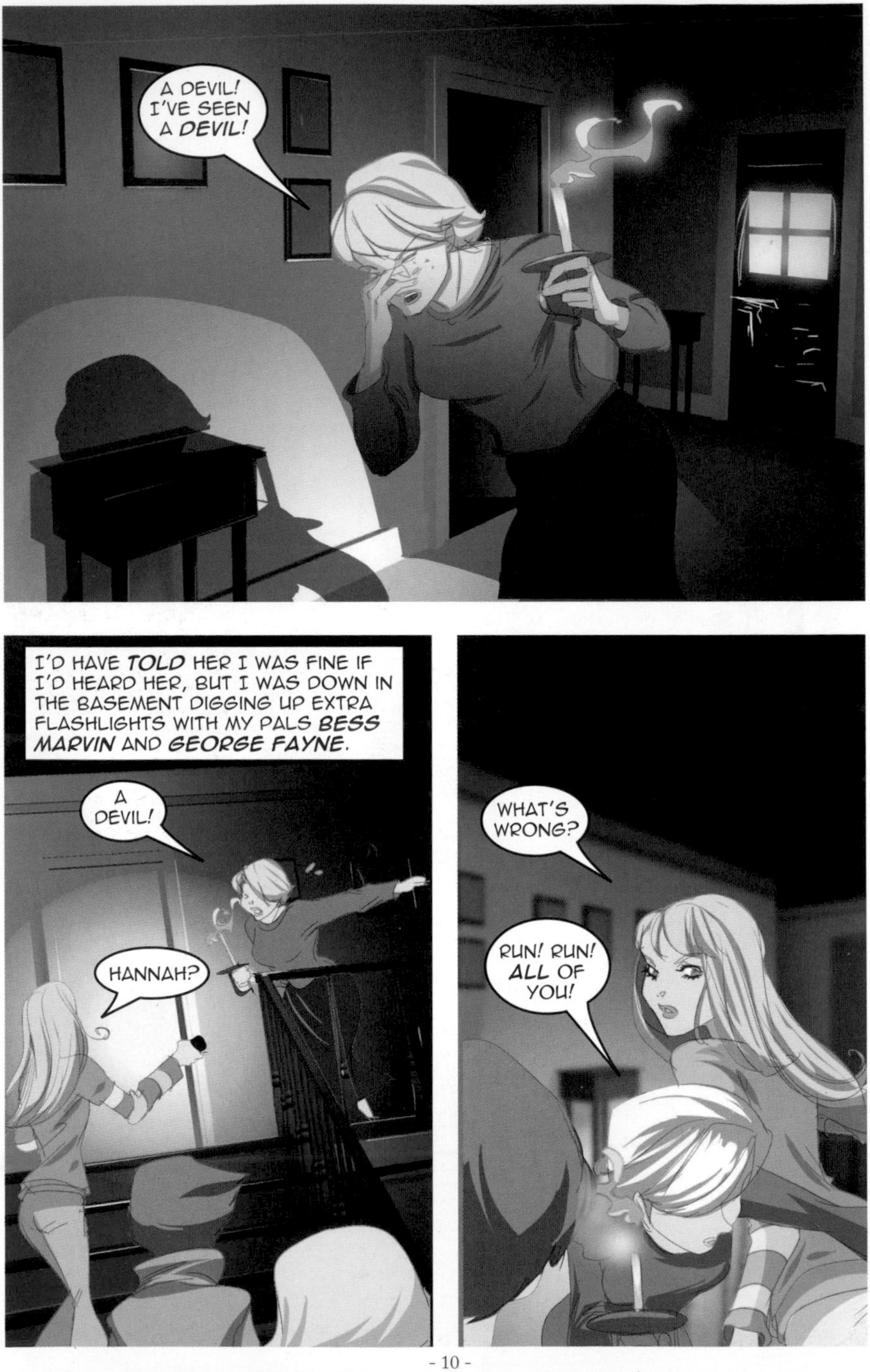
A DEVIL! I'VE SEEN A *DEVIL!*
I'D HAVE *TOLD* HER I WAS FINE IF I'D HEARD HER, BUT I WAS DOWN IN THE BASEMENT DIGGING UP EXTRA FLASHLIGHTS WITH MY PALS *BESS MARVIN* AND *GEORGE FAYNE*.
A DEVIL!
HANNAH?
WHAT'S WRONG?
RUN! RUN! *ALL* OF YOU!

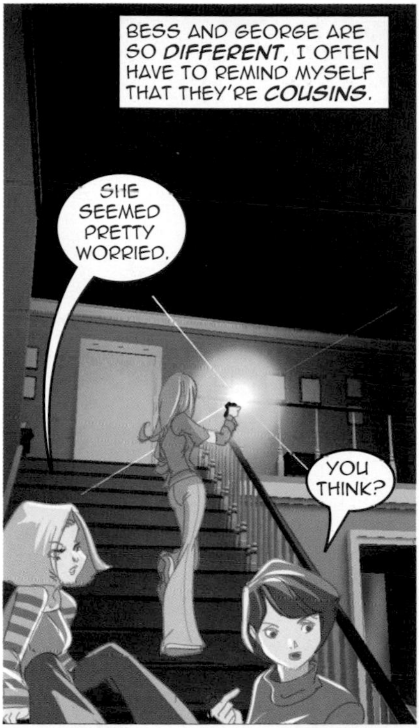
BESS AND GEORGE ARE SO DIFFERENT, I OFTEN HAVE TO REMIND MYSELF THAT THEY'RE COUSINS.
SHE SEEMED PRETTY WORRIED.
YOU THINK?

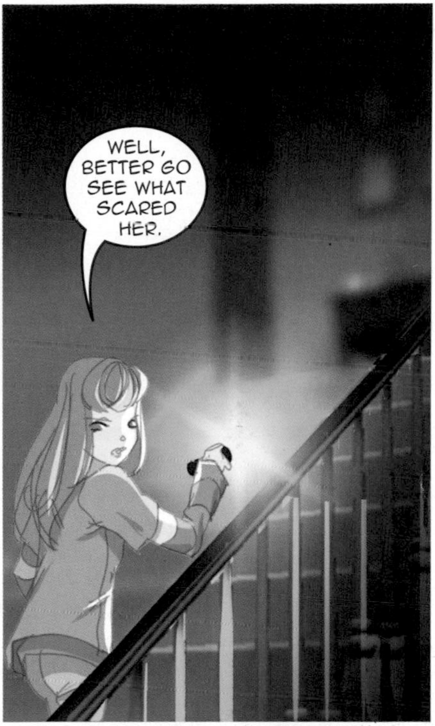
WELL, BETTER GO SEE WHAT SCARED HER.

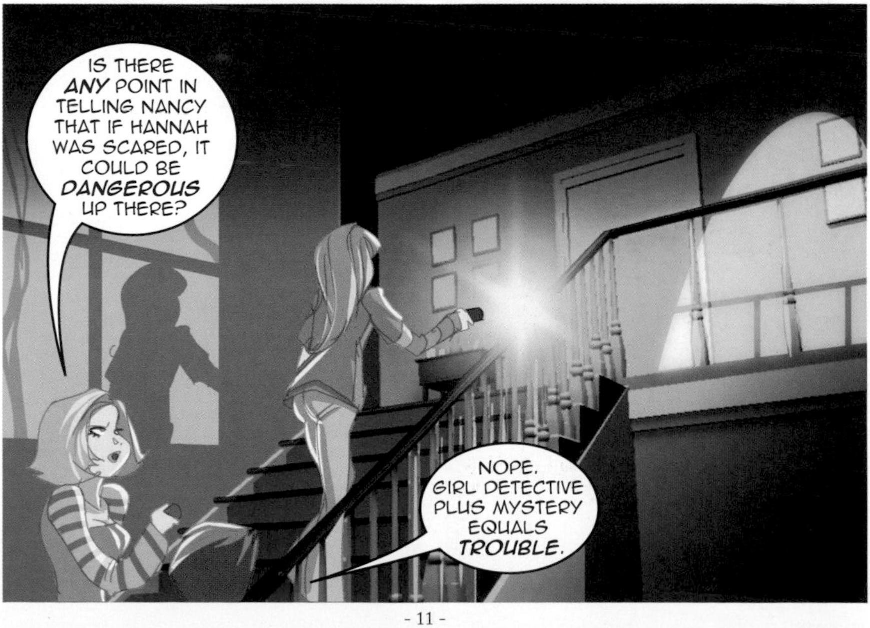
IS THERE ANY POINT IN TELLING NANCY THAT IF HANNAH WAS SCARED, IT COULD BE DANGEROUS UP THERE?
NOPE. GIRL DETECTIVE PLUS MYSTERY EQUALS TROUBLE.

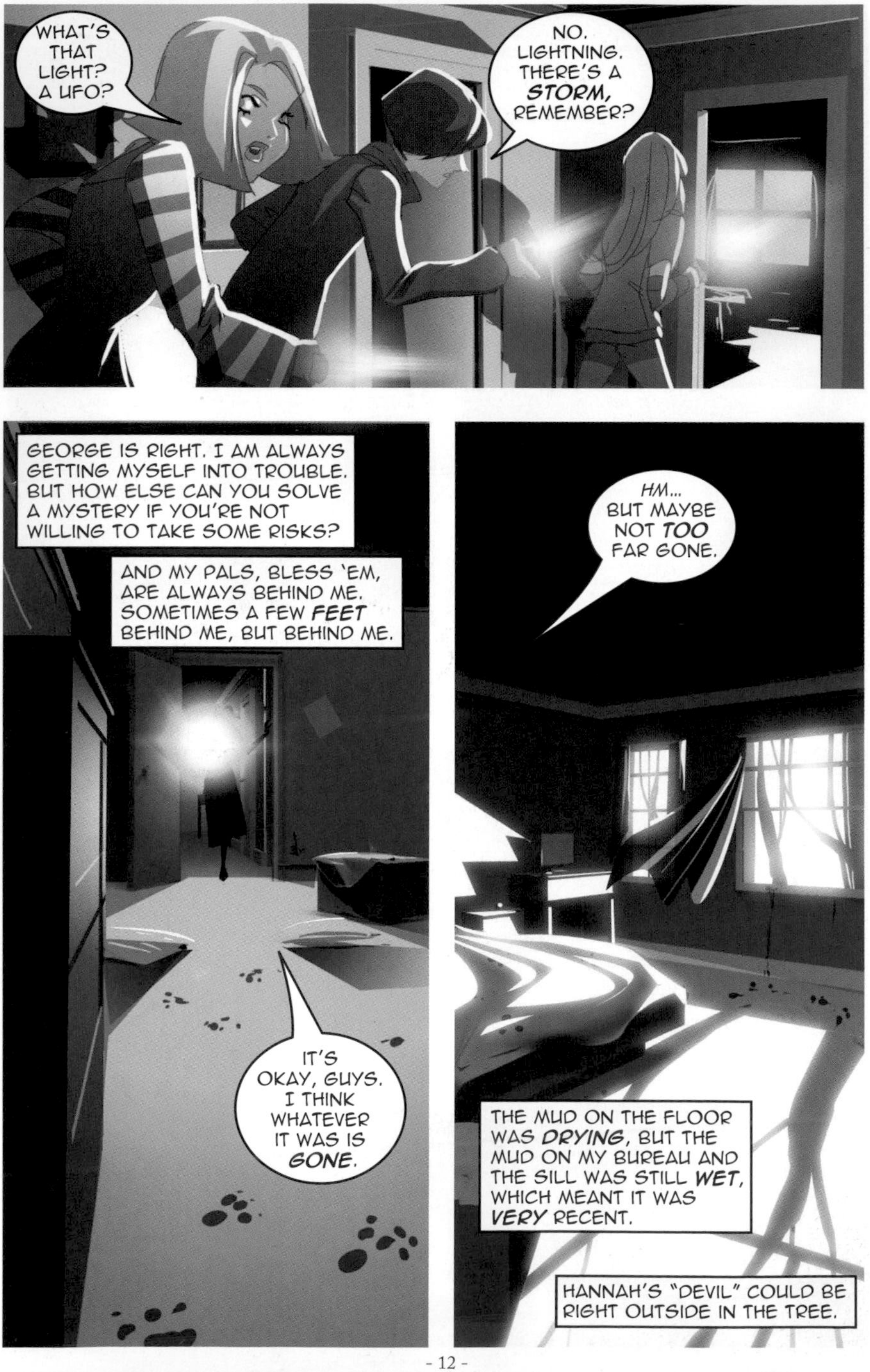
WHAT'S THAT LIGHT? A UFO?
NO. LIGHTNING. THERE'S A STORM, REMEMBER?
GEORGE IS RIGHT. I AM ALWAYS GETTING MYSELF INTO TROUBLE. BUT HOW ELSE CAN YOU SOLVE A MYSTERY IF YOU'RE NOT WILLING TO TAKE SOME RISKS?
AND MY PALS, BLESS 'EM, ARE ALWAYS BEHIND ME. SOMETIMES A FEW FEET BEHIND ME, BUT BEHIND ME.
IT'S OKAY, GUYS. I THINK WHATEVER IT WAS IS GONE.
HM... BUT MAYBE NOT TOO FAR GONE.
THE MUD ON THE FLOOR WAS DRYING, BUT THE MUD ON MY BUREAU AND THE SILL WAS STILL WET, WHICH MEANT IT WAS VERY RECENT.
HANNAH'S "DEVIL" COULD BE RIGHT OUTSIDE IN THE TREE.

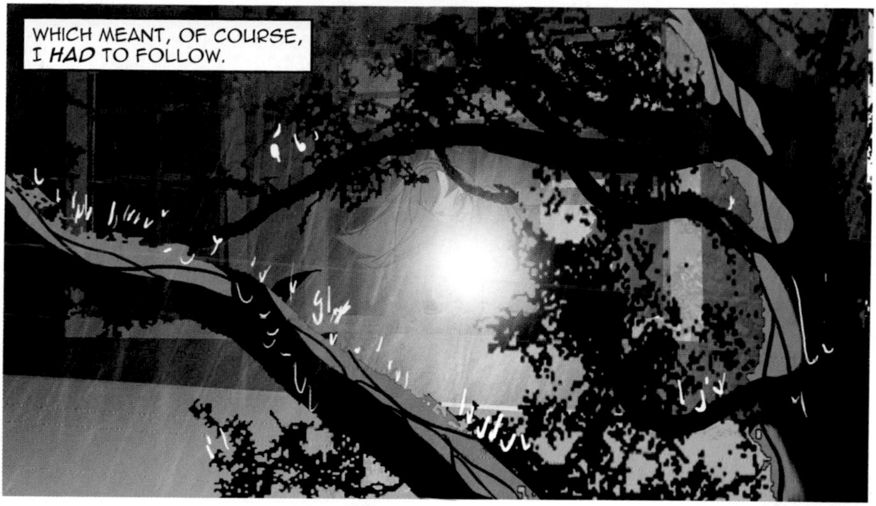
WHICH MEANT, OF COURSE, I *HAD* TO FOLLOW.

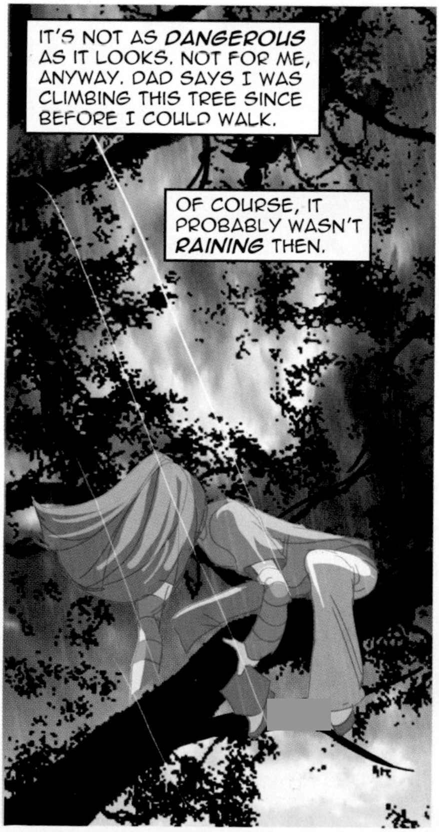
IT'S NOT AS *DANGEROUS* AS IT LOOKS. NOT FOR ME, ANYWAY. DAD SAYS I WAS CLIMBING THIS TREE SINCE BEFORE I COULD WALK.
OF COURSE, IT PROBABLY WASN'T *RAINING* THEN.

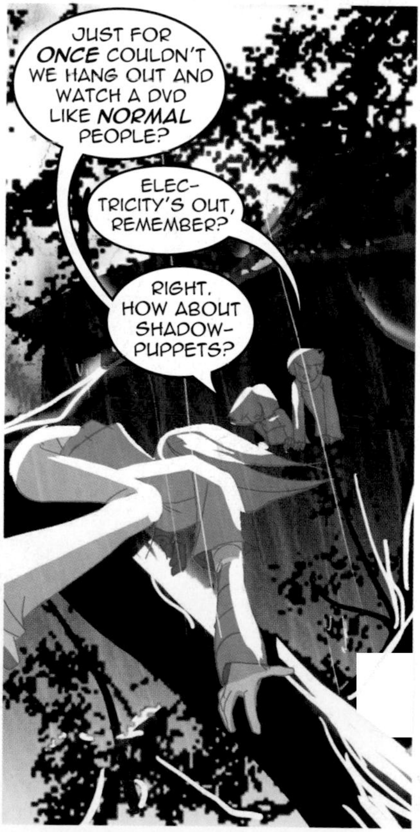
JUST FOR *ONCE* COULDN'T WE HANG OUT AND WATCH A DVD LIKE *NORMAL* PEOPLE?
ELEC-TRICITY'S OUT, REMEMBER?
RIGHT. HOW ABOUT SHADOW-PUPPETS?

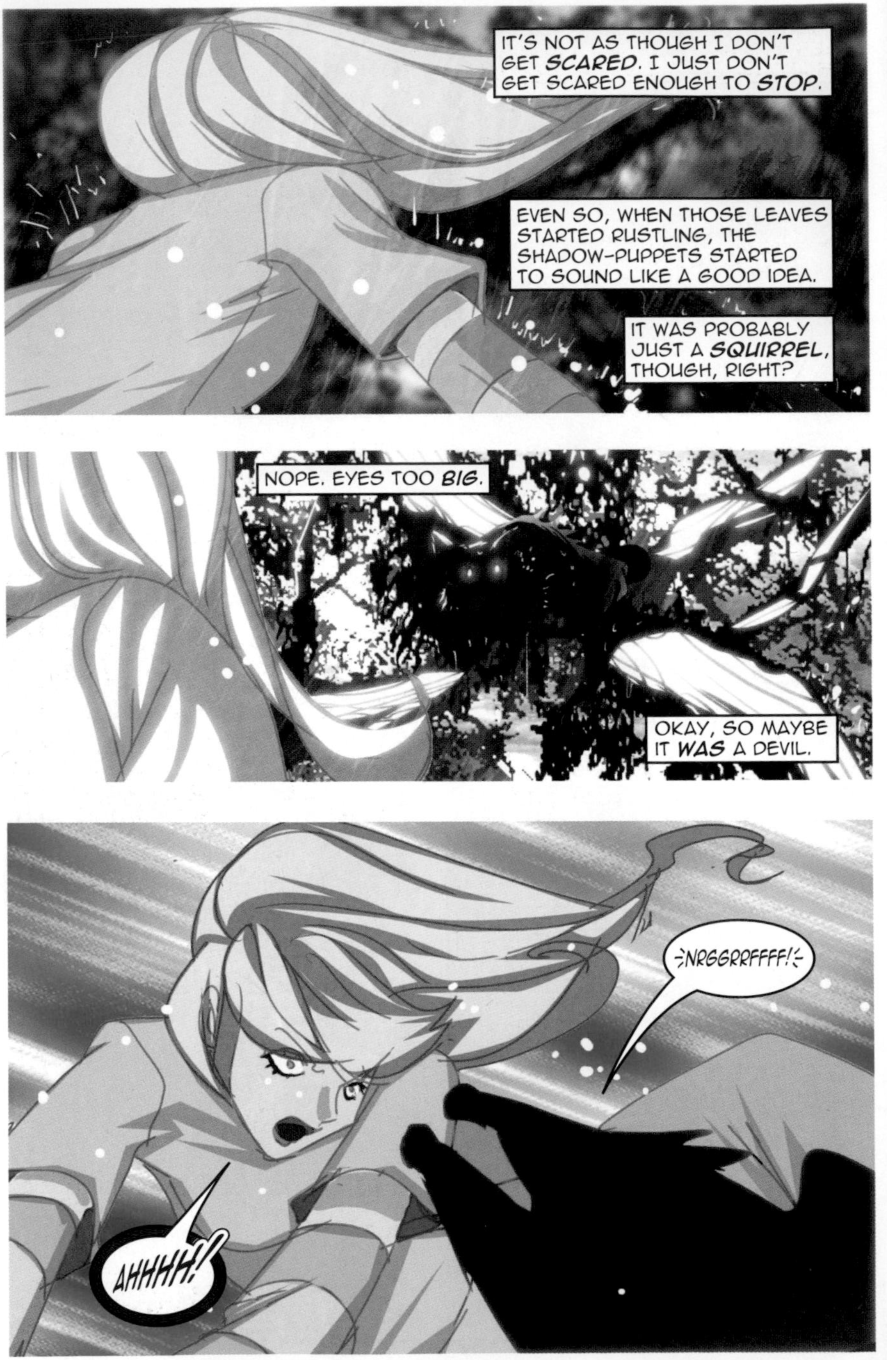
IT'S NOT AS THOUGH I DON'T GET SCARED. I JUST DON'T GET SCARED ENOUGH TO STOP.
EVEN SO, WHEN THOSE LEAVES STARTED RUSTLING, THE SHADOW-PUPPETS STARTED TO SOUND LIKE A GOOD IDEA.
IT WAS PROBABLY JUST A SQUIRREL, THOUGH, RIGHT?
NOPE. EYES TOO BIG.
OKAY, SO MAYBE IT WAS A DEVIL.
NRGGRRFFFF!
AHHHH!

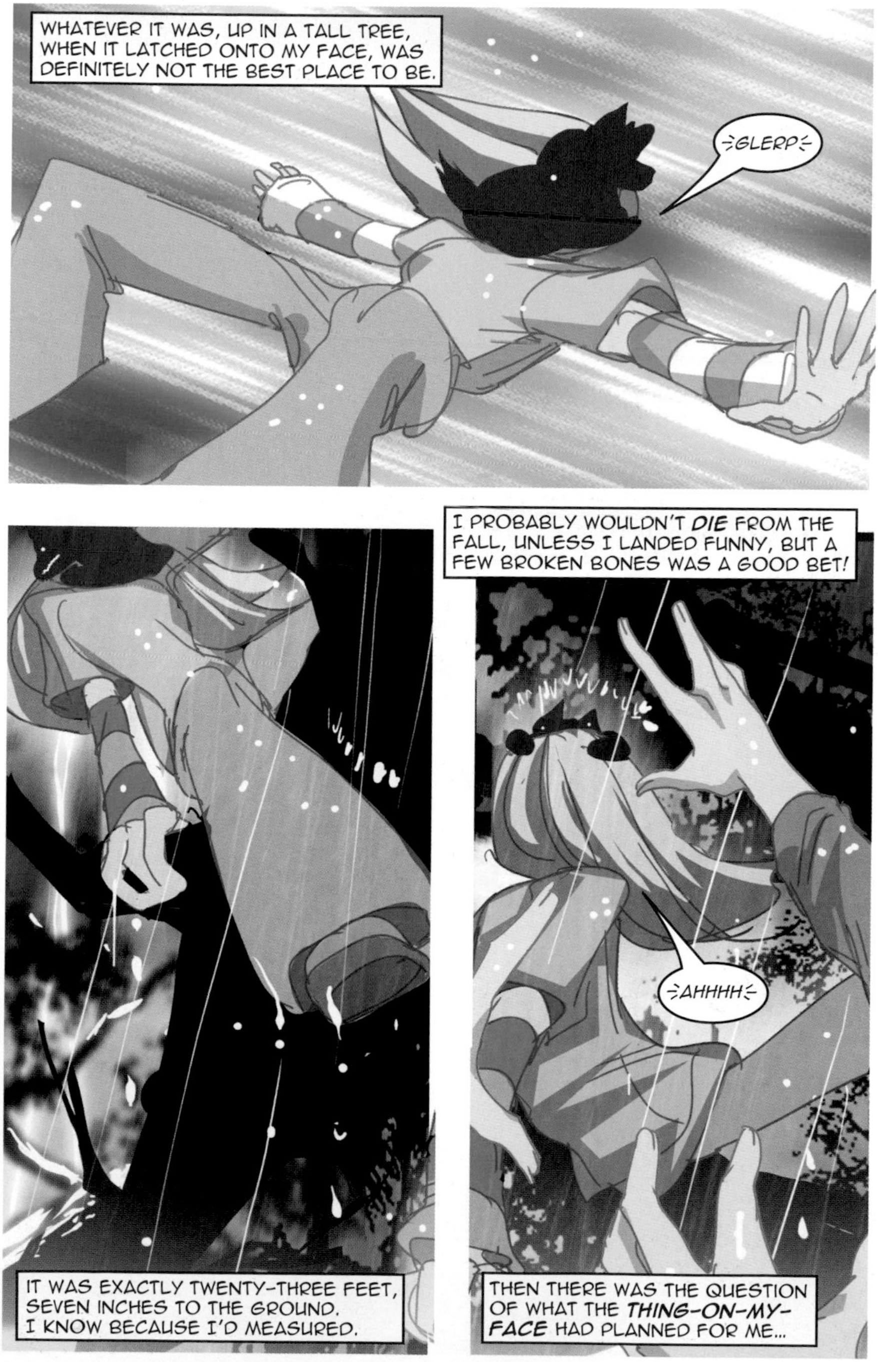

WHATEVER IT WAS, UP IN A TALL TREE, WHEN IT LATCHED ONTO MY FACE, WAS DEFINITELY NOT THE BEST PLACE TO BE.
GLERP
I PROBABLY WOULDN'T *DIE* FROM THE FALL, UNLESS I LANDED FUNNY, BUT A FEW BROKEN BONES WAS A GOOD BET!
AHHHH
IT WAS EXACTLY TWENTY-THREE FEET, SEVEN INCHES TO THE GROUND. I KNOW BECAUSE I'D MEASURED.
THEN THERE WAS THE QUESTION OF WHAT THE *THING-ON-MY-FACE* HAD PLANNED FOR ME...

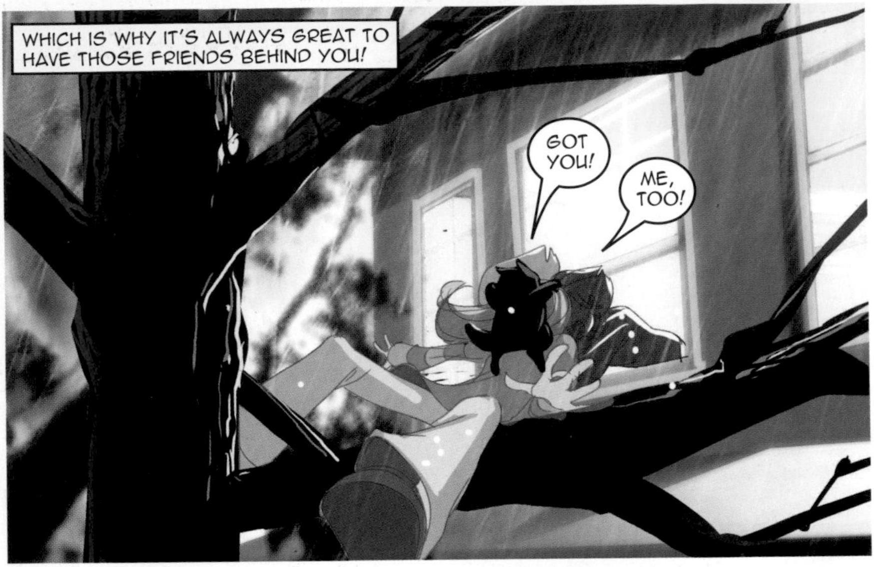
WHICH IS WHY IT'S ALWAYS GREAT TO HAVE THOSE FRIENDS BEHIND YOU!
GOT YOU!
ME, TOO!

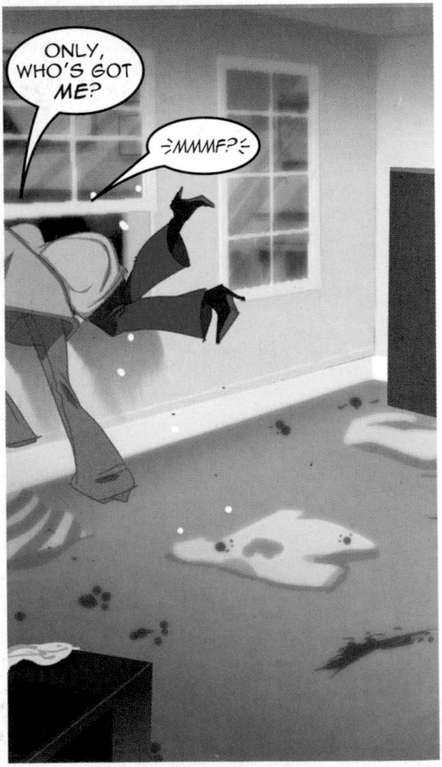
ONLY, WHO'S GOT ME?
MMMF?

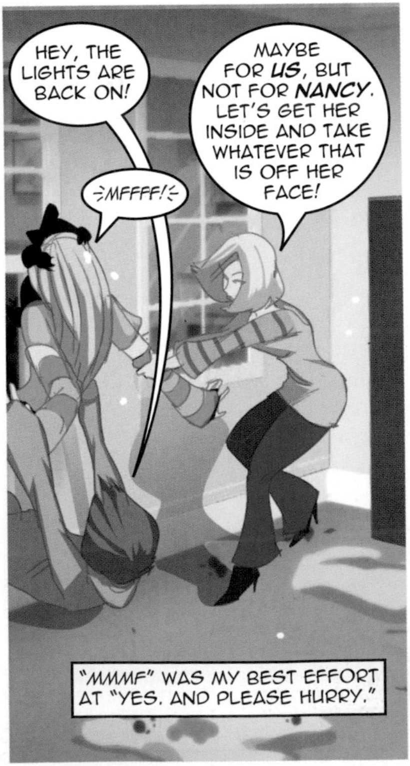
HEY, THE LIGHTS ARE BACK ON!
MAYBE FOR US, BUT NOT FOR NANCY. LET'S GET HER INSIDE AND TAKE WHATEVER THAT IS OFF HER FACE!
MFFFF!
"MMMF" WAS MY BEST EFFORT AT "YES. AND PLEASE HURRY."

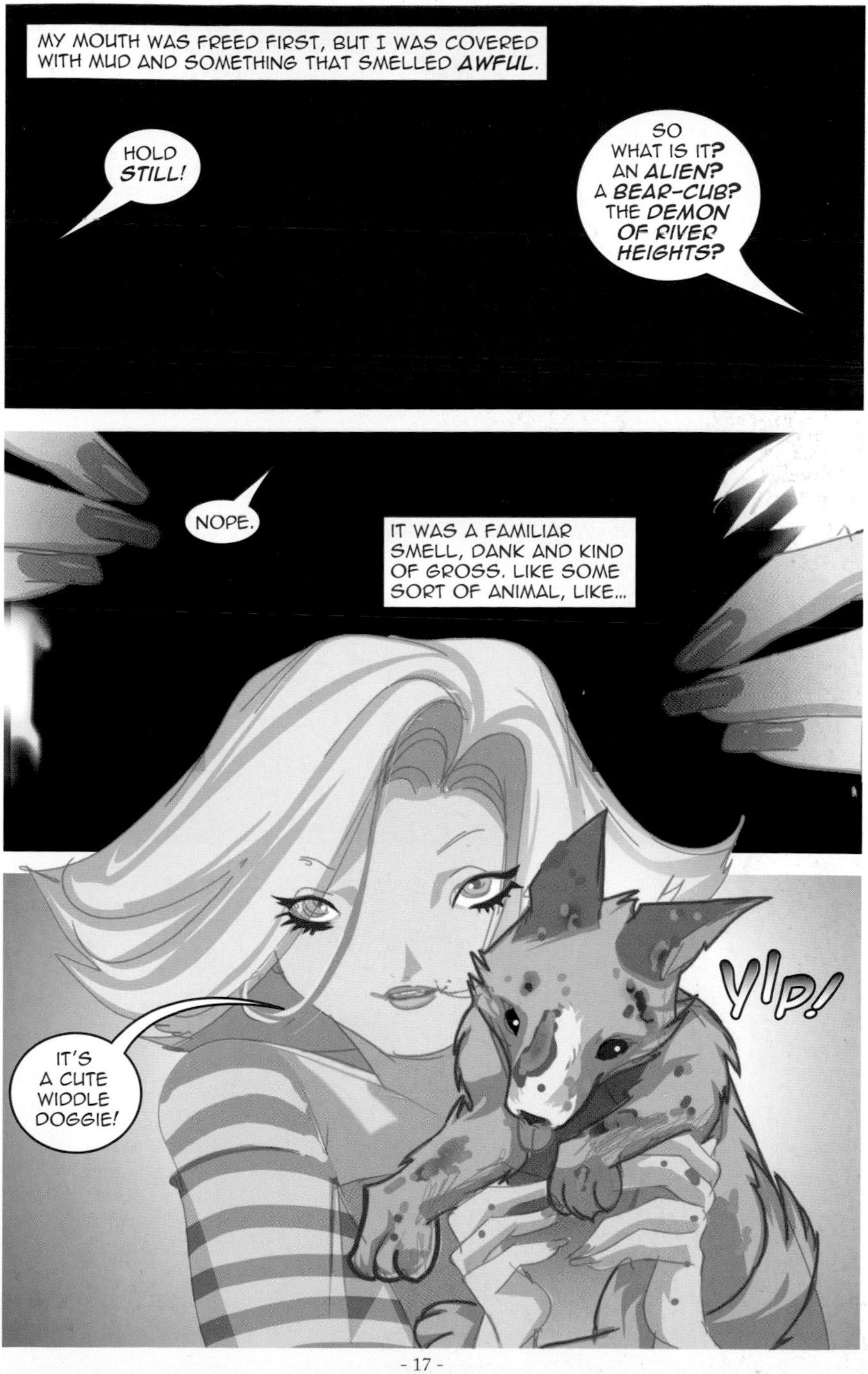
MY MOUTH WAS FREED FIRST, BUT I WAS COVERED WITH MUD AND SOMETHING THAT SMELLED AWFUL.
HOLD STILL!
SO WHAT IS IT? AN ALIEN? A BEAR-CUB? THE DEMON OF RIVER HEIGHTS?
NOPE.
IT WAS A FAMILIAR SMELL, DANK AND KIND OF GROSS. LIKE SOME SORT OF ANIMAL, LIKE...
YIP!
IT'S A CUTE WIDDLE DOGGIE!

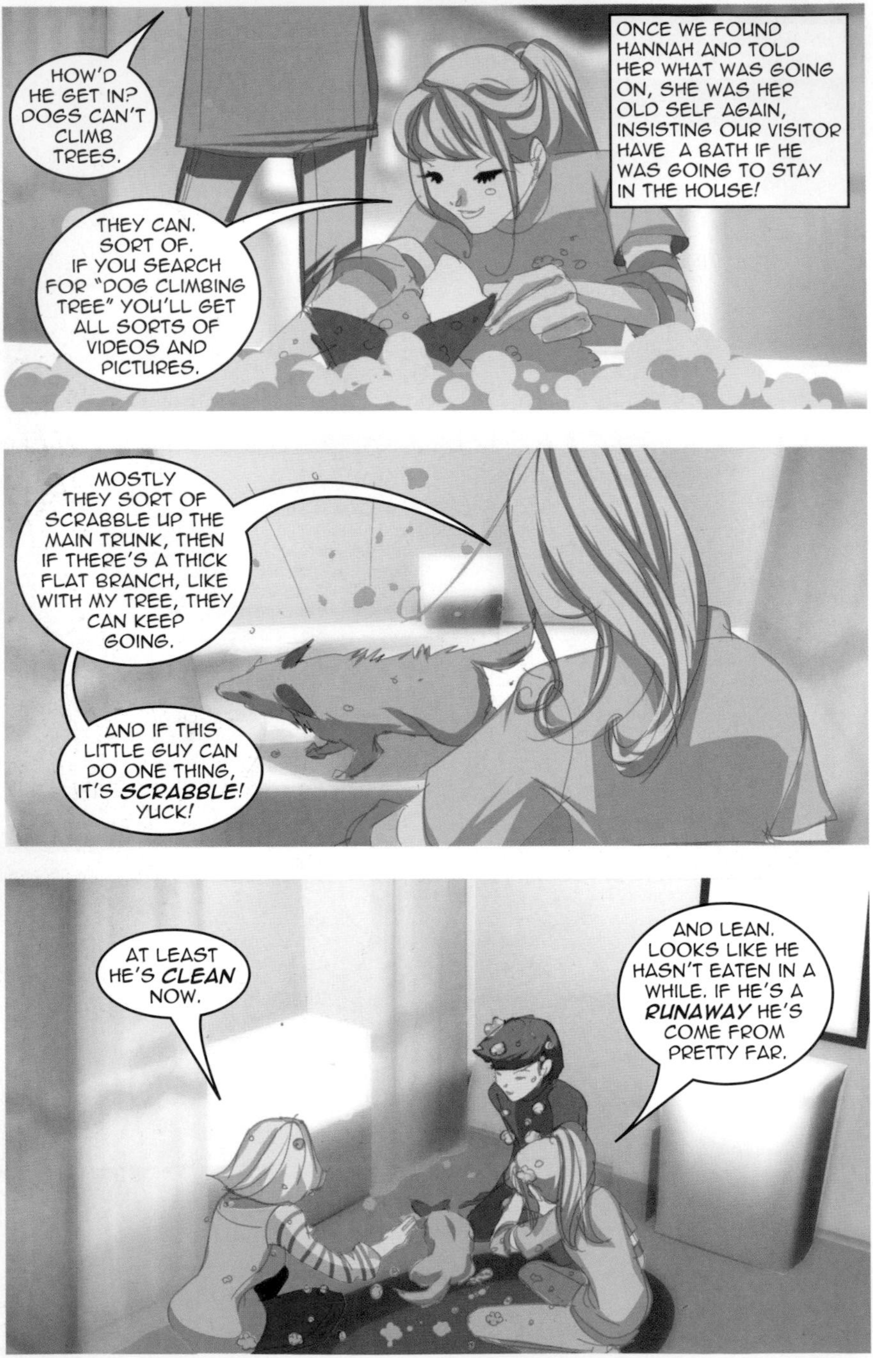
HOW'D HE GET IN? DOGS CAN'T CLIMB TREES.
ONCE WE FOUND HANNAH AND TOLD HER WHAT WAS GOING ON, SHE WAS HER OLD SELF AGAIN, INSISTING OUR VISITOR HAVE A BATH IF HE WAS GOING TO STAY IN THE HOUSE!
THEY CAN. SORT OF. IF YOU SEARCH FOR "DOG CLIMBING TREE" YOU'LL GET ALL SORTS OF VIDEOS AND PICTURES.
MOSTLY THEY SORT OF SCRABBLE UP THE MAIN TRUNK, THEN IF THERE'S A THICK FLAT BRANCH, LIKE WITH MY TREE, THEY CAN KEEP GOING.
AND IF THIS LITTLE GUY CAN DO ONE THING, IT'S ***SCRABBLE***! YUCK!
AT LEAST HE'S ***CLEAN*** NOW.
AND LEAN. LOOKS LIKE HE HASN'T EATEN IN A WHILE. IF HE'S A ***RUNAWAY*** HE'S COME FROM PRETTY FAR.

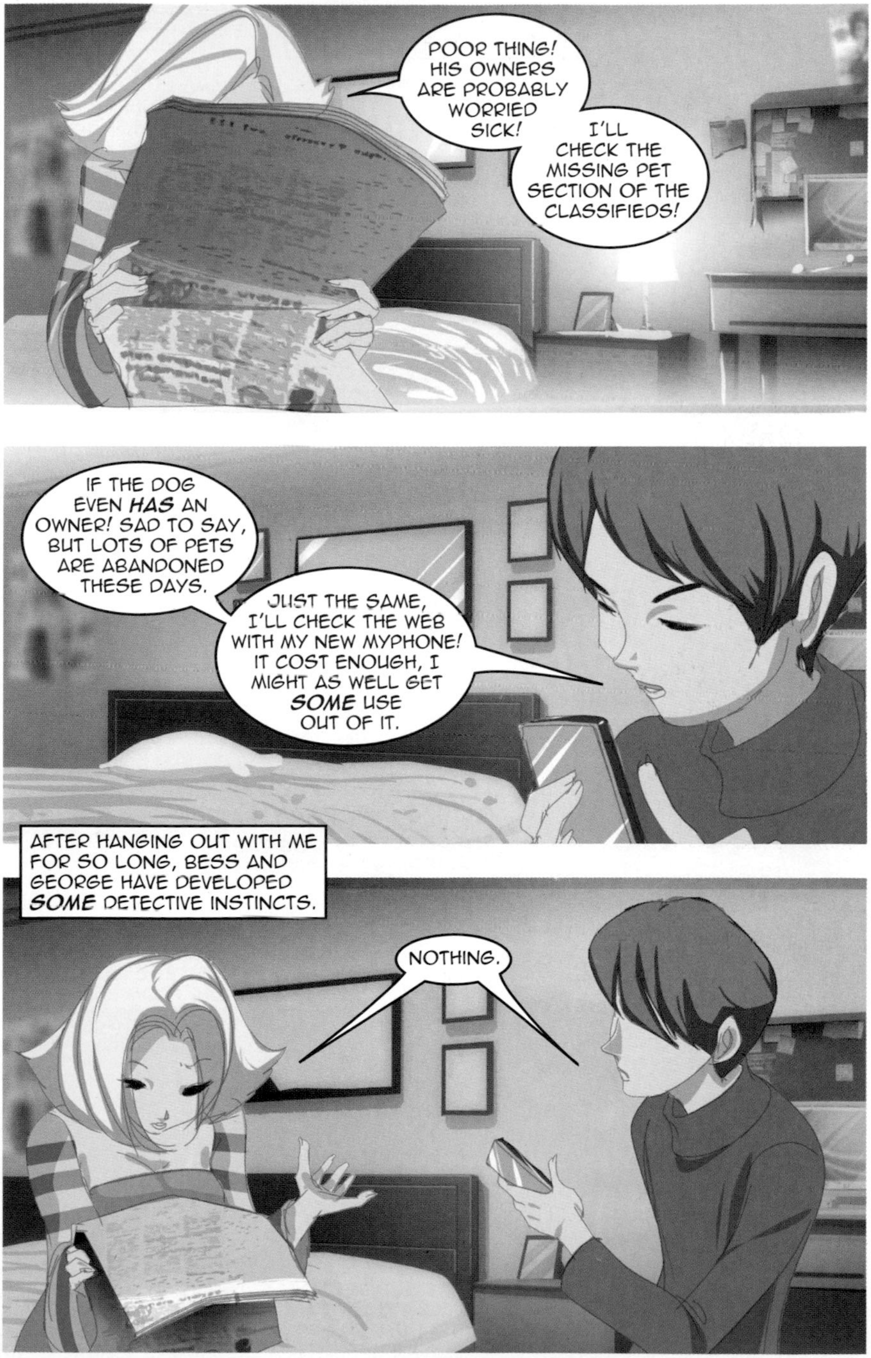
POOR THING! HIS OWNERS ARE PROBABLY WORRIED SICK!
I'LL CHECK THE MISSING PET SECTION OF THE CLASSIFIEDS!
IF THE DOG EVEN HAS AN OWNER! SAD TO SAY, BUT LOTS OF PETS ARE ABANDONED THESE DAYS.
JUST THE SAME, I'LL CHECK THE WEB WITH MY NEW MYPHONE! IT COST ENOUGH, I MIGHT AS WELL GET SOME USE OUT OF IT.
AFTER HANGING OUT WITH ME FOR SO LONG, BESS AND GEORGE HAVE DEVELOPED SOME DETECTIVE INSTINCTS.
NOTHING.

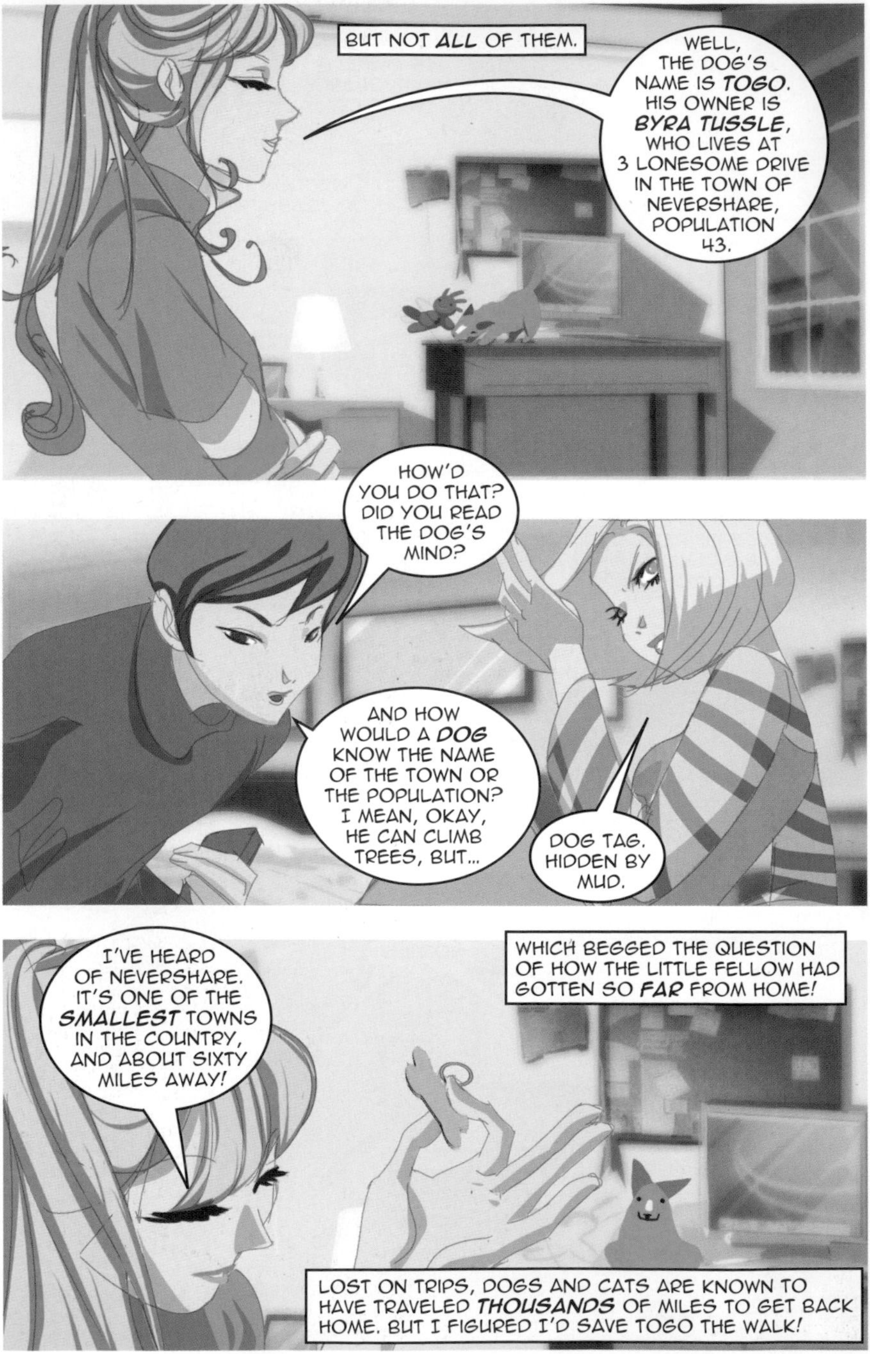
BUT NOT *ALL* OF THEM.
WELL, THE DOG'S NAME IS *TOGO*. HIS OWNER IS *BYRA TUSSLE*, WHO LIVES AT 3 LONESOME DRIVE IN THE TOWN OF NEVERSHARE, POPULATION 43.
HOW'D YOU DO THAT? DID YOU READ THE DOG'S MIND?
AND HOW WOULD A *DOG* KNOW THE NAME OF THE TOWN OR THE POPULATION? I MEAN, OKAY, HE CAN CLIMB TREES, BUT...
DOG TAG. HIDDEN BY MUD.
I'VE HEARD OF NEVERSHARE. IT'S ONE OF THE *SMALLEST* TOWNS IN THE COUNTRY, AND ABOUT SIXTY MILES AWAY!
WHICH BEGGED THE QUESTION OF HOW THE LITTLE FELLOW HAD GOTTEN SO *FAR* FROM HOME!
LOST ON TRIPS, DOGS AND CATS ARE KNOWN TO HAVE TRAVELED *THOUSANDS* OF MILES TO GET BACK HOME. BUT I FIGURED I'D SAVE TOGO THE WALK!

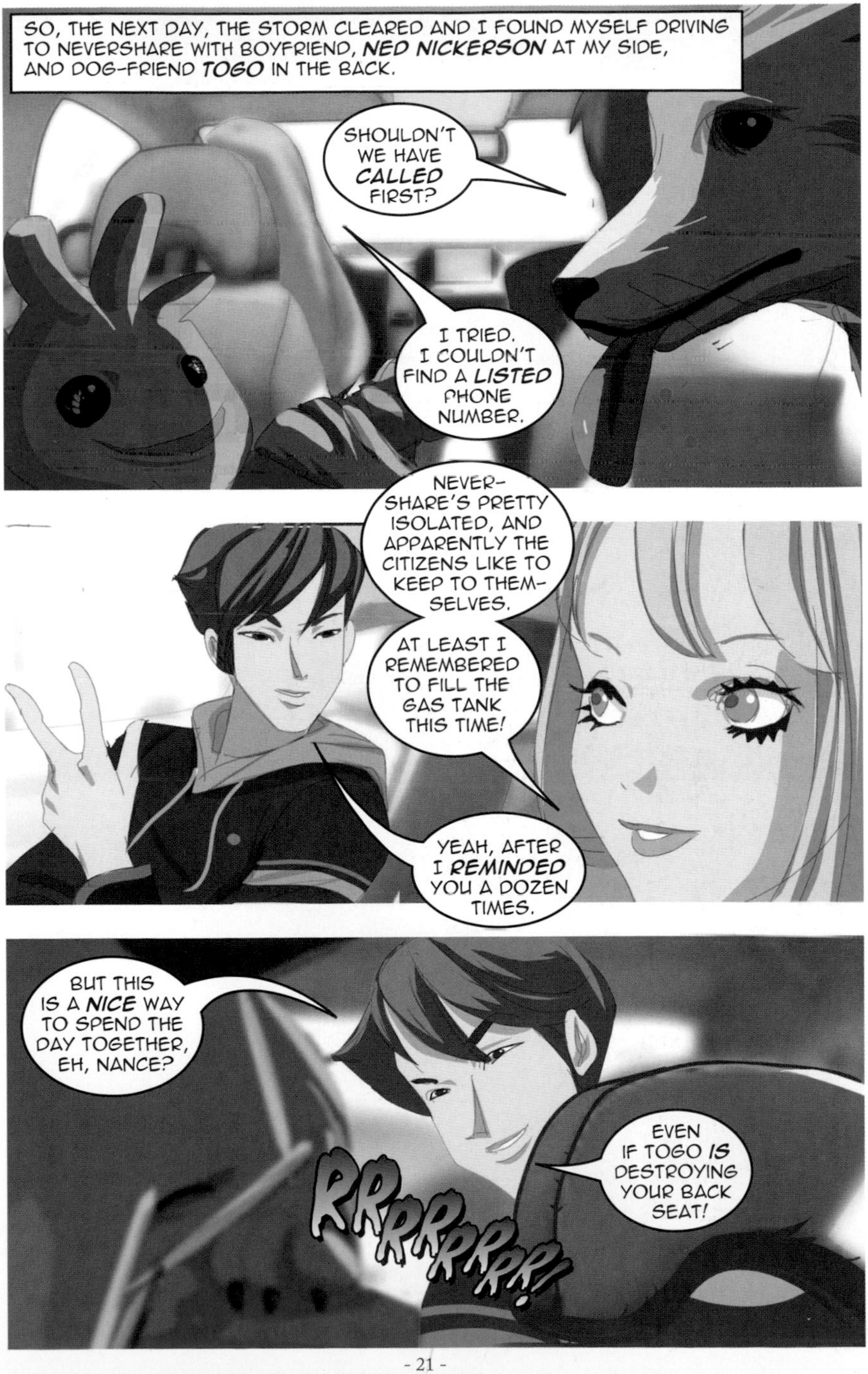

SO, THE NEXT DAY, THE STORM CLEARED AND I FOUND MYSELF DRIVING TO NEVERSHARE WITH BOYFRIEND, NED NICKERSON AT MY SIDE, AND DOG-FRIEND TOGO IN THE BACK.
SHOULDN'T WE HAVE CALLED FIRST?
I TRIED. I COULDN'T FIND A LISTED PHONE NUMBER.
NEVER-SHARE'S PRETTY ISOLATED, AND APPARENTLY THE CITIZENS LIKE TO KEEP TO THEM-SELVES.
AT LEAST I REMEMBERED TO FILL THE GAS TANK THIS TIME!
YEAH, AFTER I REMINDED YOU A DOZEN TIMES.
BUT THIS IS A NICE WAY TO SPEND THE DAY TOGETHER, EH, NANCE?
EVEN IF TOGO IS DESTROYING YOUR BACK SEAT!
RRRRRRRR!

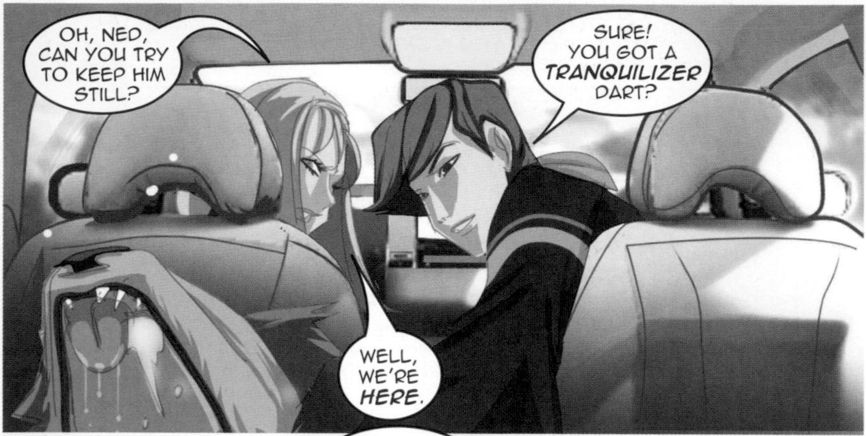
OH, NED, CAN YOU TRY TO KEEP HIM STILL?
SURE! YOU GOT A TRANQUILIZER DART?
WELL, WE'RE HERE.

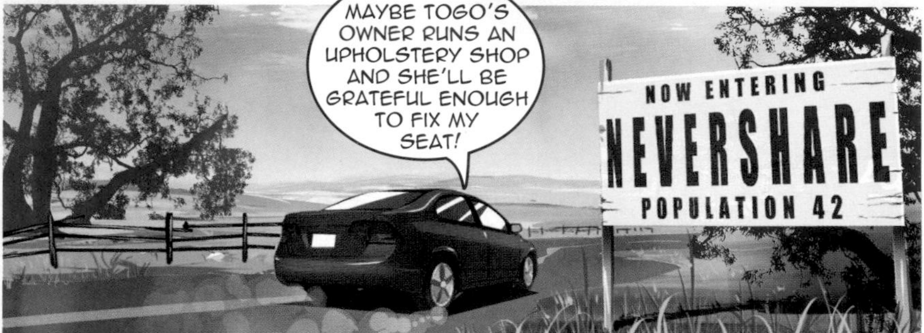
MAYBE TOGO'S OWNER RUNS AN UPHOLSTERY SHOP AND SHE'LL BE GRATEFUL ENOUGH TO FIX MY SEAT!
NOW ENTERING
NEVERSHARE
POPULATION 42

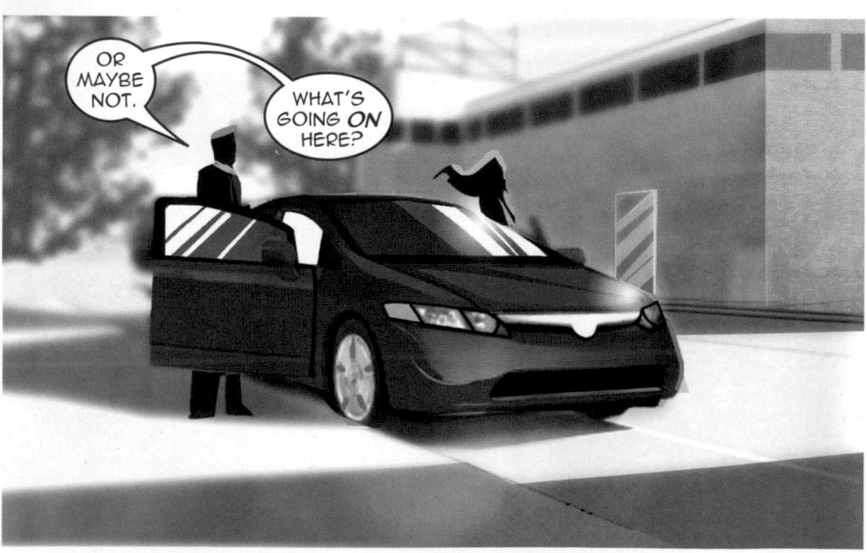
OR MAYBE NOT.
WHAT'S GOING ON HERE?

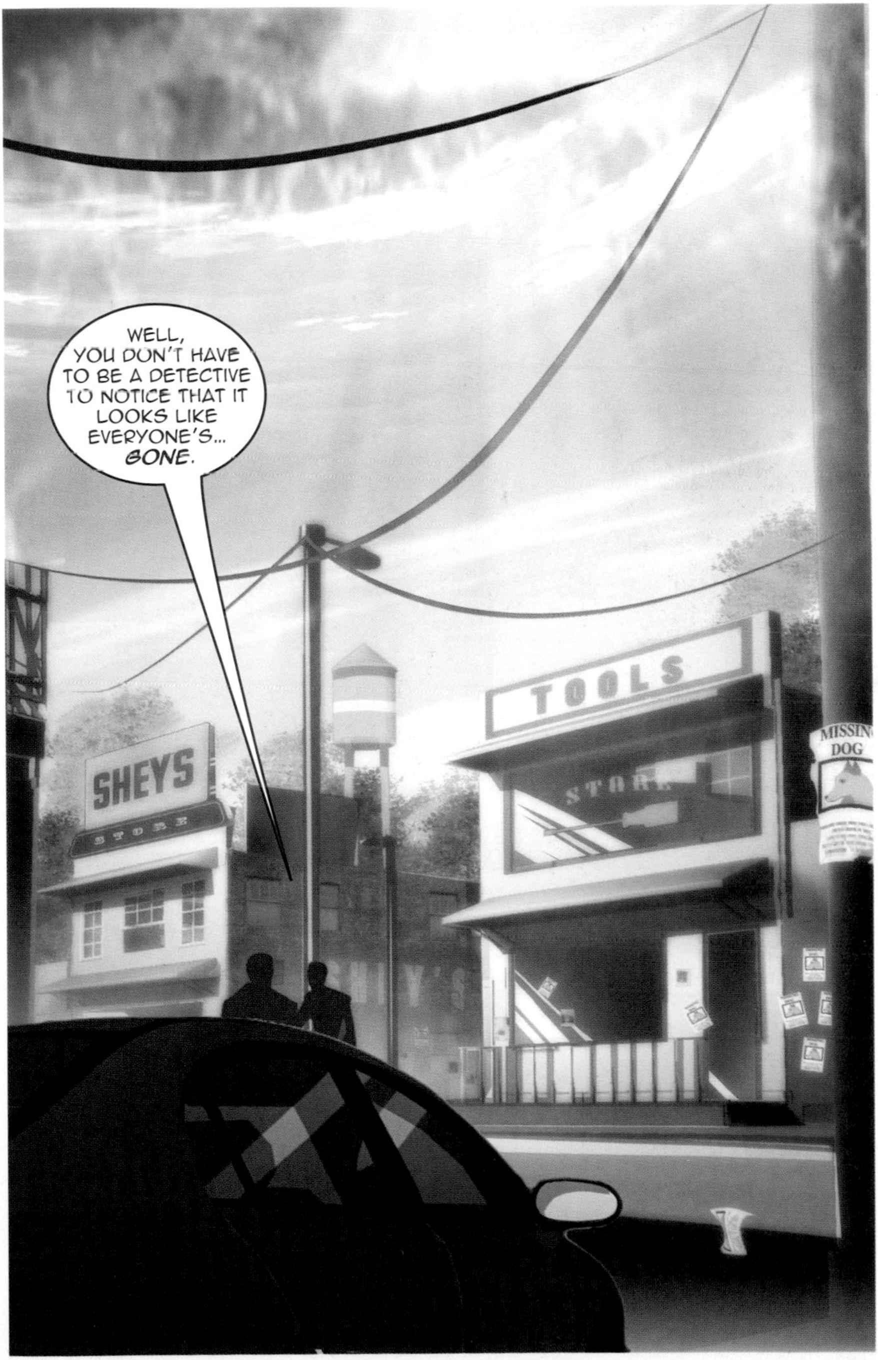
WELL, YOU DON'T HAVE TO BE A DETECTIVE TO NOTICE THAT IT LOOKS LIKE EVERYONE'S... GONE.
SHEYS
STORE
TOOLS
STORE
MISSING DOG

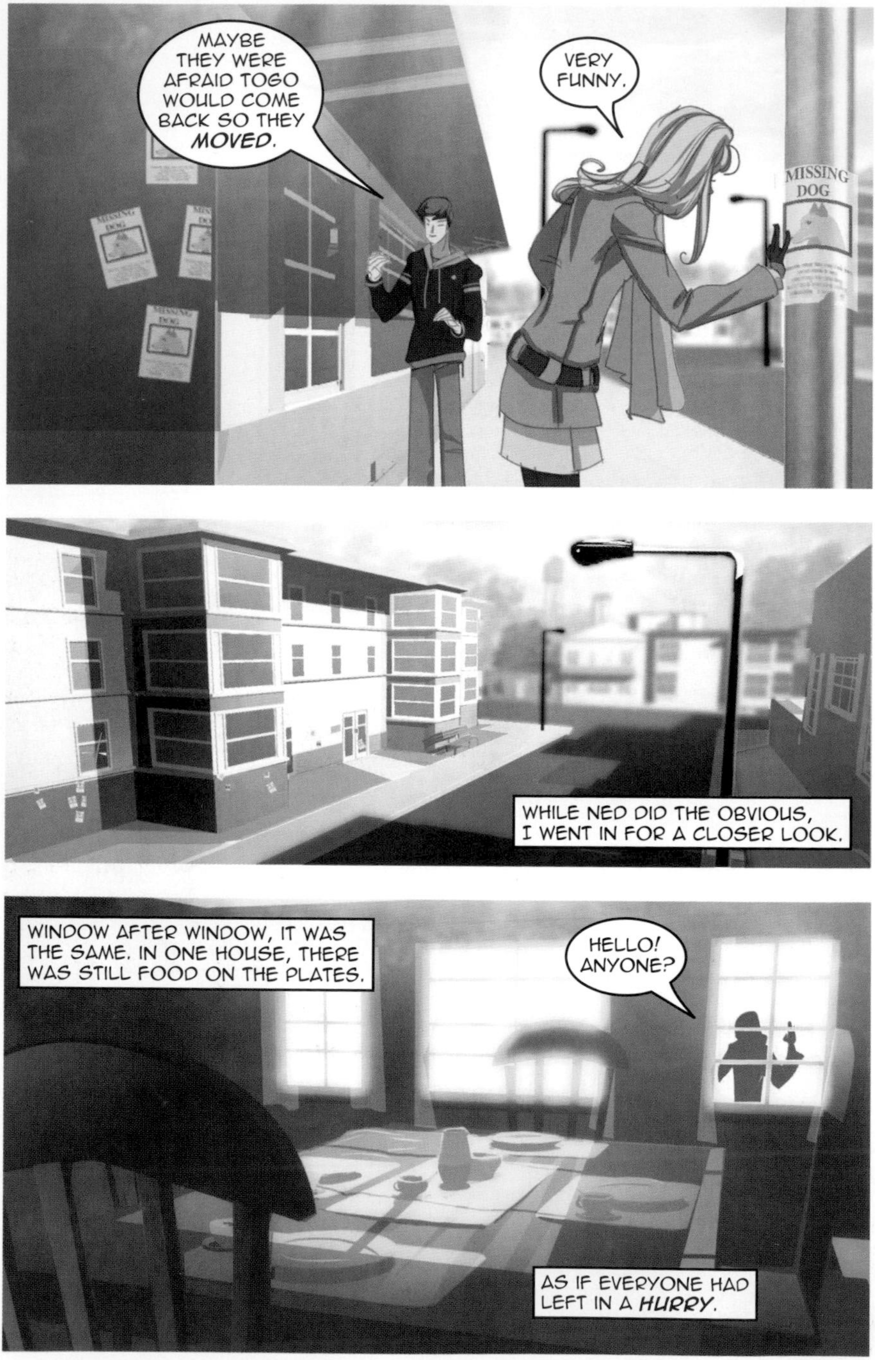
MAYBE THEY WERE AFRAID TOGO WOULD COME BACK SO THEY *MOVED*.
VERY FUNNY.
MISSING DOG
WHILE NED DID THE OBVIOUS, I WENT IN FOR A CLOSER LOOK.
WINDOW AFTER WINDOW, IT WAS THE SAME. IN ONE HOUSE, THERE WAS STILL FOOD ON THE PLATES.
HELLO! ANYONE?
AS IF EVERYONE HAD LEFT IN A *HURRY*.

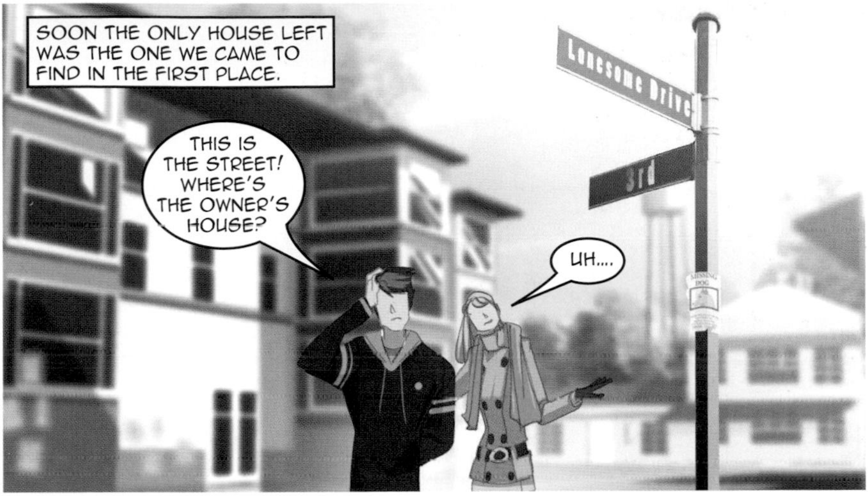
SOON THE ONLY HOUSE LEFT WAS THE ONE WE CAME TO FIND IN THE FIRST PLACE.
Lonesome Drive
3rd
THIS IS THE STREET! WHERE'S THE OWNER'S HOUSE?
UH....

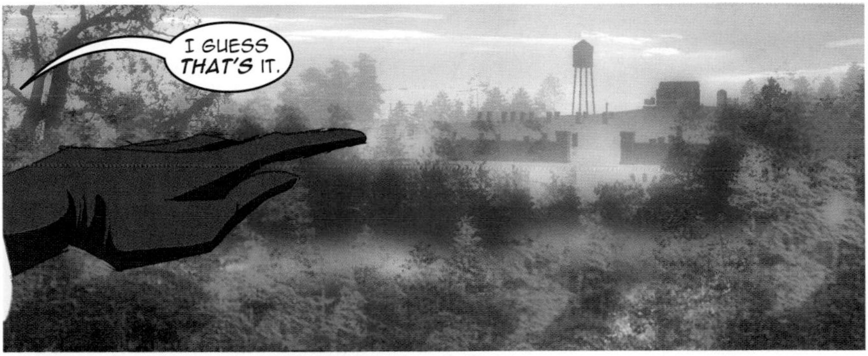
I GUESS *THAT'S* IT.

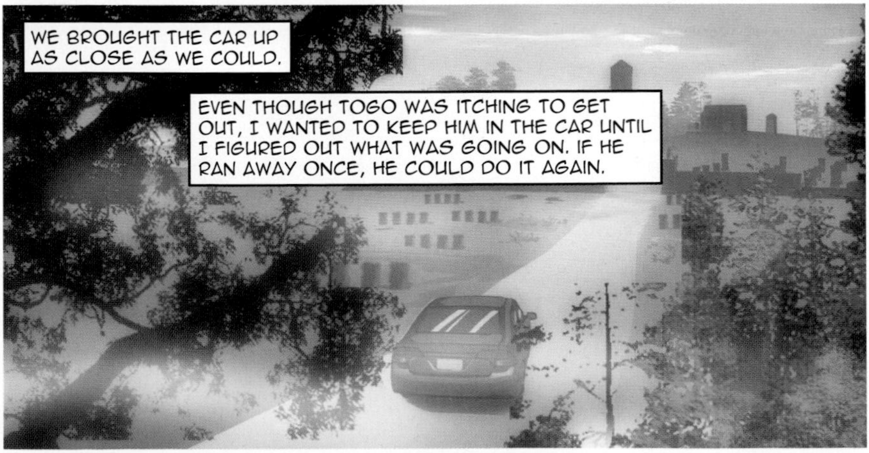
WE BROUGHT THE CAR UP AS CLOSE AS WE COULD.
EVEN THOUGH TOGO WAS ITCHING TO GET OUT, I WANTED TO KEEP HIM IN THE CAR UNTIL I FIGURED OUT WHAT WAS GOING ON. IF HE RAN AWAY ONCE, HE COULD DO IT AGAIN.

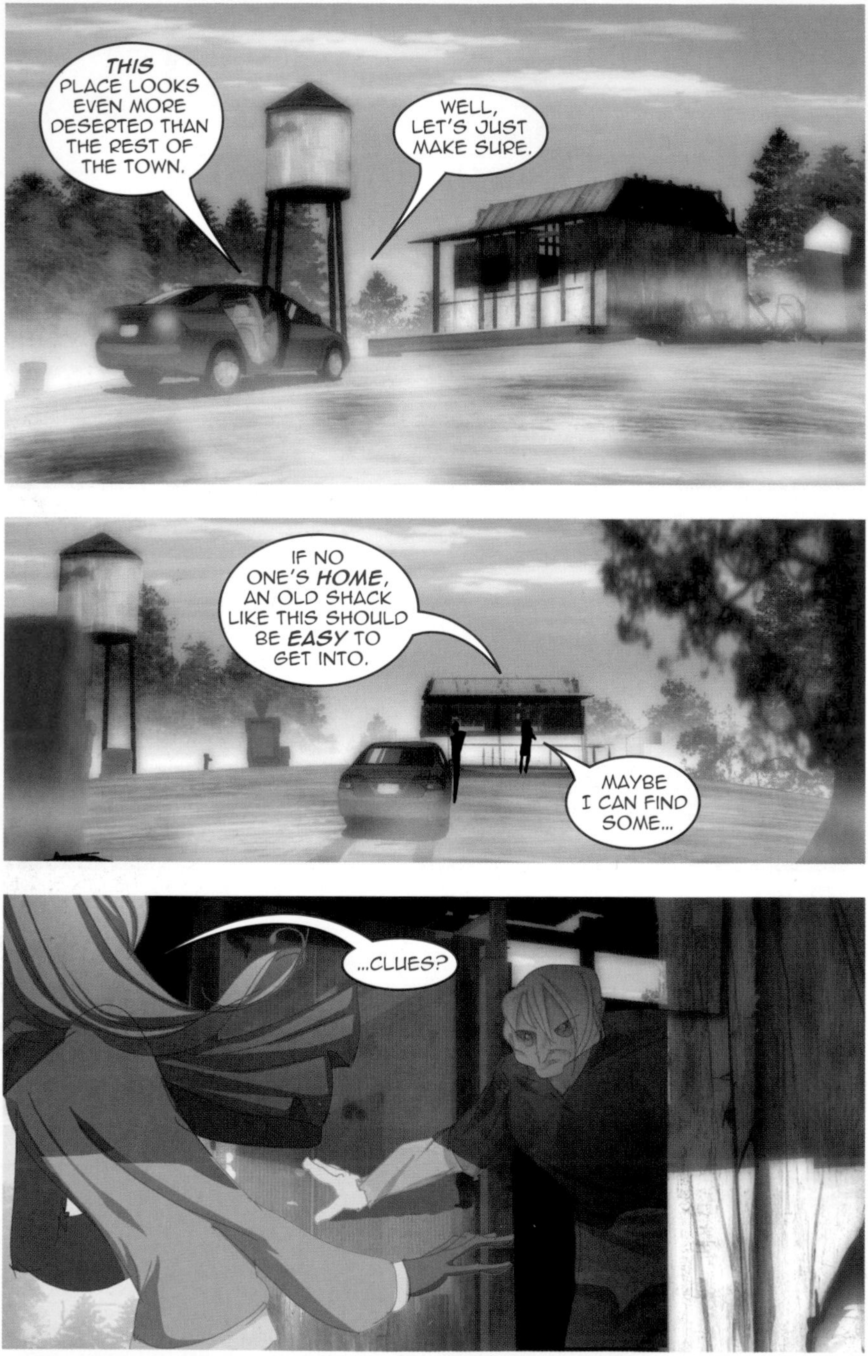
THIS PLACE LOOKS EVEN MORE DESERTED THAN THE REST OF THE TOWN.
WELL, LET'S JUST MAKE SURE.
IF NO ONE'S HOME, AN OLD SHACK LIKE THIS SHOULD BE EASY TO GET INTO.
MAYBE I CAN FIND SOME...
...CLUES?

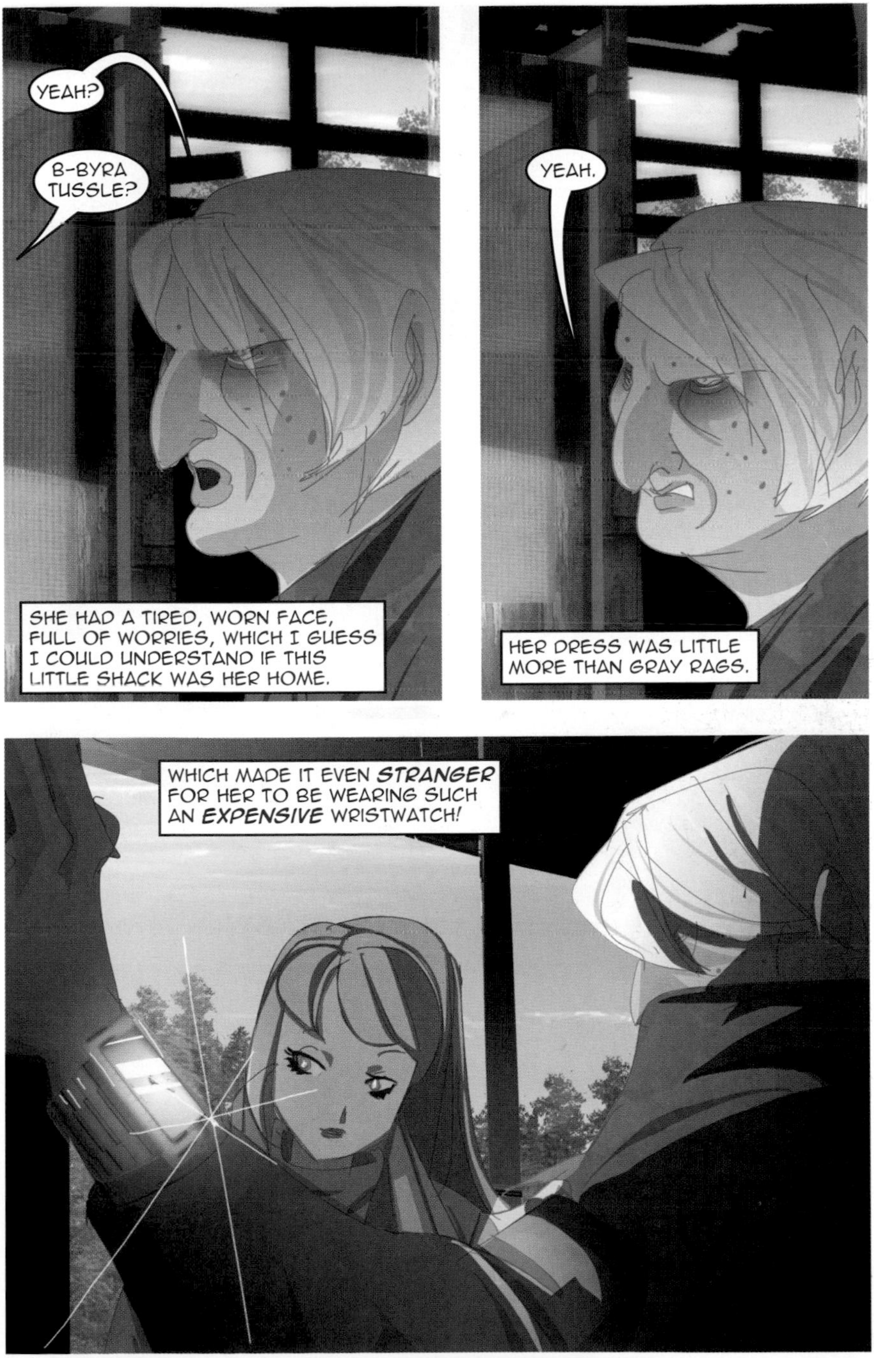
YEAH?
B-BYRA TUSSLE?
SHE HAD A TIRED, WORN FACE, FULL OF WORRIES, WHICH I GUESS I COULD UNDERSTAND IF THIS LITTLE SHACK WAS HER HOME.
YEAH.
HER DRESS WAS LITTLE MORE THAN GRAY RAGS.
WHICH MADE IT EVEN STRANGER FOR HER TO BE WEARING SUCH AN EXPENSIVE WRISTWATCH!

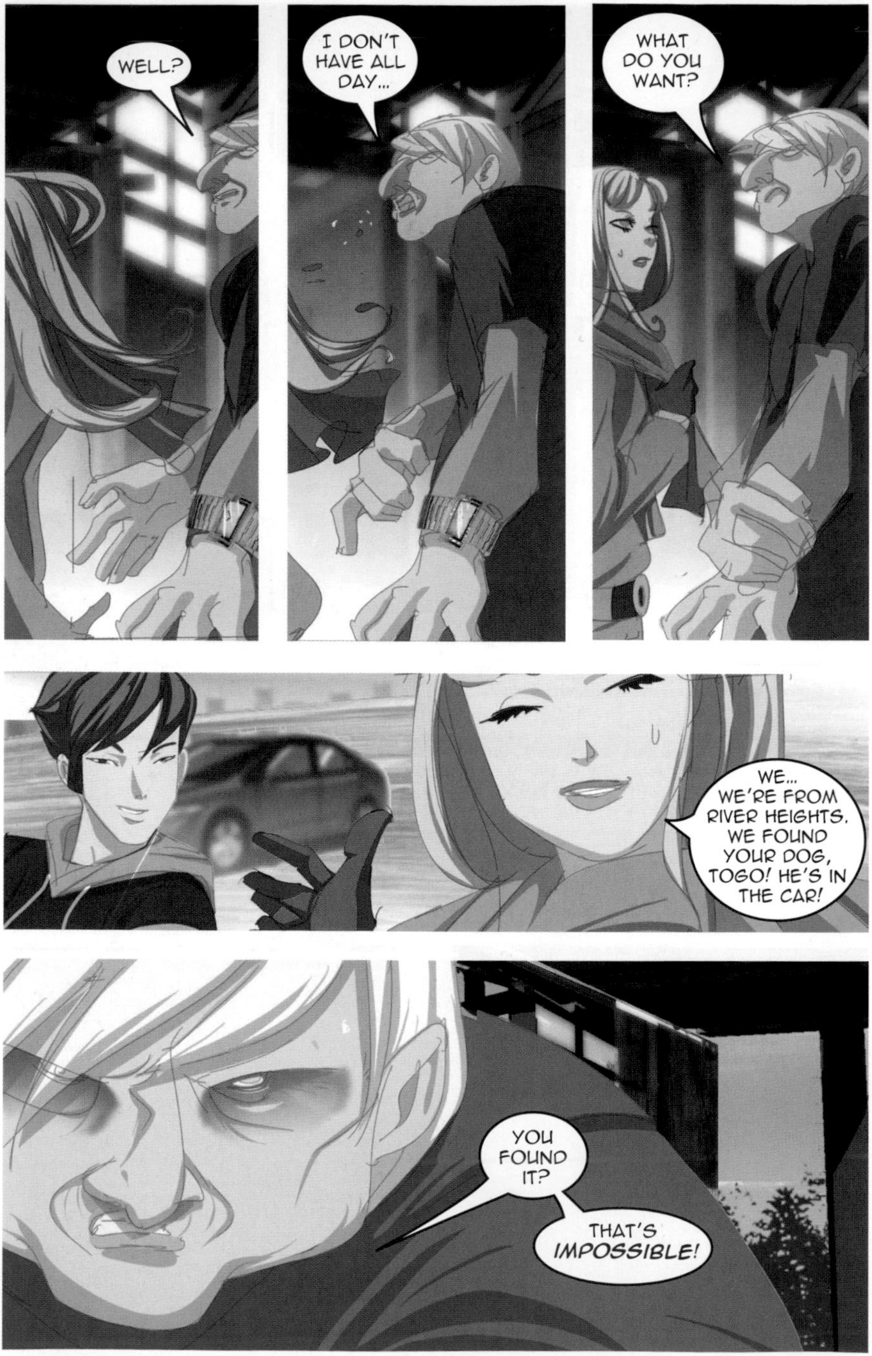
WELL?
I DON'T HAVE ALL DAY...
WHAT DO YOU WANT?
WE... WE'RE FROM RIVER HEIGHTS. WE FOUND YOUR DOG, TOGO! HE'S IN THE CAR!
YOU FOUND IT?
THAT'S *IMPOSSIBLE!*

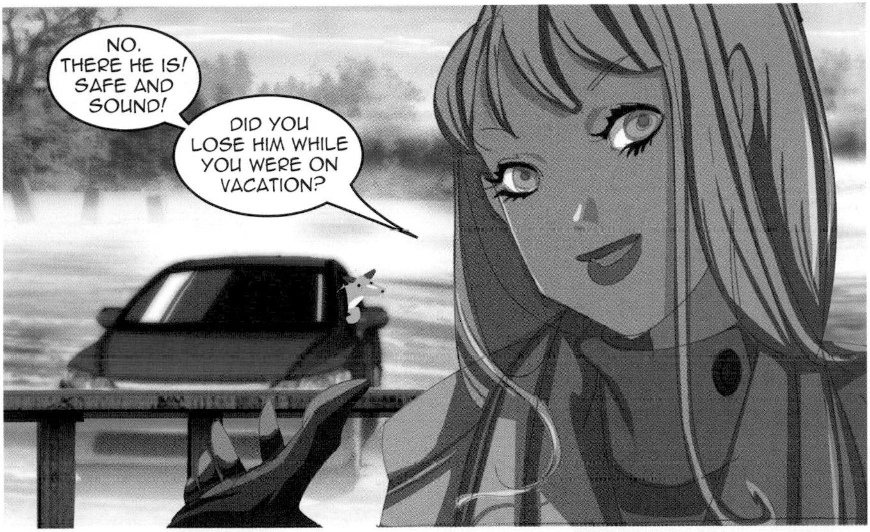
NO. THERE HE IS! SAFE AND SOUND!
DID YOU LOSE HIM WHILE YOU WERE ON VACATION?

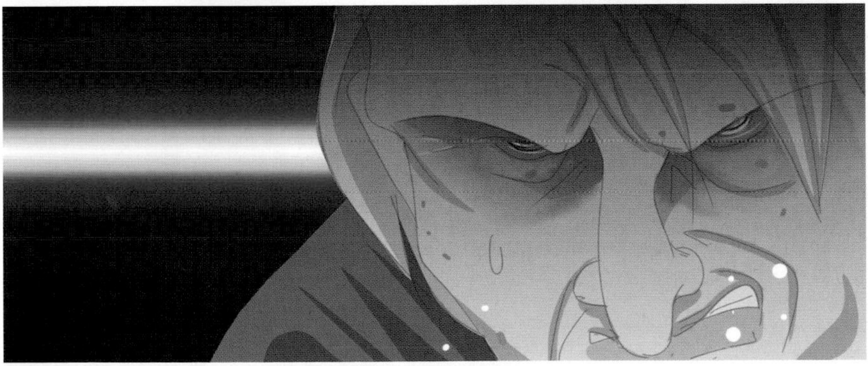

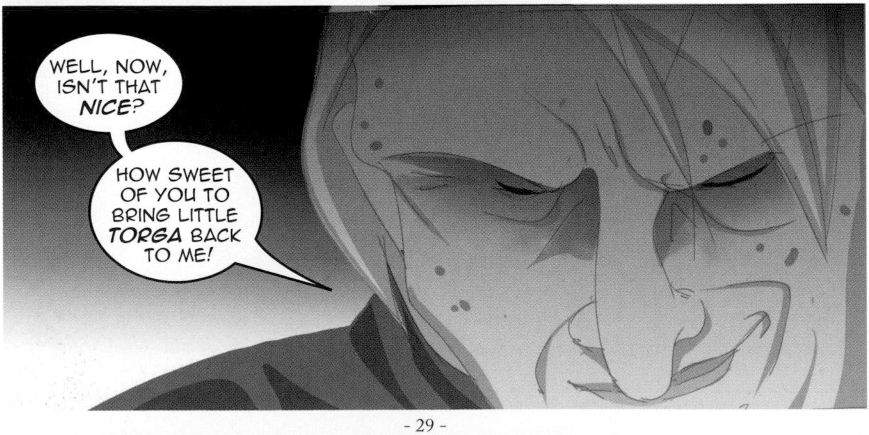
WELL, NOW, ISN'T THAT NICE?
HOW SWEET OF YOU TO BRING LITTLE TORGA BACK TO ME!

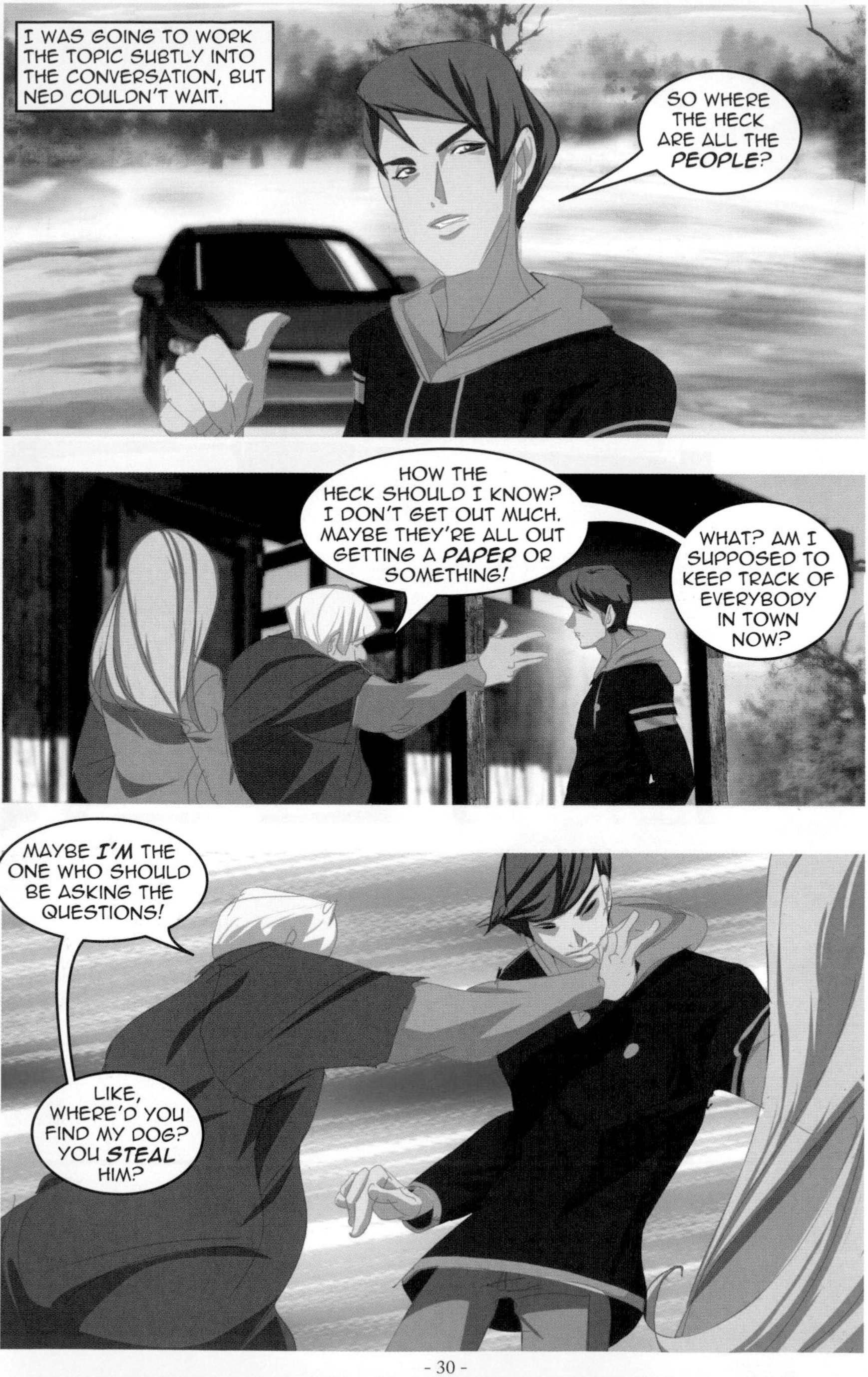
I WAS GOING TO WORK THE TOPIC SUBTLY INTO THE CONVERSATION, BUT NED COULDN'T WAIT.
SO WHERE THE HECK ARE ALL THE PEOPLE?
HOW THE HECK SHOULD I KNOW? I DON'T GET OUT MUCH. MAYBE THEY'RE ALL OUT GETTING A PAPER OR SOMETHING!
WHAT? AM I SUPPOSED TO KEEP TRACK OF EVERYBODY IN TOWN NOW?
MAYBE I'M THE ONE WHO SHOULD BE ASKING THE QUESTIONS!
LIKE, WHERE'D YOU FIND MY DOG? YOU STEAL HIM?

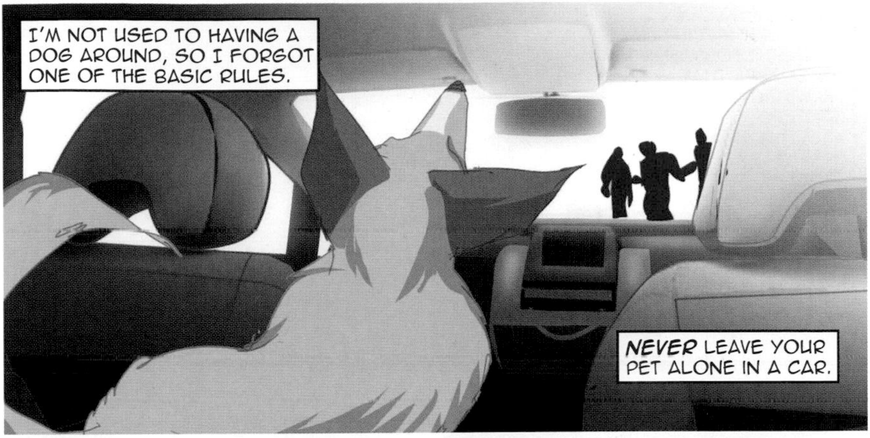
I'M NOT USED TO HAVING A DOG AROUND, SO I FORGOT ONE OF THE BASIC RULES.
NEVER LEAVE YOUR PET ALONE IN A CAR.

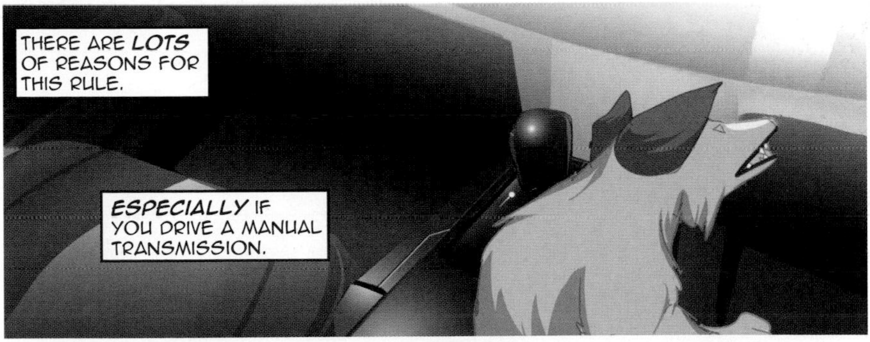
THERE ARE LOTS OF REASONS FOR THIS RULE.
ESPECIALLY IF YOU DRIVE A MANUAL TRANSMISSION.

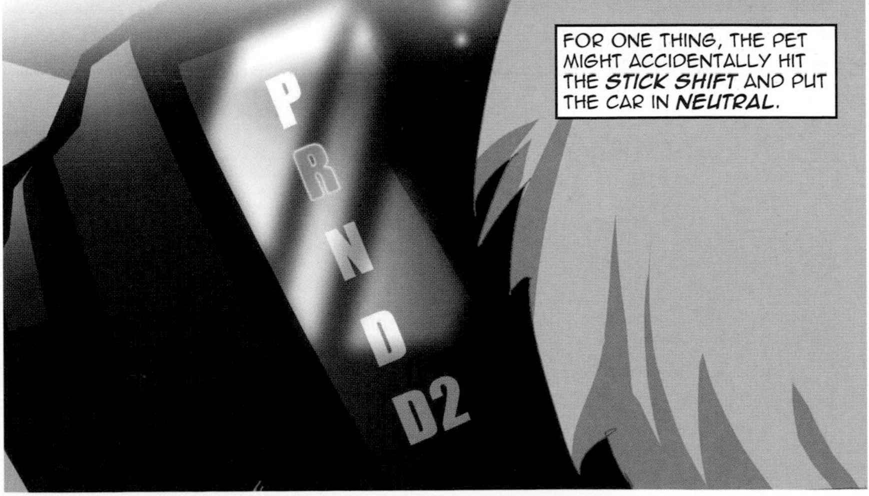
FOR ONE THING, THE PET MIGHT ACCIDENTALLY HIT THE STICK SHIFT AND PUT THE CAR IN NEUTRAL.
P
R
N
D
D2

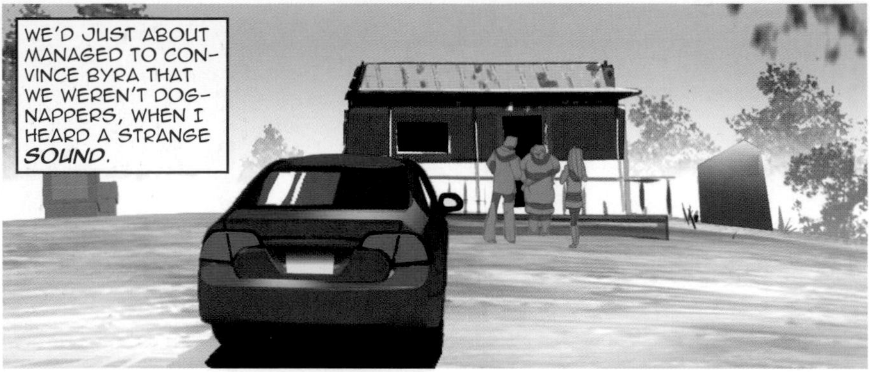
WE'D JUST ABOUT MANAGED TO CONVINCE BYRA THAT WE WEREN'T DOG-NAPPERS, WHEN I HEARD A STRANGE *SOUND*.

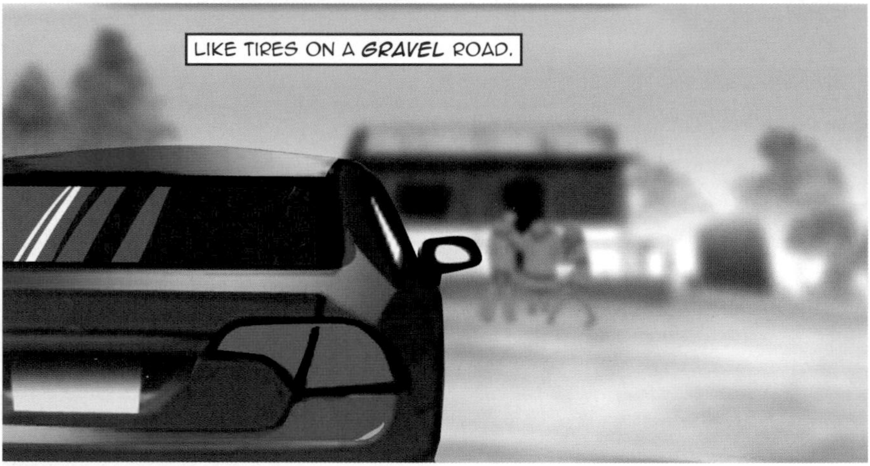
LIKE TIRES ON A *GRAVEL* ROAD.

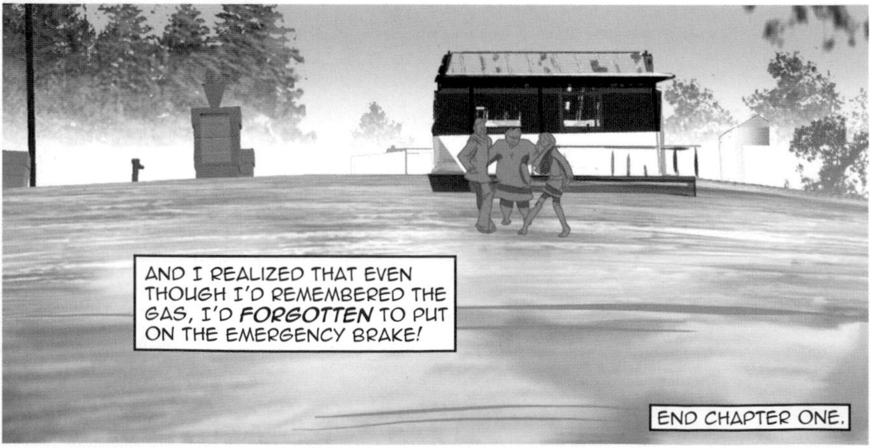
AND I REALIZED THAT EVEN THOUGH I'D REMEMBERED THE GAS, I'D *FORGOTTEN* TO PUT ON THE EMERGENCY BRAKE!
END CHAPTER ONE.

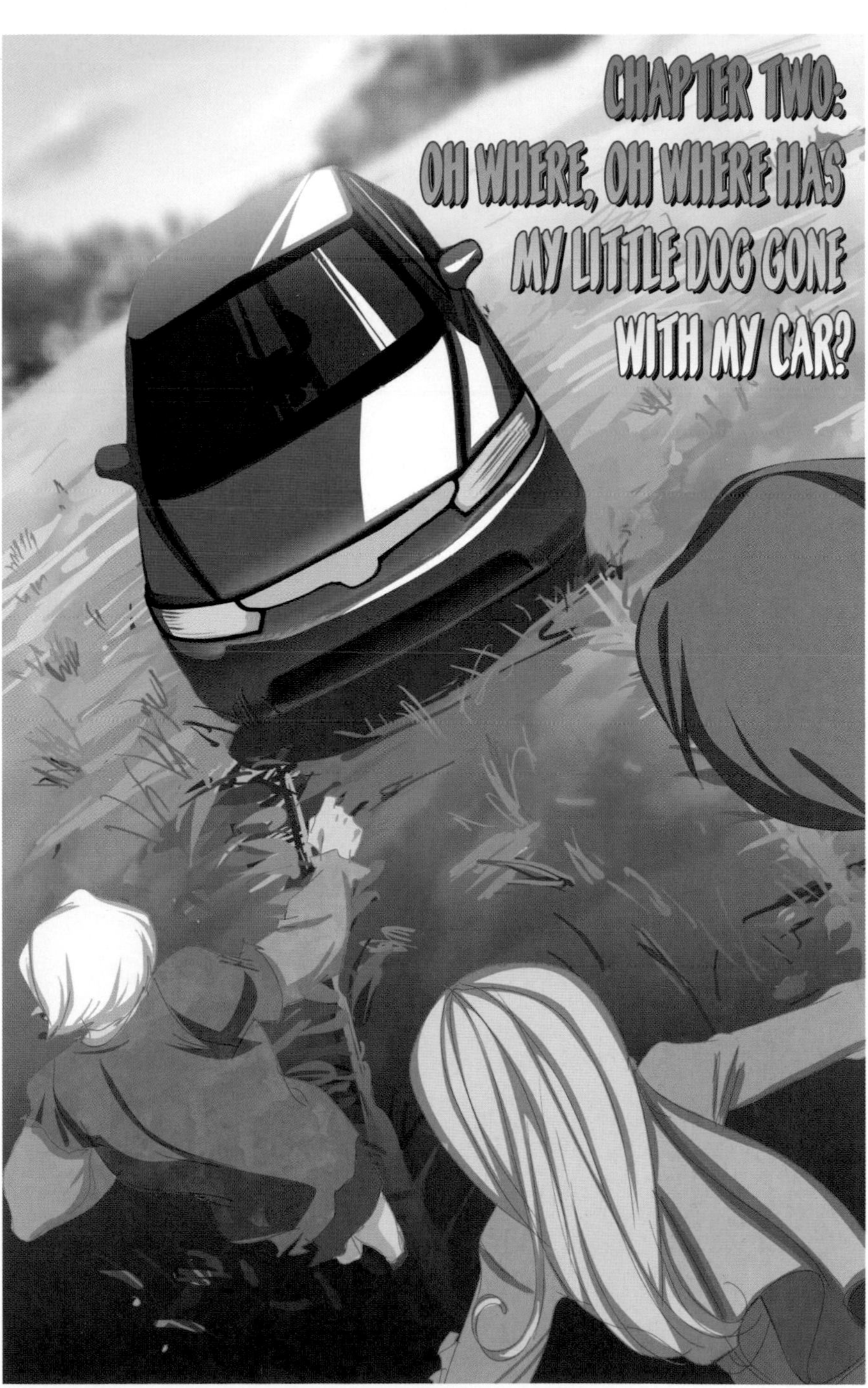
CHAPTER TWO:
OH WHERE, OH WHERE HAS
MY LITTLE DOG GONE
WITH MY CAR?

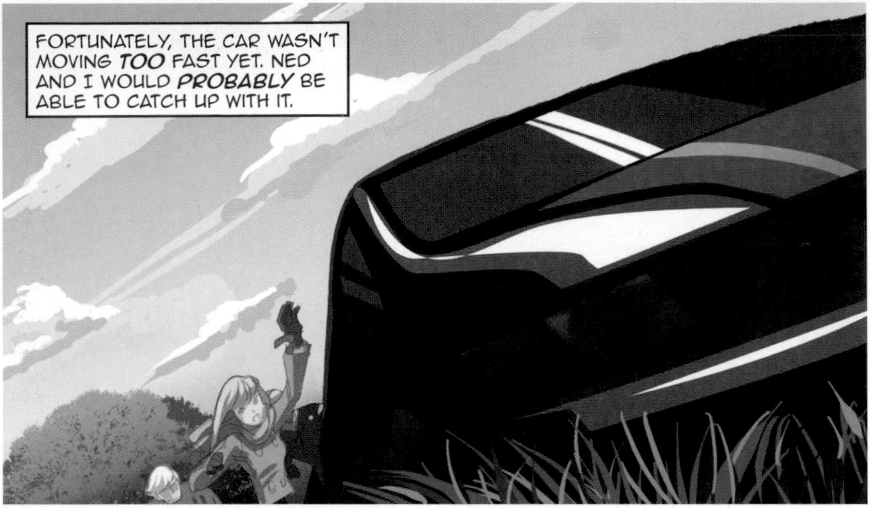
FORTUNATELY, THE CAR WASN'T MOVING *TOO* FAST YET. NED AND I WOULD *PROBABLY* BE ABLE TO CATCH UP WITH IT.

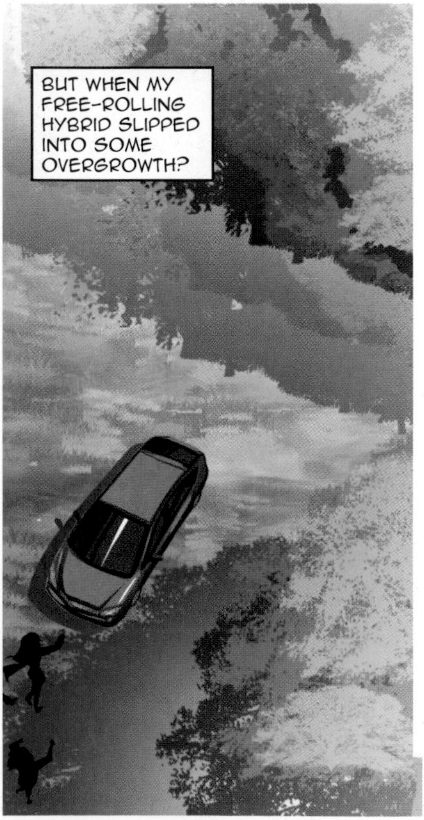
BUT WHEN MY FREE-ROLLING HYBRID SLIPPED INTO SOME OVERGROWTH?

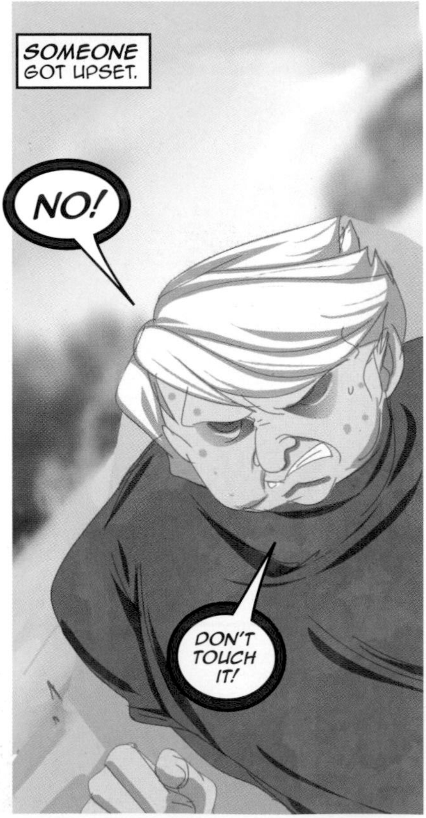
SOMEONE GOT UPSET.
NO!
DON'T TOUCH IT!

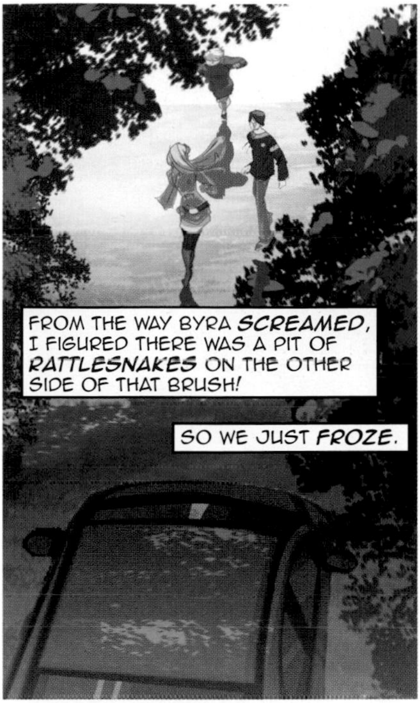
FROM THE WAY BYRA *SCREAMED*, I FIGURED THERE WAS A PIT OF *RATTLESNAKES* ON THE OTHER SIDE OF THAT BRUSH!
SO WE JUST *FROZE*.

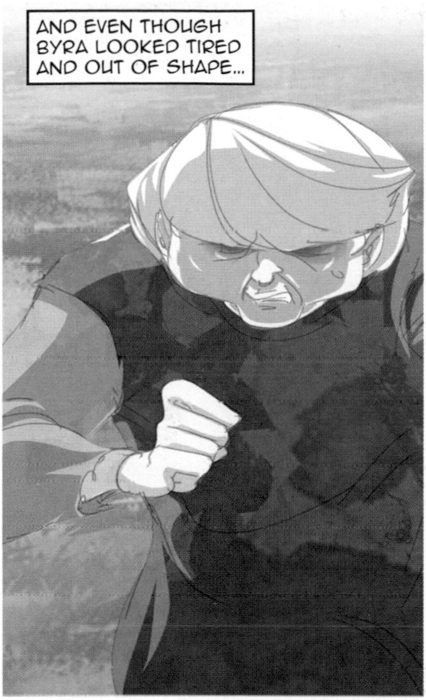
AND EVEN THOUGH BYRA LOOKED TIRED AND OUT OF SHAPE...

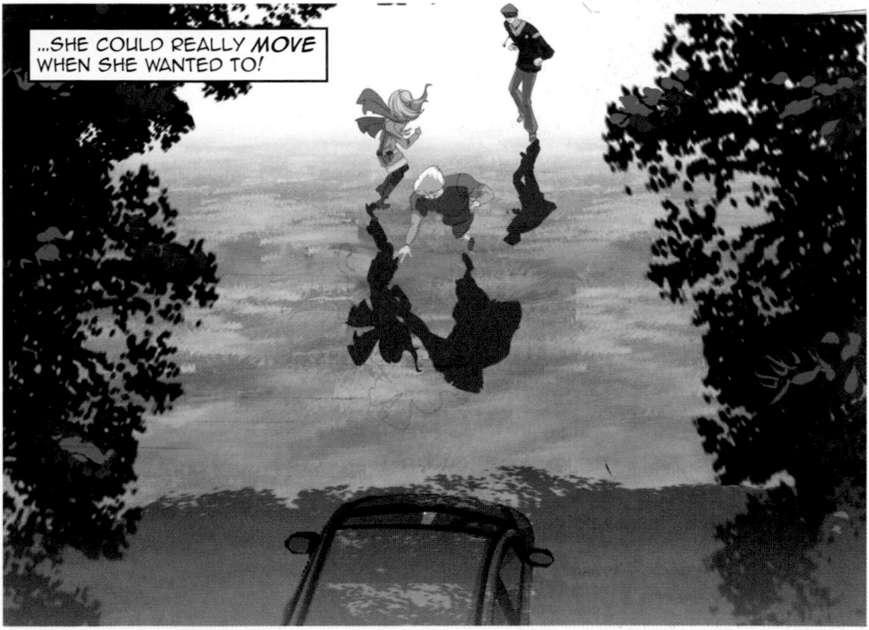
...SHE COULD REALLY *MOVE* WHEN SHE WANTED TO!

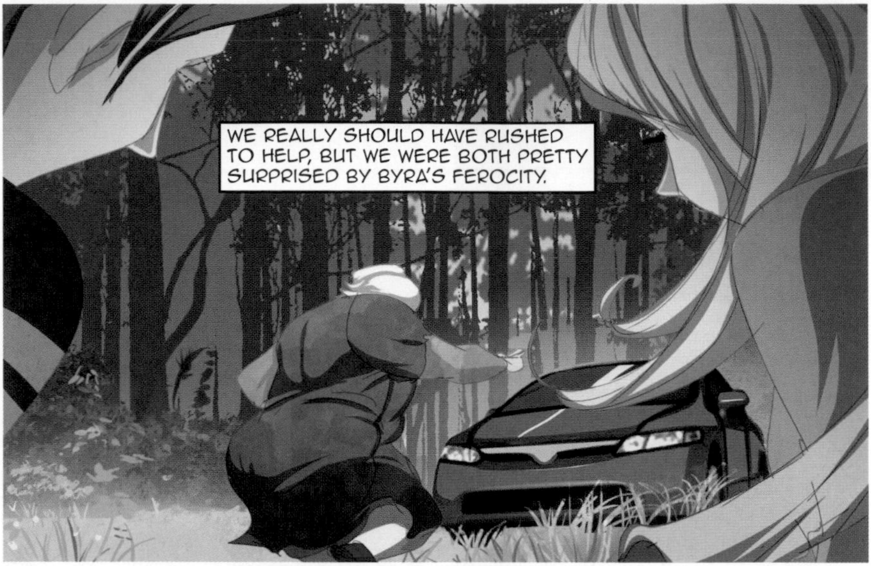
WE REALLY SHOULD HAVE RUSHED TO HELP, BUT WE WERE BOTH PRETTY SURPRISED BY BYRA'S FEROCITY.

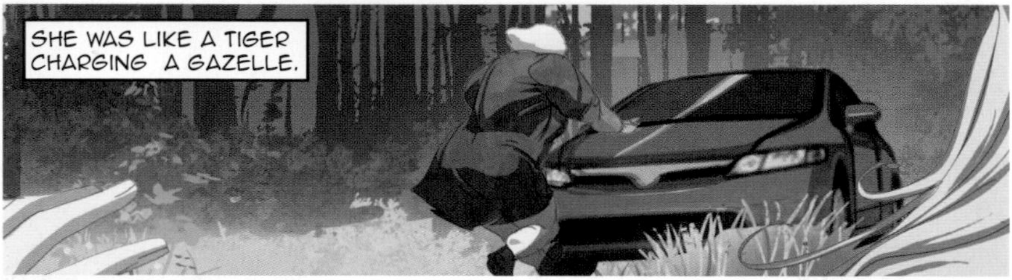
SHE WAS LIKE A TIGER CHARGING A GAZELLE.

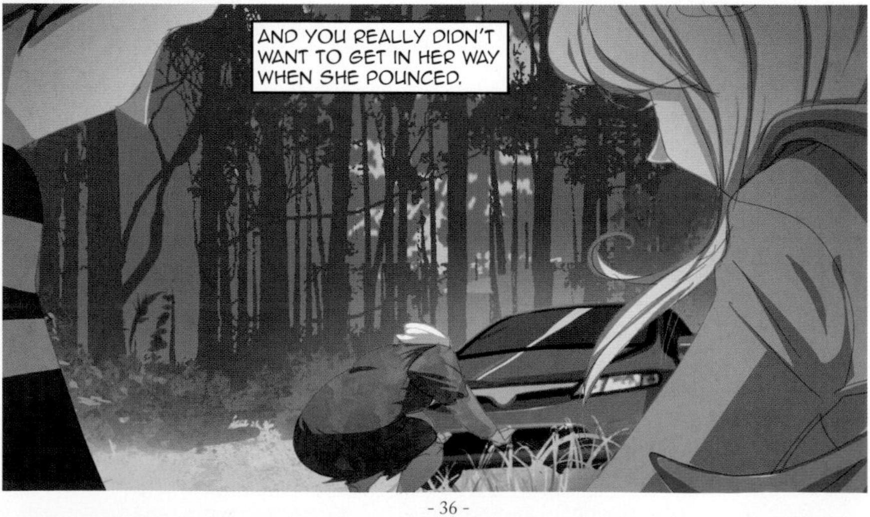
AND YOU REALLY DIDN'T WANT TO GET IN HER WAY WHEN SHE POUNCED.

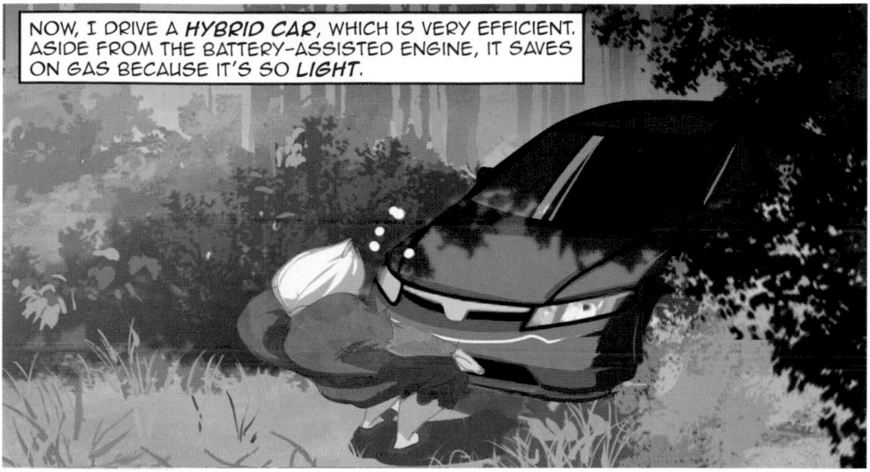
NOW, I DRIVE A HYBRID CAR, WHICH IS VERY EFFICIENT. ASIDE FROM THE BATTERY-ASSISTED ENGINE, IT SAVES ON GAS BECAUSE IT'S SO LIGHT.

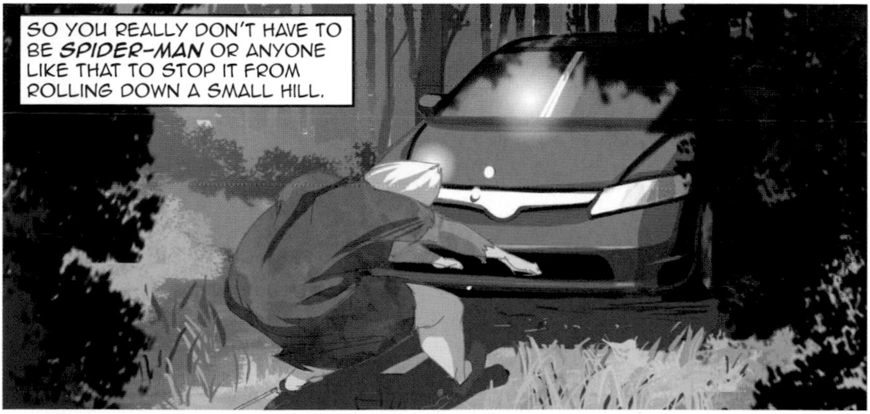
SO YOU REALLY DON'T HAVE TO BE SPIDER-MAN OR ANYONE LIKE THAT TO STOP IT FROM ROLLING DOWN A SMALL HILL.

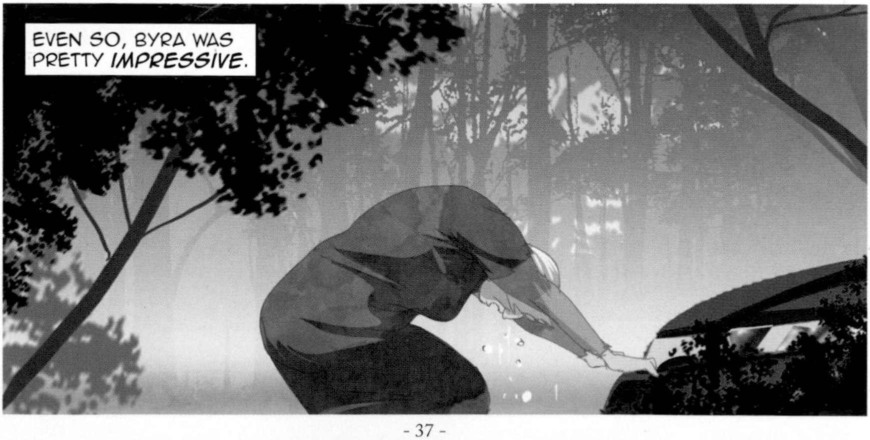
EVEN SO, BYRA WAS PRETTY IMPRESSIVE.

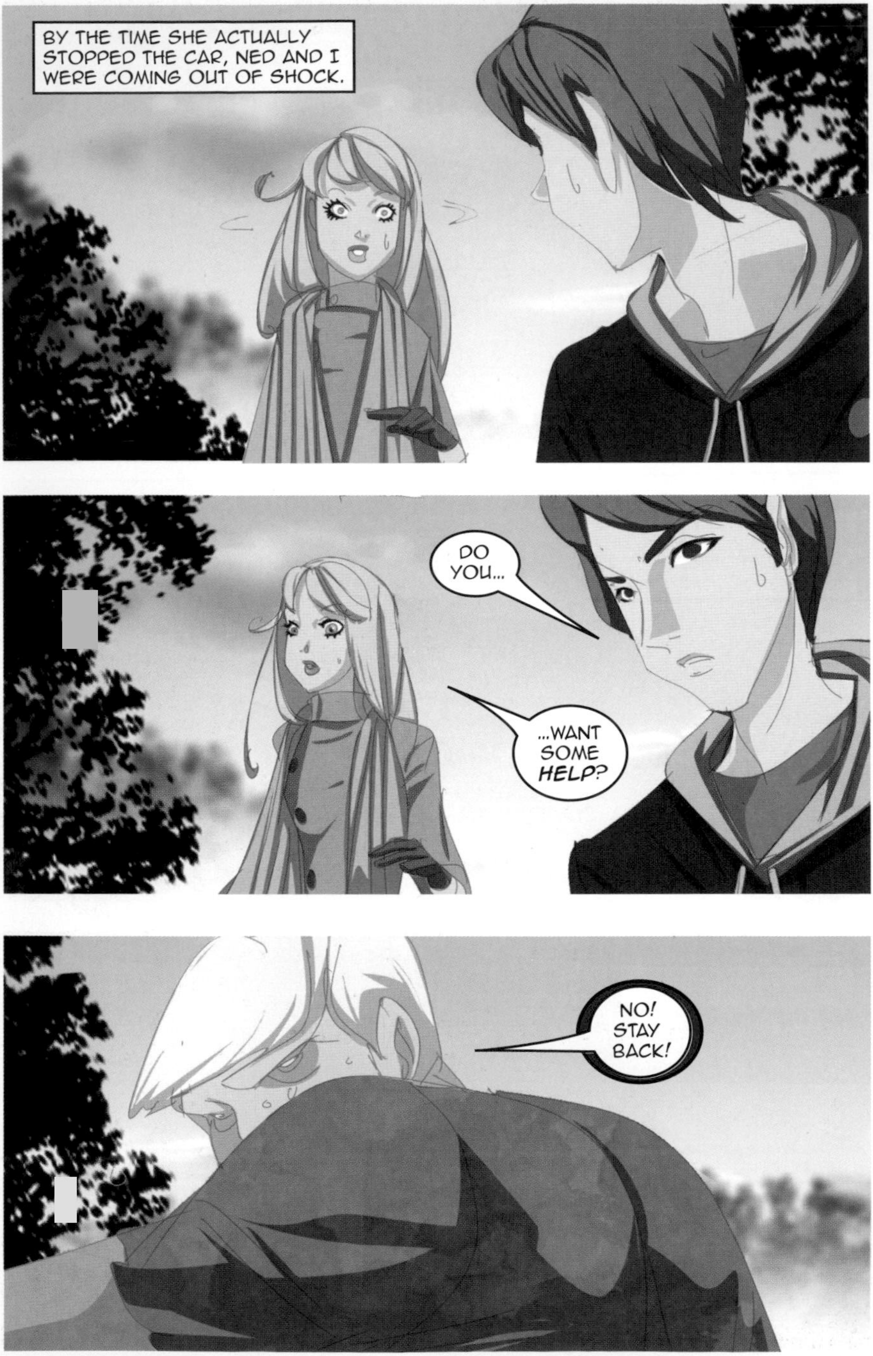
BY THE TIME SHE ACTUALLY STOPPED THE CAR, NED AND I WERE COMING OUT OF SHOCK.
DO YOU...
...WANT SOME HELP?
NO! STAY BACK!

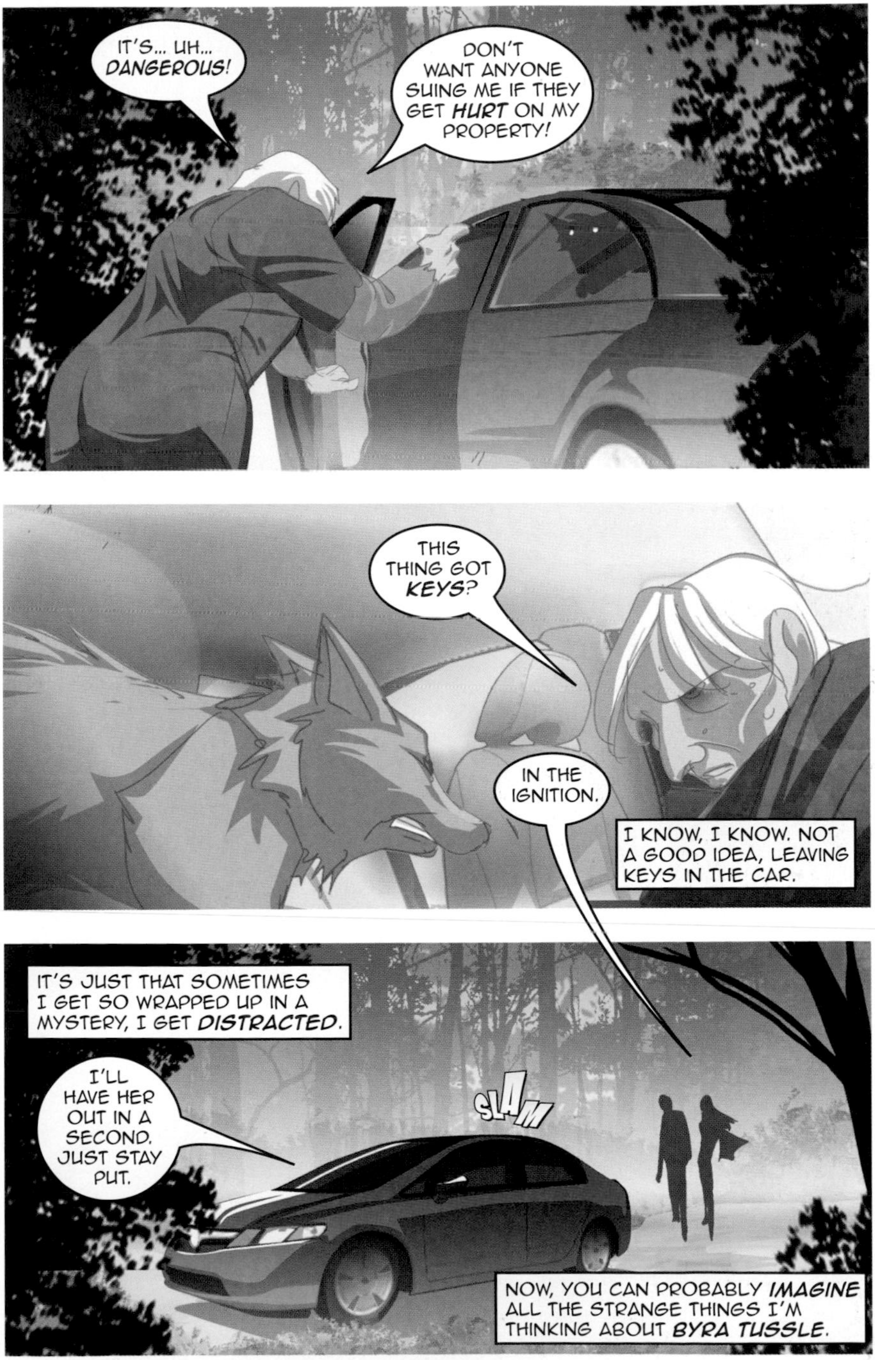
IT'S... UH... DANGEROUS!
DON'T WANT ANYONE SUING ME IF THEY GET HURT ON MY PROPERTY!
THIS THING GOT KEYS?
IN THE IGNITION.
I KNOW, I KNOW. NOT A GOOD IDEA, LEAVING KEYS IN THE CAR.
IT'S JUST THAT SOMETIMES I GET SO WRAPPED UP IN A MYSTERY, I GET DISTRACTED.
I'LL HAVE HER OUT IN A SECOND. JUST STAY PUT.
SLAM
NOW, YOU CAN PROBABLY IMAGINE ALL THE STRANGE THINGS I'M THINKING ABOUT BYRA TUSSLE.

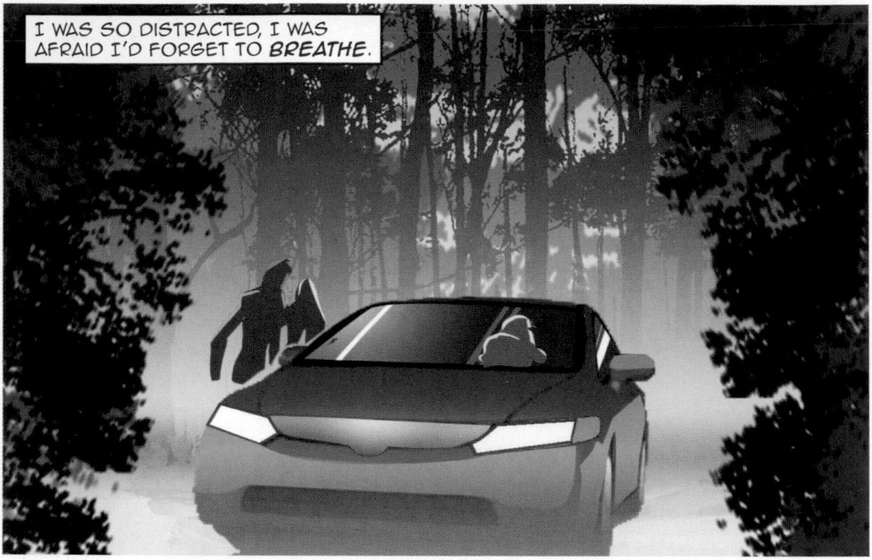
I WAS SO DISTRACTED, I WAS AFRAID I'D FORGET TO *BREATHE*.

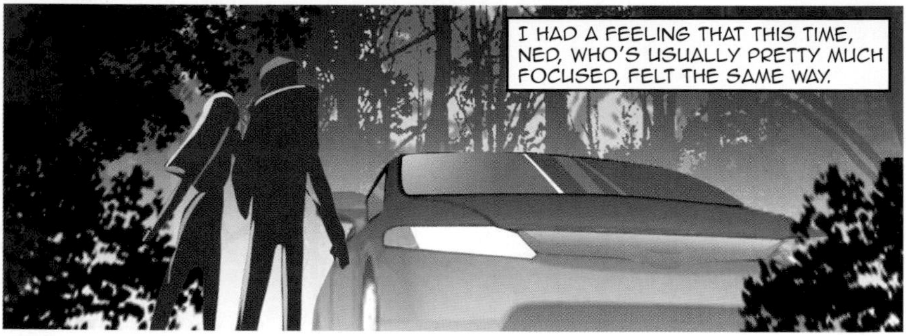
I HAD A FEELING THAT THIS TIME, NED, WHO'S USUALLY PRETTY MUCH FOCUSED, FELT THE SAME WAY.

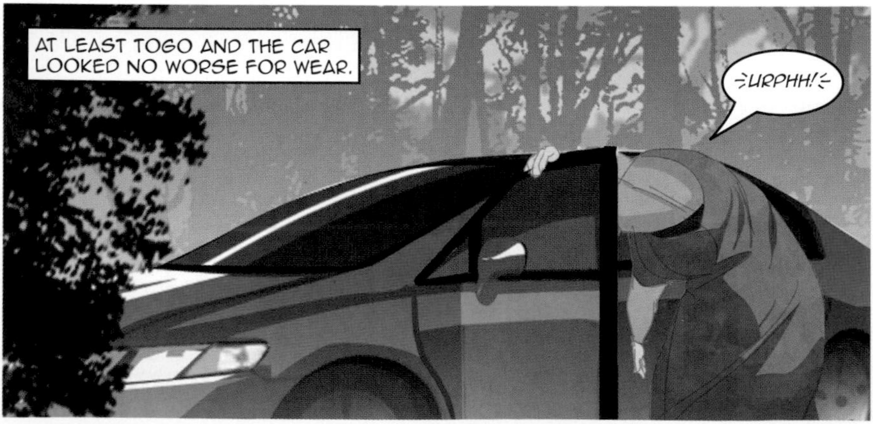
AT LEAST TOGO AND THE CAR LOOKED NO WORSE FOR WEAR.
URPHH!

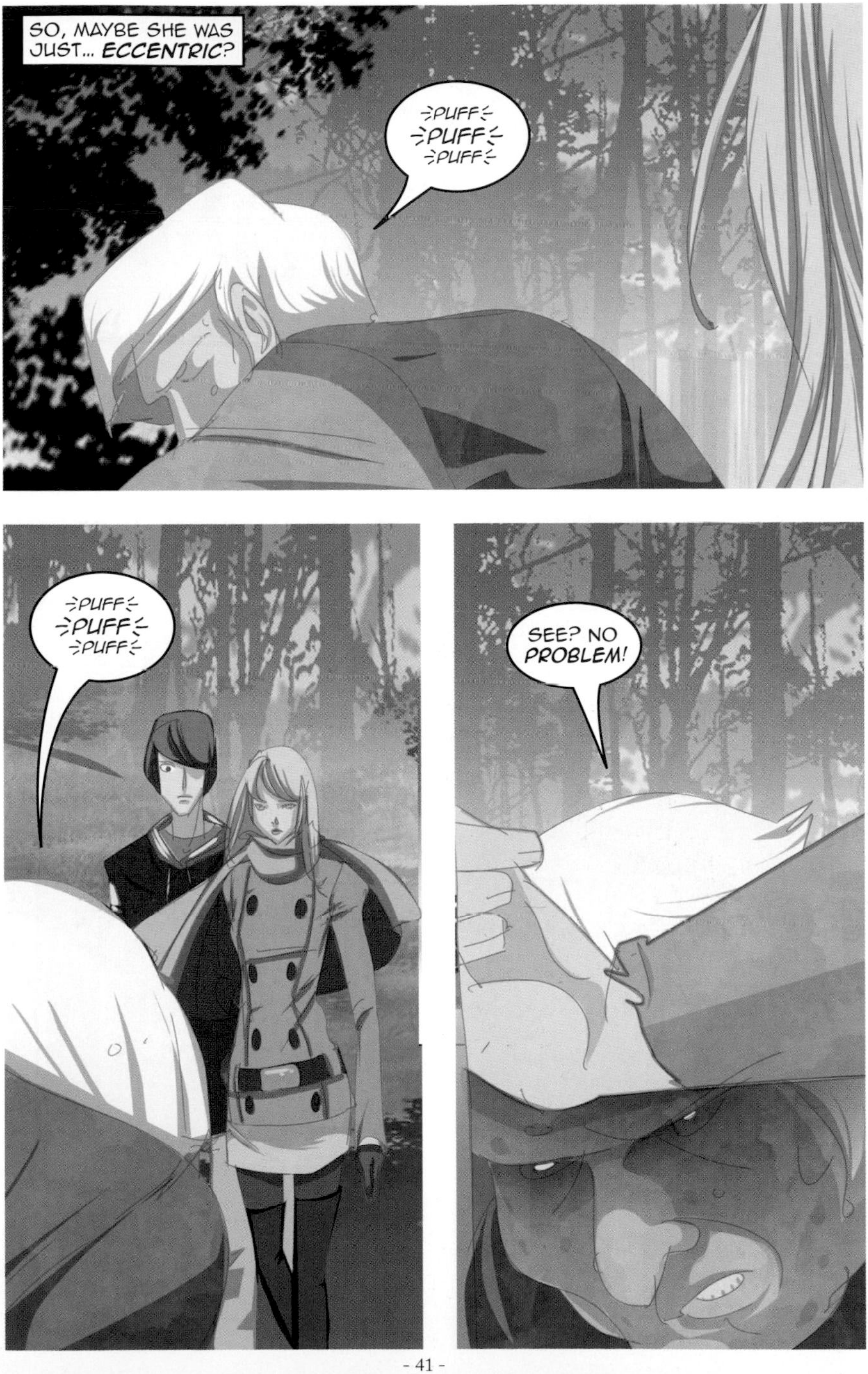
SO, MAYBE SHE WAS JUST... ECCENTRIC?
PUFF PUFF PUFF
PUFF PUFF PUFF
SEE? NO PROBLEM!

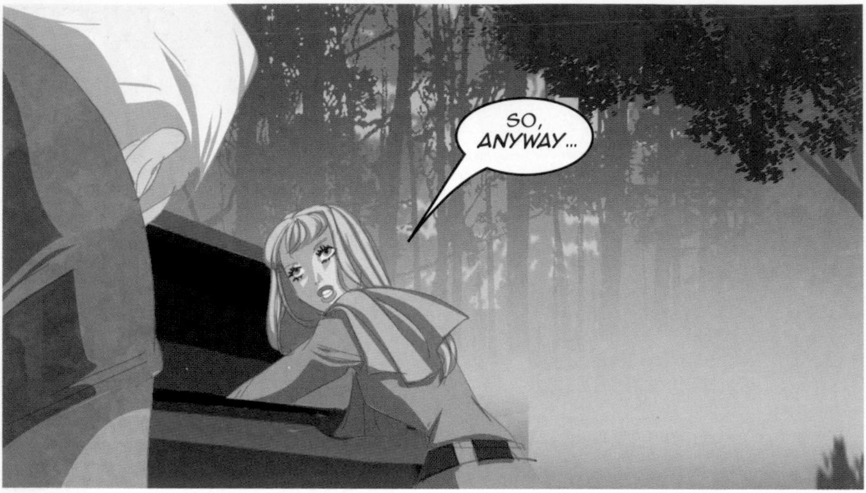
SO, ANYWAY...

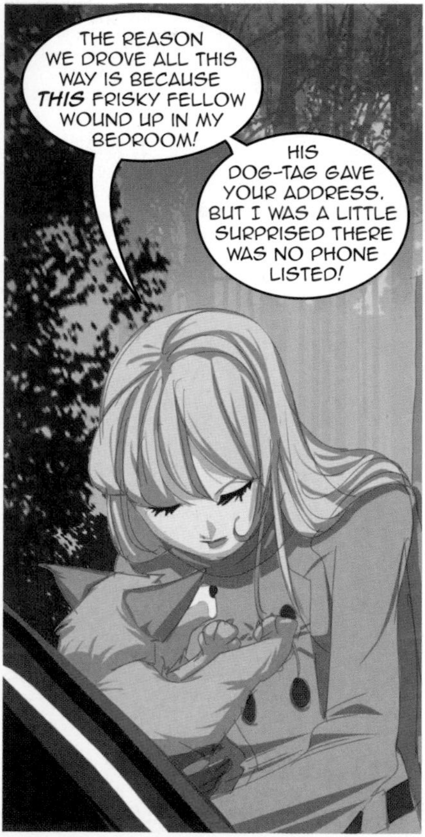
THE REASON WE DROVE ALL THIS WAY IS BECAUSE THIS FRISKY FELLOW WOUND UP IN MY BEDROOM!
HIS DOG-TAG GAVE YOUR ADDRESS. BUT I WAS A LITTLE SURPRISED THERE WAS NO PHONE LISTED!

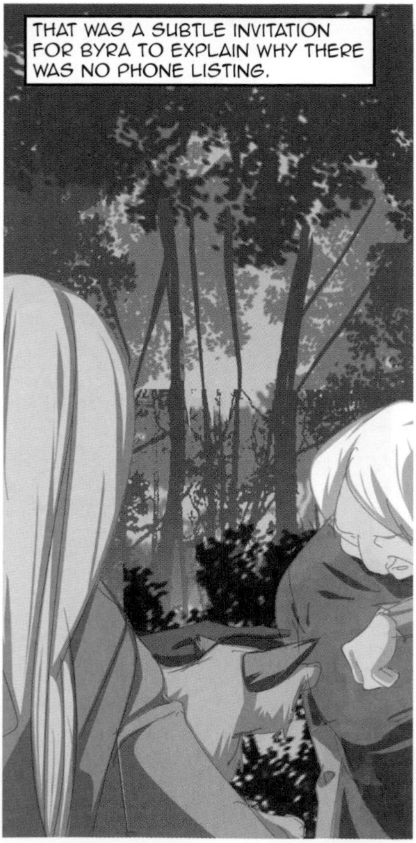
THAT WAS A SUBTLE INVITATION FOR BYRA TO EXPLAIN WHY THERE WAS NO PHONE LISTING.

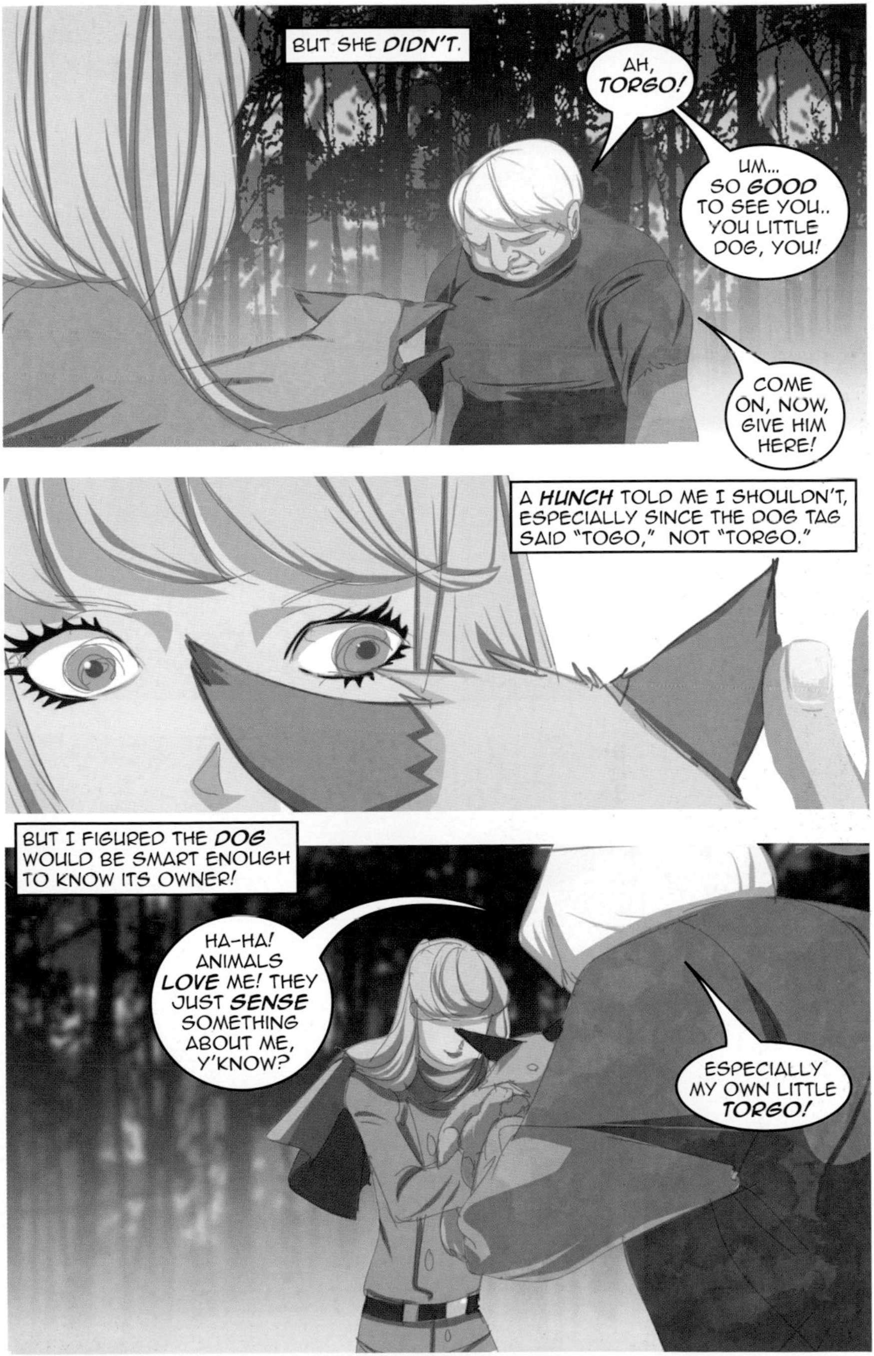
BUT SHE DIDN'T.
AH, TORGO!
UM... SO GOOD TO SEE YOU.. YOU LITTLE DOG, YOU!
COME ON, NOW, GIVE HIM HERE!
A HUNCH TOLD ME I SHOULDN'T, ESPECIALLY SINCE THE DOG TAG SAID "TOGO," NOT "TORGO."
BUT I FIGURED THE DOG WOULD BE SMART ENOUGH TO KNOW ITS OWNER!
HA-HA! ANIMALS LOVE ME! THEY JUST SENSE SOMETHING ABOUT ME, Y'KNOW?
ESPECIALLY MY OWN LITTLE TORGO!

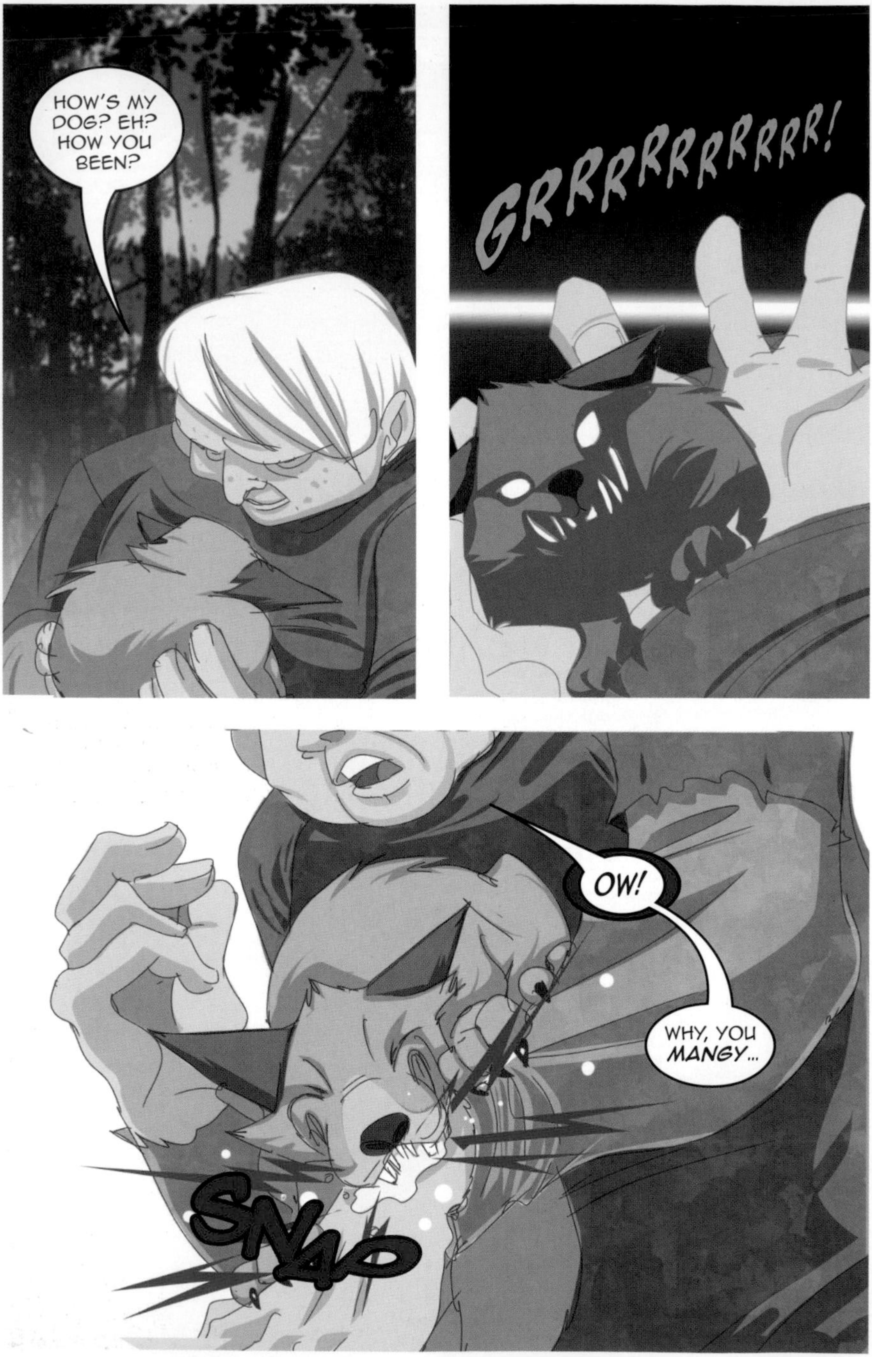
HOW'S MY DOG? EH? HOW YOU BEEN?
GRRRRRRRRRRR!
OW!
WHY, YOU MANGY...
SNAP

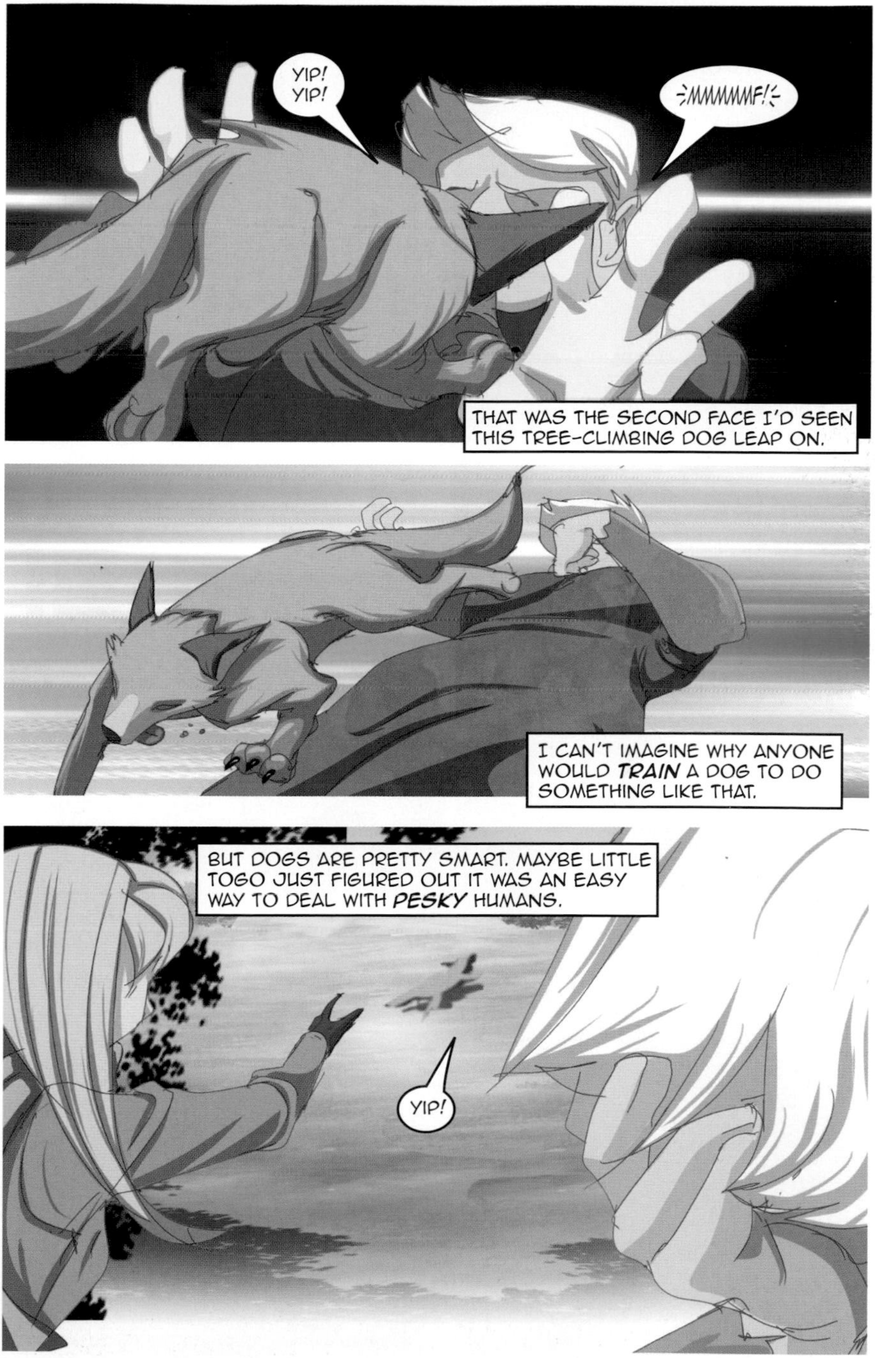
YIP! YIP!
MMMMMMF!
THAT WAS THE SECOND FACE I'D SEEN THIS TREE-CLIMBING DOG LEAP ON.
I CAN'T IMAGINE WHY ANYONE WOULD TRAIN A DOG TO DO SOMETHING LIKE THAT.
BUT DOGS ARE PRETTY SMART. MAYBE LITTLE TOGO JUST FIGURED OUT IT WAS AN EASY WAY TO DEAL WITH PESKY HUMANS.
YIP!

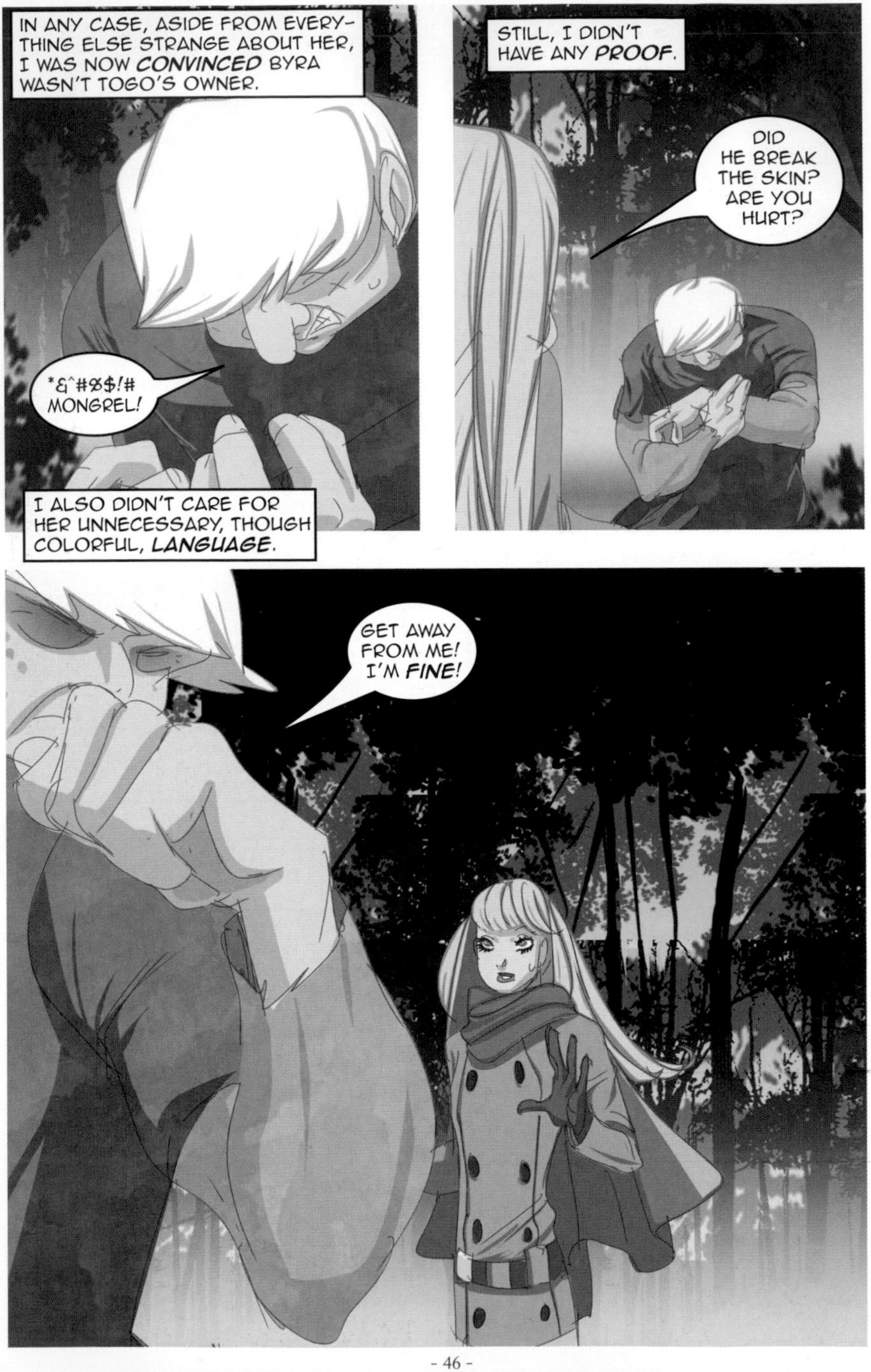
IN ANY CASE, ASIDE FROM EVERYTHING ELSE STRANGE ABOUT HER, I WAS NOW CONVINCED BYRA WASN'T TOGO'S OWNER.
*&^#%$!# MONGREL!
I ALSO DIDN'T CARE FOR HER UNNECESSARY, THOUGH COLORFUL, LANGUAGE.
STILL, I DIDN'T HAVE ANY PROOF.
DID HE BREAK THE SKIN? ARE YOU HURT?
GET AWAY FROM ME! I'M FINE!

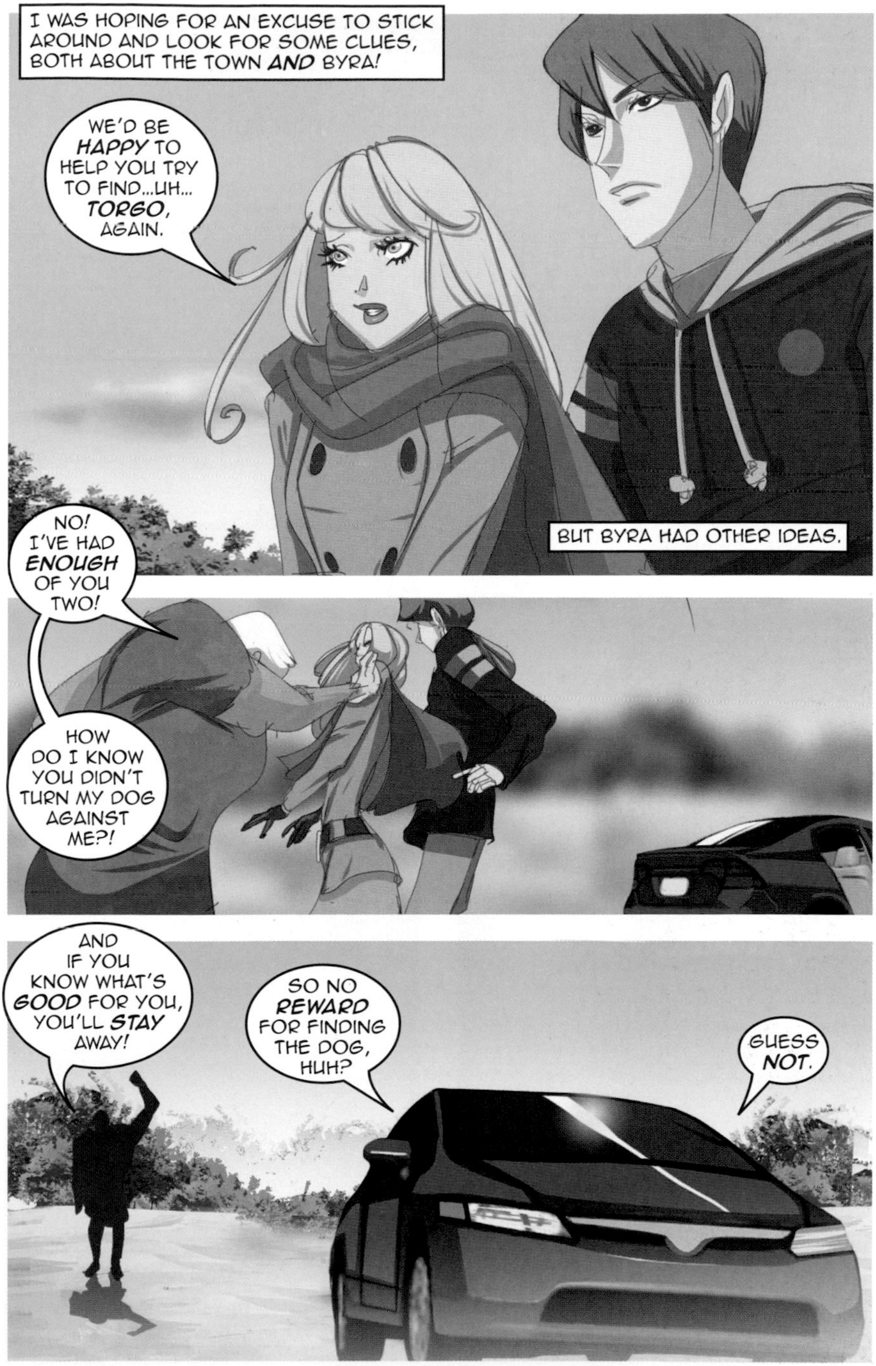
I WAS HOPING FOR AN EXCUSE TO STICK AROUND AND LOOK FOR SOME CLUES, BOTH ABOUT THE TOWN AND BYRA!
WE'D BE HAPPY TO HELP YOU TRY TO FIND...UH... TORGO, AGAIN.
BUT BYRA HAD OTHER IDEAS.
NO! I'VE HAD ENOUGH OF YOU TWO!
HOW DO I KNOW YOU DIDN'T TURN MY DOG AGAINST ME?!
AND IF YOU KNOW WHAT'S GOOD FOR YOU, YOU'LL STAY AWAY!
SO NO REWARD FOR FINDING THE DOG, HUH?
GUESS NOT.

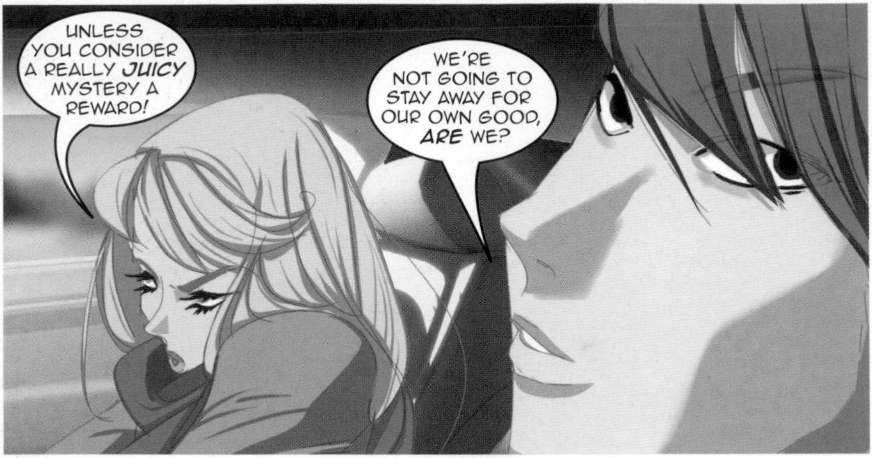
UNLESS YOU CONSIDER A REALLY JUICY MYSTERY A REWARD!
WE'RE NOT GOING TO STAY AWAY FOR OUR OWN GOOD, ARE WE?

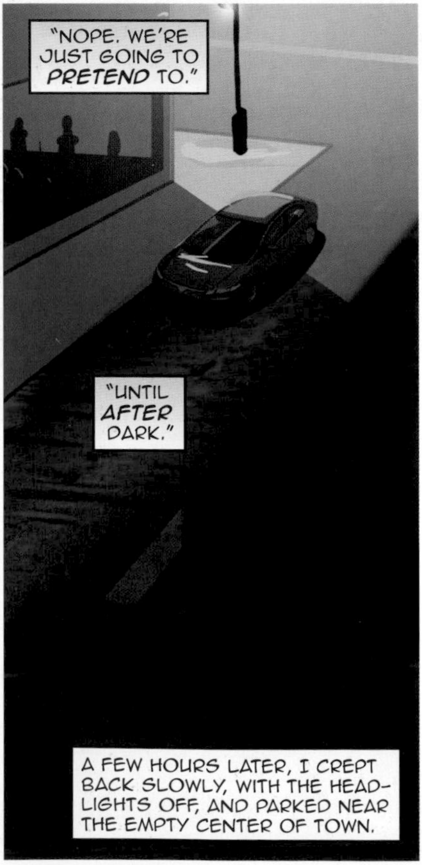
"NOPE. WE'RE JUST GOING TO PRETEND TO."
"UNTIL AFTER DARK."
A FEW HOURS LATER, I CREPT BACK SLOWLY, WITH THE HEAD-LIGHTS OFF, AND PARKED NEAR THE EMPTY CENTER OF TOWN.

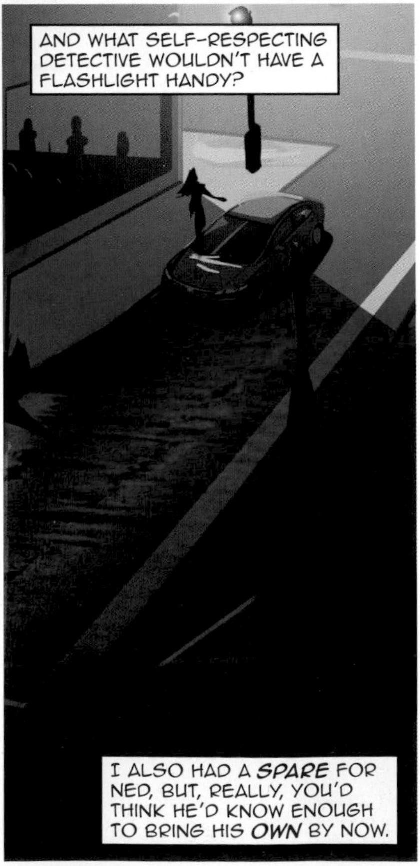
AND WHAT SELF-RESPECTING DETECTIVE WOULDN'T HAVE A FLASHLIGHT HANDY?
I ALSO HAD A SPARE FOR NED, BUT, REALLY, YOU'D THINK HE'D KNOW ENOUGH TO BRING HIS OWN BY NOW.

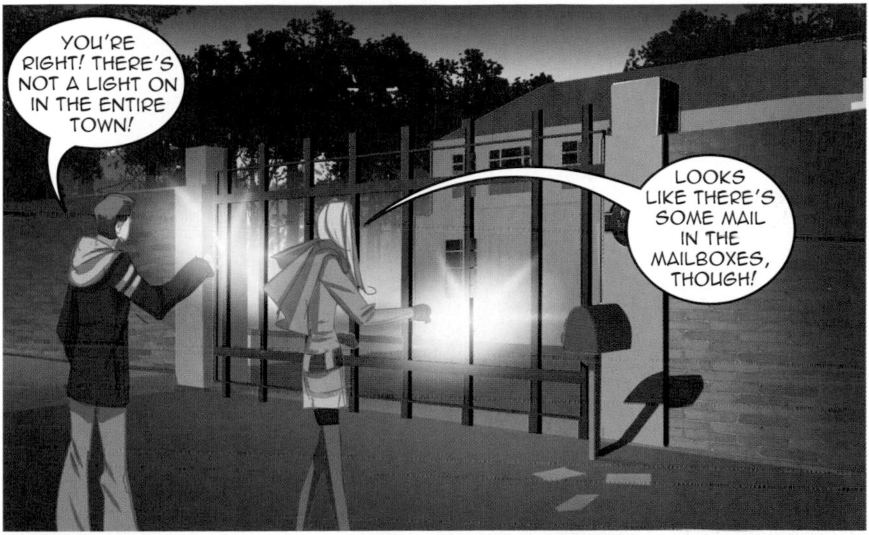
YOU'RE RIGHT! THERE'S NOT A LIGHT ON IN THE ENTIRE TOWN!
LOOKS LIKE THERE'S SOME MAIL IN THE MAILBOXES, THOUGH!

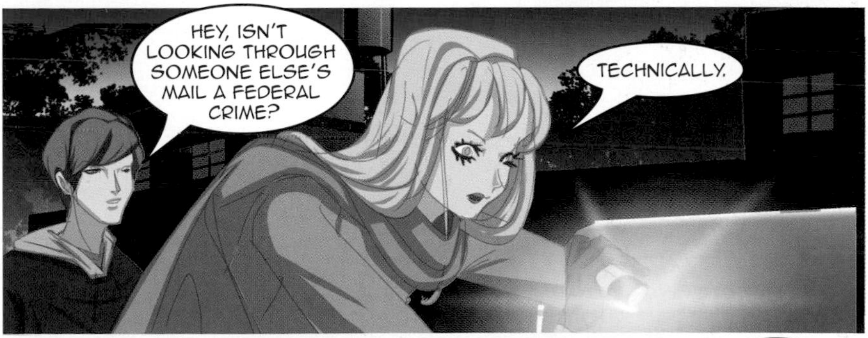
HEY, ISN'T LOOKING THROUGH SOMEONE ELSE'S MAIL A FEDERAL CRIME?
TECHNICALLY.

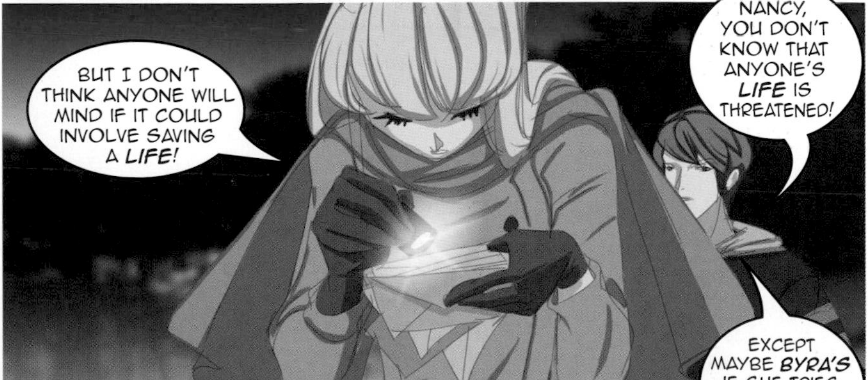
BUT I DON'T THINK ANYONE WILL MIND IF IT COULD INVOLVE SAVING A *LIFE*!
NANCY, YOU DON'T KNOW THAT ANYONE'S *LIFE* IS THREATENED!
EXCEPT MAYBE *BYRA'S* IF SHE TRIES PICKING UP *TOGO* AGAIN.

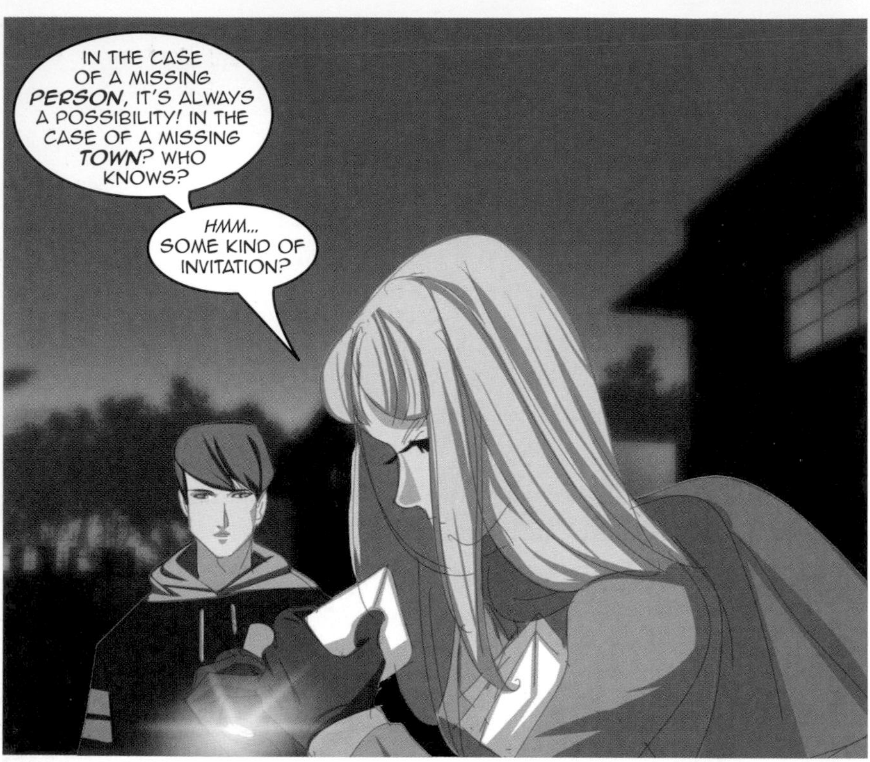
IN THE CASE OF A MISSING PERSON, IT'S ALWAYS A POSSIBILITY! IN THE CASE OF A MISSING TOWN? WHO KNOWS?
HMM... SOME KIND OF INVITATION?

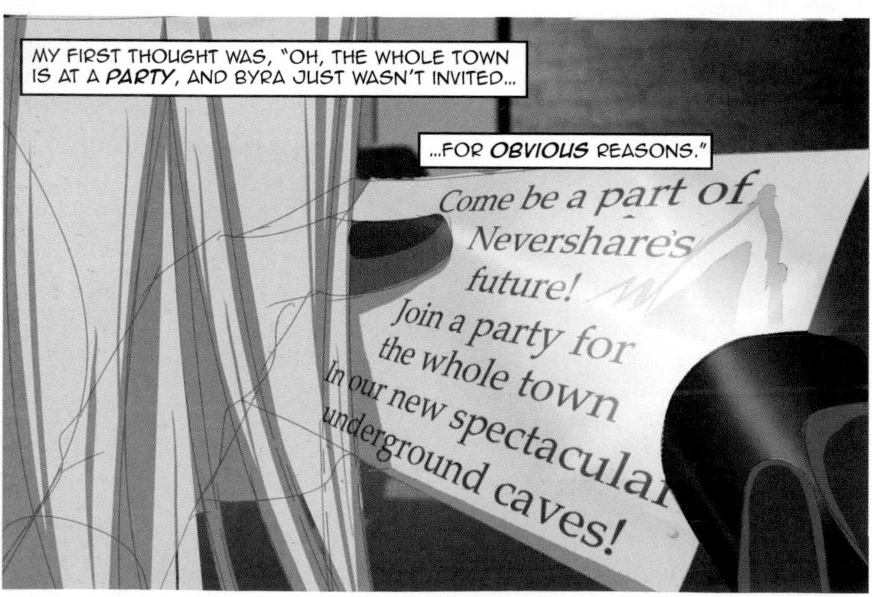
MY FIRST THOUGHT WAS, "OH, THE WHOLE TOWN IS AT A PARTY, AND BYRA JUST WASN'T INVITED...
...FOR OBVIOUS REASONS."
Come be a part of Nevershare's future! Join a party for the whole town In our new spectacular underground caves!

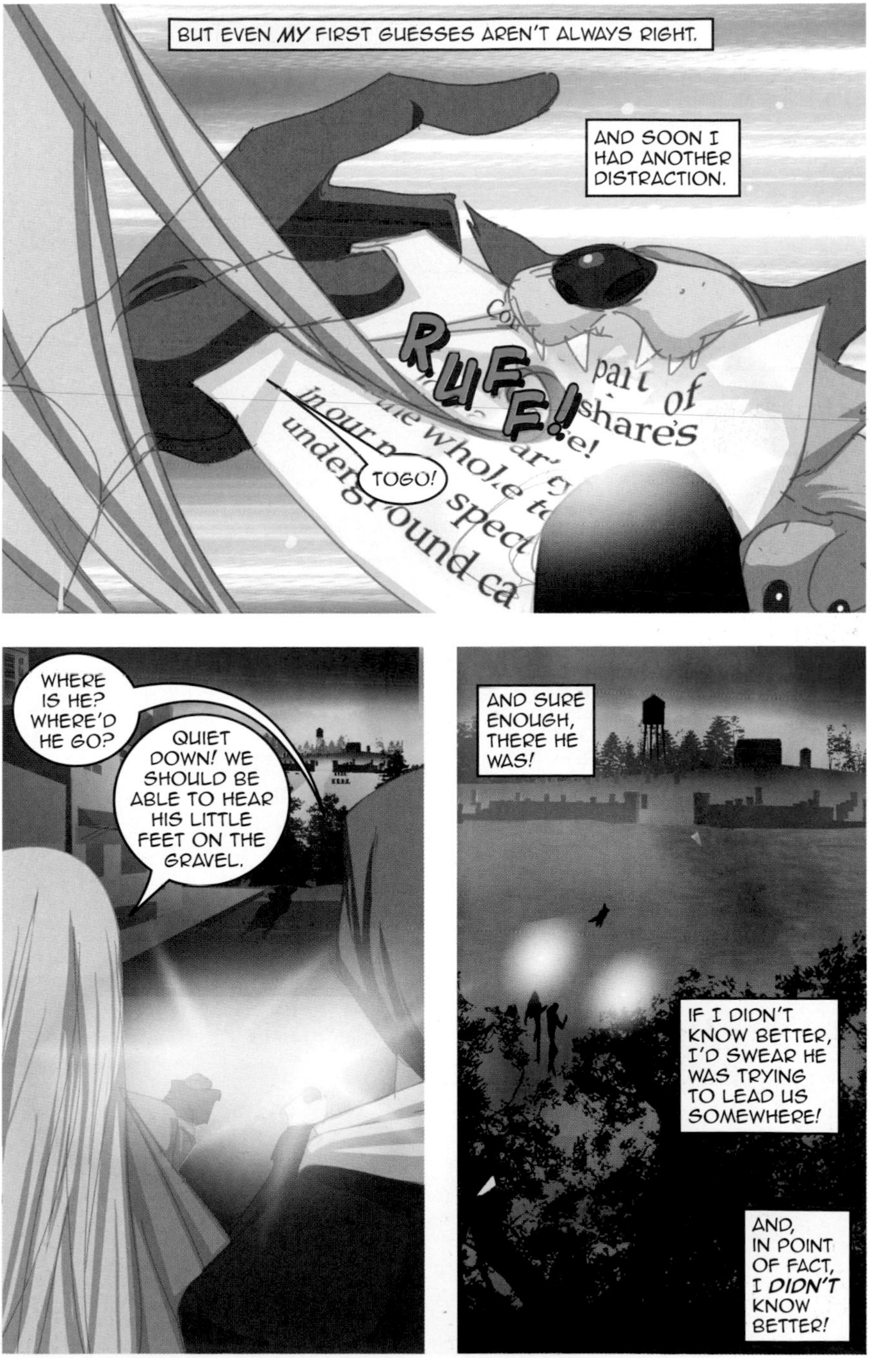
BUT EVEN MY FIRST GUESSES AREN'T ALWAYS RIGHT.
AND SOON I HAD ANOTHER DISTRACTION.
RUFF!
TOGO!
WHERE IS HE? WHERE'D HE GO?
QUIET DOWN! WE SHOULD BE ABLE TO HEAR HIS LITTLE FEET ON THE GRAVEL.
AND SURE ENOUGH, THERE HE WAS!
IF I DIDN'T KNOW BETTER, I'D SWEAR HE WAS TRYING TO LEAD US SOMEWHERE!
AND, IN POINT OF FACT, I DIDN'T KNOW BETTER!

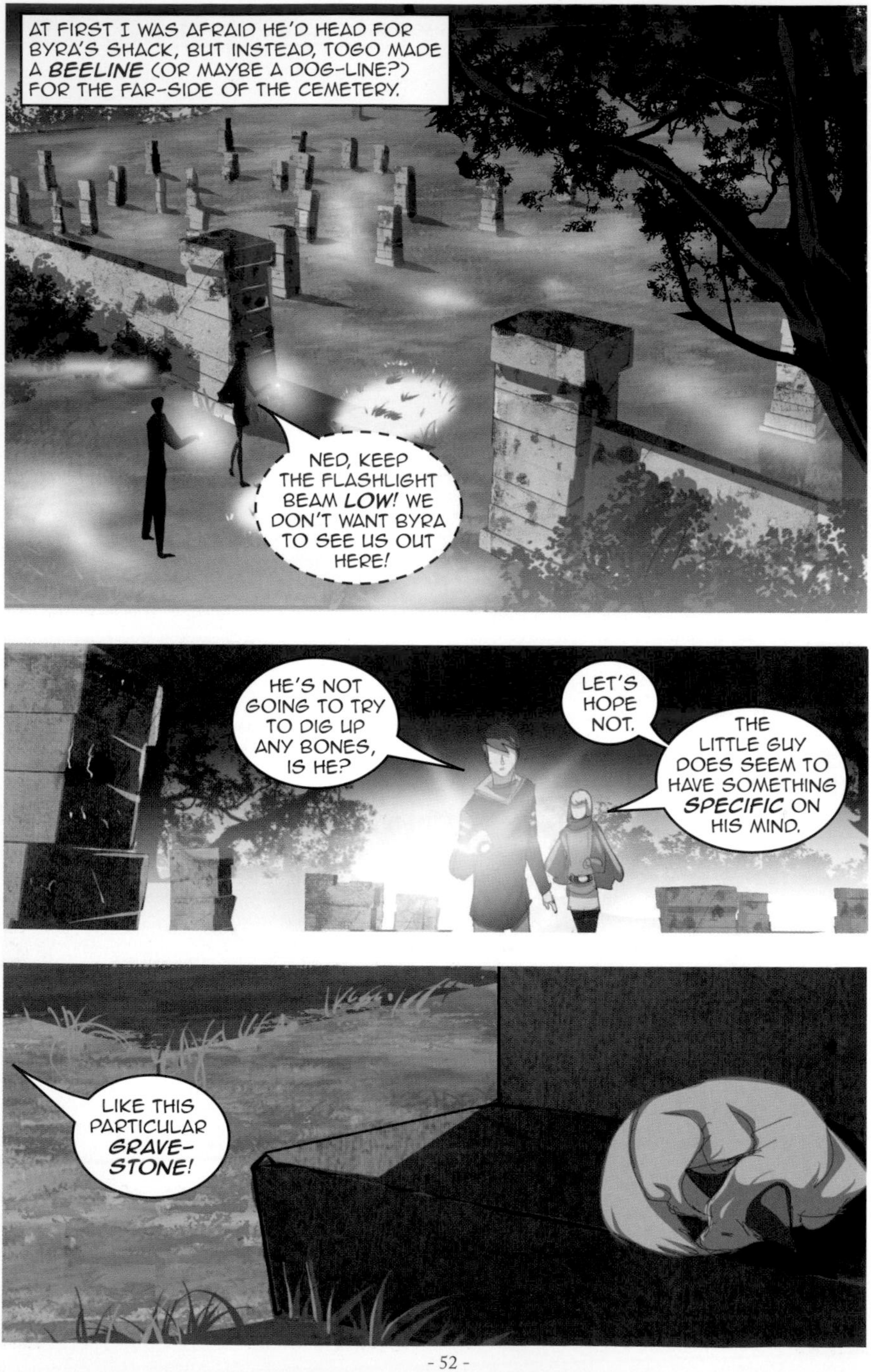
AT FIRST I WAS AFRAID HE'D HEAD FOR BYRA'S SHACK, BUT INSTEAD, TOGO MADE A BEELINE (OR MAYBE A DOG-LINE?) FOR THE FAR-SIDE OF THE CEMETERY.
NED, KEEP THE FLASHLIGHT BEAM LOW! WE DON'T WANT BYRA TO SEE US OUT HERE!
HE'S NOT GOING TO TRY TO DIG UP ANY BONES, IS HE?
LET'S HOPE NOT.
THE LITTLE GUY DOES SEEM TO HAVE SOMETHING SPECIFIC ON HIS MIND.
LIKE THIS PARTICULAR GRAVE-STONE!

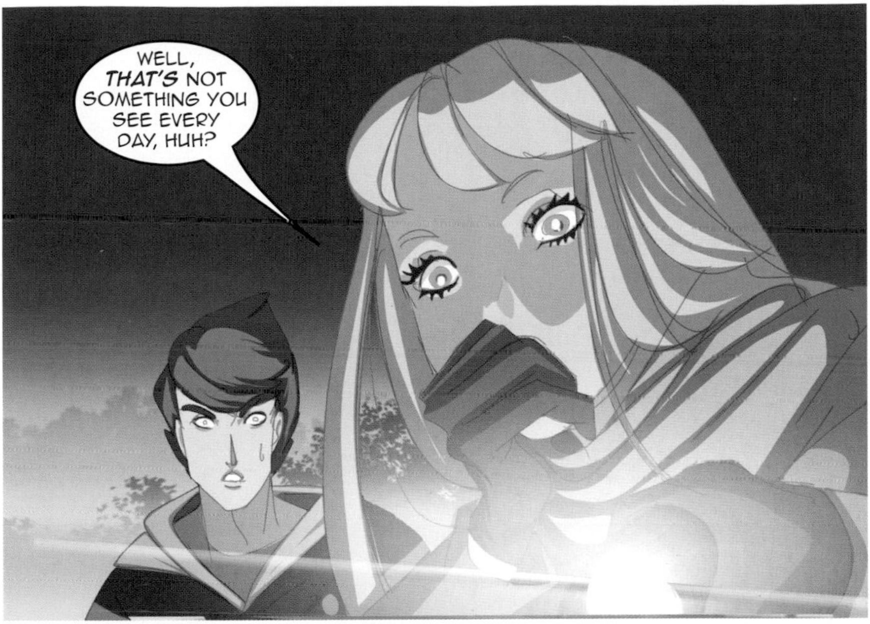
WELL, *THAT'S* NOT SOMETHING YOU SEE EVERY DAY, HUH?

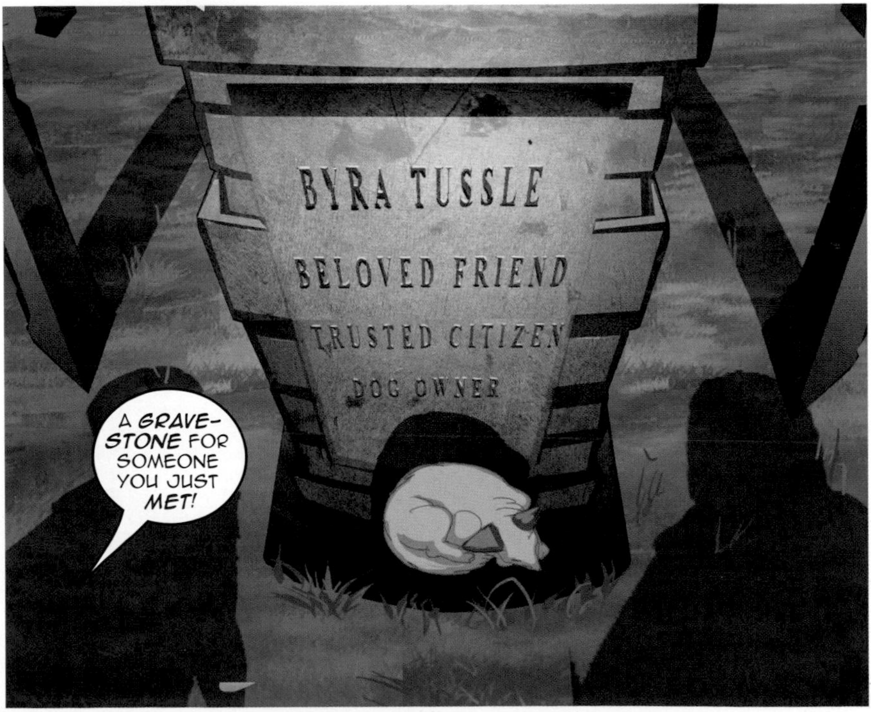
BYRA TUSSLE
BELOVED FRIEND
TRUSTED CITIZEN
DOG OWNER
A *GRAVE-STONE* FOR SOMEONE YOU JUST *MET*!

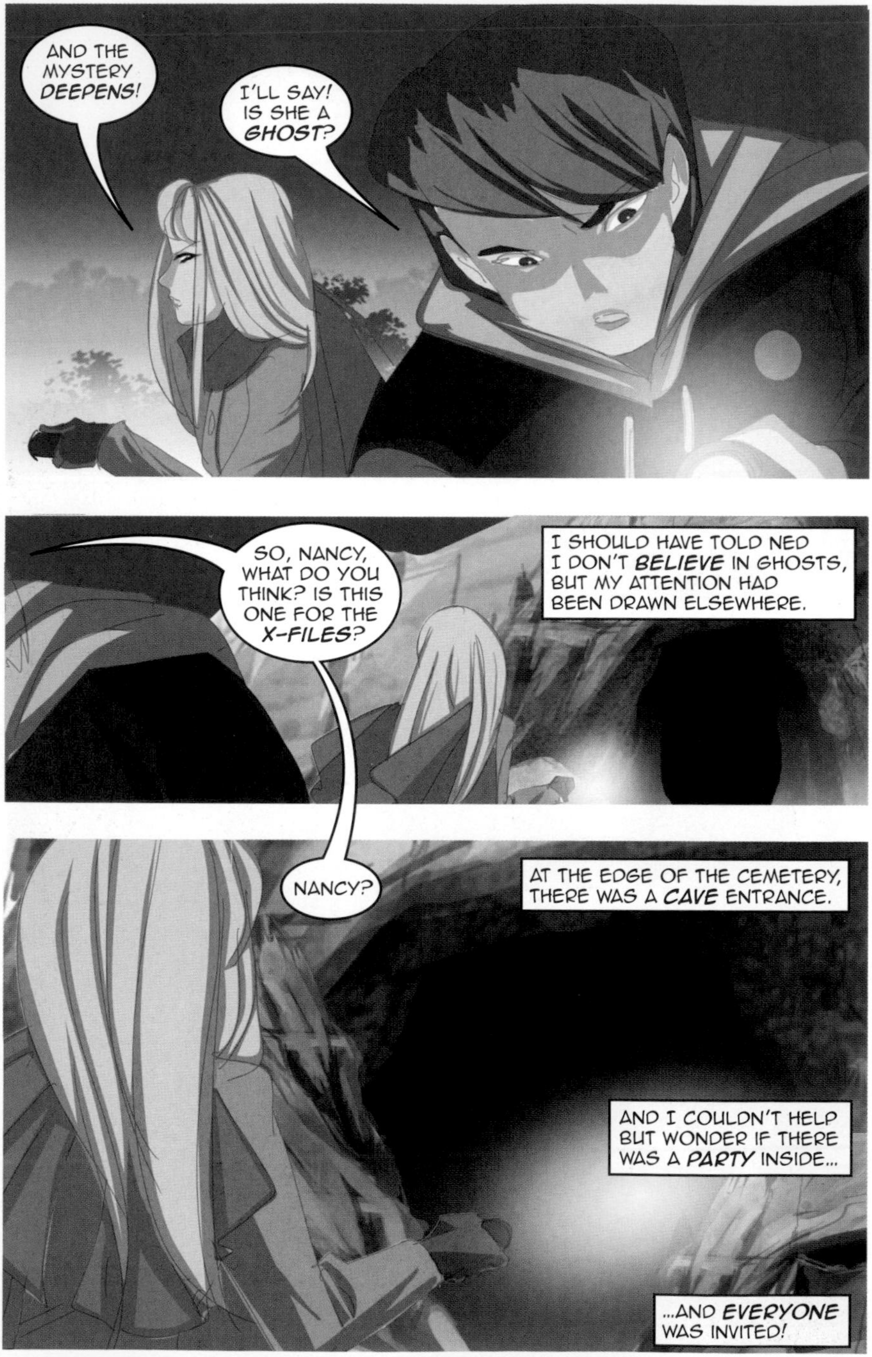
AND THE MYSTERY *DEEPENS!*
I'LL SAY! IS SHE A *GHOST?*
SO, NANCY, WHAT DO YOU THINK? IS THIS ONE FOR THE *X-FILES?*
I SHOULD HAVE TOLD NED I DON'T *BELIEVE* IN GHOSTS, BUT MY ATTENTION HAD BEEN DRAWN ELSEWHERE.
NANCY?
AT THE EDGE OF THE CEMETERY, THERE WAS A *CAVE* ENTRANCE.
AND I COULDN'T HELP BUT WONDER IF THERE WAS A *PARTY* INSIDE...
...AND *EVERYONE* WAS INVITED!

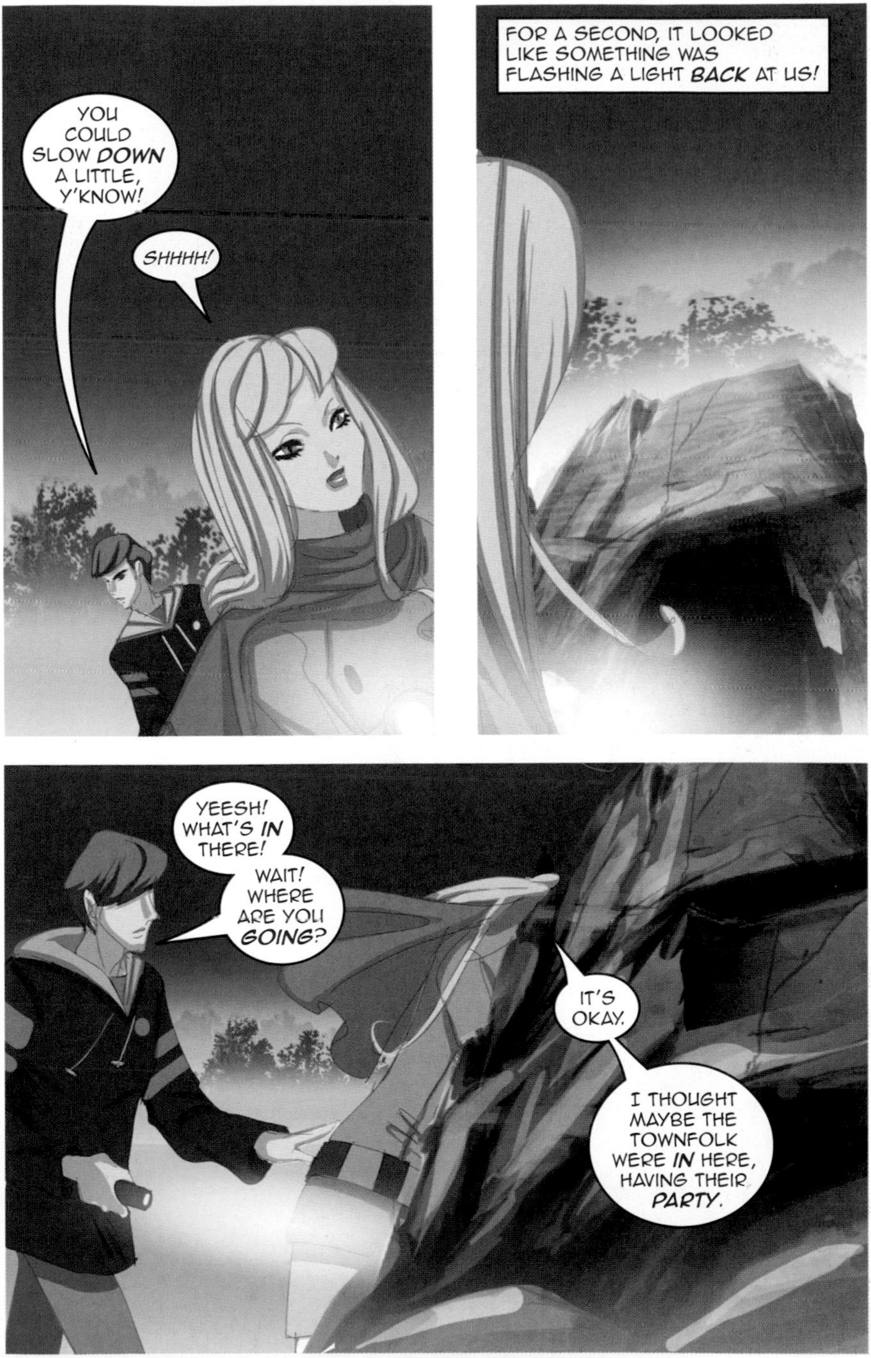
YOU COULD SLOW DOWN A LITTLE, Y'KNOW!
SHHHH!
FOR A SECOND, IT LOOKED LIKE SOMETHING WAS FLASHING A LIGHT BACK AT US!
YEESH! WHAT'S IN THERE!
WAIT! WHERE ARE YOU GOING?
IT'S OKAY.
I THOUGHT MAYBE THE TOWNFOLK WERE IN HERE, HAVING THEIR PARTY.

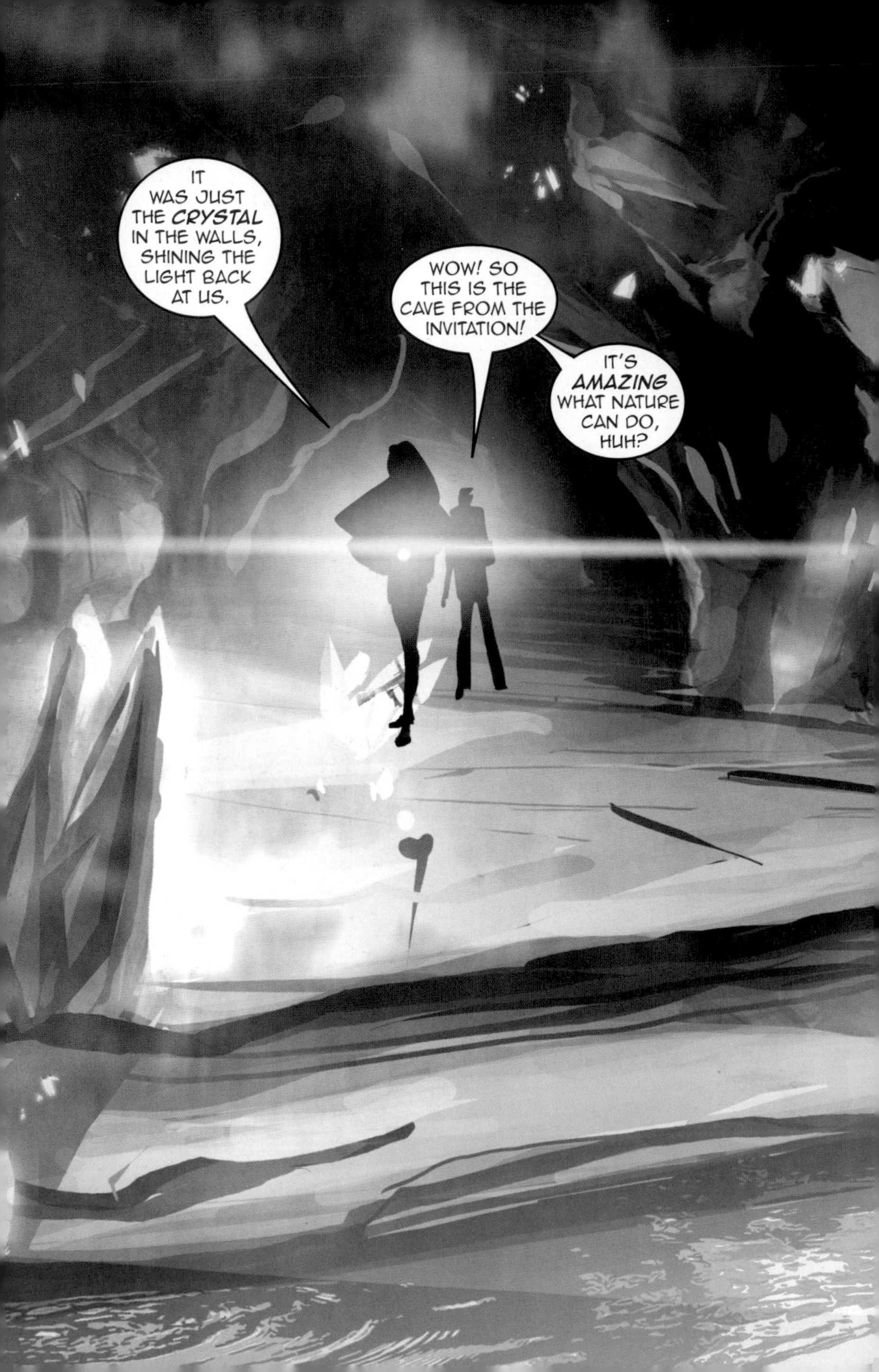
IT WAS JUST THE CRYSTAL IN THE WALLS, SHINING THE LIGHT BACK AT US.
WOW! SO THIS IS THE CAVE FROM THE INVITATION!
IT'S AMAZING WHAT NATURE CAN DO, HUH?

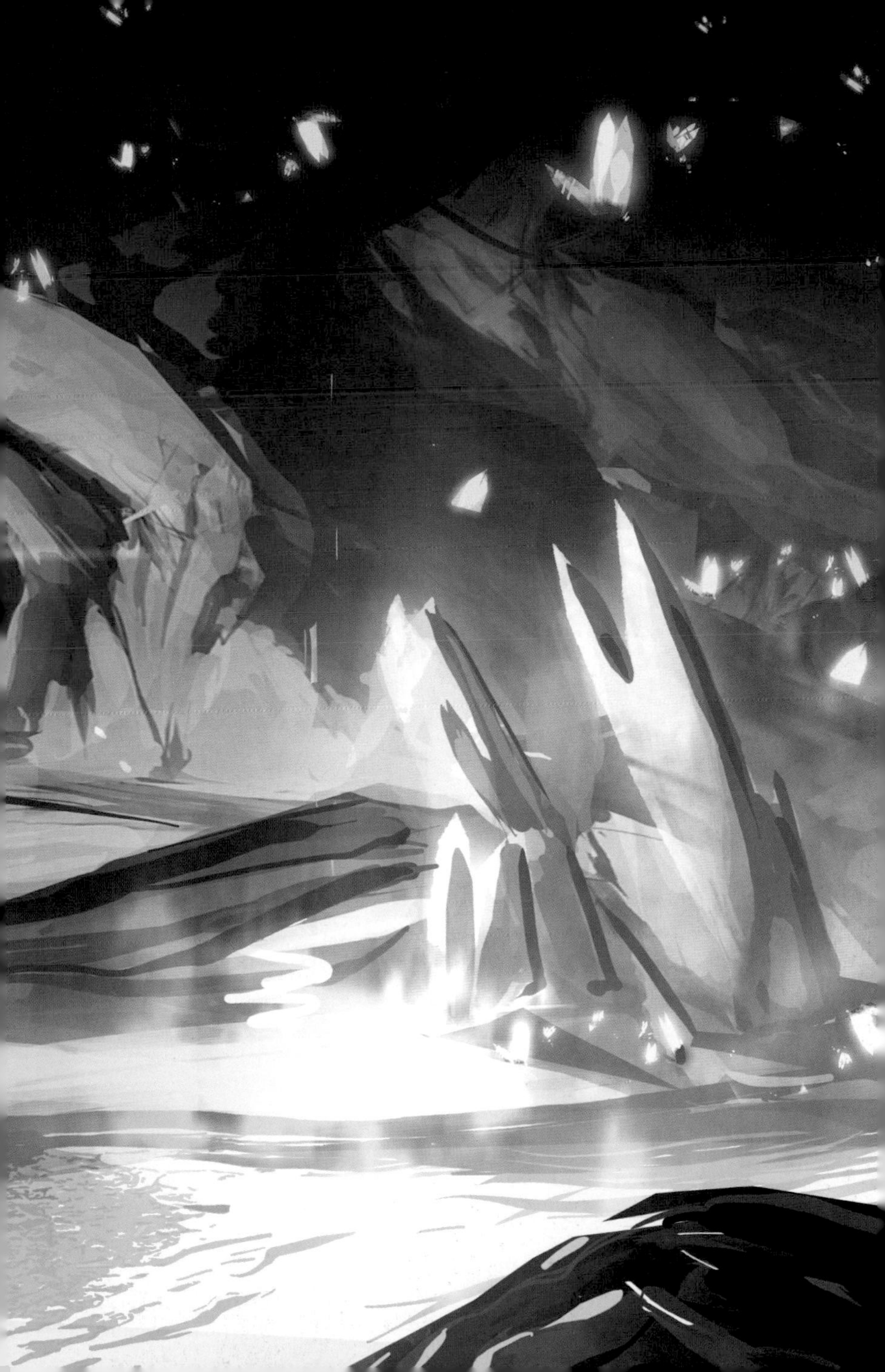

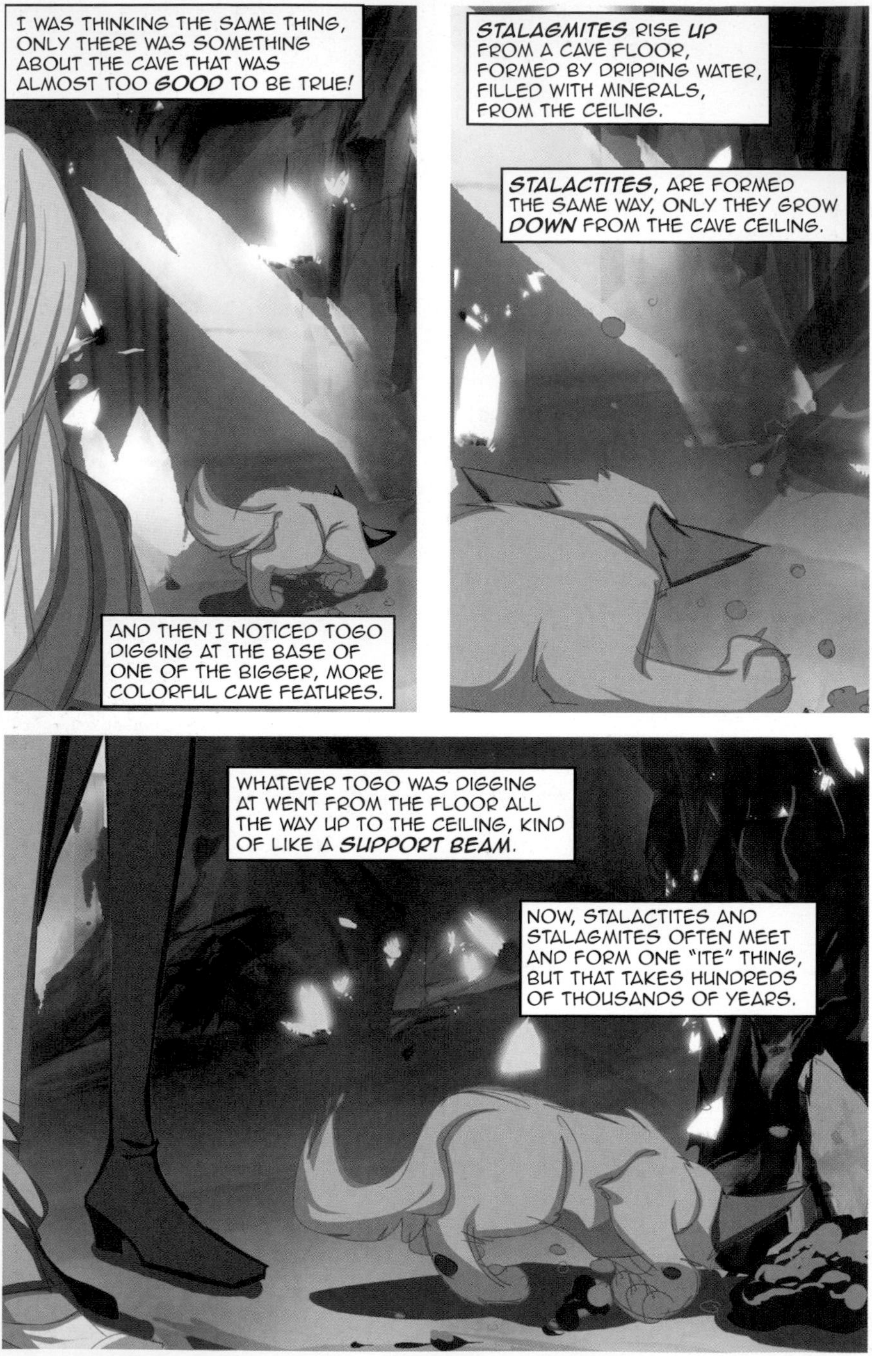
I WAS THINKING THE SAME THING, ONLY THERE WAS SOMETHING ABOUT THE CAVE THAT WAS ALMOST TOO GOOD TO BE TRUE!
AND THEN I NOTICED TOGO DIGGING AT THE BASE OF ONE OF THE BIGGER, MORE COLORFUL CAVE FEATURES.
STALAGMITES RISE UP FROM A CAVE FLOOR, FORMED BY DRIPPING WATER, FILLED WITH MINERALS, FROM THE CEILING.
STALACTITES, ARE FORMED THE SAME WAY, ONLY THEY GROW DOWN FROM THE CAVE CEILING.
WHATEVER TOGO WAS DIGGING AT WENT FROM THE FLOOR ALL THE WAY UP TO THE CEILING, KIND OF LIKE A SUPPORT BEAM.
NOW, STALACTITES AND STALAGMITES OFTEN MEET AND FORM ONE "ITE" THING, BUT THAT TAKES HUNDREDS OF THOUSANDS OF YEARS.

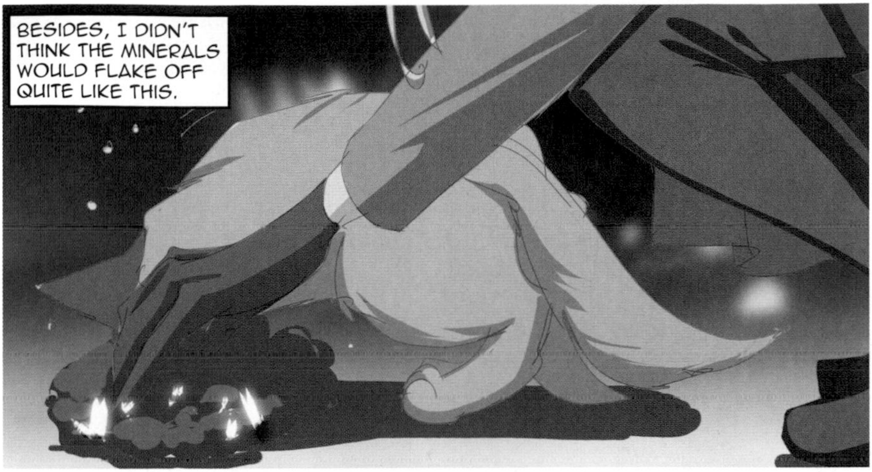
BESIDES, I DIDN'T THINK THE MINERALS WOULD FLAKE OFF QUITE LIKE THIS.

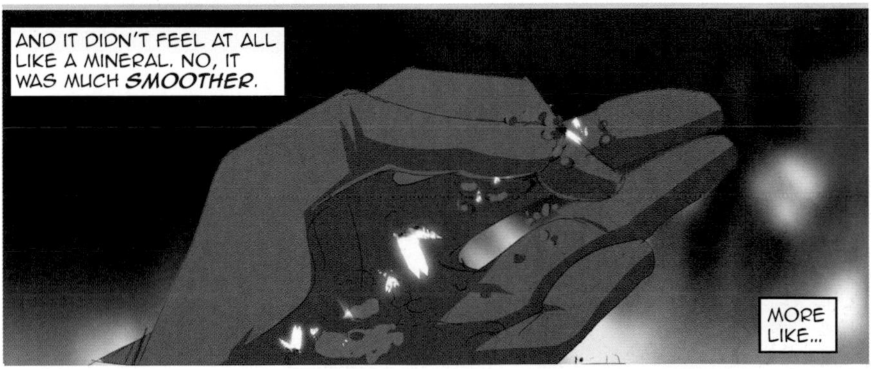
AND IT DIDN'T FEEL AT ALL LIKE A MINERAL. NO, IT WAS MUCH *SMOOTHER*.
MORE LIKE...

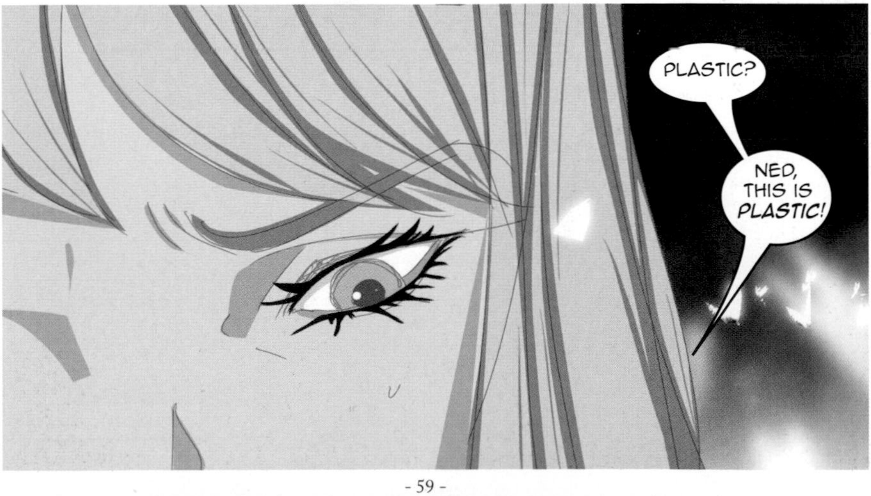
PLASTIC?
NED, THIS IS *PLASTIC!*

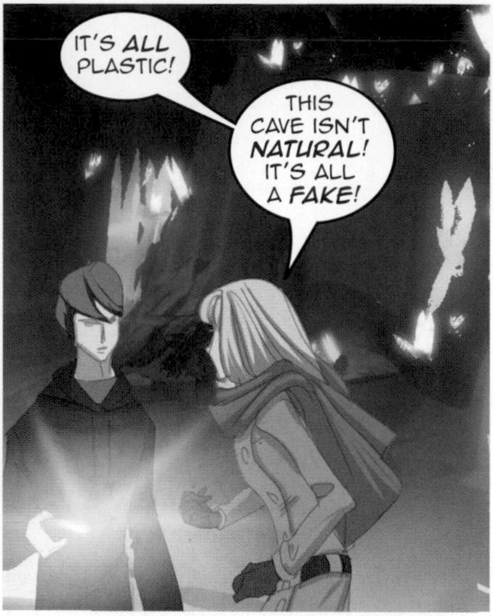
IT'S ALL PLASTIC!
THIS CAVE ISN'T NATURAL! IT'S ALL A FAKE!

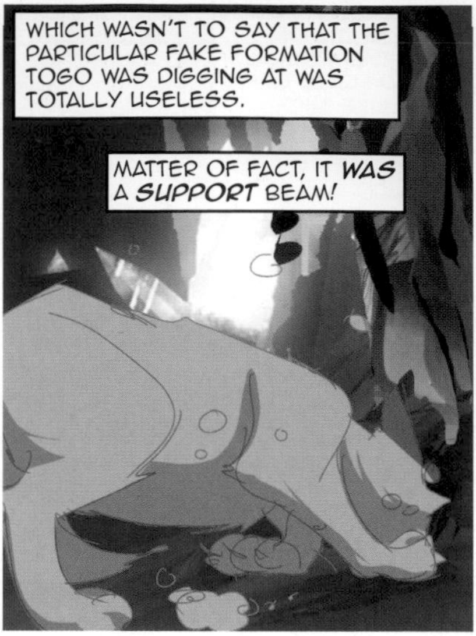
WHICH WASN'T TO SAY THAT THE PARTICULAR FAKE FORMATION TOGO WAS DIGGING AT WAS TOTALLY USELESS.
MATTER OF FACT, IT WAS A SUPPORT BEAM!

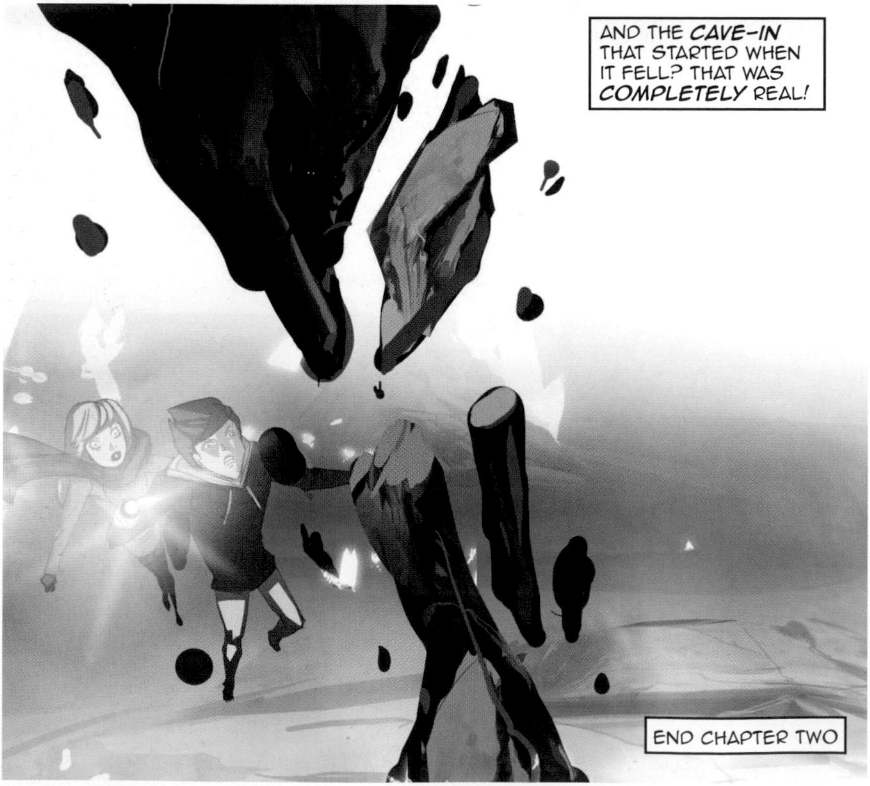
AND THE CAVE-IN THAT STARTED WHEN IT FELL? THAT WAS COMPLETELY REAL!
END CHAPTER TWO

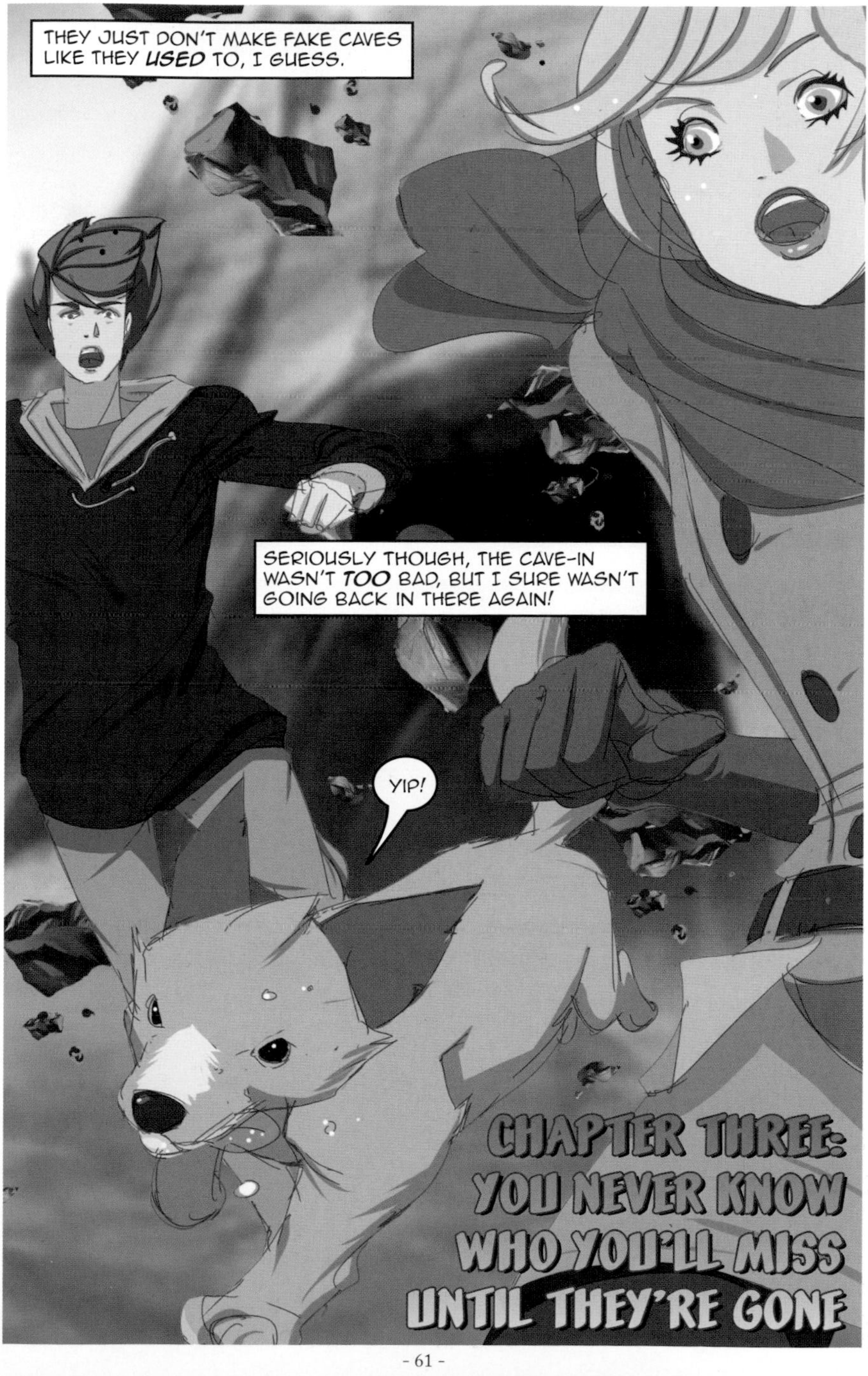
THEY JUST DON'T MAKE FAKE CAVES LIKE THEY *USED* TO, I GUESS.
SERIOUSLY THOUGH, THE CAVE-IN WASN'T *TOO* BAD, BUT I SURE WASN'T GOING BACK IN THERE AGAIN!
YIP!
CHAPTER THREE: YOU NEVER KNOW WHO YOU'LL MISS UNTIL THEY'RE GONE

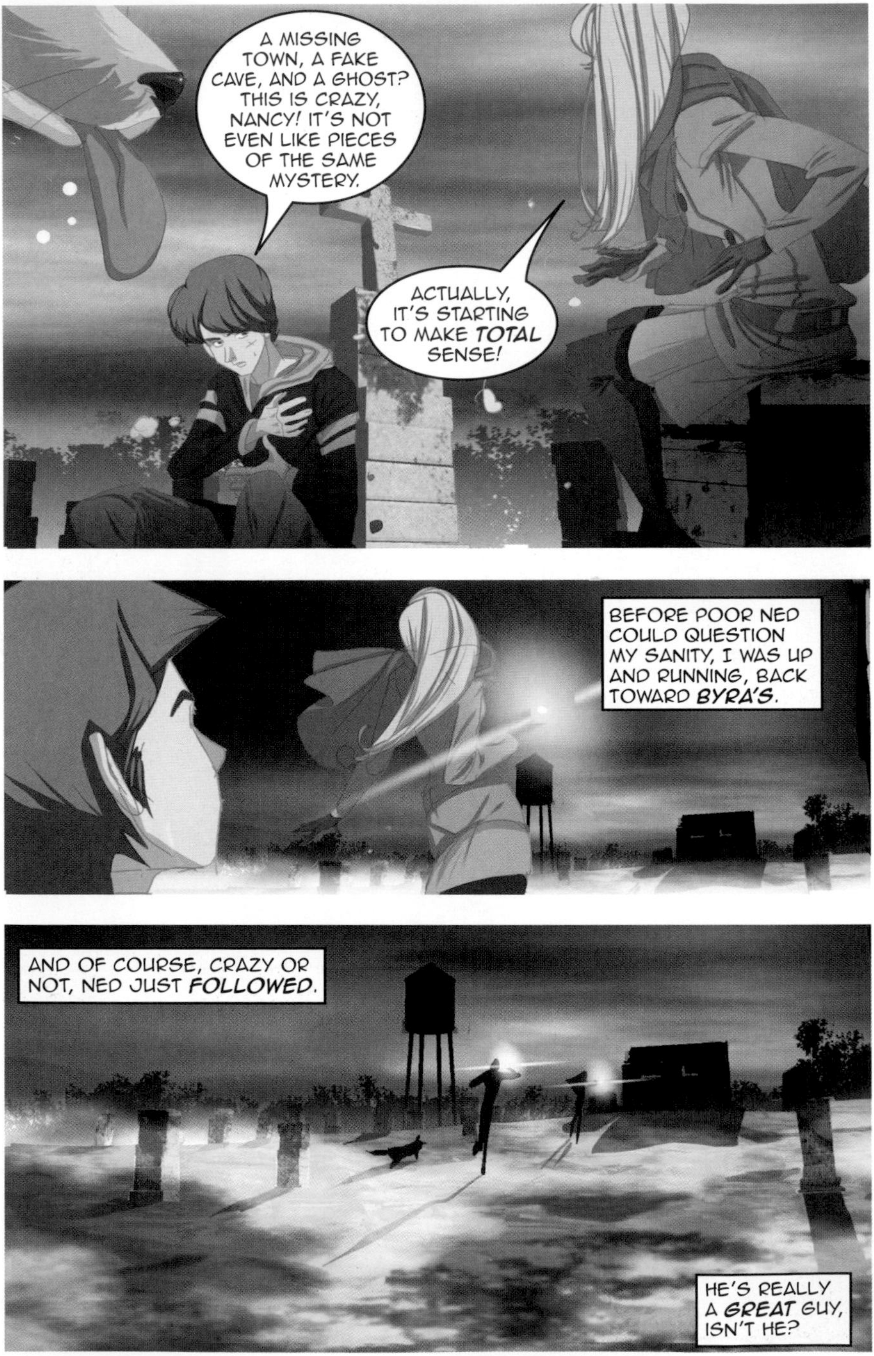
A MISSING TOWN, A FAKE CAVE, AND A GHOST? THIS IS CRAZY, NANCY! IT'S NOT EVEN LIKE PIECES OF THE SAME MYSTERY.
ACTUALLY, IT'S STARTING TO MAKE TOTAL SENSE!
BEFORE POOR NED COULD QUESTION MY SANITY, I WAS UP AND RUNNING, BACK TOWARD BYRA'S.
AND OF COURSE, CRAZY OR NOT, NED JUST FOLLOWED.
HE'S REALLY A GREAT GUY, ISN'T HE?

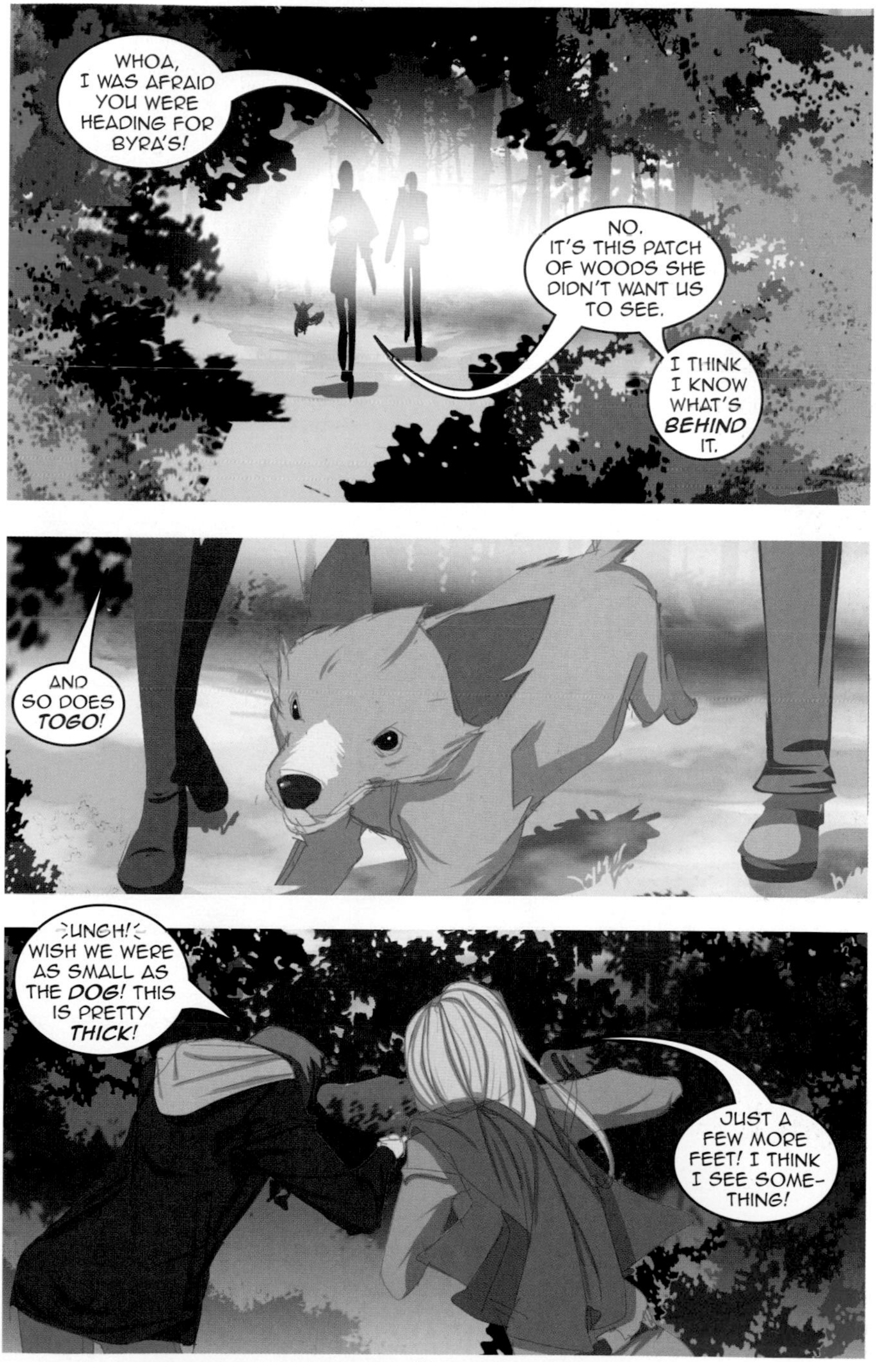
WHOA, I WAS AFRAID YOU WERE HEADING FOR BYRA'S!
NO. IT'S THIS PATCH OF WOODS SHE DIDN'T WANT US TO SEE.
I THINK I KNOW WHAT'S *BEHIND* IT.
AND SO DOES *TOGO!*
UNGH! WISH WE WERE AS SMALL AS THE *DOG!* THIS IS PRETTY *THICK!*
JUST A FEW MORE FEET! I THINK I SEE SOME-THING!

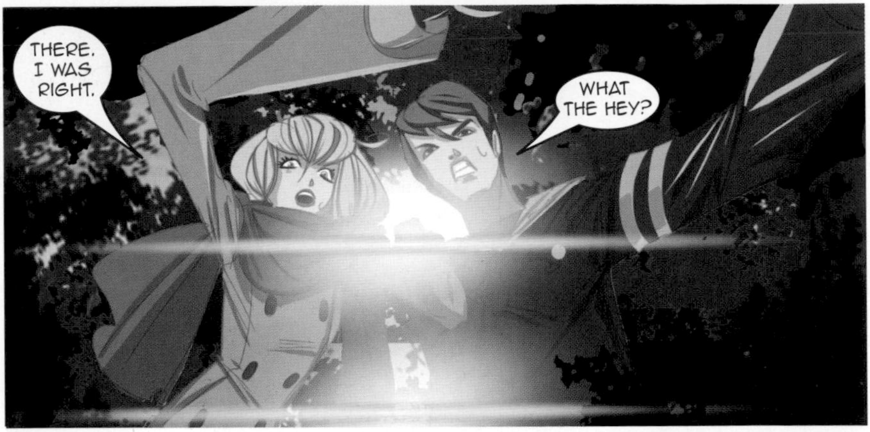
THERE. I WAS RIGHT.
WHAT THE HEY?

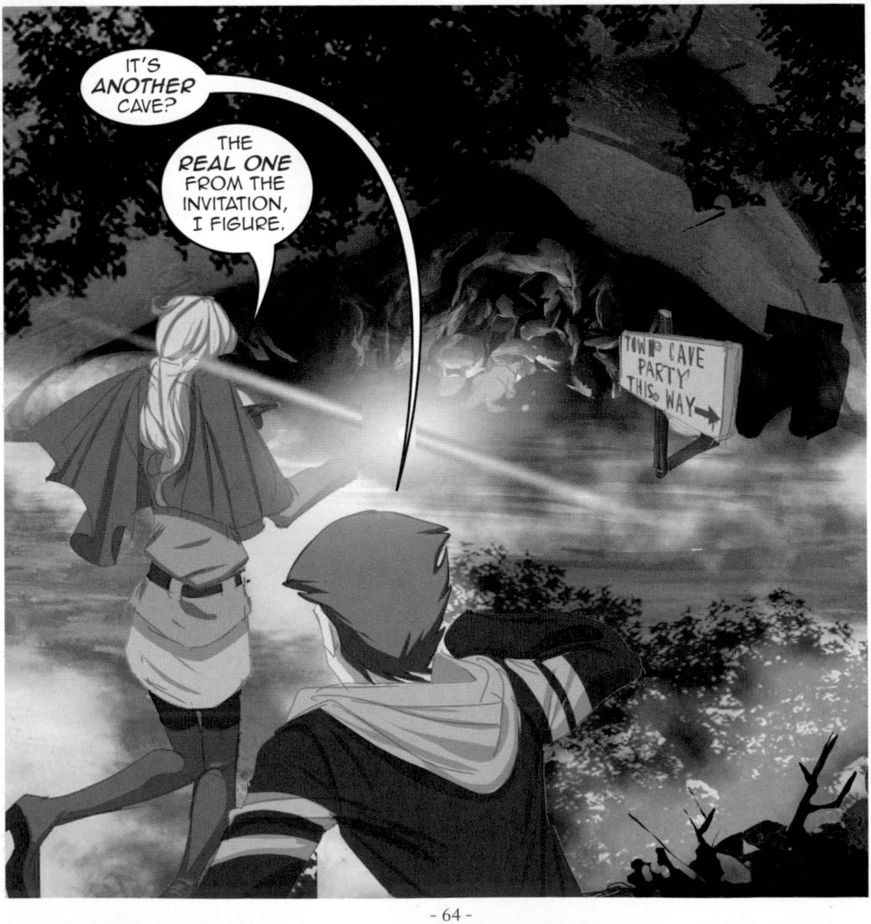
IT'S *ANOTHER* CAVE?
THE *REAL ONE* FROM THE INVITATION, I FIGURE.
TOWN CAVE PARTY THIS WAY

LOOK! THERE'S A SMALL GAP IN THE COLLAPSED STONES! TOGO'S HEADING IN! IT LOOKS JUST BIG ENOUGH FOR ME, TOO!
NANCY, DON'T EVEN THINK ABOUT IT...
OKAY, I WON'T THINK! I'LL JUST DO IT!
NO! NANCY, THOSE ROCKS ARE STILL LOOSE!
UNFORTUNATELY, NED WAS RIGHT!
NANCY!
CRUNK

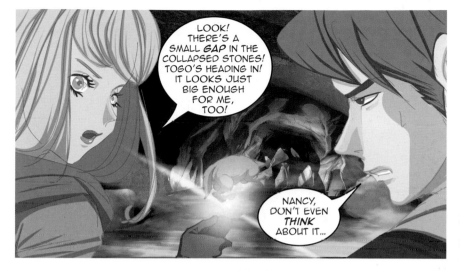

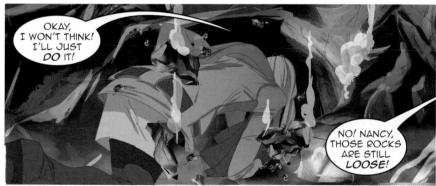

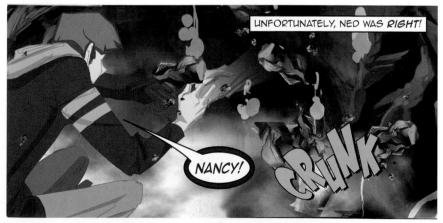

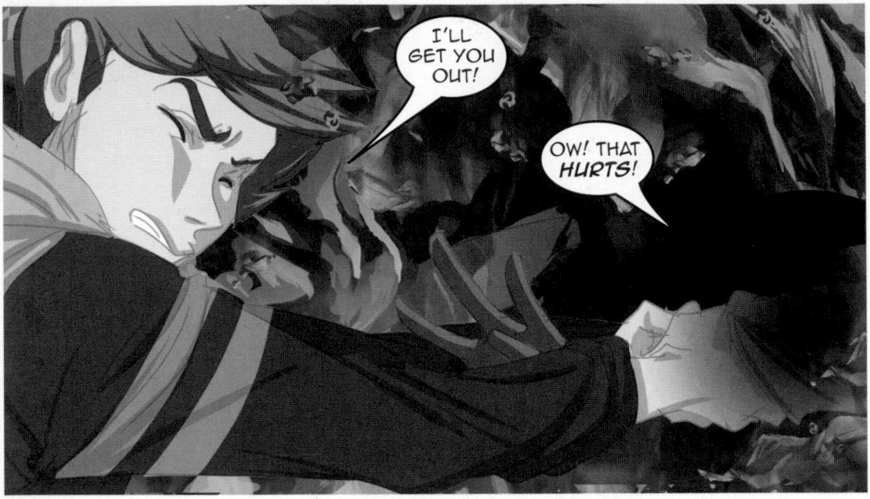
I'LL GET YOU OUT!
OW! THAT **HURTS**!

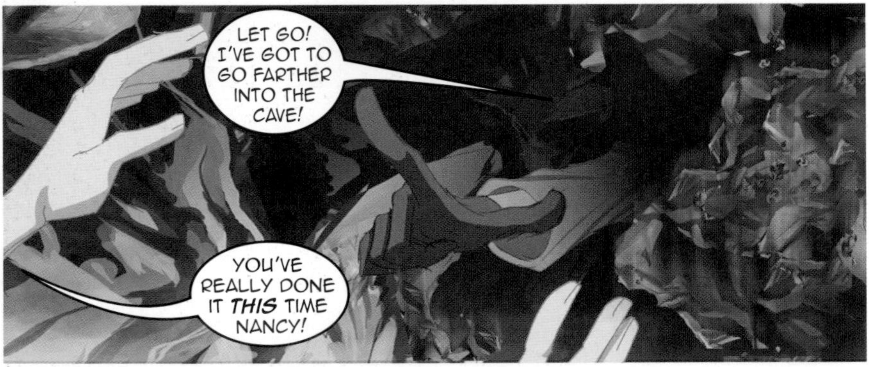
LET GO! I'VE GOT TO GO FARTHER INTO THE CAVE!
YOU'VE REALLY DONE IT **THIS** TIME NANCY!

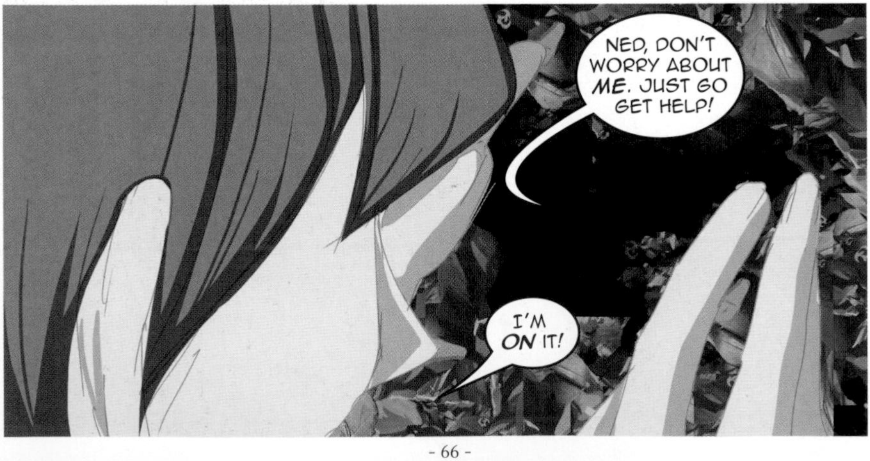
NED, DON'T WORRY ABOUT **ME**. JUST GO GET HELP!
I'M **ON** IT!

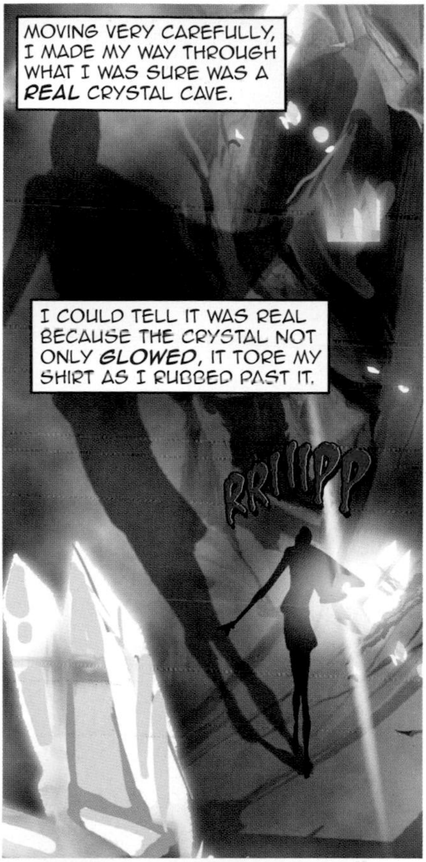
MOVING VERY CAREFULLY, I MADE MY WAY THROUGH WHAT I WAS SURE WAS A **REAL** CRYSTAL CAVE.
I COULD TELL IT WAS REAL BECAUSE THE CRYSTAL NOT ONLY **GLOWED**, IT TORE MY SHIRT AS I RUBBED PAST IT.
RRIIIPP

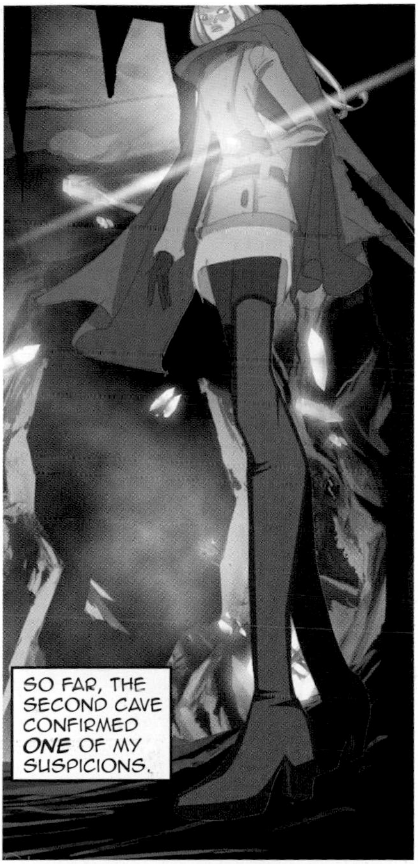
SO FAR, THE SECOND CAVE CONFIRMED **ONE** OF MY SUSPICIONS.

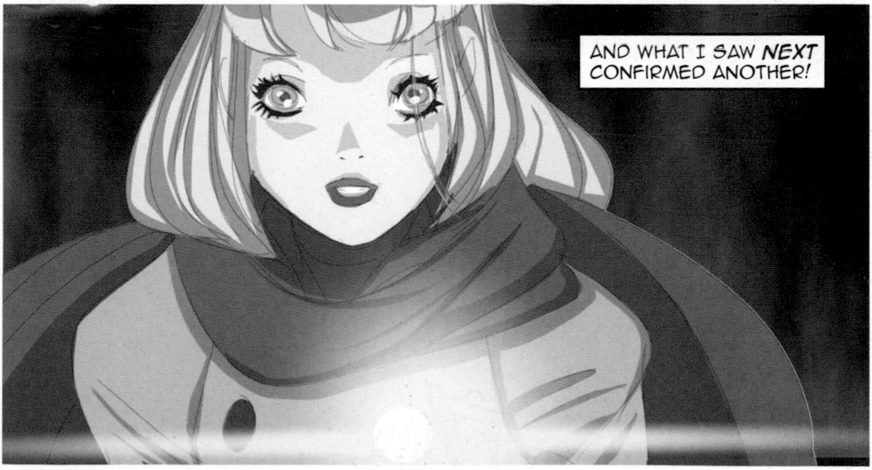
AND WHAT I SAW **NEXT** CONFIRMED ANOTHER!

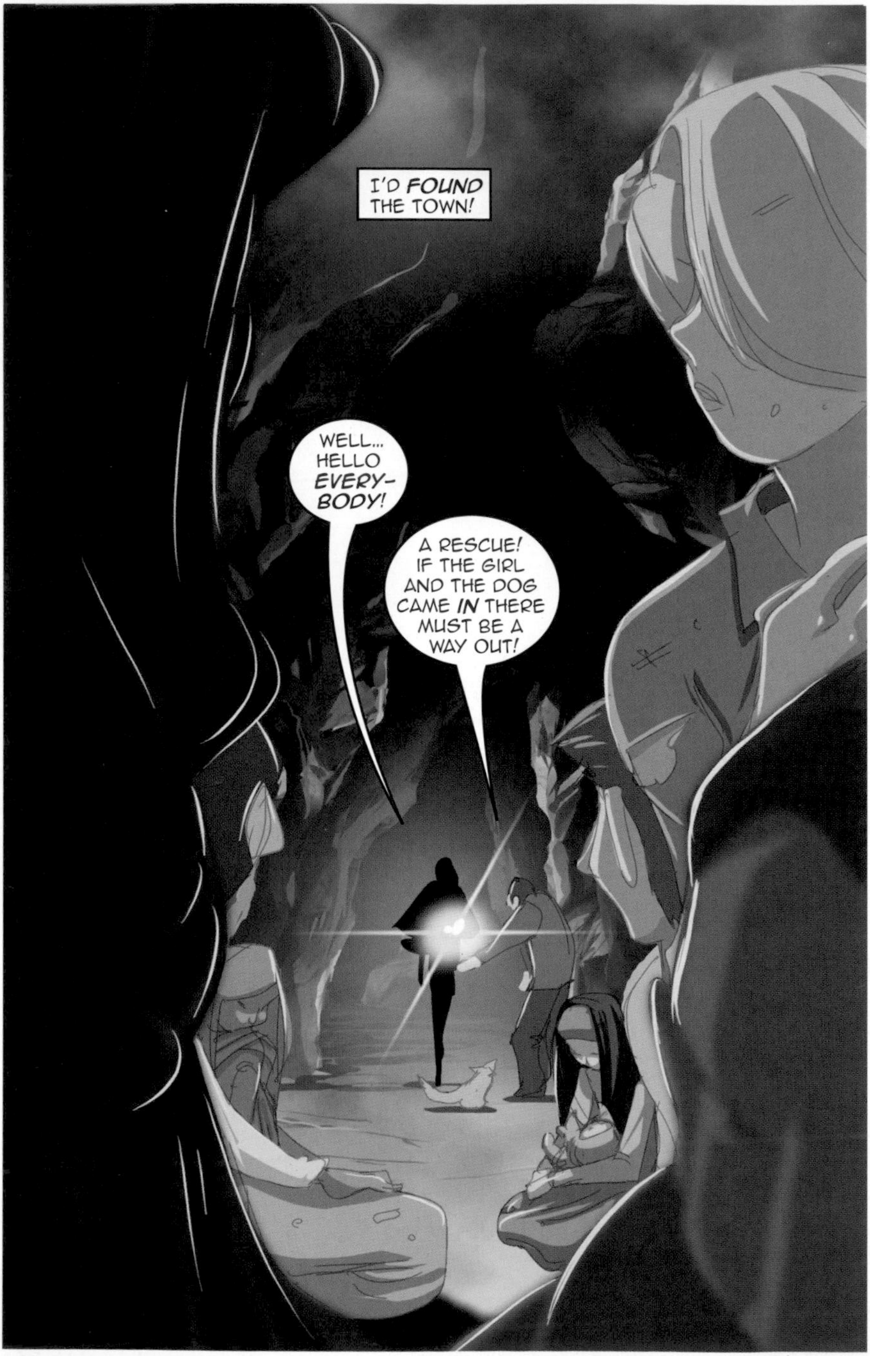
I'D FOUND THE TOWN!
WELL... HELLO EVERY-BODY!
A RESCUE! IF THE GIRL AND THE DOG CAME IN THERE MUST BE A WAY OUT!

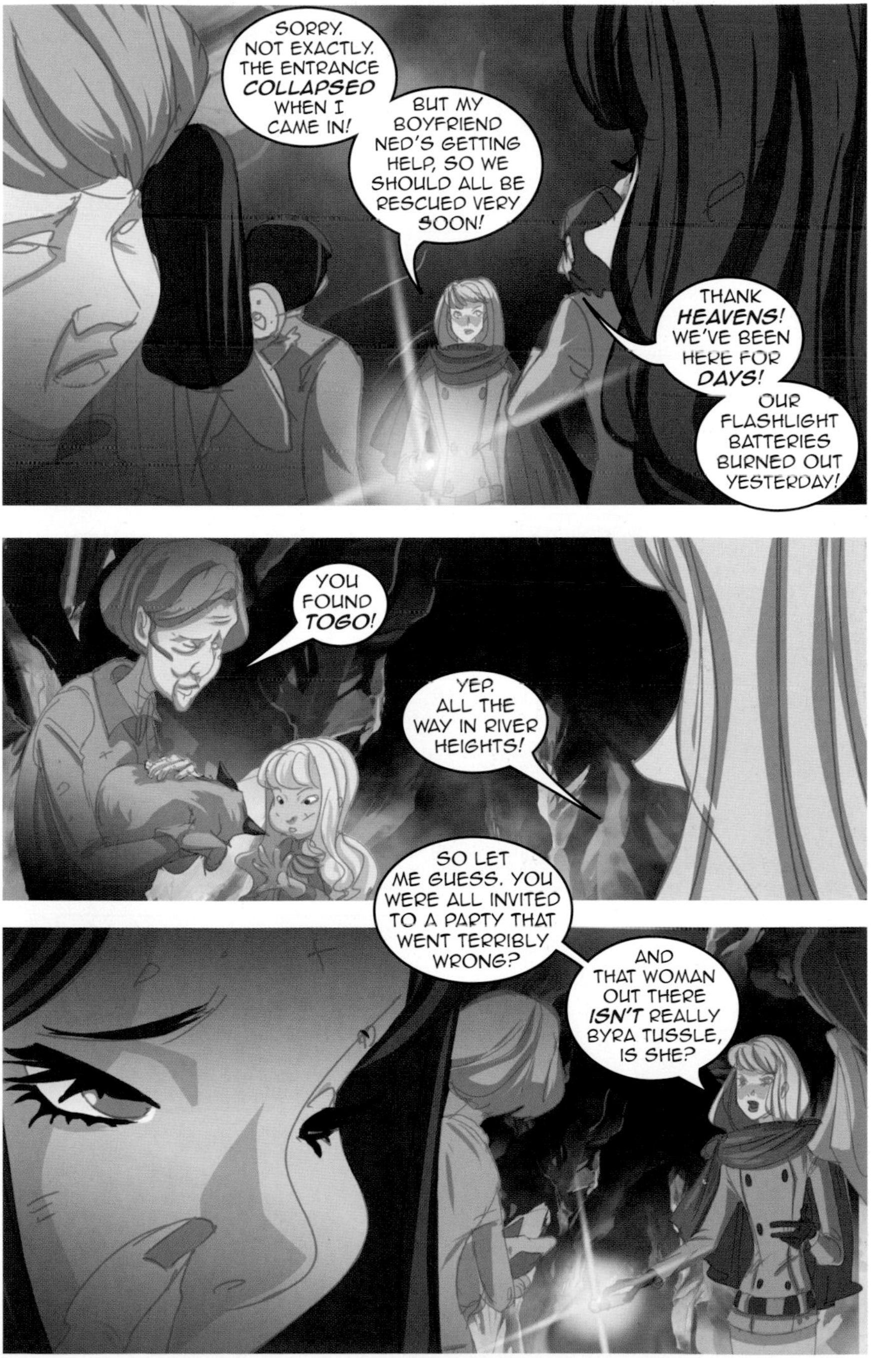
SORRY. NOT EXACTLY. THE ENTRANCE *COLLAPSED* WHEN I CAME IN!
BUT MY BOYFRIEND NED'S GETTING HELP, SO WE SHOULD ALL BE RESCUED VERY *SOON!*
THANK *HEAVENS!* WE'VE BEEN HERE FOR *DAYS!*
OUR FLASHLIGHT BATTERIES BURNED OUT YESTERDAY!
YOU FOUND *TOGO!*
YEP. ALL THE WAY IN RIVER HEIGHTS!
SO LET ME GUESS. YOU WERE ALL INVITED TO A PARTY THAT WENT TERRIBLY WRONG?
AND THAT WOMAN OUT THERE *ISN'T* REALLY BYRA TUSSLE, IS SHE?

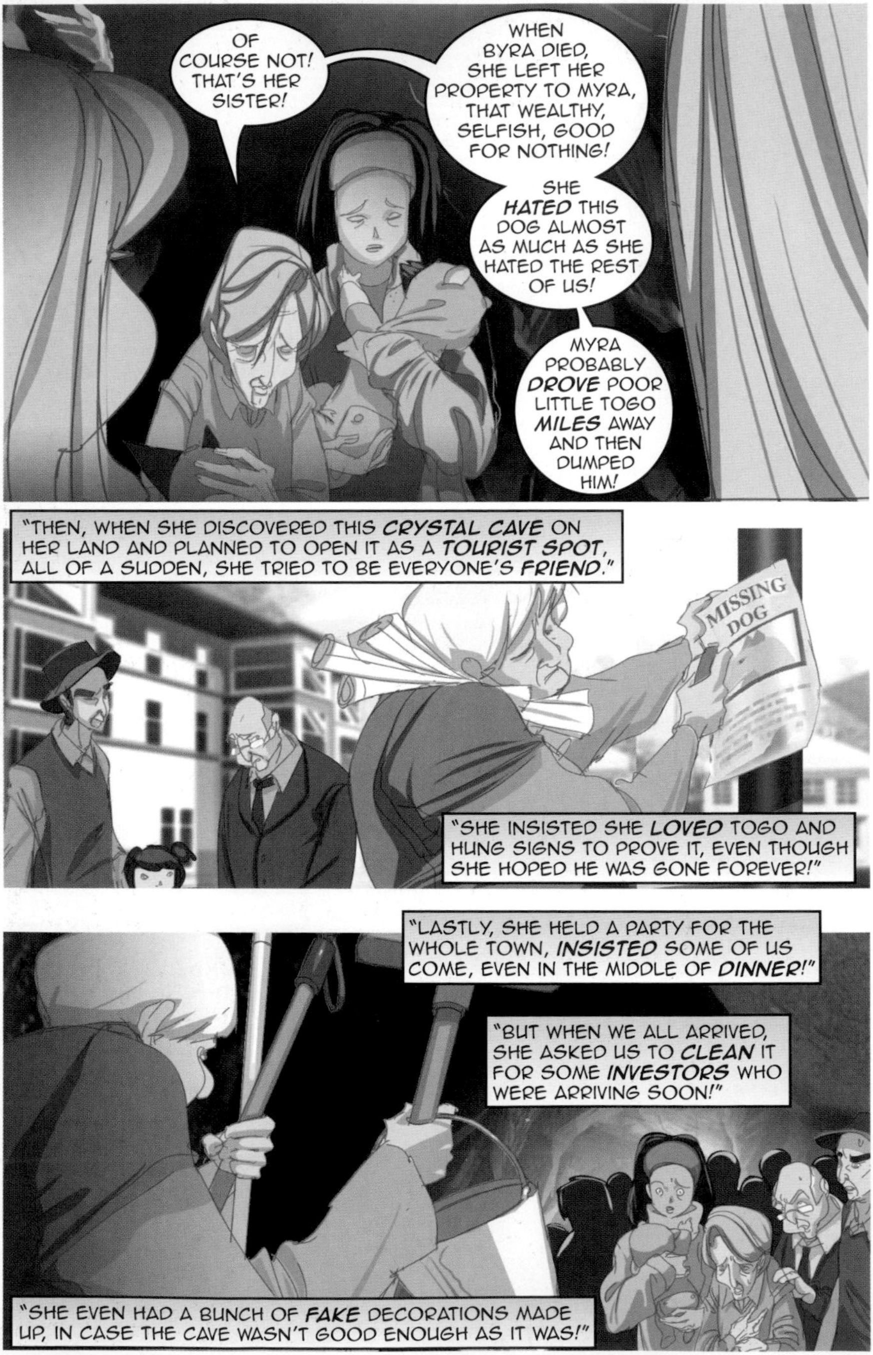
OF COURSE NOT! THAT'S HER SISTER!
WHEN BYRA DIED, SHE LEFT HER PROPERTY TO MYRA, THAT WEALTHY, SELFISH, GOOD FOR NOTHING!
SHE HATED THIS DOG ALMOST AS MUCH AS SHE HATED THE REST OF US!
MYRA PROBABLY DROVE POOR LITTLE TOGO MILES AWAY AND THEN DUMPED HIM!
"THEN, WHEN SHE DISCOVERED THIS CRYSTAL CAVE ON HER LAND AND PLANNED TO OPEN IT AS A TOURIST SPOT, ALL OF A SUDDEN, SHE TRIED TO BE EVERYONE'S FRIEND."
MISSING DOG
"SHE INSISTED SHE LOVED TOGO AND HUNG SIGNS TO PROVE IT, EVEN THOUGH SHE HOPED HE WAS GONE FOREVER!"
"LASTLY, SHE HELD A PARTY FOR THE WHOLE TOWN, INSISTED SOME OF US COME, EVEN IN THE MIDDLE OF DINNER!"
"BUT WHEN WE ALL ARRIVED, SHE ASKED US TO CLEAN IT FOR SOME INVESTORS WHO WERE ARRIVING SOON!"
"SHE EVEN HAD A BUNCH OF FAKE DECORATIONS MADE UP, IN CASE THE CAVE WASN'T GOOD ENOUGH AS IT WAS!"

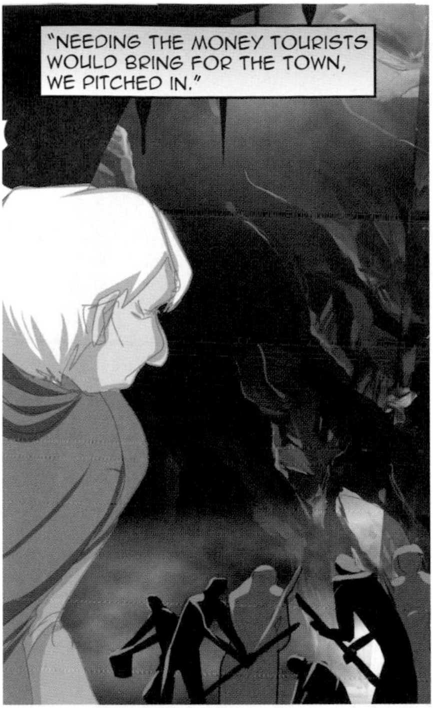
"NEEDING THE MONEY TOURISTS WOULD BRING FOR THE TOWN, WE PITCHED IN."

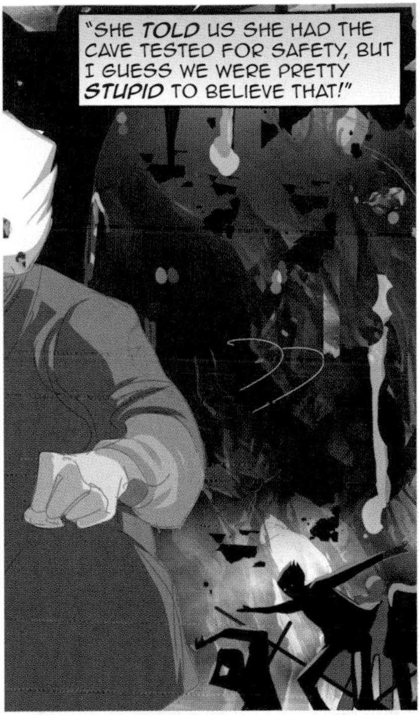
"SHE *TOLD* US SHE HAD THE CAVE TESTED FOR SAFETY, BUT I GUESS WE WERE PRETTY *STUPID* TO BELIEVE THAT!"

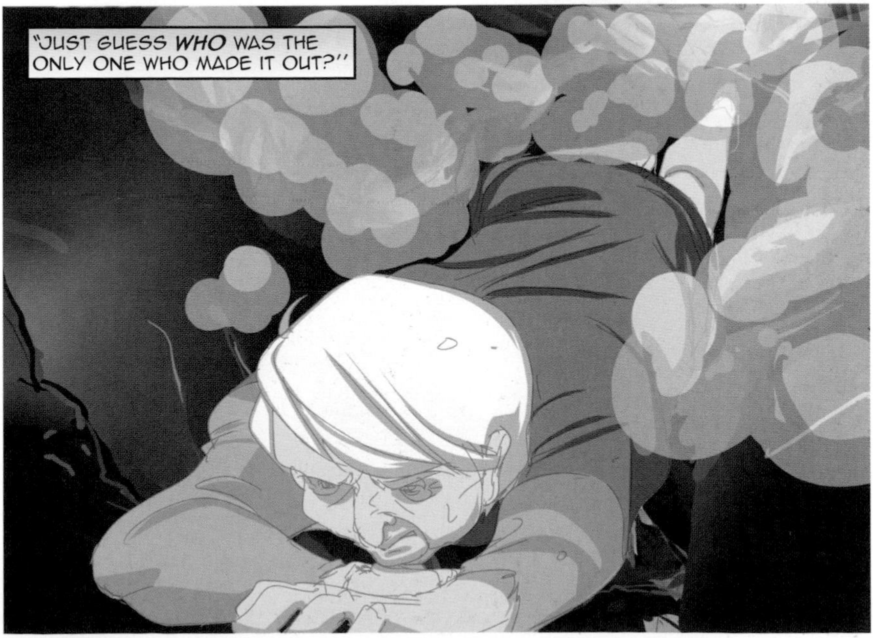
"JUST GUESS *WHO* WAS THE ONLY ONE WHO MADE IT OUT?"

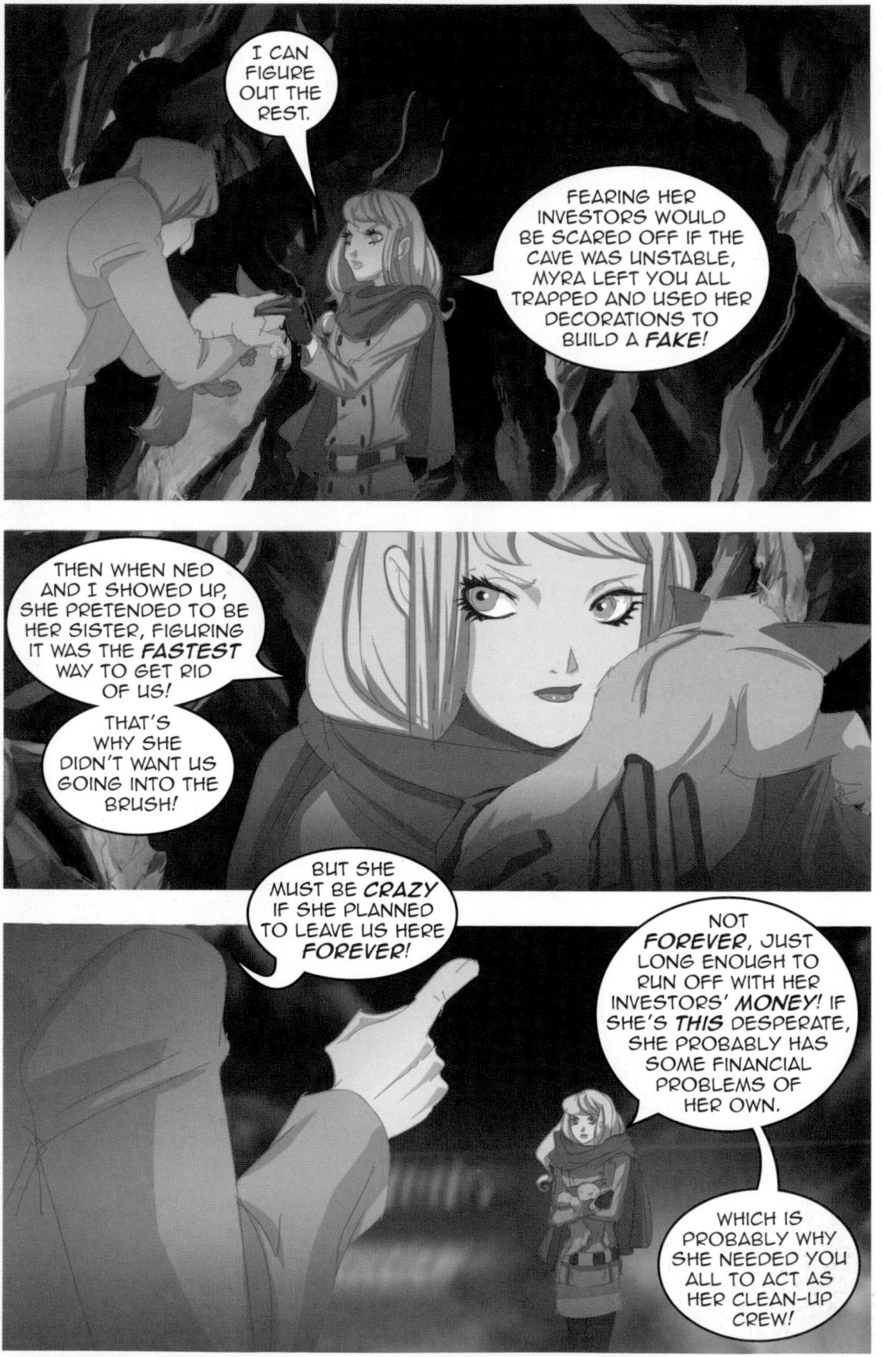
I CAN FIGURE OUT THE REST.
FEARING HER INVESTORS WOULD BE SCARED OFF IF THE CAVE WAS UNSTABLE, MYRA LEFT YOU ALL TRAPPED AND USED HER DECORATIONS TO BUILD A *FAKE*!
THEN WHEN NED AND I SHOWED UP, SHE PRETENDED TO BE HER SISTER, FIGURING IT WAS THE *FASTEST* WAY TO GET RID OF US!
THAT'S WHY SHE DIDN'T WANT US GOING INTO THE BRUSH!
BUT SHE MUST BE *CRAZY* IF SHE PLANNED TO LEAVE US HERE *FOREVER*!
NOT *FOREVER*, JUST LONG ENOUGH TO RUN OFF WITH HER INVESTORS' *MONEY*! IF SHE'S *THIS* DESPERATE, SHE PROBABLY HAS SOME FINANCIAL PROBLEMS OF HER OWN.
WHICH IS PROBABLY WHY SHE NEEDED YOU ALL TO ACT AS HER CLEAN-UP CREW!

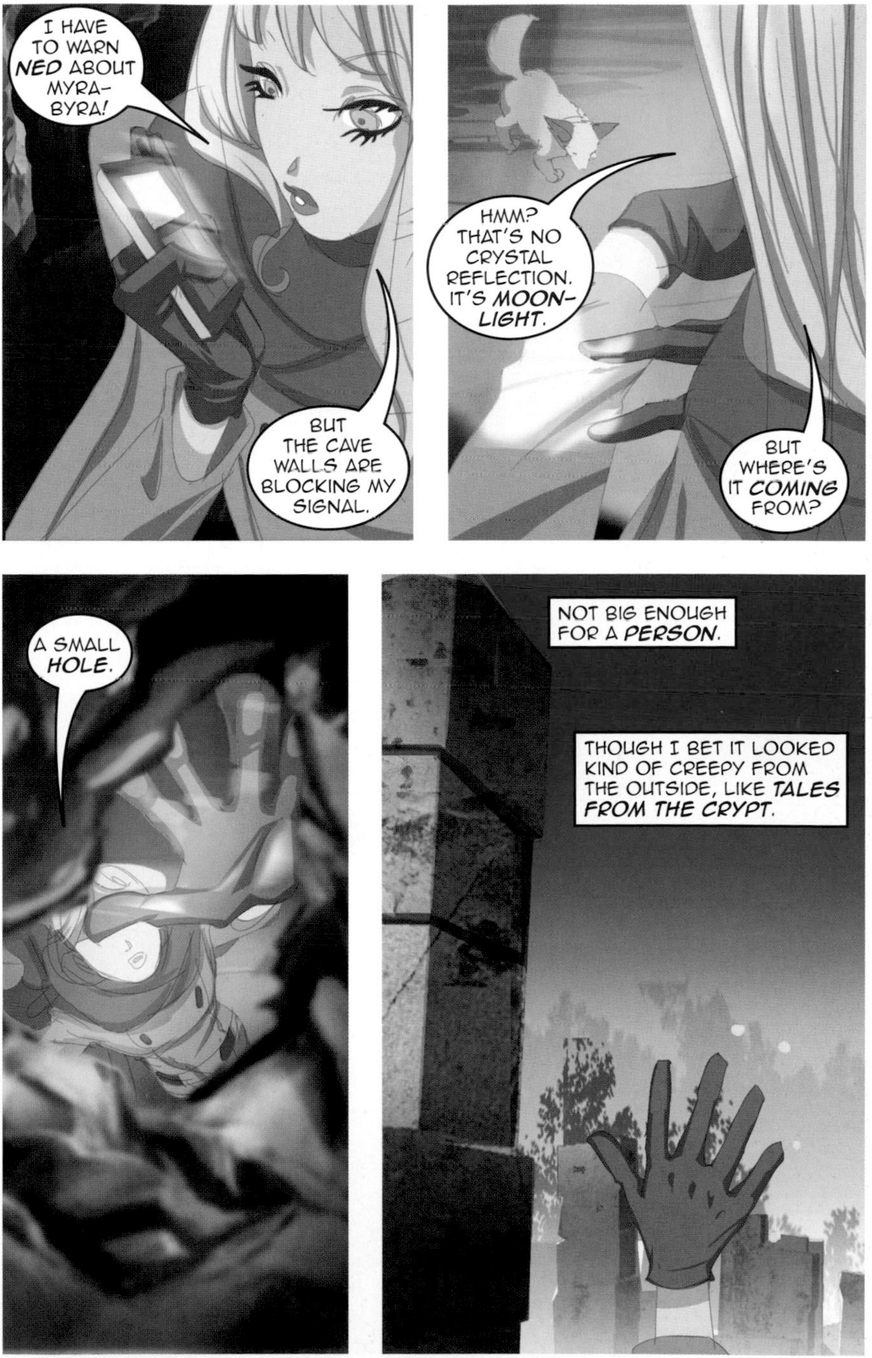
I HAVE TO WARN NED ABOUT MYRA-BYRA!
BUT THE CAVE WALLS ARE BLOCKING MY SIGNAL.
HMM? THAT'S NO CRYSTAL REFLECTION. IT'S MOON-LIGHT.
BUT WHERE'S IT COMING FROM?
A SMALL HOLE.
NOT BIG ENOUGH FOR A PERSON.
THOUGH I BET IT LOOKED KIND OF CREEPY FROM THE OUTSIDE, LIKE TALES FROM THE CRYPT.

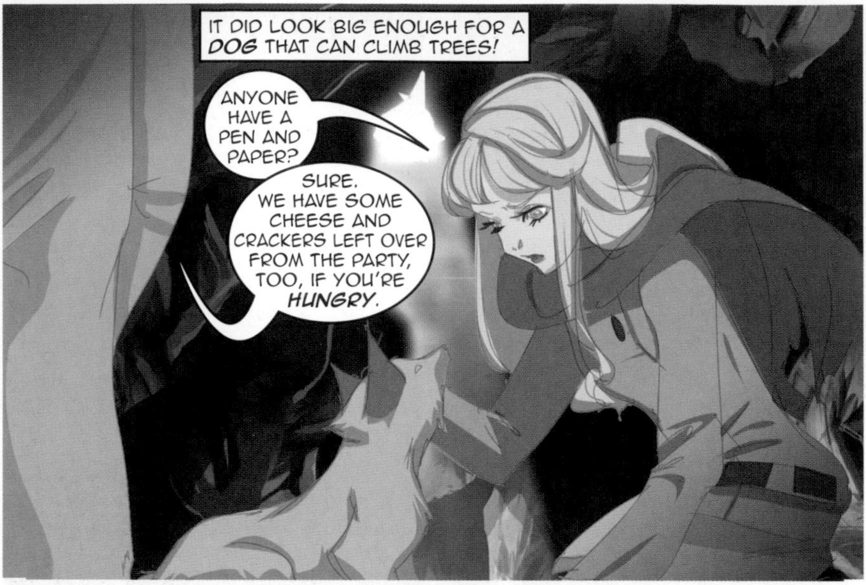
IT DID LOOK BIG ENOUGH FOR A DOG THAT CAN CLIMB TREES!
ANYONE HAVE A PEN AND PAPER?
SURE. WE HAVE SOME CHEESE AND CRACKERS LEFT OVER FROM THE PARTY, TOO, IF YOU'RE HUNGRY.

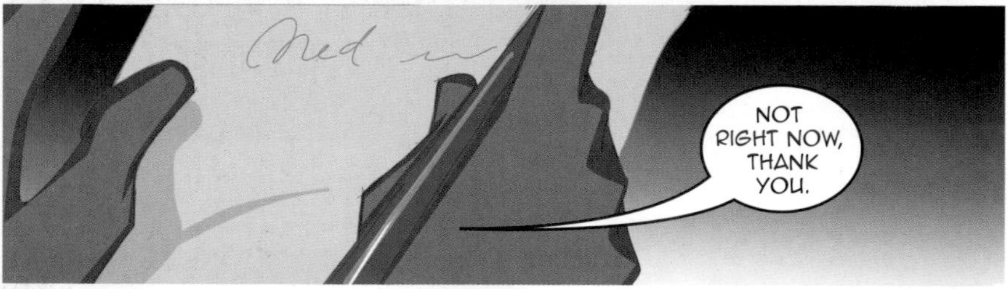
Ned
NOT RIGHT NOW, THANK YOU.

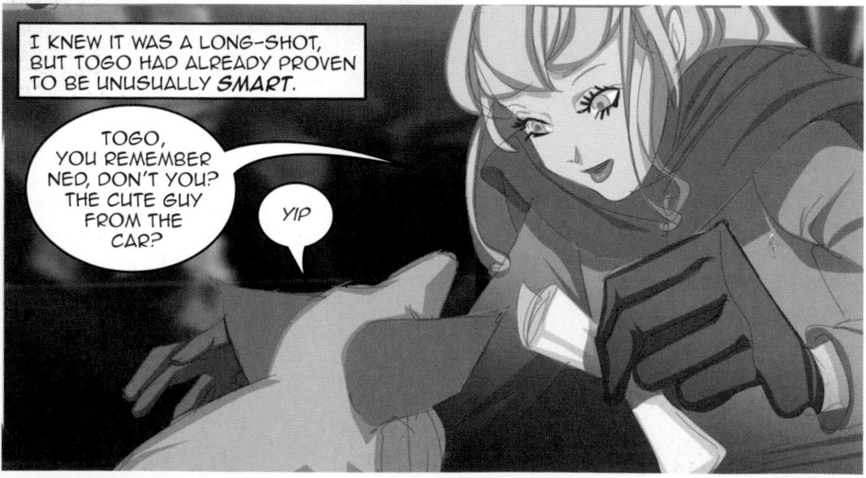
I KNEW IT WAS A LONG-SHOT, BUT TOGO HAD ALREADY PROVEN TO BE UNUSUALLY SMART.
TOGO, YOU REMEMBER NED, DON'T YOU? THE CUTE GUY FROM THE CAR?
YIP

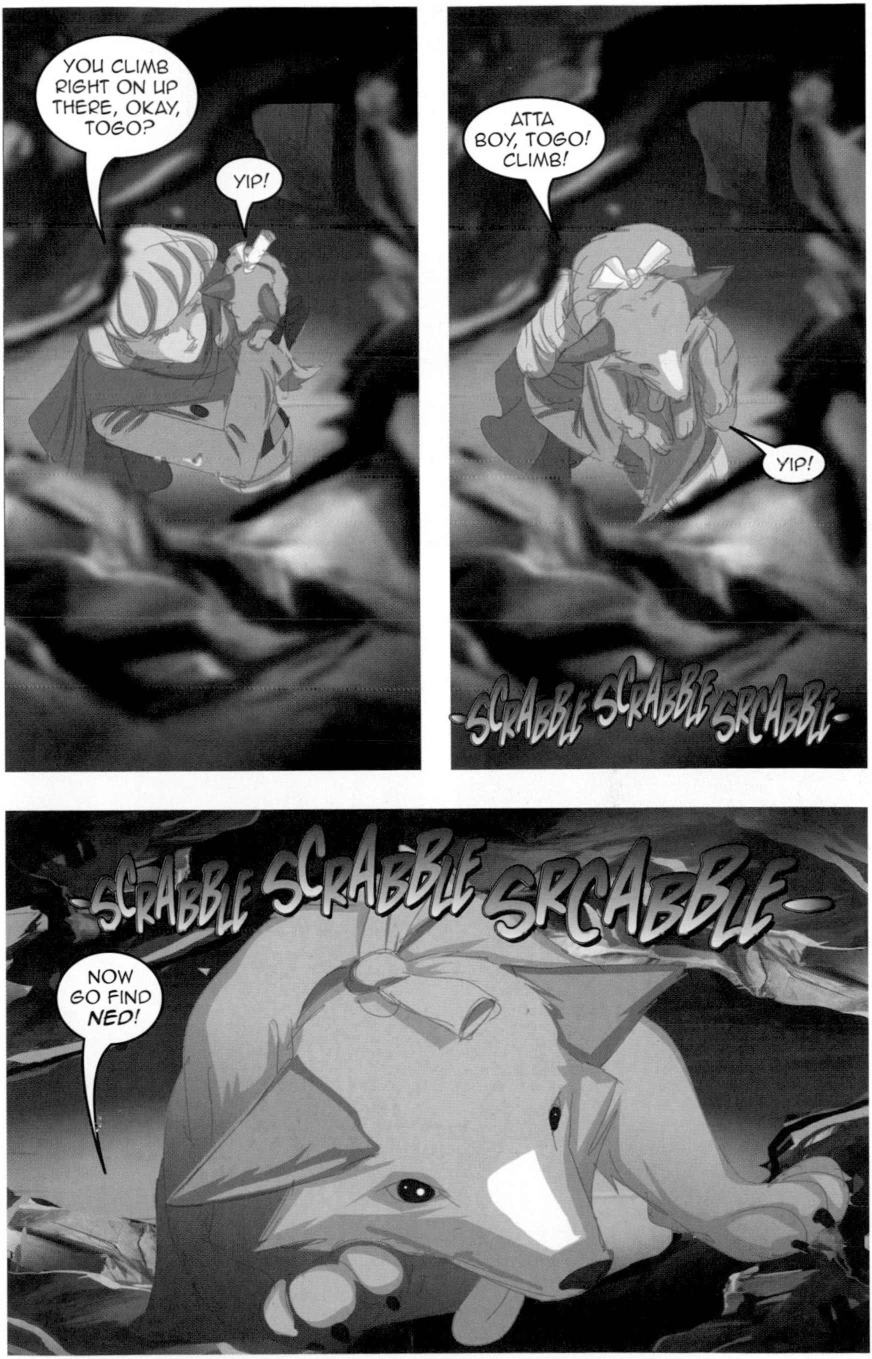
YOU CLIMB RIGHT ON UP THERE, OKAY, TOGO?
YIP!
ATTA BOY, TOGO! CLIMB!
YIP!
-SCRABBLE SCRABBLE SRCABBLE-
-SCRABBLE SCRABBLE SRCABBLE-
NOW GO FIND *NED*!

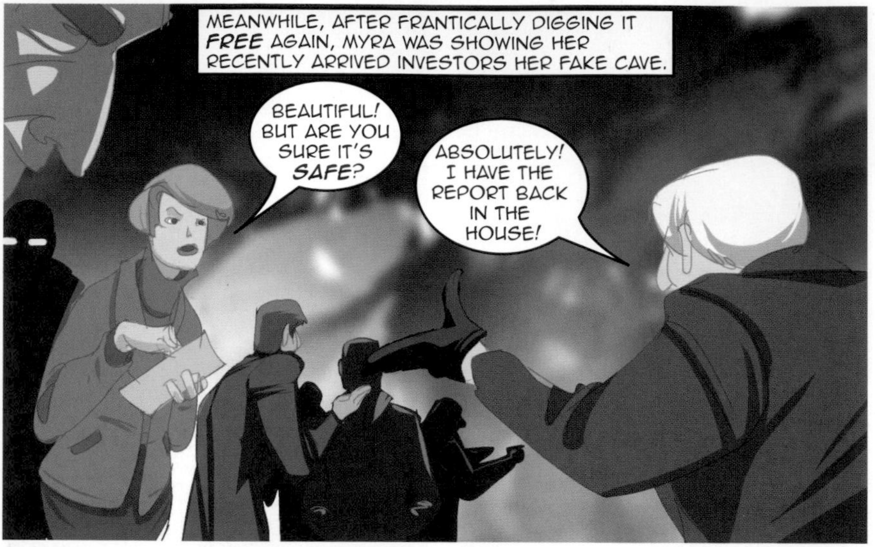
MEANWHILE, AFTER FRANTICALLY DIGGING IT FREE AGAIN, MYRA WAS SHOWING HER RECENTLY ARRIVED INVESTORS HER FAKE CAVE.
BEAUTIFUL! BUT ARE YOU SURE IT'S SAFE?
ABSOLUTELY! I HAVE THE REPORT BACK IN THE HOUSE!

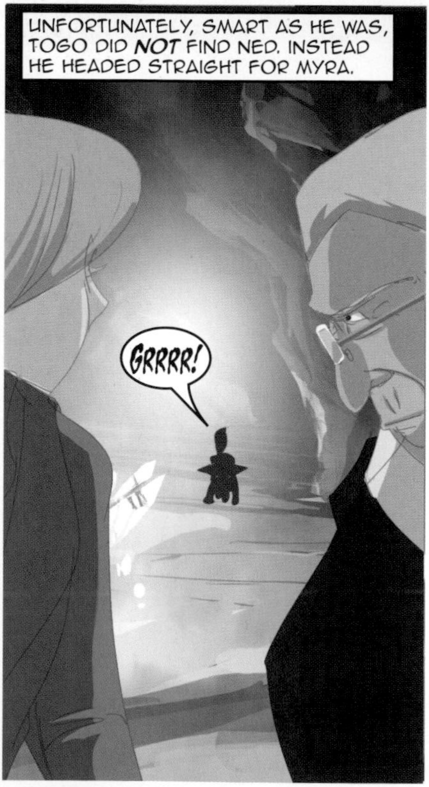
UNFORTUNATELY, SMART AS HE WAS, TOGO DID NOT FIND NED. INSTEAD HE HEADED STRAIGHT FOR MYRA.
GRRRR!

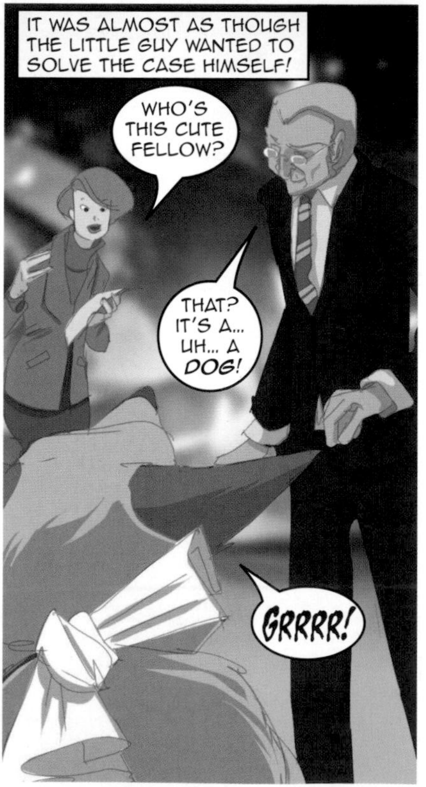
IT WAS ALMOST AS THOUGH THE LITTLE GUY WANTED TO SOLVE THE CASE HIMSELF!
WHO'S THIS CUTE FELLOW?
THAT? IT'S A... UH... A DOG!
GRRRR!

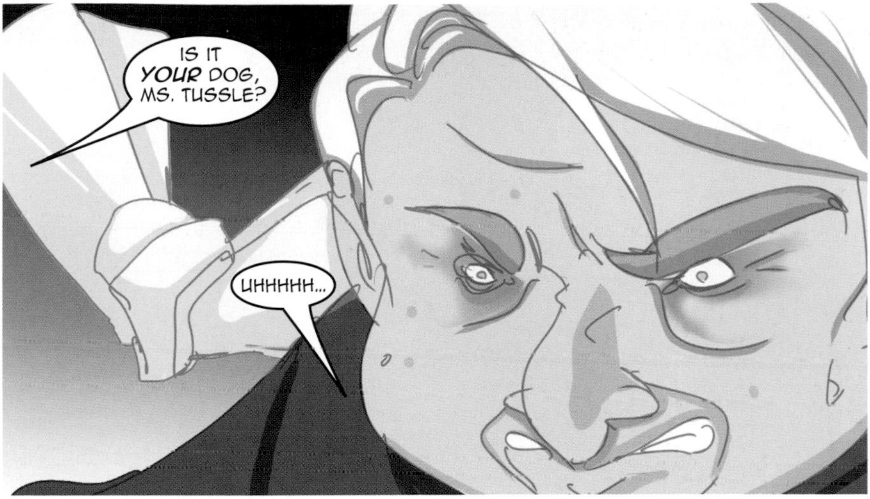
IS IT YOUR DOG, MS. TUSSLE?
UHHHHH...

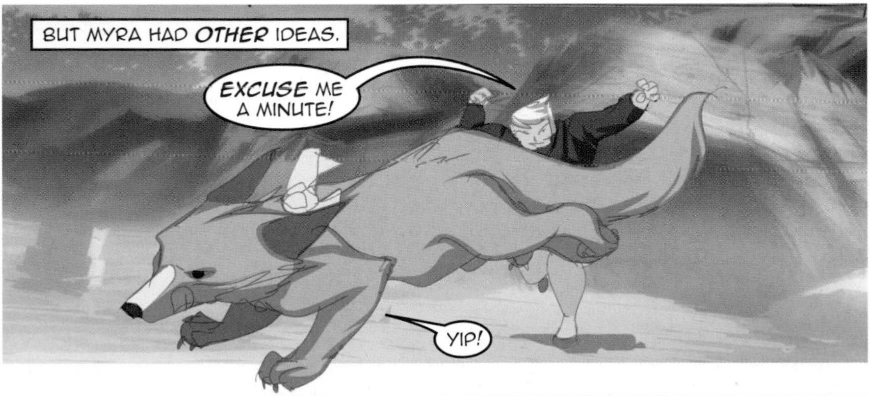
BUT MYRA HAD OTHER IDEAS.
EXCUSE ME A MINUTE!
YIP!

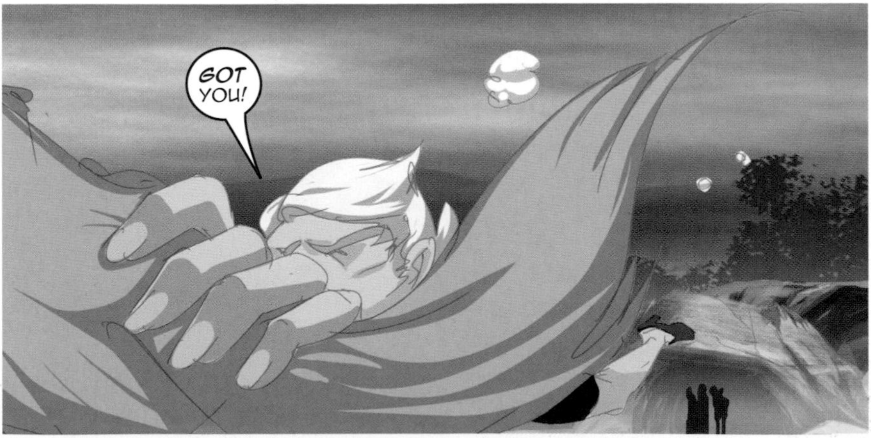
GOT YOU!

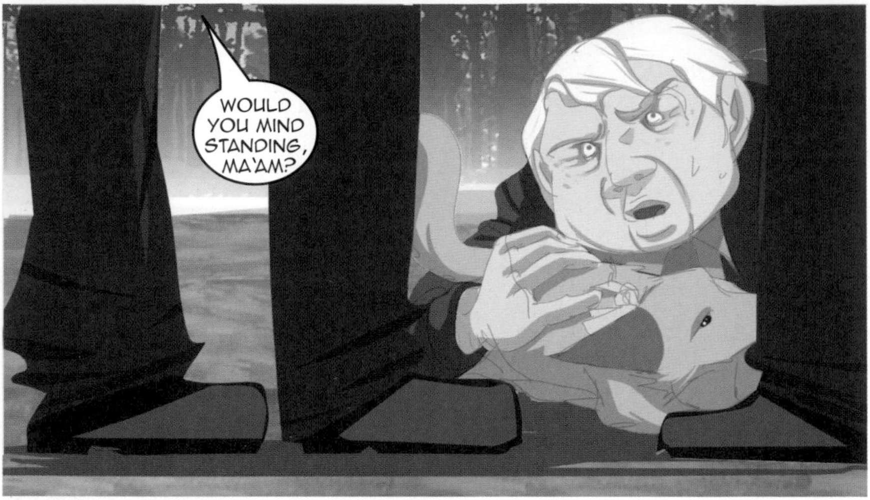
WOULD YOU MIND STANDING, MA'AM?

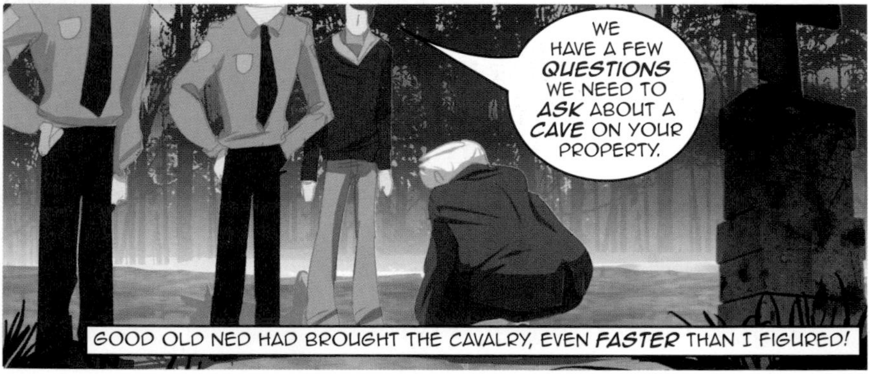
WE HAVE A FEW QUESTIONS WE NEED TO ASK ABOUT A CAVE ON YOUR PROPERTY.
GOOD OLD NED HAD BROUGHT THE CAVALRY, EVEN FASTER THAN I FIGURED!

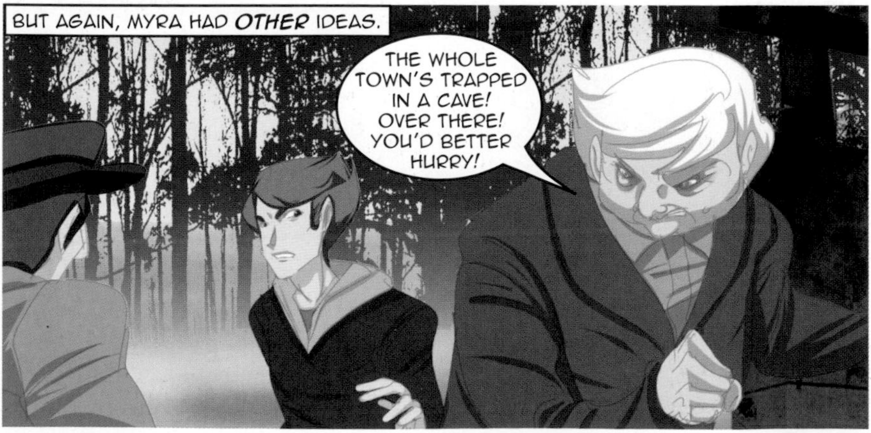
BUT AGAIN, MYRA HAD OTHER IDEAS.
THE WHOLE TOWN'S TRAPPED IN A CAVE! OVER THERE! YOU'D BETTER HURRY!

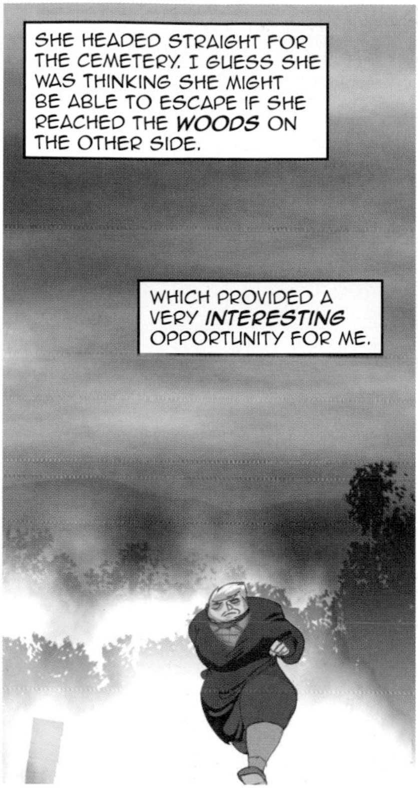
SHE HEADED STRAIGHT FOR THE CEMETERY. I GUESS SHE WAS THINKING SHE MIGHT BE ABLE TO ESCAPE IF SHE REACHED THE ***WOODS*** ON THE OTHER SIDE.
WHICH PROVIDED A VERY ***INTERESTING*** OPPORTUNITY FOR ME.

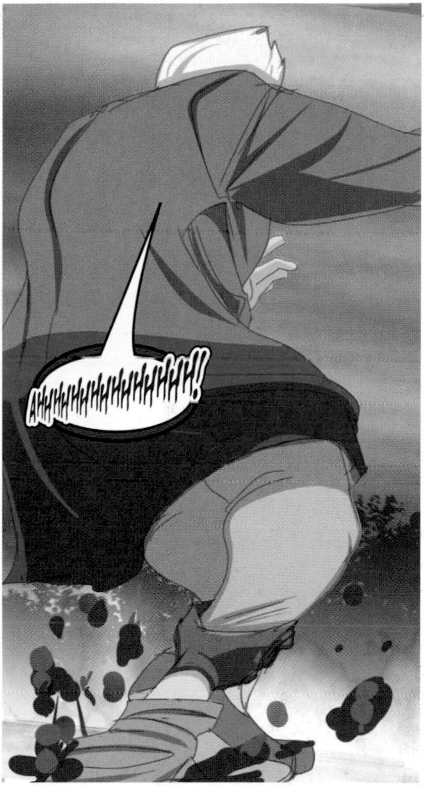
AHHHHHHHHHHHHHH!!

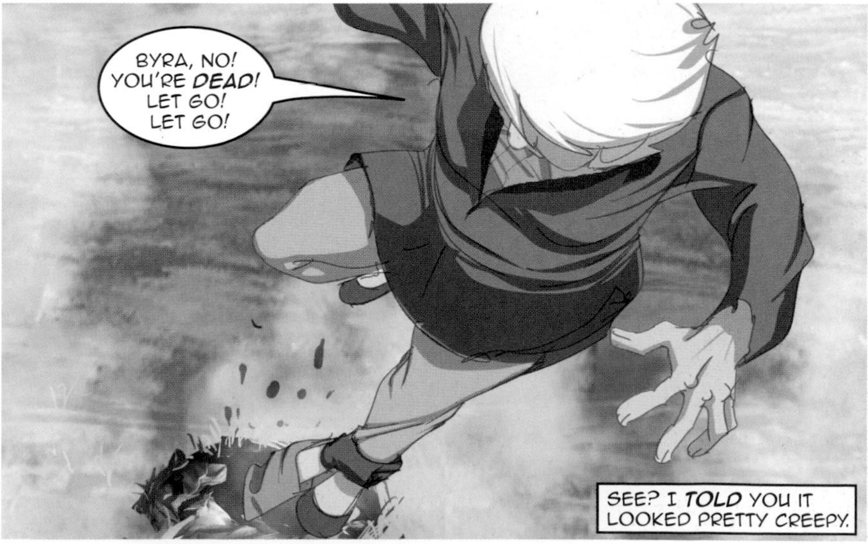
BYRA, NO! YOU'RE ***DEAD!*** LET GO! LET GO!
SEE? I ***TOLD*** YOU IT LOOKED PRETTY CREEPY.

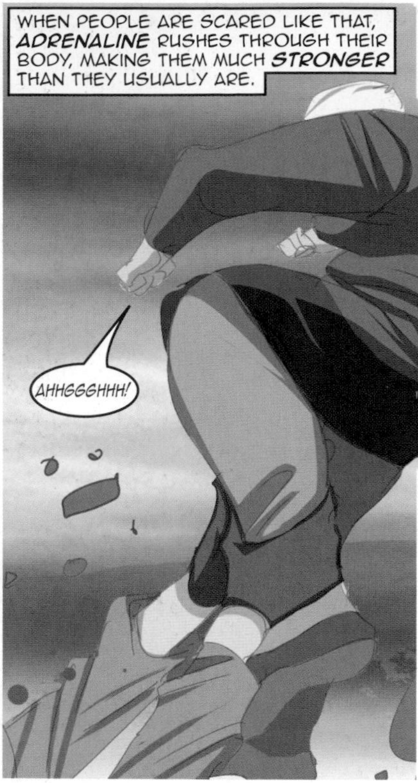
WHEN PEOPLE ARE SCARED LIKE THAT, ADRENALINE RUSHES THROUGH THEIR BODY, MAKING THEM MUCH STRONGER THAN THEY USUALLY ARE.
AHHGGGHHH!

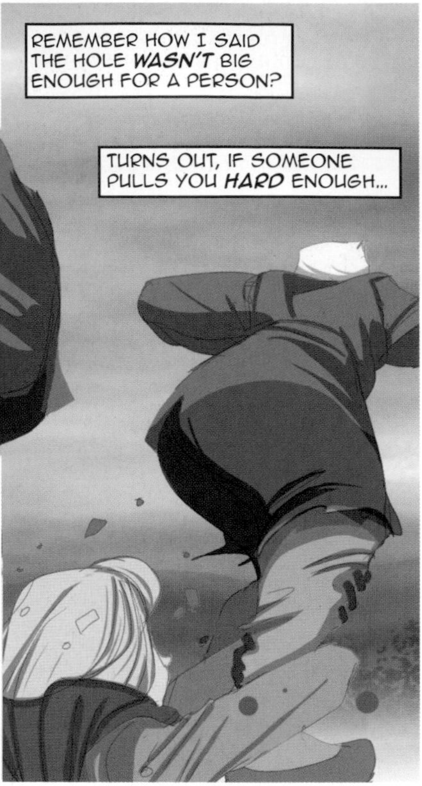
REMEMBER HOW I SAID THE HOLE WASN'T BIG ENOUGH FOR A PERSON?
TURNS OUT, IF SOMEONE PULLS YOU HARD ENOUGH...

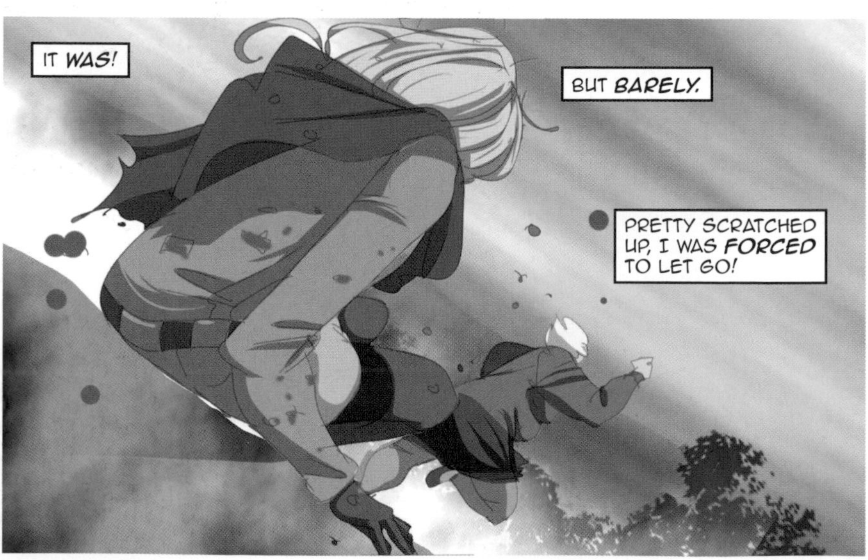
IT WAS!
BUT BARELY.
PRETTY SCRATCHED UP, I WAS FORCED TO LET GO!

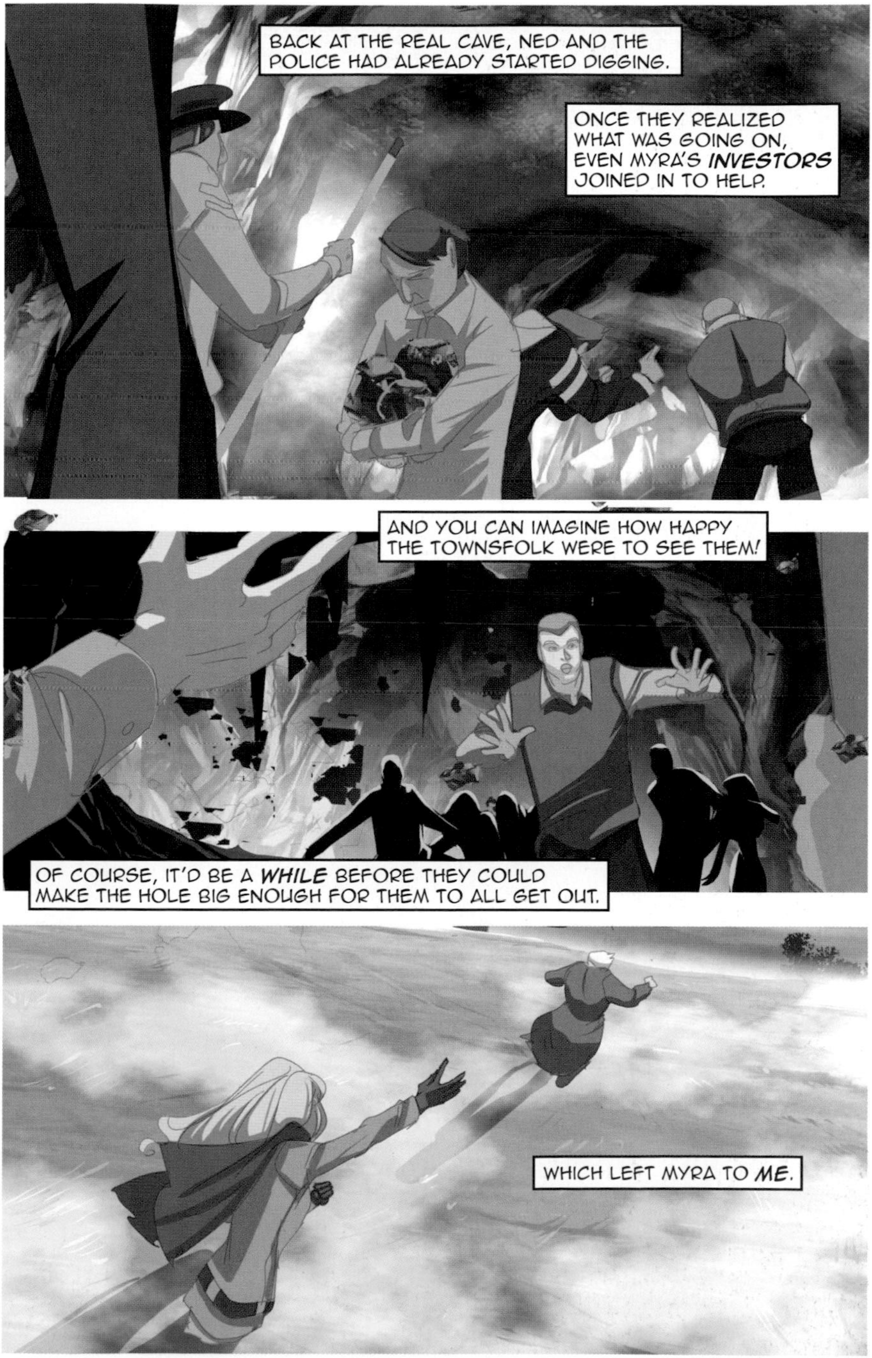
BACK AT THE REAL CAVE, NED AND THE POLICE HAD ALREADY STARTED DIGGING.
ONCE THEY REALIZED WHAT WAS GOING ON, EVEN MYRA'S INVESTORS JOINED IN TO HELP.
AND YOU CAN IMAGINE HOW HAPPY THE TOWNSFOLK WERE TO SEE THEM!
OF COURSE, IT'D BE A WHILE BEFORE THEY COULD MAKE THE HOLE BIG ENOUGH FOR THEM TO ALL GET OUT.
WHICH LEFT MYRA TO ME.

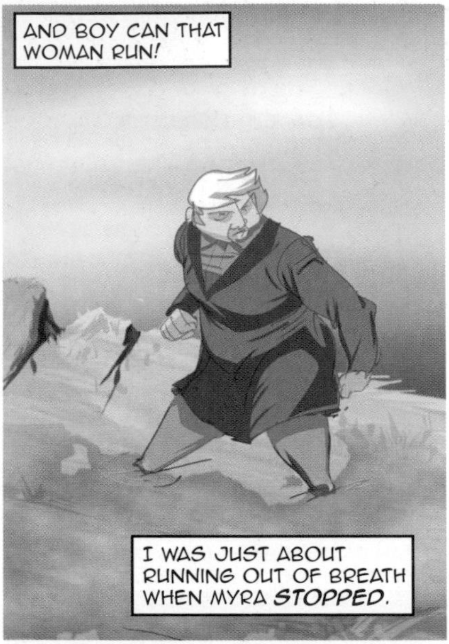
AND BOY CAN THAT WOMAN RUN!
I WAS JUST ABOUT RUNNING OUT OF BREATH WHEN MYRA STOPPED.

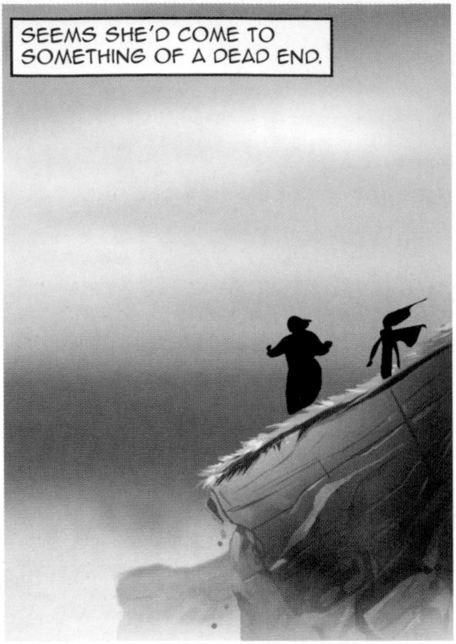
SEEMS SHE'D COME TO SOMETHING OF A DEAD END.

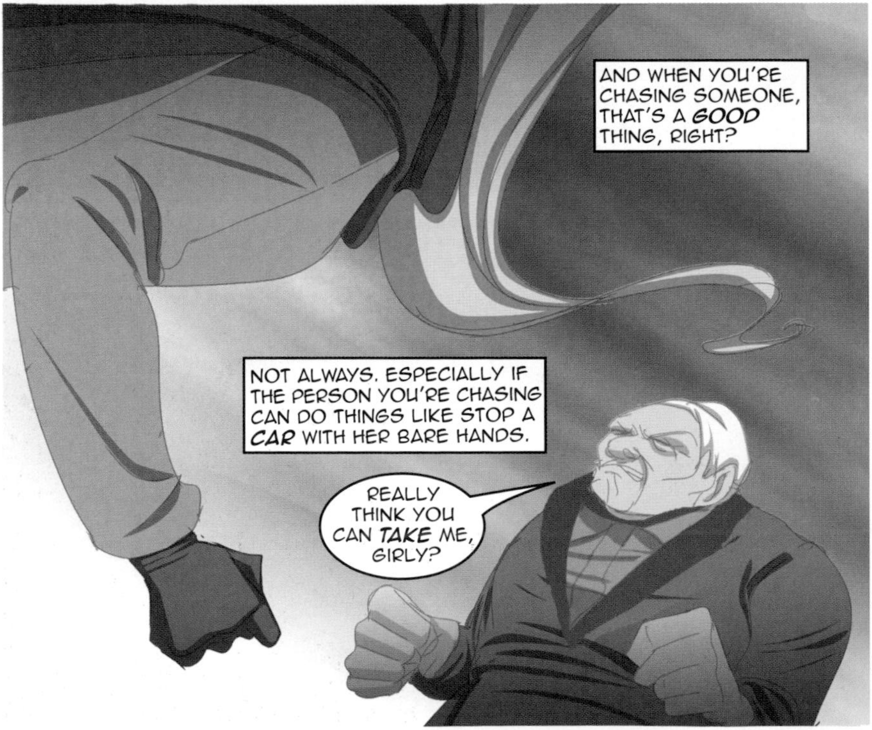
AND WHEN YOU'RE CHASING SOMEONE, THAT'S A GOOD THING, RIGHT?
NOT ALWAYS. ESPECIALLY IF THE PERSON YOU'RE CHASING CAN DO THINGS LIKE STOP A CAR WITH HER BARE HANDS.
REALLY THINK YOU CAN TAKE ME, GIRLY?

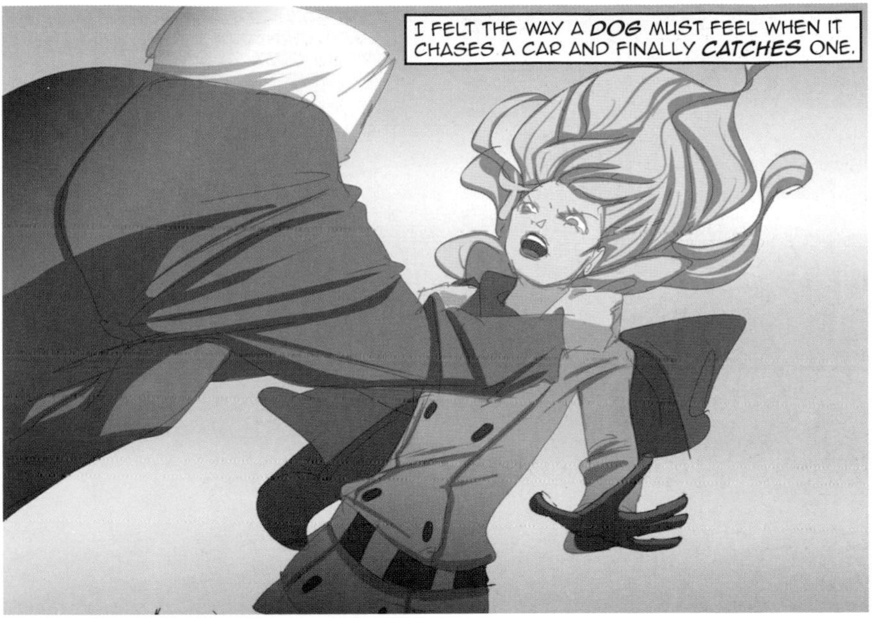
I FELT THE WAY A DOG MUST FEEL WHEN IT CHASES A CAR AND FINALLY CATCHES ONE.

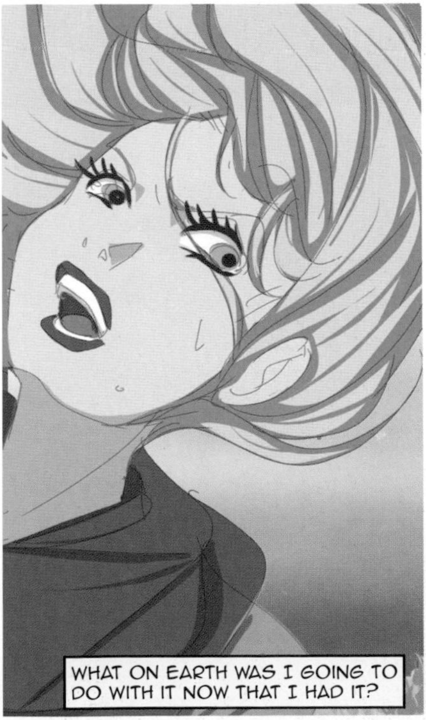
WHAT ON EARTH WAS I GOING TO DO WITH IT NOW THAT I HAD IT?

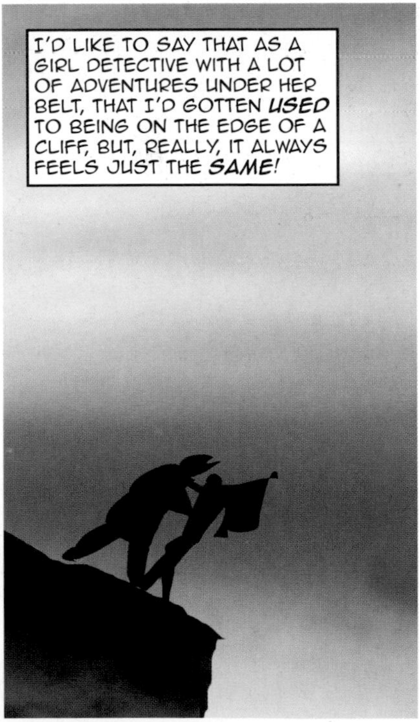
I'D LIKE TO SAY THAT AS A GIRL DETECTIVE WITH A LOT OF ADVENTURES UNDER HER BELT, THAT I'D GOTTEN USED TO BEING ON THE EDGE OF A CLIFF, BUT, REALLY, IT ALWAYS FEELS JUST THE SAME!

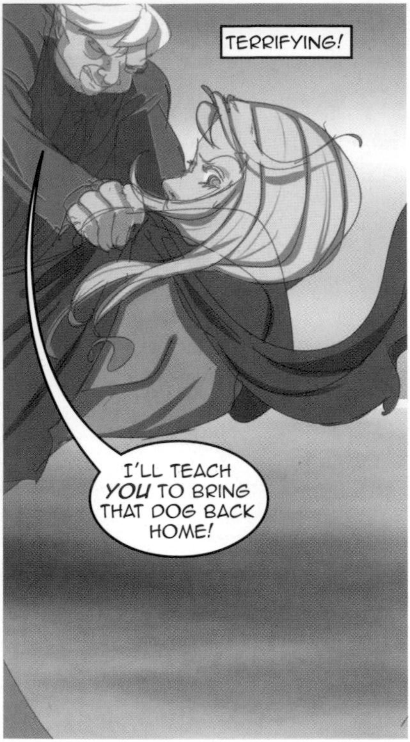
TERRIFYING!
I'LL TEACH YOU TO BRING THAT DOG BACK HOME!

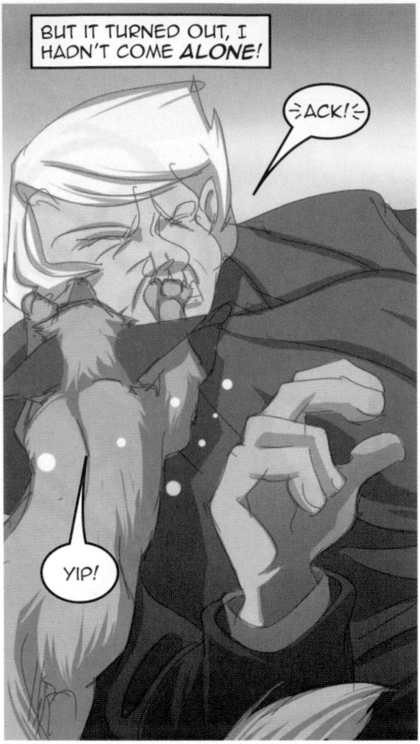
BUT IT TURNED OUT, I HADN'T COME ALONE!
ACK!
YIP!

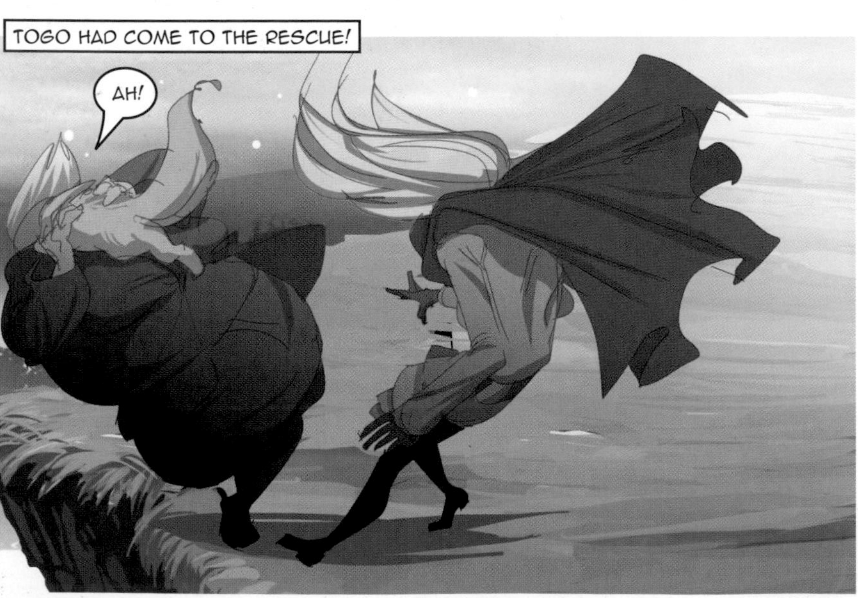
TOGO HAD COME TO THE RESCUE!
AH!

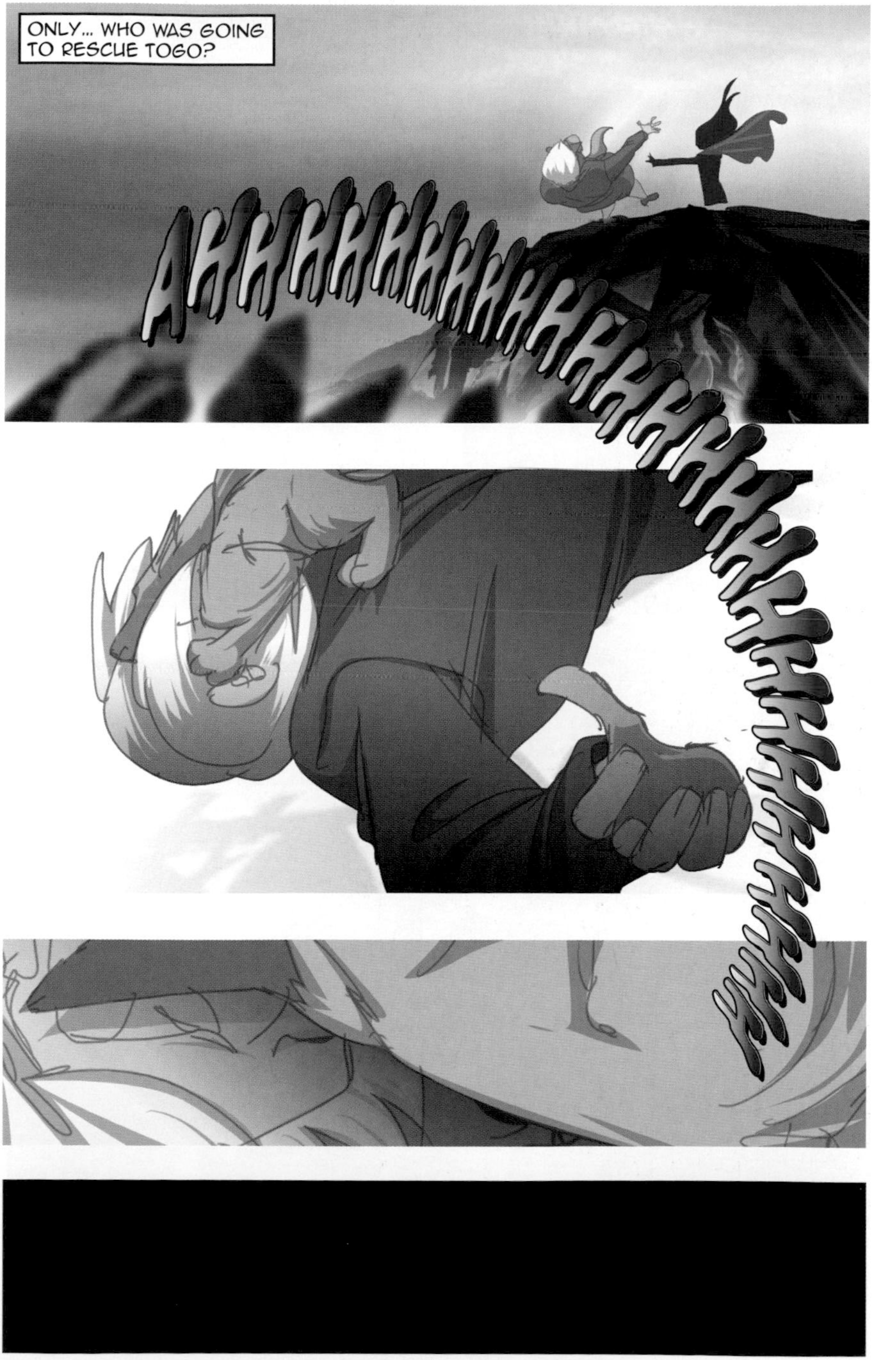
ONLY... WHO WAS GOING TO RESCUE TOGO?
AHHHHHHHHHHHHHHHHHHHHHHHHHHHHHHHHHHHHH

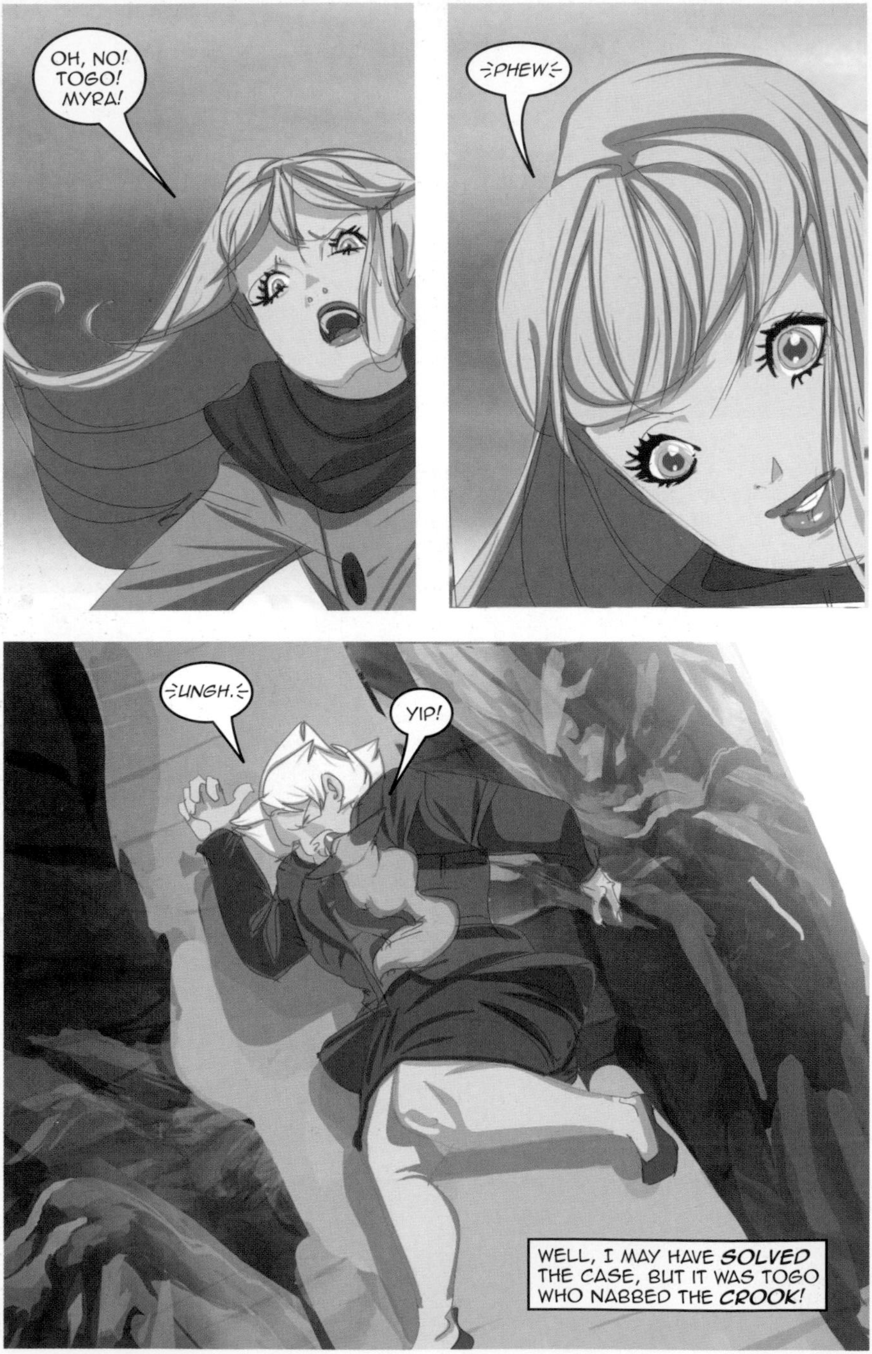
OH, NO! TOGO! MYRA!
PHEW
UNGH.
YIP!
WELL, I MAY HAVE *SOLVED* THE CASE, BUT IT WAS TOGO WHO NABBED THE *CROOK*!

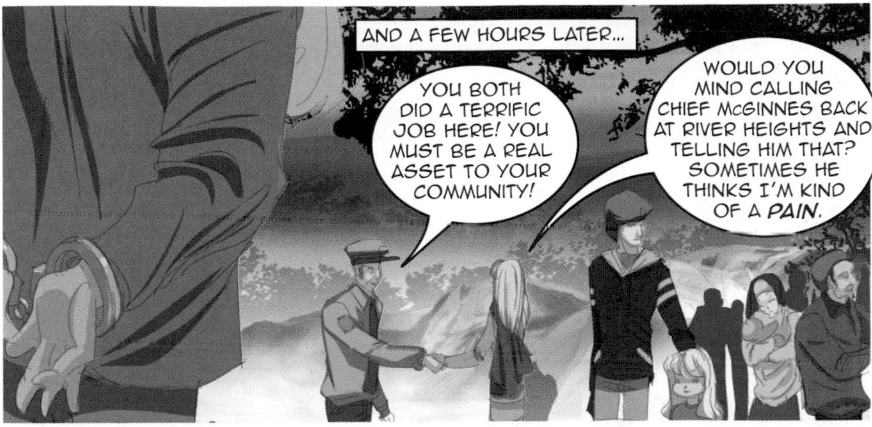
AND A FEW HOURS LATER...
YOU BOTH DID A TERRIFIC JOB HERE! YOU MUST BE A REAL ASSET TO YOUR COMMUNITY!
WOULD YOU MIND CALLING CHIEF McGINNES BACK AT RIVER HEIGHTS AND TELLING HIM THAT? SOMETIMES HE THINKS I'M KIND OF A ***PAIN***.

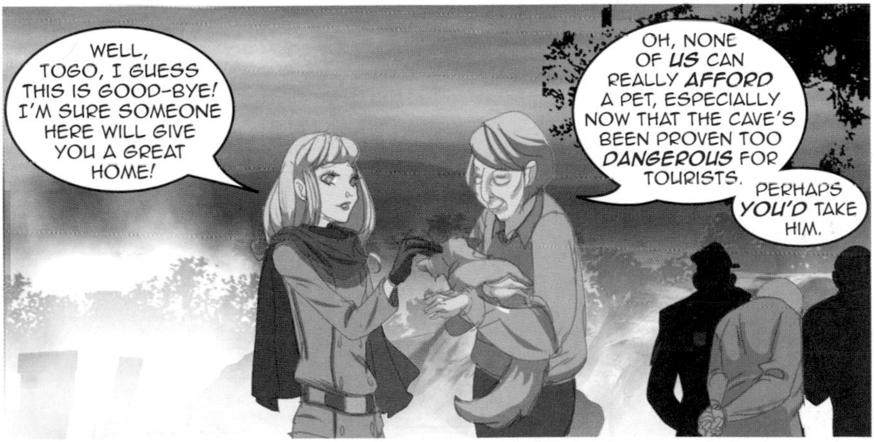
WELL, TOGO, I GUESS THIS IS GOOD-BYE! I'M SURE SOMEONE HERE WILL GIVE YOU A GREAT HOME!
OH, NONE OF ***US*** CAN REALLY ***AFFORD*** A PET, ESPECIALLY NOW THAT THE CAVE'S BEEN PROVEN TOO ***DANGEROUS*** FOR TOURISTS.
PERHAPS ***YOU'D*** TAKE HIM.

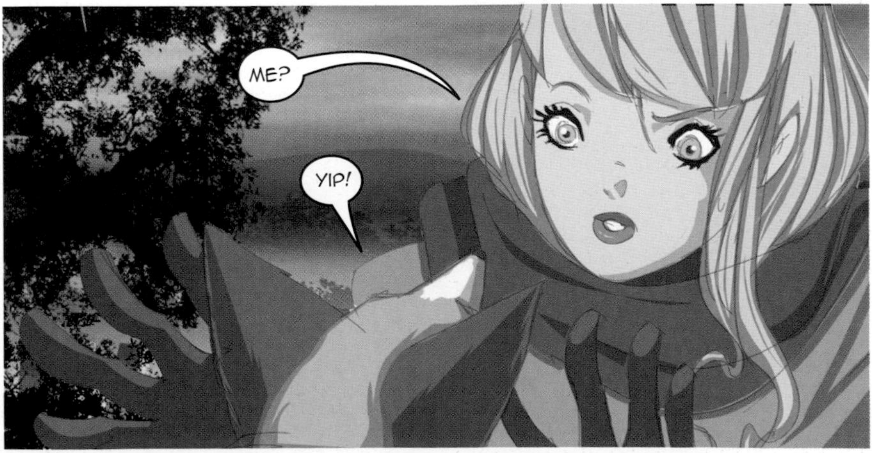
ME?
YIP!

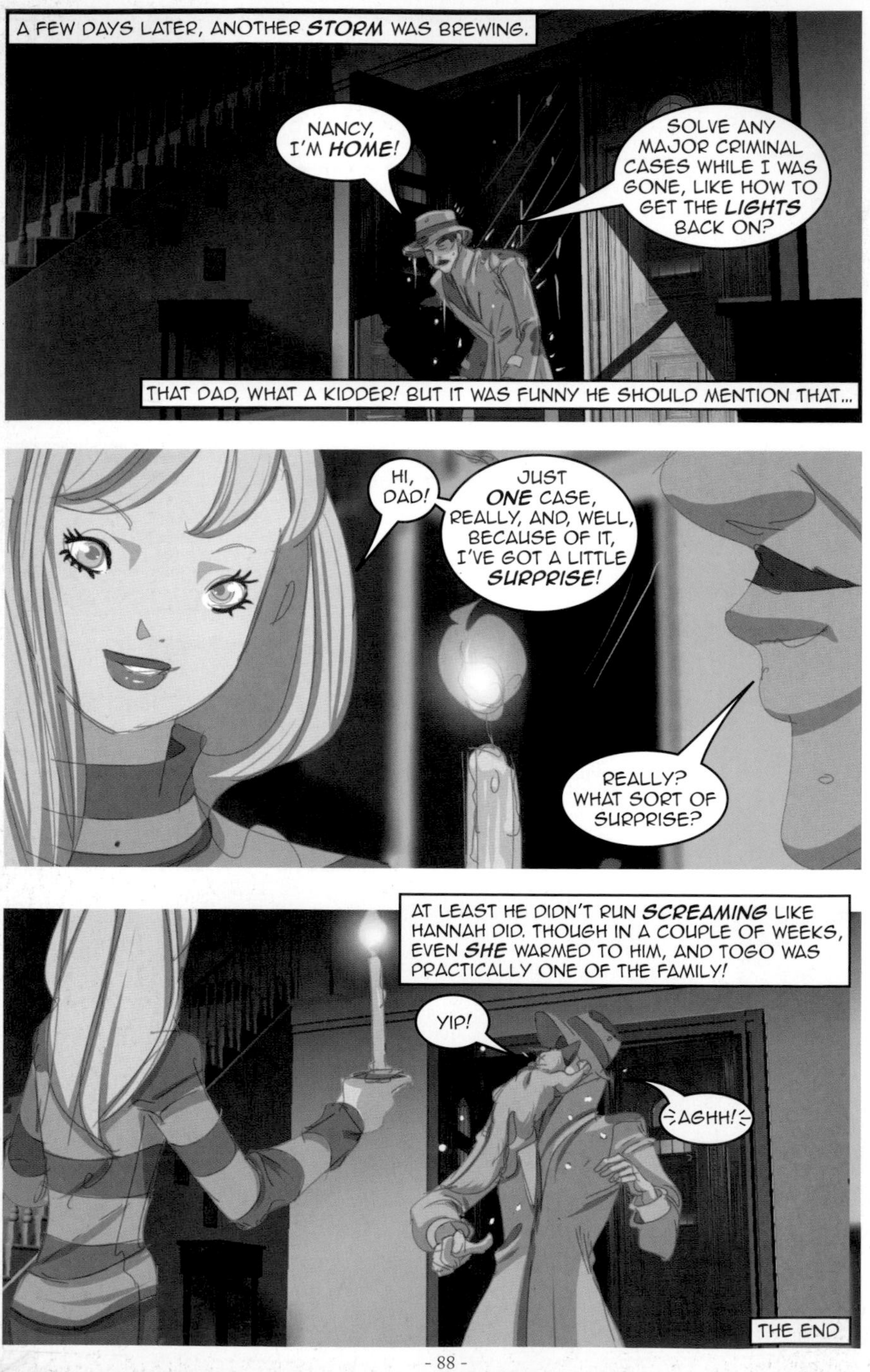
A FEW DAYS LATER, ANOTHER STORM WAS BREWING.
NANCY, I'M HOME!
SOLVE ANY MAJOR CRIMINAL CASES WHILE I WAS GONE, LIKE HOW TO GET THE LIGHTS BACK ON?
THAT DAD, WHAT A KIDDER! BUT IT WAS FUNNY HE SHOULD MENTION THAT...
HI, DAD!
JUST ONE CASE, REALLY, AND, WELL, BECAUSE OF IT, I'VE GOT A LITTLE SURPRISE!
REALLY? WHAT SORT OF SURPRISE?
AT LEAST HE DIDN'T RUN SCREAMING LIKE HANNAH DID. THOUGH IN A COUPLE OF WEEKS, EVEN SHE WARMED TO HIM, AND TOGO WAS PRACTICALLY ONE OF THE FAMILY!
YIP!
AGHH!
THE END

Nancy Drew: Sea of Darkness

Set a Course for Danger and Discovery!

The celebrated ship "Heerlijkheid," is usually the centerpiece of an Icelandic town's local festival. Now that its captain has disappeared, the renovated vessel has become an eerie distraction. Did Captain Magnus sail away with a legendary treasure, or was he carried off into the night? Take the helm as detective Nancy Drew and set a course for the Sea of Darkness!

Buy Nancy Drew games online at www.herinteractive.com. Dare to Play!

WIN MAC DVD-ROM SOFTWARE

EVERYONE 10+
Alcohol Reference
Mild Blood
Violent References
ESRB CONTENT RATING   www.esrb.org

Copyright © 2016 Her Interactive, Inc. HER INTERACTIVE, the HER INTERACTIVE logo and DARE TO PLAY are trademarks of Her Interactive, Inc. NANCY DREW is a registered trademark of Simon & Schuster, Inc. Licensed by permission of Simon & Schuster, Inc. Other brands or product names are trademarks of their respective holders.

WATCH OUT FOR PAPERCUTZ

©2016 Viacom International Inc.

Hi, mystery-lovers! Welcome to the seventh, search-filled NANCY DREW DIARIES graphic novel by Stefan Petrucha, Sarah Kinney, Sho Murase, and Carlos Jose Guzman from Papercutz—those magical, dog-loving, armchair detectives dedicated to publishing great graphic novels for all ages. I'm Jim Salicrup, the Editor-in-Chief and amateur dog-walker.

As you may or may not know, NANCY DREW DIARIES re-presents NANCY DREW GIRL DETECTIVE graphic novels that were originally published, in this case, eight years ago. Just like many of the original Nancy Drew Mysteries are based on novels originally published up to 85 years ago. So, it's fun for me to revisit these stories, make an editorial tweak here and there, and experience the thrill of Nancy Drew solving a couple of clever mysteries all over again.

For example, I got a kick out of seeing Nancy's flip phone. I'm sure Nancy is now using a smart phone, and probably dropping it in unusual places as well. I doubt that a smart phone can survive being dropped in a sewer—unless it's waterproof (And don't think too hard about how Nancy got her cell phone back after it fell in a sewer—yuck!). When that giant snake swallowed her phone, and Ned started talking to Nancy (We won't question how the phone was answered and how the speaker got turned on, either!) it reminded me of another all-new series we're publishing at Papercutz—SANJAY AND CRAIG!

That's right, the very same SANJAY AND CRAIG that you enjoy on Nickelodeon is also a Papercutz

graphic novel series, featuring all-new stories starring Sanjay Patel and Craig, his talking snake. Funny, I never questioned why Craig could talk before, and it certainly never occurred to me that he might've swallowed a cell phone! Even weirder is that when Craig wears a cap and t-shirt, he's able to pass as just another one of Sanjay's human friends, such as Hector or Megan. By the way, SANJAY AND CRAIG aren't the only Nickelodeon characters Papercutz is currently publishing, look for graphic novels featuring BREADWINNERS, HARVEY BEAKS, and PIG GOAT BANANA CRICKET as well. Or to get a taste of what these comics are like, pick up the latest issue of NICKELODEON MAGAZINE. Each issue is jam-packed with comics featuring many of the characters I just mentioned.

"Doggone Town" reminded me of a series both Papercutz publisher Terry Nantier and I liked when we were kids—Lassie. Lassie was a TV series, as well as a long-running comicbook series, that featured the adventures of a boy (Timmy) and his non-talking dog (a collie named Lassie). The classic parody of Lassie, is that he would often be able to lead sheriffs to trouble spots, such as old mines, just like Togo does. In fact, in just last week's New York Post, I read this amazing story:

It was a scene straight out of an episode of 'Lassie.'

"Police in western Massachusetts say a dog approached an officer on Tuesday barking frantically and then led the officer across a field and down an icy, 30-foot embankment, where the dog's canine companion had become entangled in the undergrowth."

I'm lucky if my dog, Mr. Snuggles, remembers me. Finally, with all this talk of various TV shows, guess who might be getting her own prime time TV series on CBS? Nothing's official yet, but wouldn't it be great to see a certain Girl Detective back on TV? Until we know more, let's just look forward to NANCY DREW DIARIES #8 featuring "Tiger Counter" and "What Goes Up…," coming soon! We suspect you'll love it!

Thanks,

JIM

STAY IN TOUCH!

EMAIL: salicrup@papercutz.com
WEB: www.papercutz.com
TWITTER: @papercutzgn
FACEBOOK: PAPERCUTZGRAPHICNOVELS
REGULAR MAIL: Papercutz, 160 Broadway, Suite 700, East Wing, New York, NY 10038

©2016 Viacom International Inc.

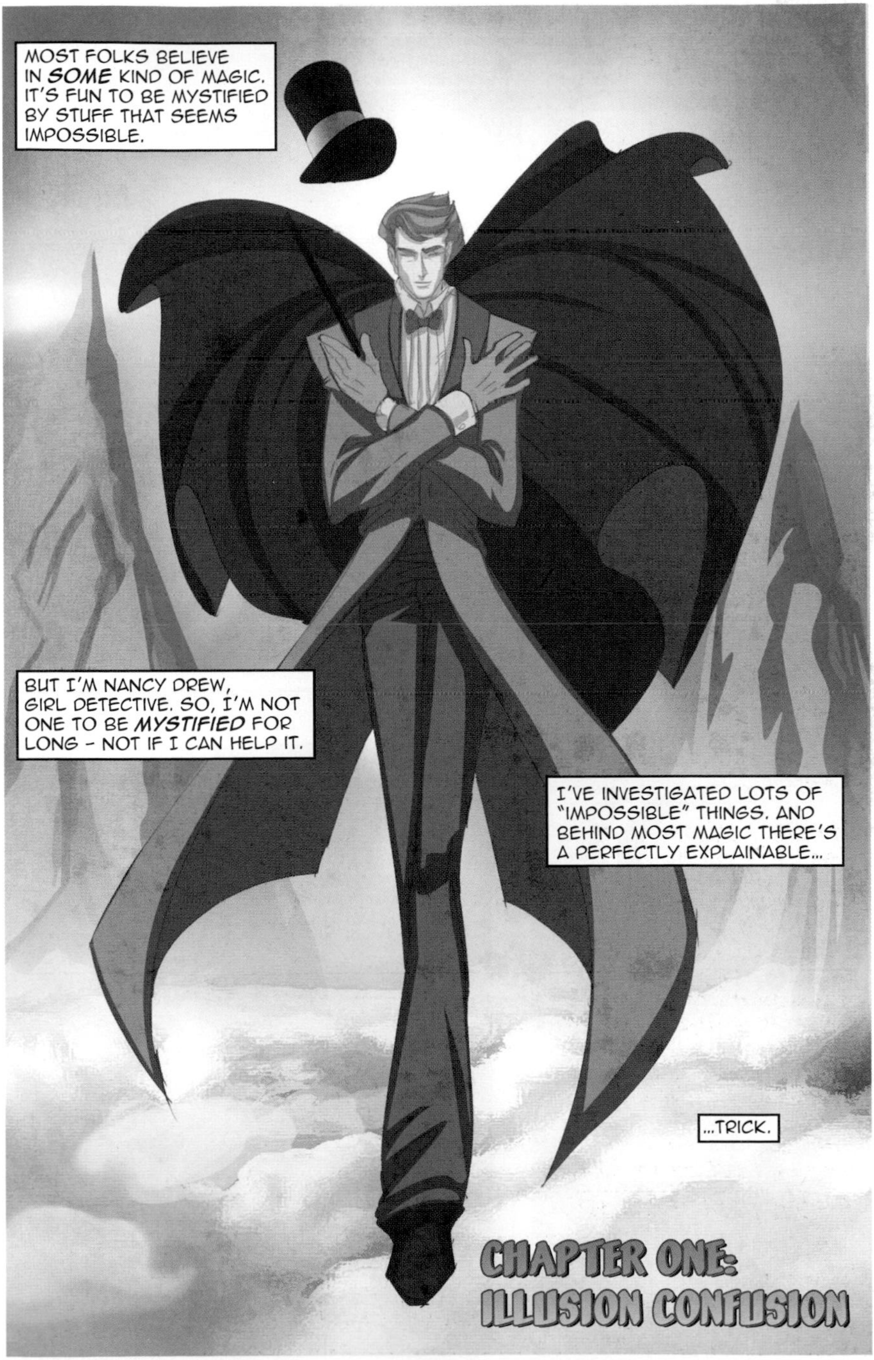
MOST FOLKS BELIEVE IN *SOME* KIND OF MAGIC. IT'S FUN TO BE MYSTIFIED BY STUFF THAT SEEMS IMPOSSIBLE.
BUT I'M NANCY DREW, GIRL DETECTIVE. SO, I'M NOT ONE TO BE *MYSTIFIED* FOR LONG - NOT IF I CAN HELP IT.
I'VE INVESTIGATED LOTS OF "IMPOSSIBLE" THINGS. AND BEHIND MOST MAGIC THERE'S A PERFECTLY EXPLAINABLE...
...TRICK.
CHAPTER ONE: ILLUSION CONFUSION

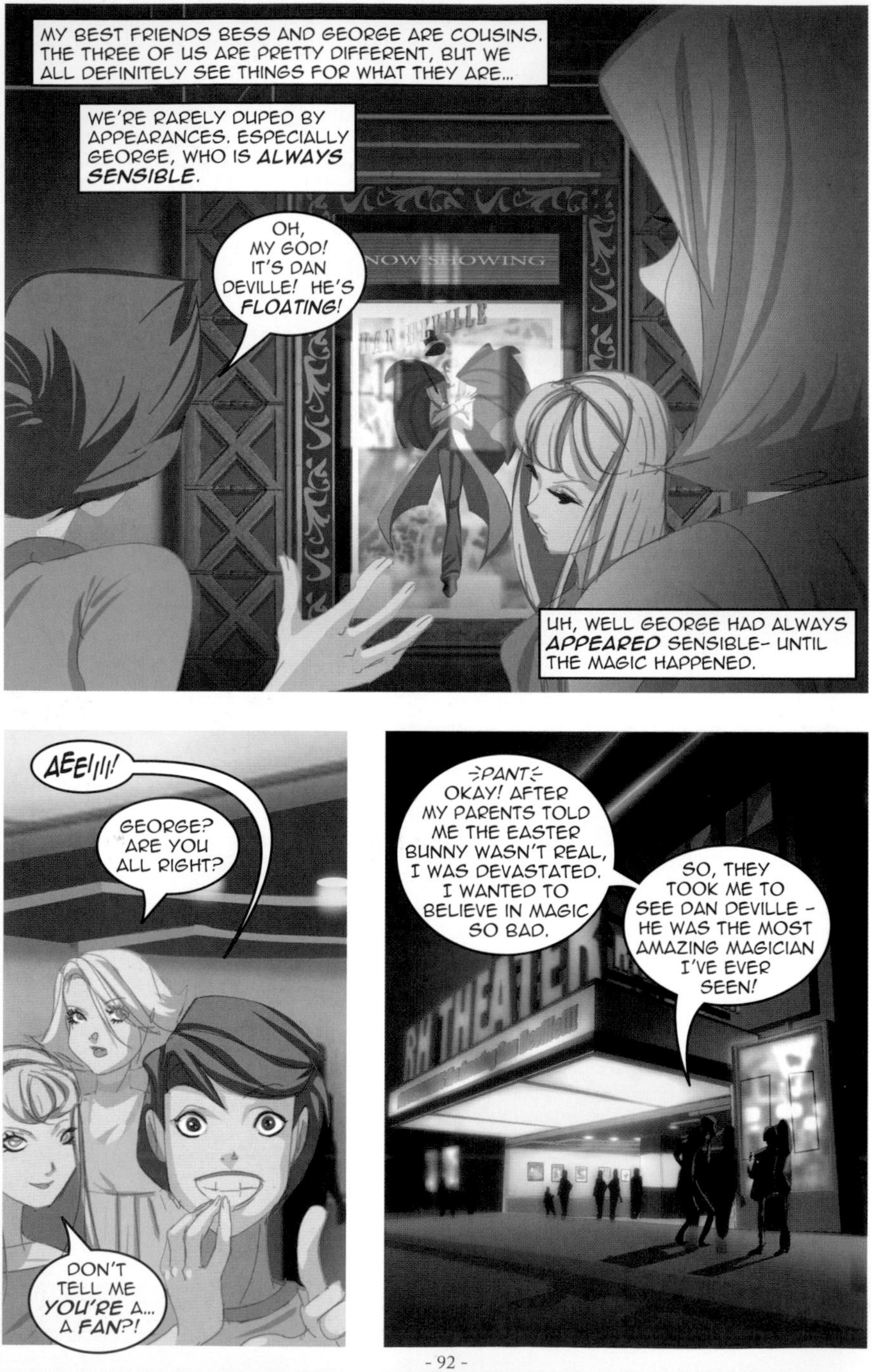
MY BEST FRIENDS BESS AND GEORGE ARE COUSINS. THE THREE OF US ARE PRETTY DIFFERENT, BUT WE ALL DEFINITELY SEE THINGS FOR WHAT THEY ARE...
WE'RE RARELY DUPED BY APPEARANCES. ESPECIALLY GEORGE, WHO IS *ALWAYS SENSIBLE*.
OH, MY GOD! IT'S DAN DEVILLE! HE'S *FLOATING*!
NOW SHOWING
UH, WELL GEORGE HAD ALWAYS *APPEARED* SENSIBLE- UNTIL THE MAGIC HAPPENED.
AEEIIII!
GEORGE? ARE YOU ALL RIGHT?
DON'T TELL ME *YOU'RE* A... A *FAN*?!
PANT
OKAY! AFTER MY PARENTS TOLD ME THE EASTER BUNNY WASN'T REAL, I WAS DEVASTATED. I WANTED TO BELIEVE IN MAGIC SO BAD.
SO, THEY TOOK ME TO SEE DAN DEVILLE - HE WAS THE MOST AMAZING MAGICIAN I'VE EVER SEEN!

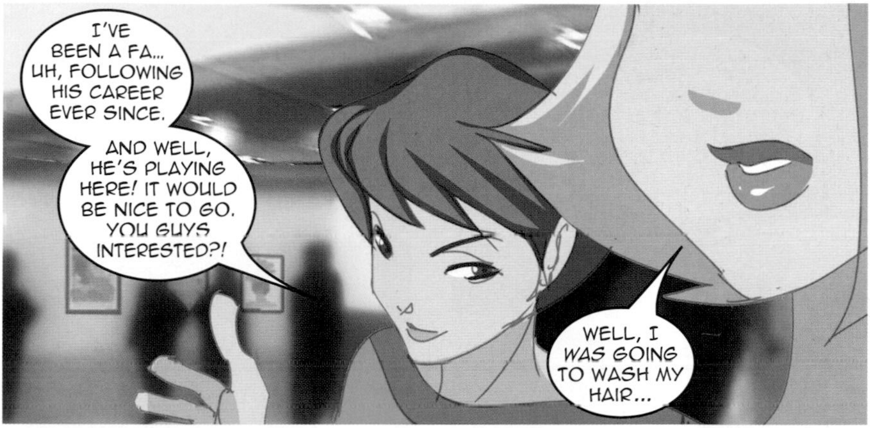
I'VE BEEN A FA... UH, FOLLOWING HIS CAREER EVER SINCE.
AND WELL, HE'S PLAYING HERE! IT WOULD BE NICE TO GO. YOU GUYS INTERESTED?!
WELL, I WAS GOING TO WASH MY HAIR...

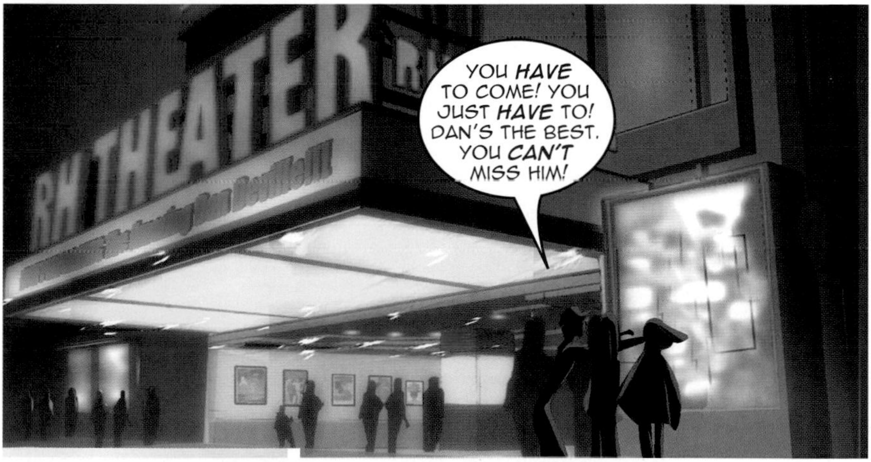
RX THEATER
YOU *HAVE* TO COME! YOU JUST *HAVE* TO! DAN'S THE BEST. YOU *CAN'T* MISS HIM!

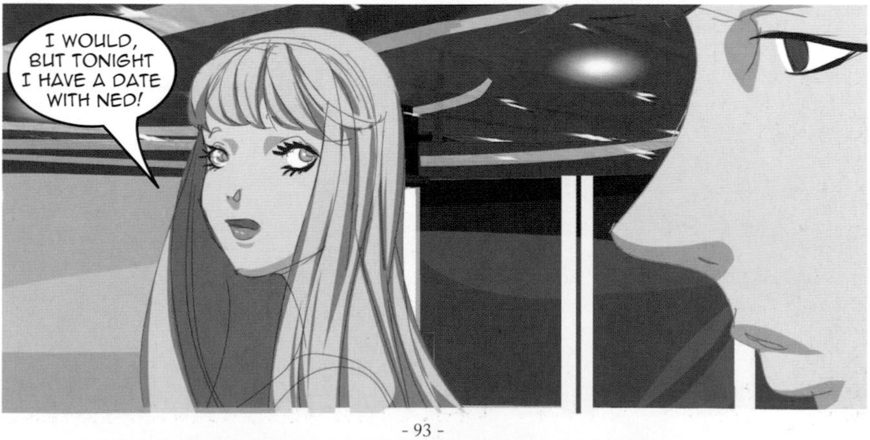
I WOULD, BUT TONIGHT I HAVE A DATE WITH NED!

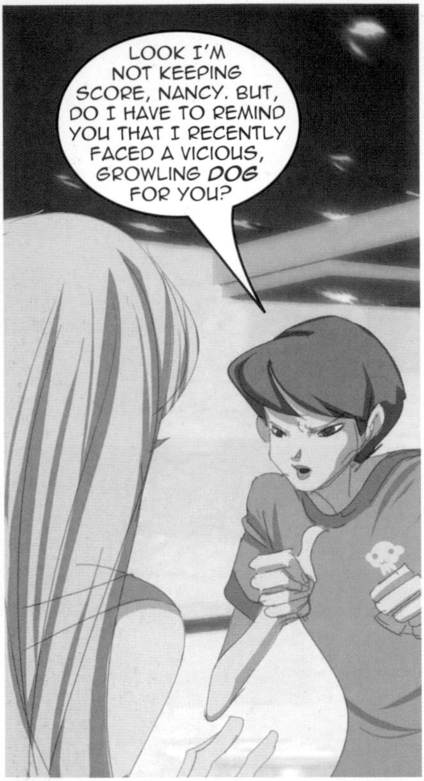
LOOK I'M NOT KEEPING SCORE, NANCY. BUT, DO I HAVE TO REMIND YOU THAT I RECENTLY FACED A VICIOUS, GROWLING DOG FOR YOU?

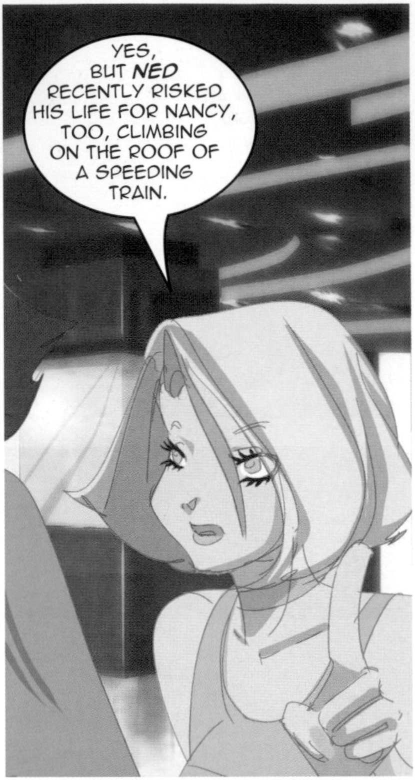
YES, BUT NED RECENTLY RISKED HIS LIFE FOR NANCY, TOO, CLIMBING ON THE ROOF OF A SPEEDING TRAIN.

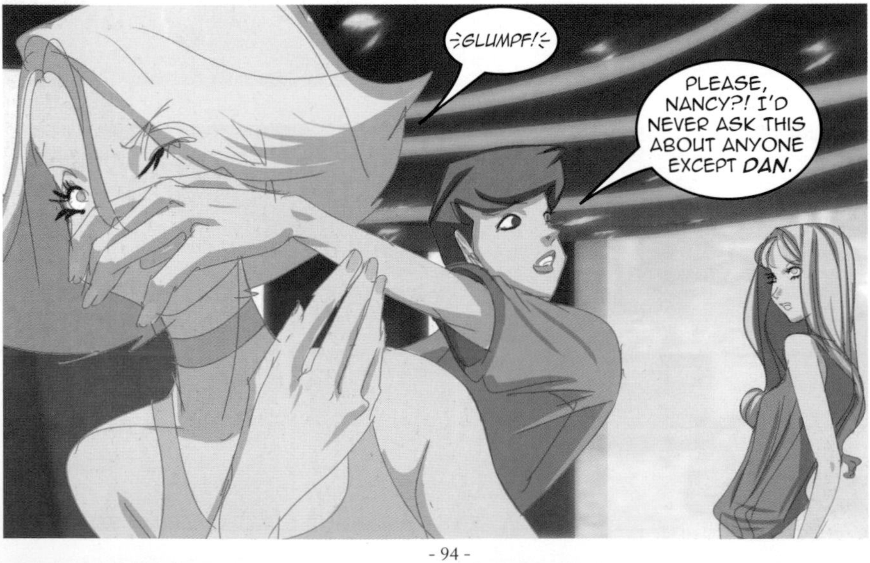
GLUMPF!
PLEASE, NANCY?! I'D NEVER ASK THIS ABOUT ANYONE EXCEPT DAN.

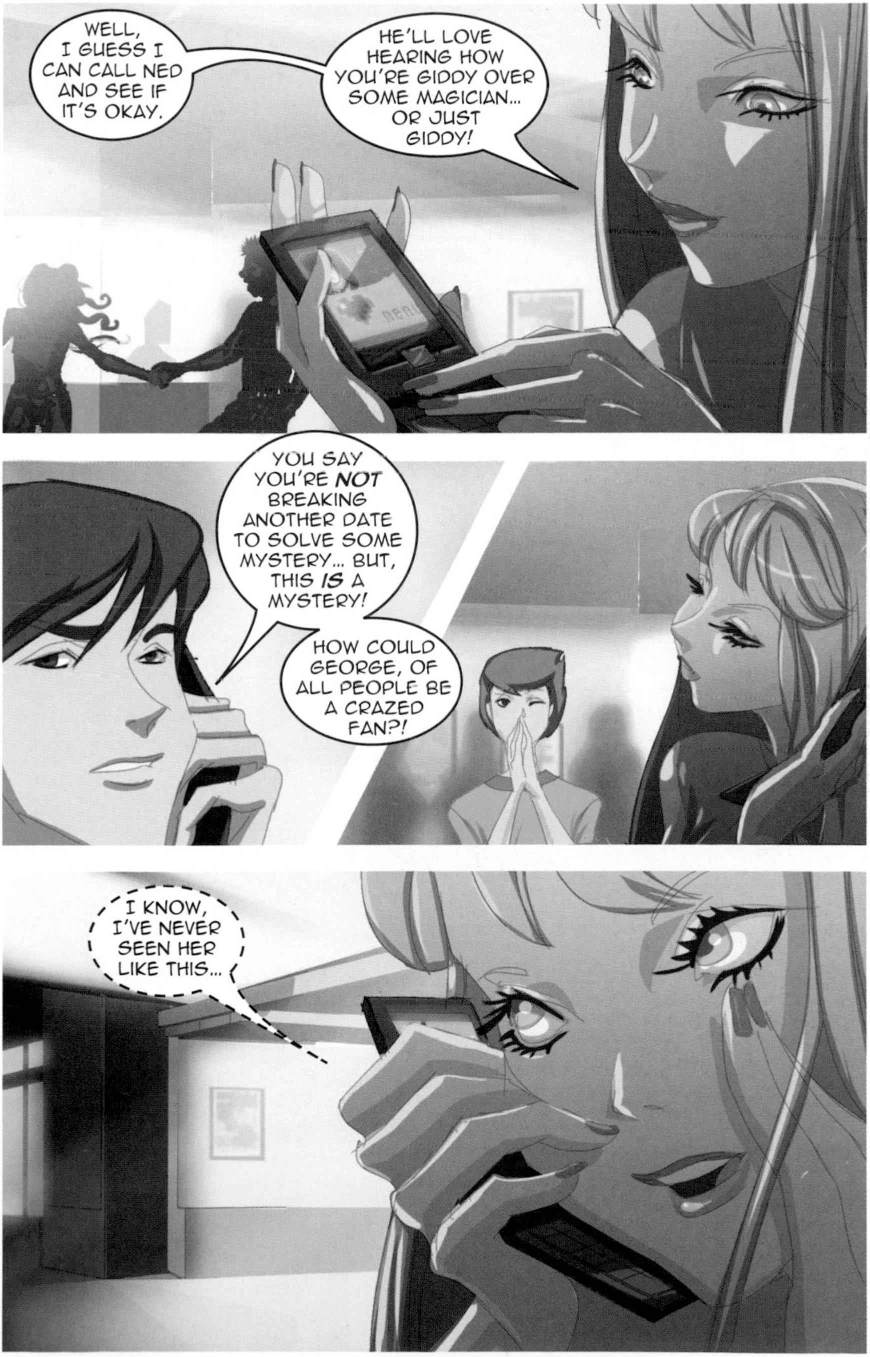
WELL, I GUESS I CAN CALL NED AND SEE IF IT'S OKAY.
HE'LL LOVE HEARING HOW YOU'RE GIDDY OVER SOME MAGICIAN... OR JUST GIDDY!
YOU SAY YOU'RE **NOT** BREAKING ANOTHER DATE TO SOLVE SOME MYSTERY... BUT, THIS ***IS*** A MYSTERY!
HOW COULD GEORGE, OF ALL PEOPLE BE A CRAZED FAN?!
I KNOW, I'VE NEVER SEEN HER LIKE THIS...

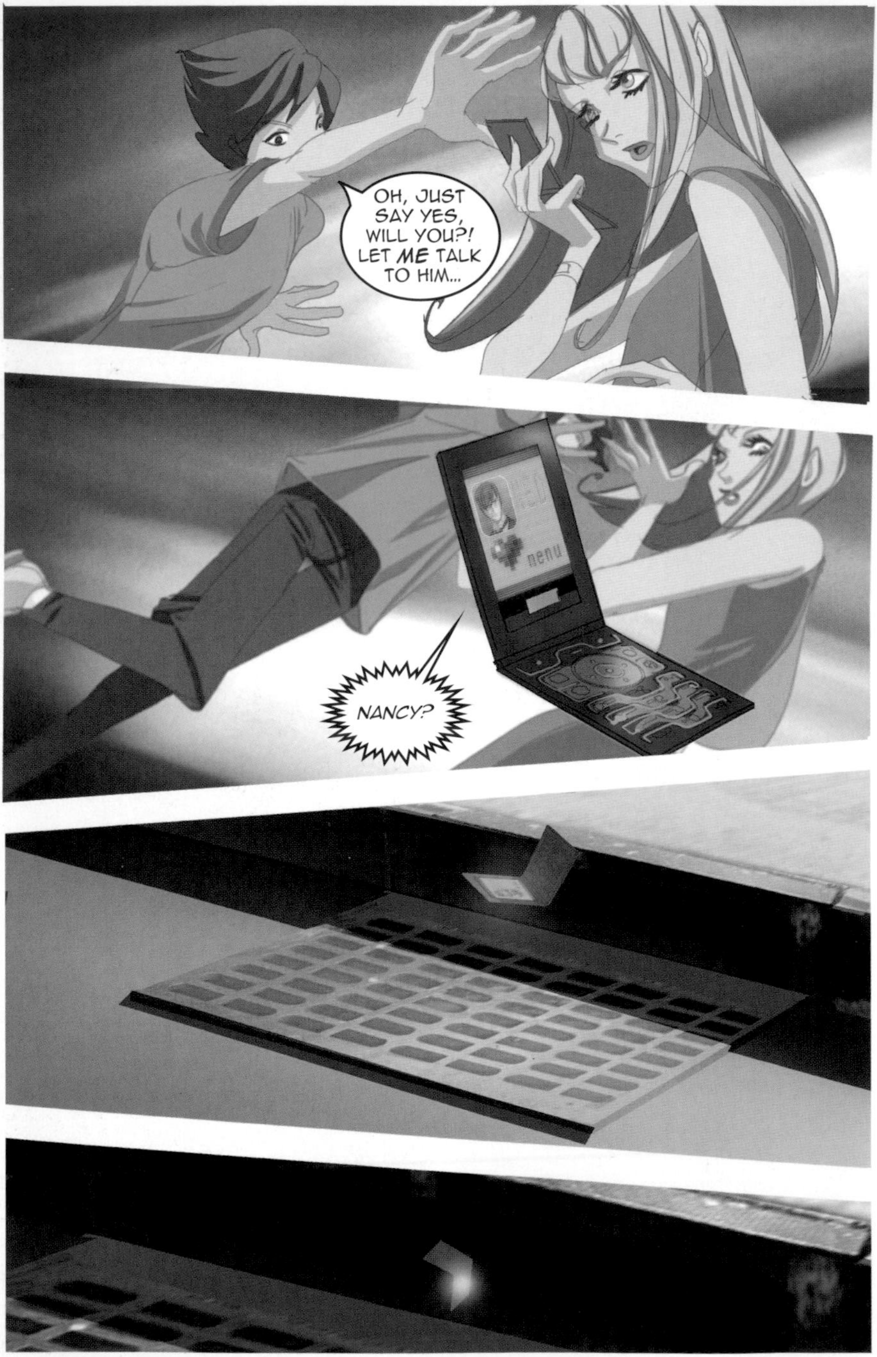
OH, JUST SAY YES, WILL YOU?! LET *ME* TALK TO HIM...
NANCY?

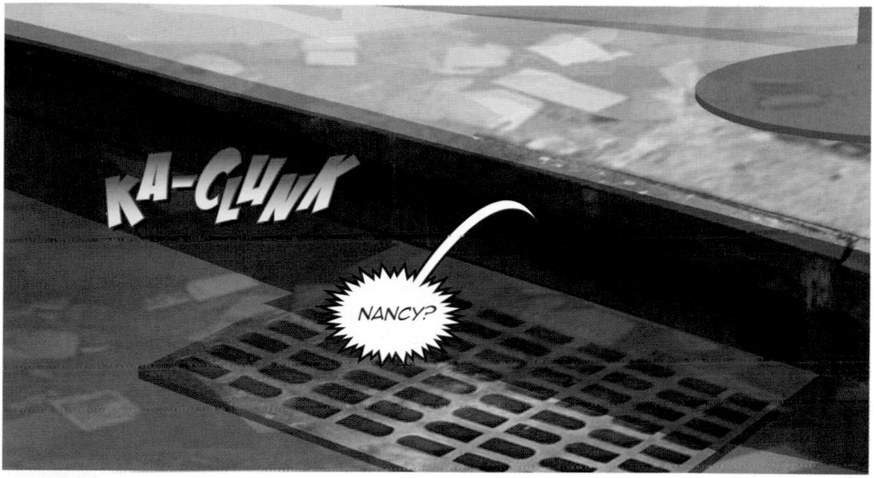
KA-CLUNK
NANCY?

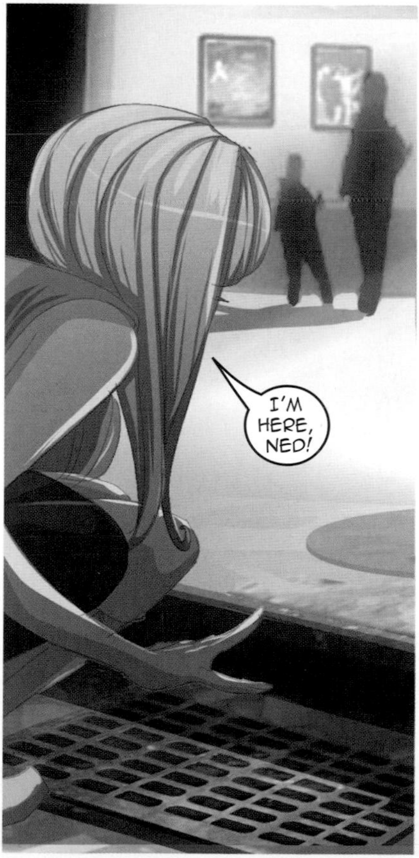
I'M HERE, NED!

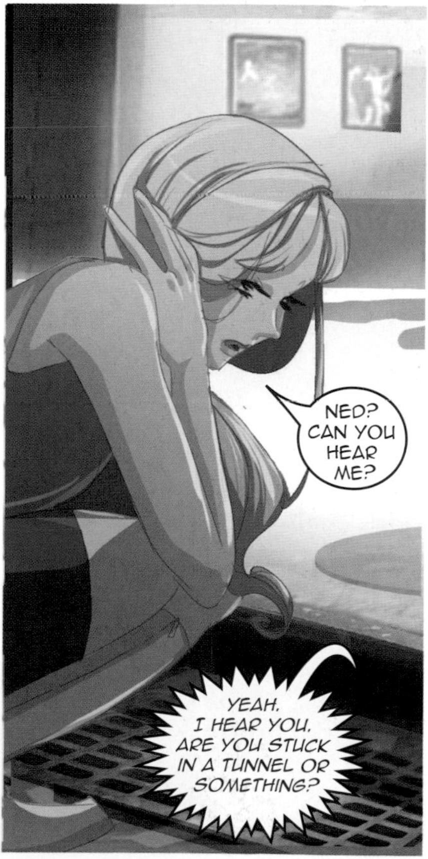
NED? CAN YOU HEAR ME?
YEAH. I HEAR YOU. ARE YOU STUCK IN A TUNNEL OR SOMETHING?

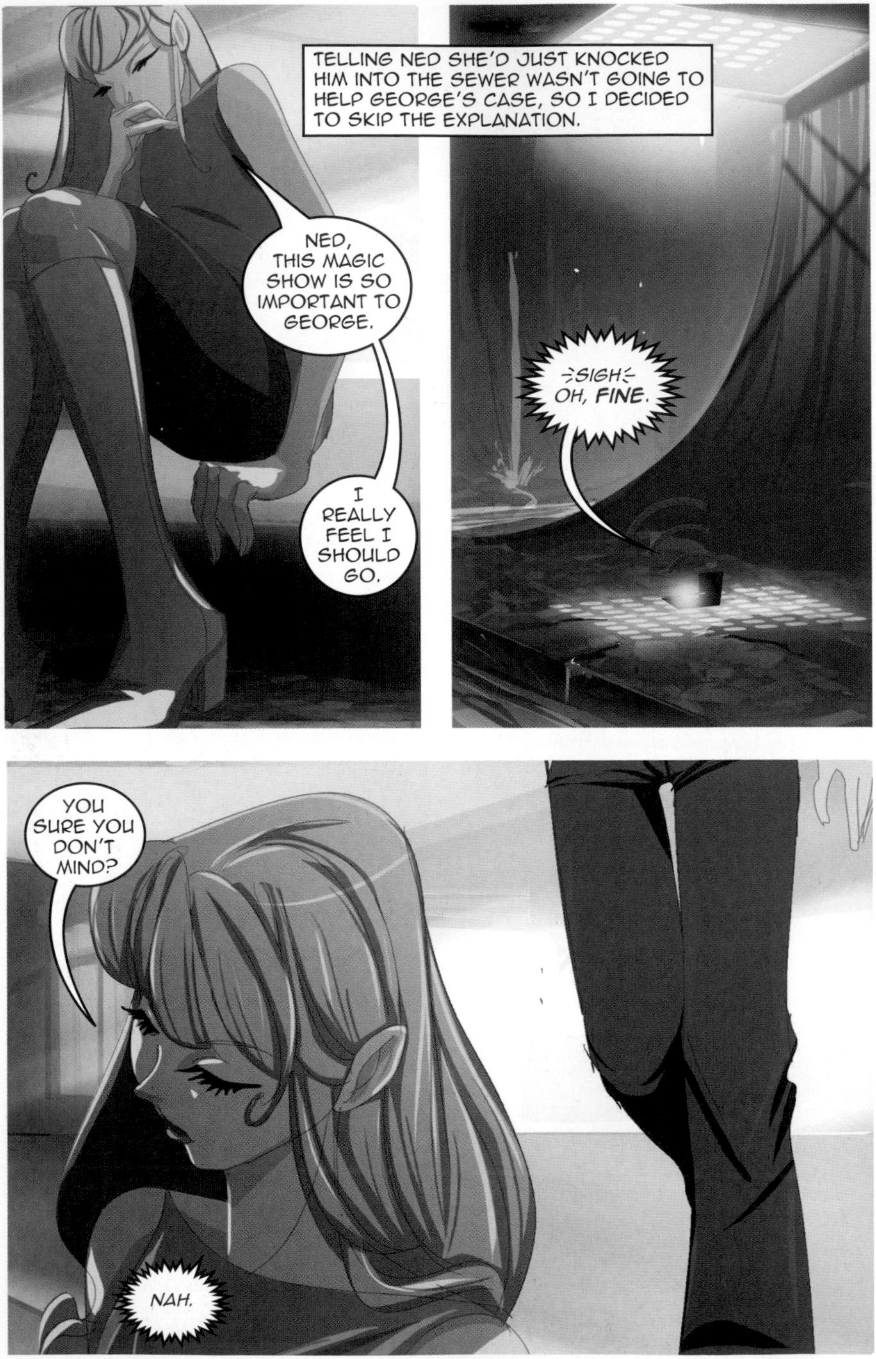
TELLING NED SHE'D JUST KNOCKED HIM INTO THE SEWER WASN'T GOING TO HELP GEORGE'S CASE, SO I DECIDED TO SKIP THE EXPLANATION.
NED, THIS MAGIC SHOW IS SO IMPORTANT TO GEORGE.
I REALLY FEEL I SHOULD GO.
SIGH OH, FINE.
YOU SURE YOU DON'T MIND?
NAH.

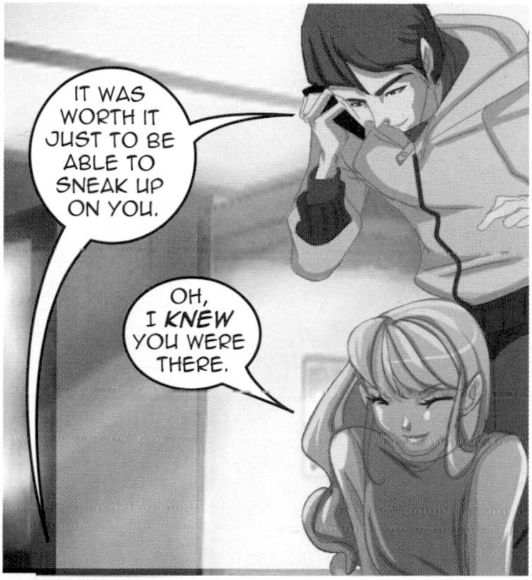
IT WAS WORTH IT JUST TO BE ABLE TO SNEAK UP ON YOU.
OH, I *KNEW* YOU WERE THERE.
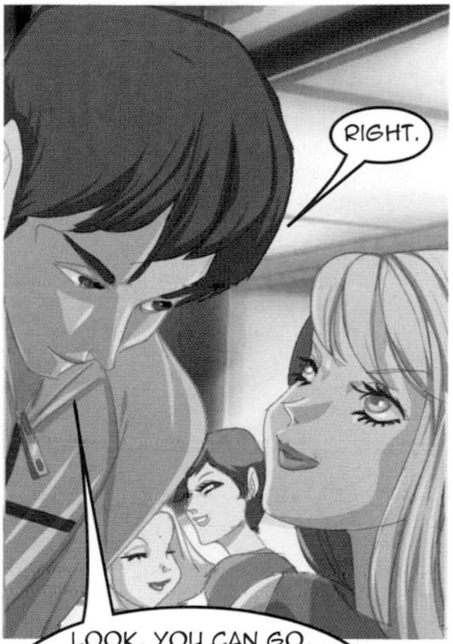
RIGHT.
LOOK, YOU CAN GO, BUT YOU HAVE TO PROMISE TO SHOW UP FOR A *NEW* DATE AT A FANCY RESTAURANT TOMORROW NIGHT, MYSTERY OR NO.
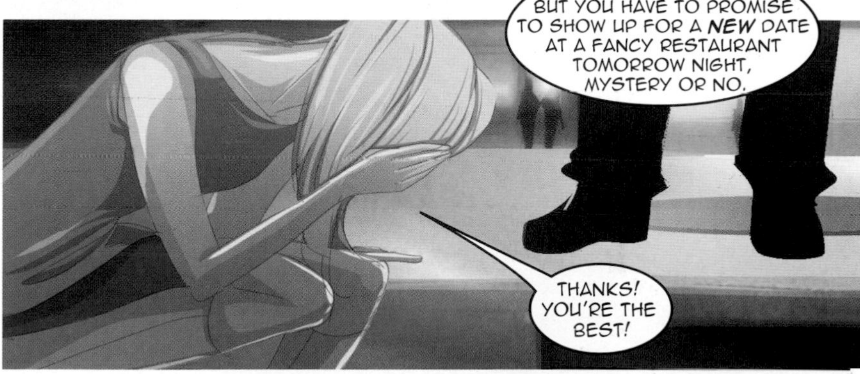
THANKS! YOU'RE THE BEST!
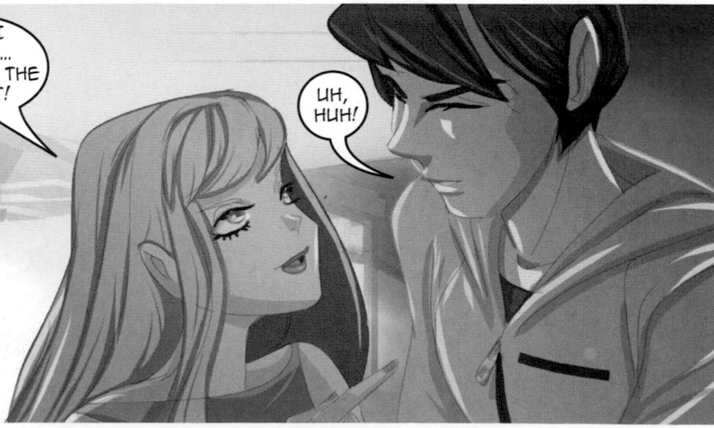
OH, I MEAN... *YOU'RE* THE BEST!
UH, HUH!

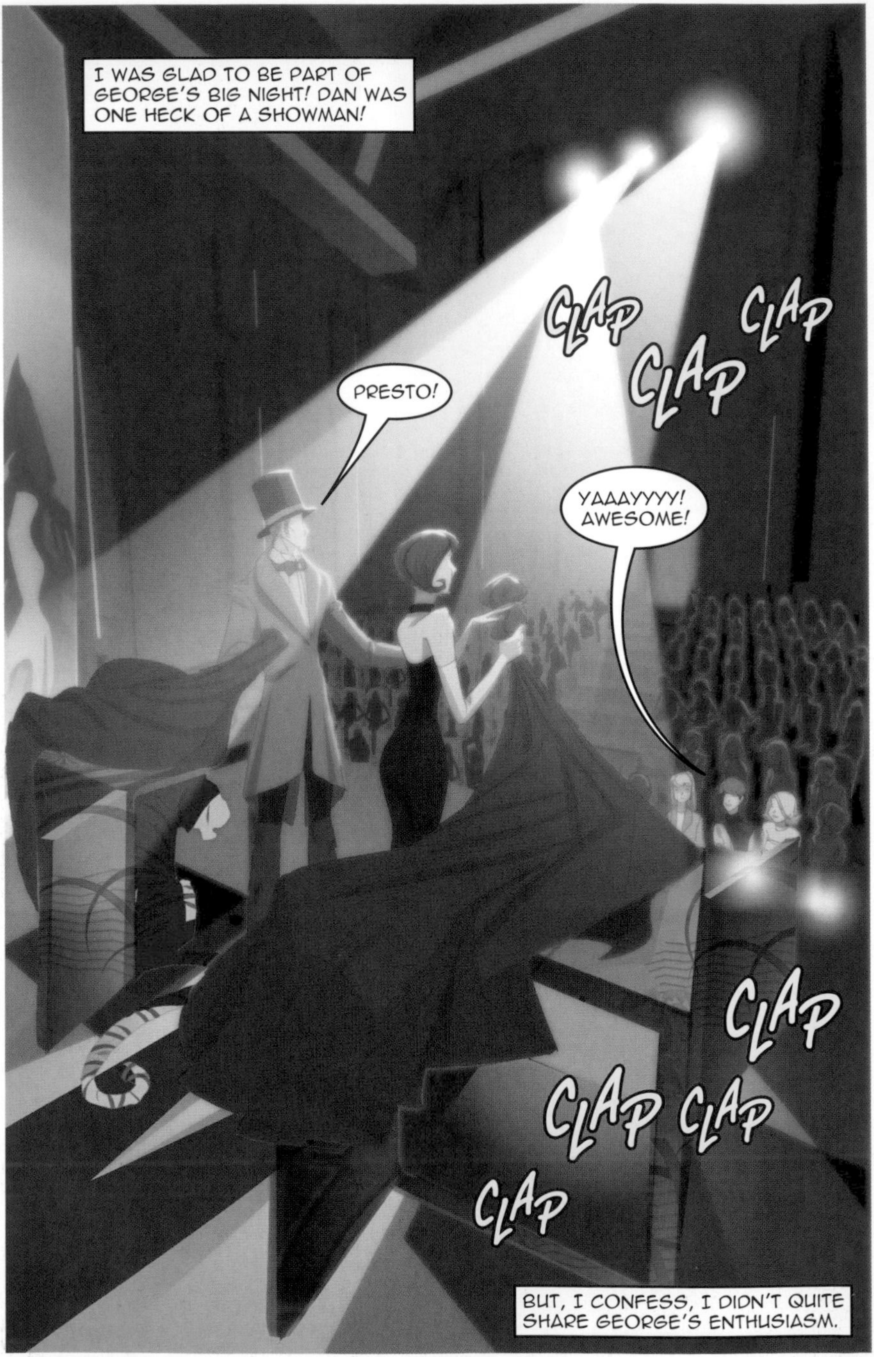
I WAS GLAD TO BE PART OF GEORGE'S BIG NIGHT! DAN WAS ONE HECK OF A SHOWMAN!
PRESTO!
CLAP
CLAP
CLAP
YAAAYYYY! AWESOME!
CLAP
CLAP
CLAP
CLAP
BUT, I CONFESS, I DIDN'T QUITE SHARE GEORGE'S ENTHUSIASM.

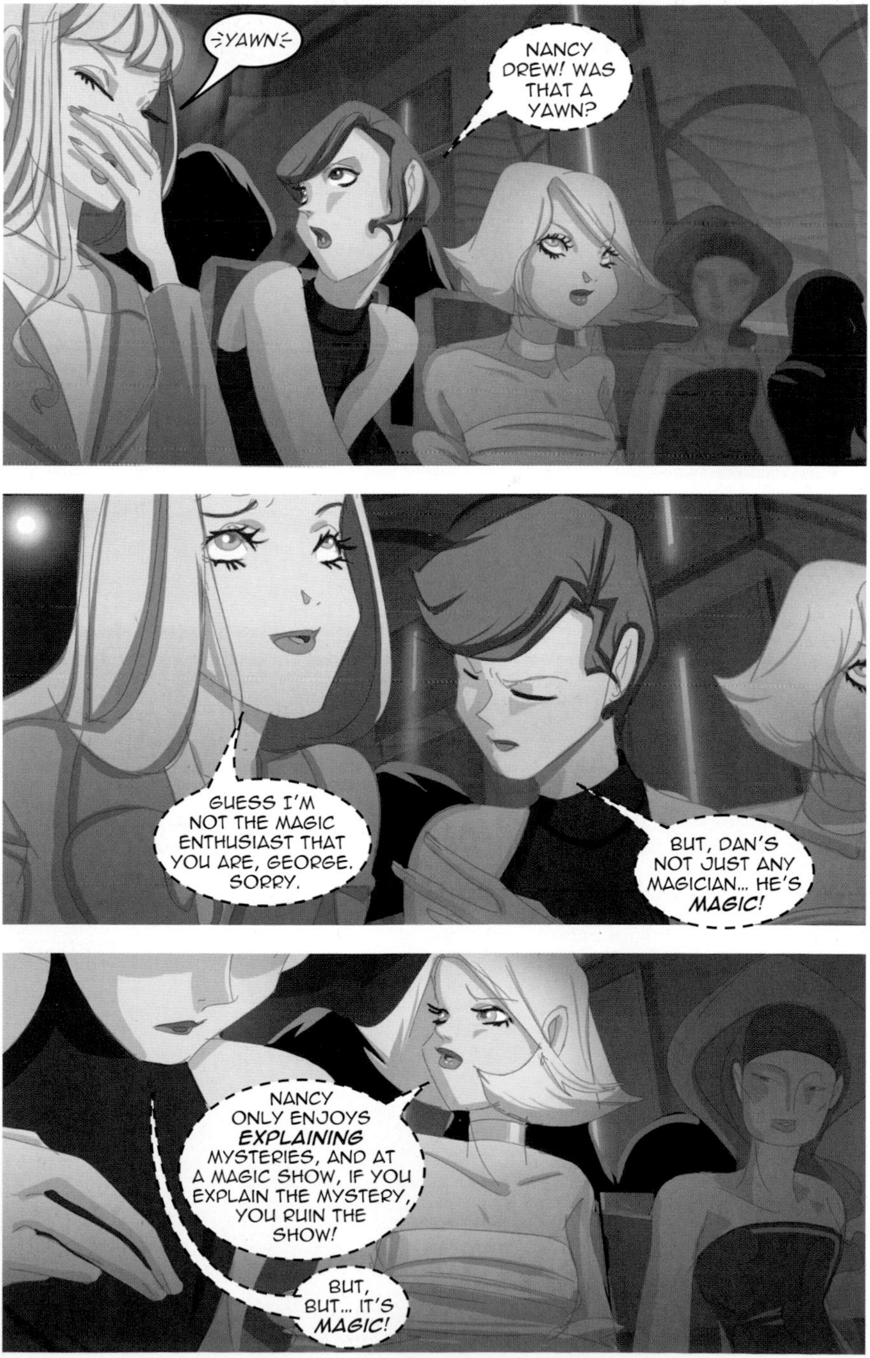

YAWN
NANCY DREW! WAS THAT A YAWN?
GUESS I'M NOT THE MAGIC ENTHUSIAST THAT YOU ARE, GEORGE. SORRY.
BUT, DAN'S NOT JUST ANY MAGICIAN... HE'S MAGIC!
NANCY ONLY ENJOYS EXPLAINING MYSTERIES, AND AT A MAGIC SHOW, IF YOU EXPLAIN THE MYSTERY, YOU RUIN THE SHOW!
BUT, BUT... IT'S MAGIC!

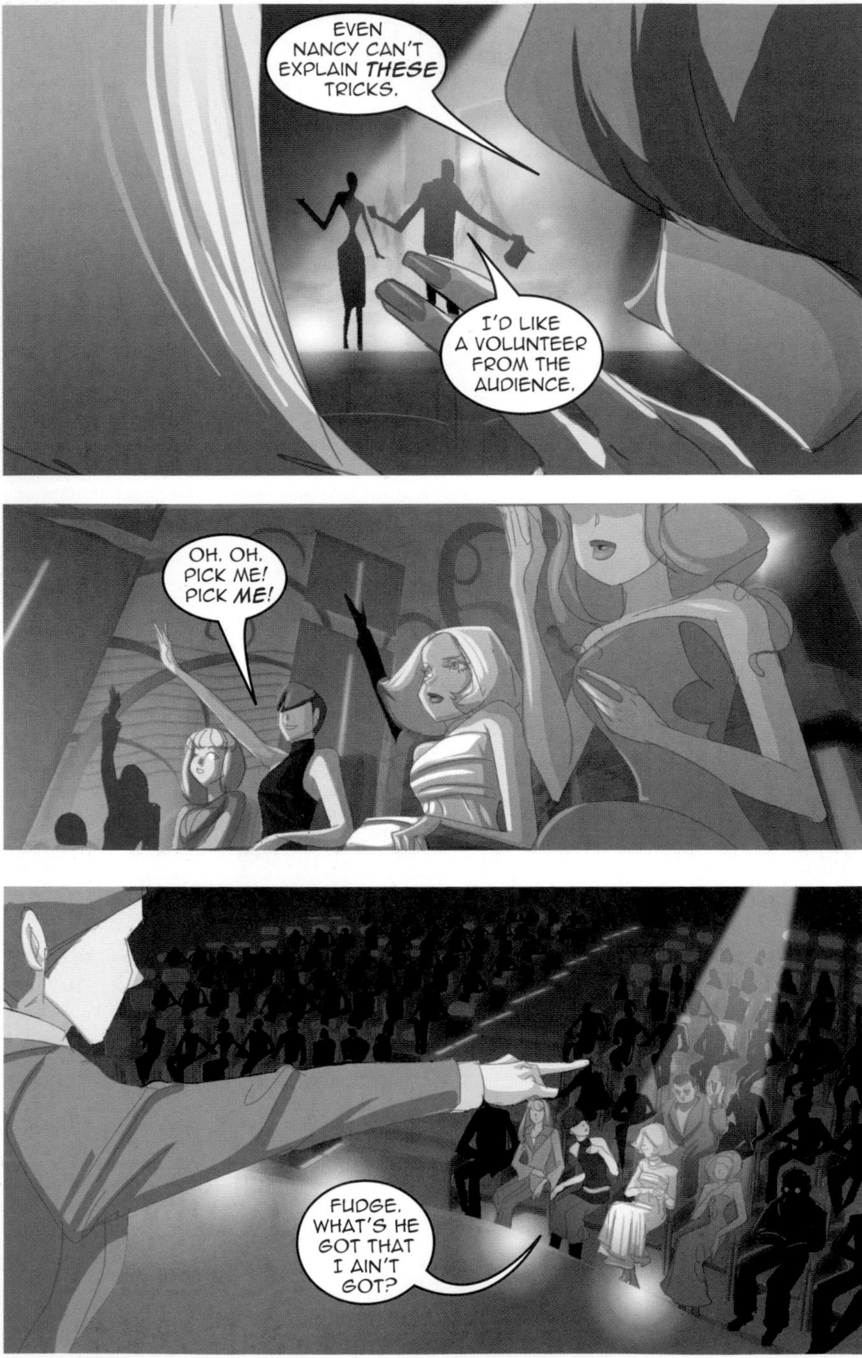
EVEN NANCY CAN'T EXPLAIN *THESE* TRICKS.
I'D LIKE A VOLUNTEER FROM THE AUDIENCE.
OH. OH. PICK ME! PICK *ME*!
FUDGE. WHAT'S HE GOT THAT I AIN'T GOT?

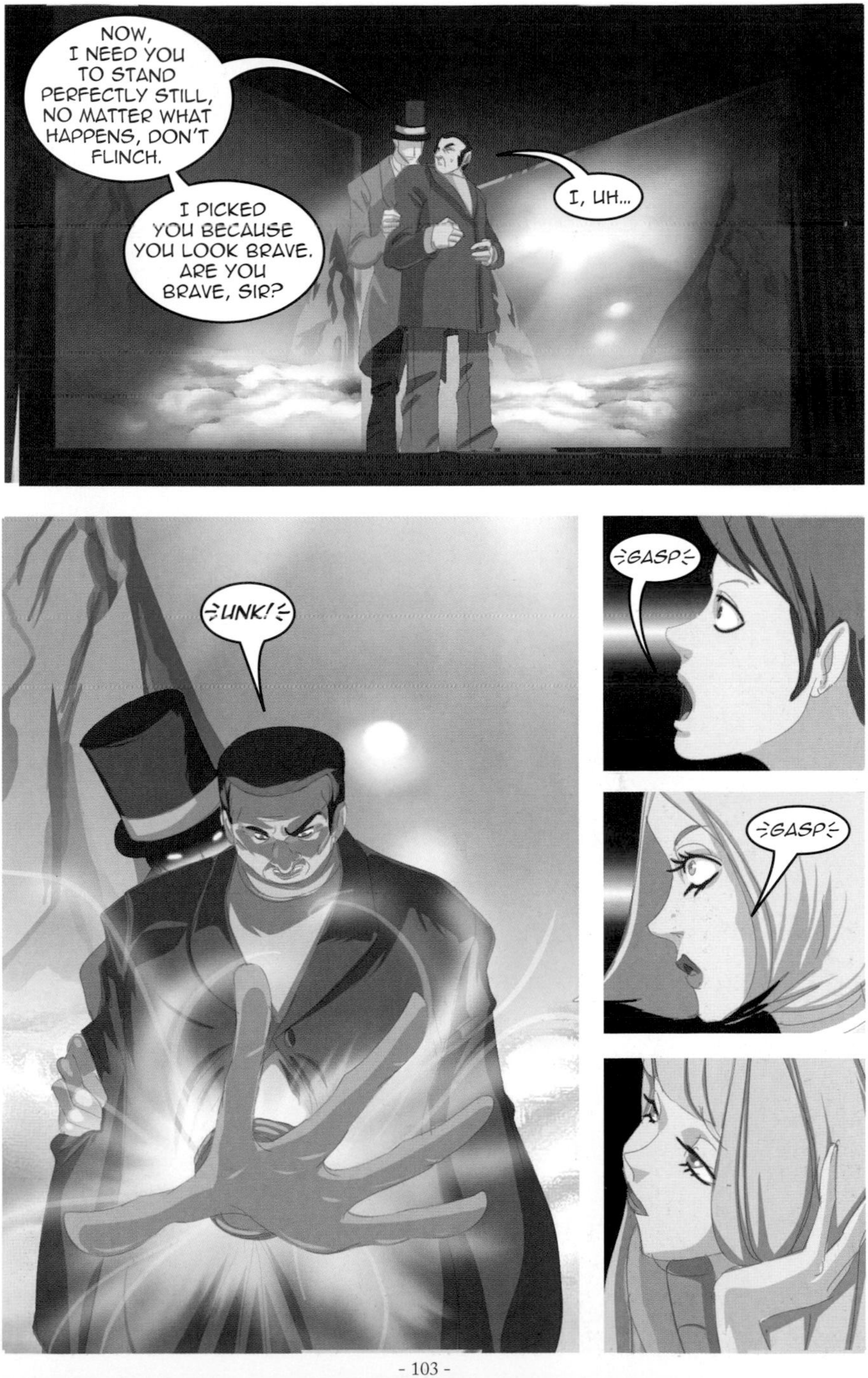
NOW, I NEED YOU TO STAND PERFECTLY STILL, NO MATTER WHAT HAPPENS, DON'T FLINCH.
I PICKED YOU BECAUSE YOU LOOK BRAVE. ARE YOU BRAVE, SIR?
I, UH...
UNK!
GASP
GASP

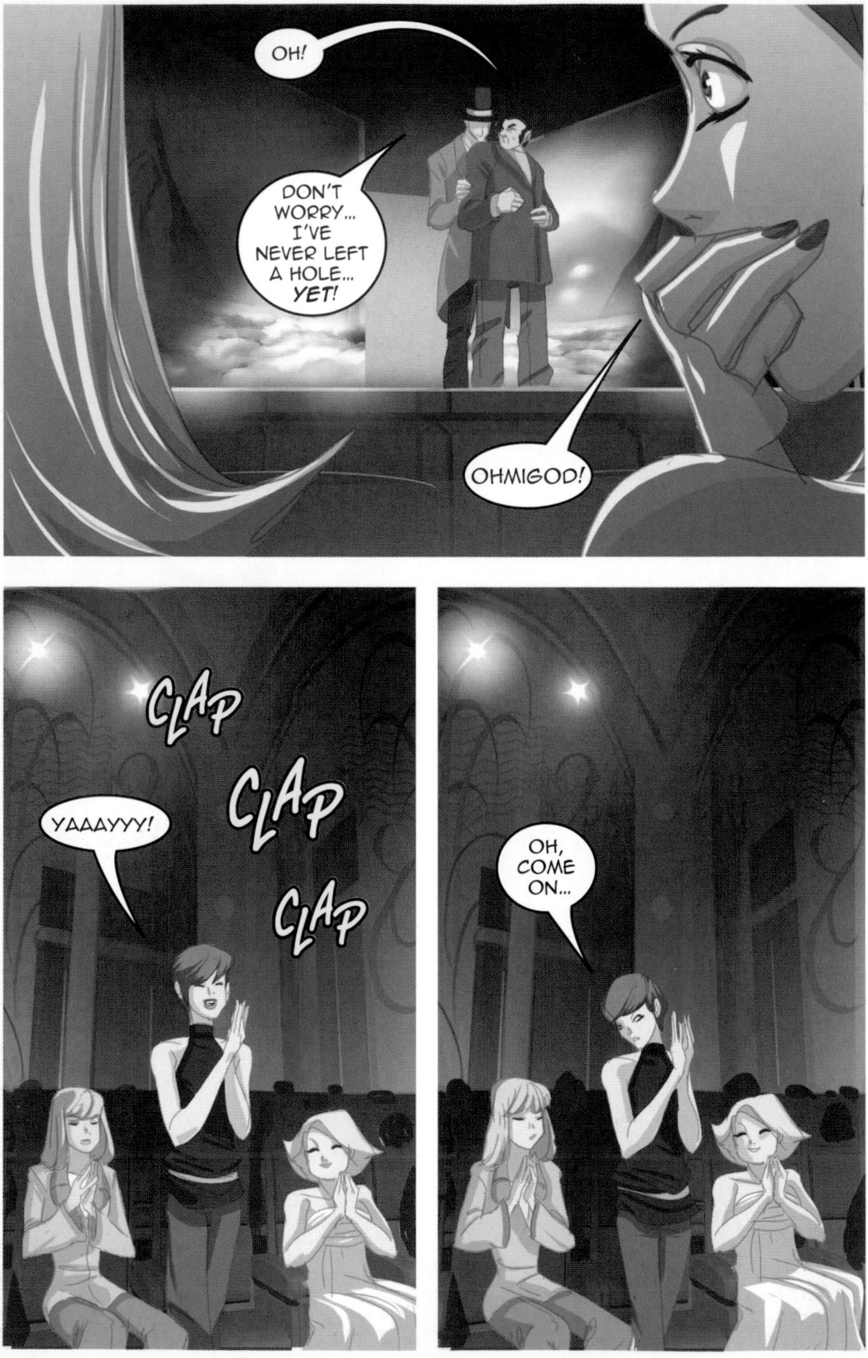
OH!
DON'T WORRY... I'VE NEVER LEFT A HOLE... YET!
OHMIGOD!
CLAP
CLAP
YAAAYYY!
CLAP
OH, COME ON...

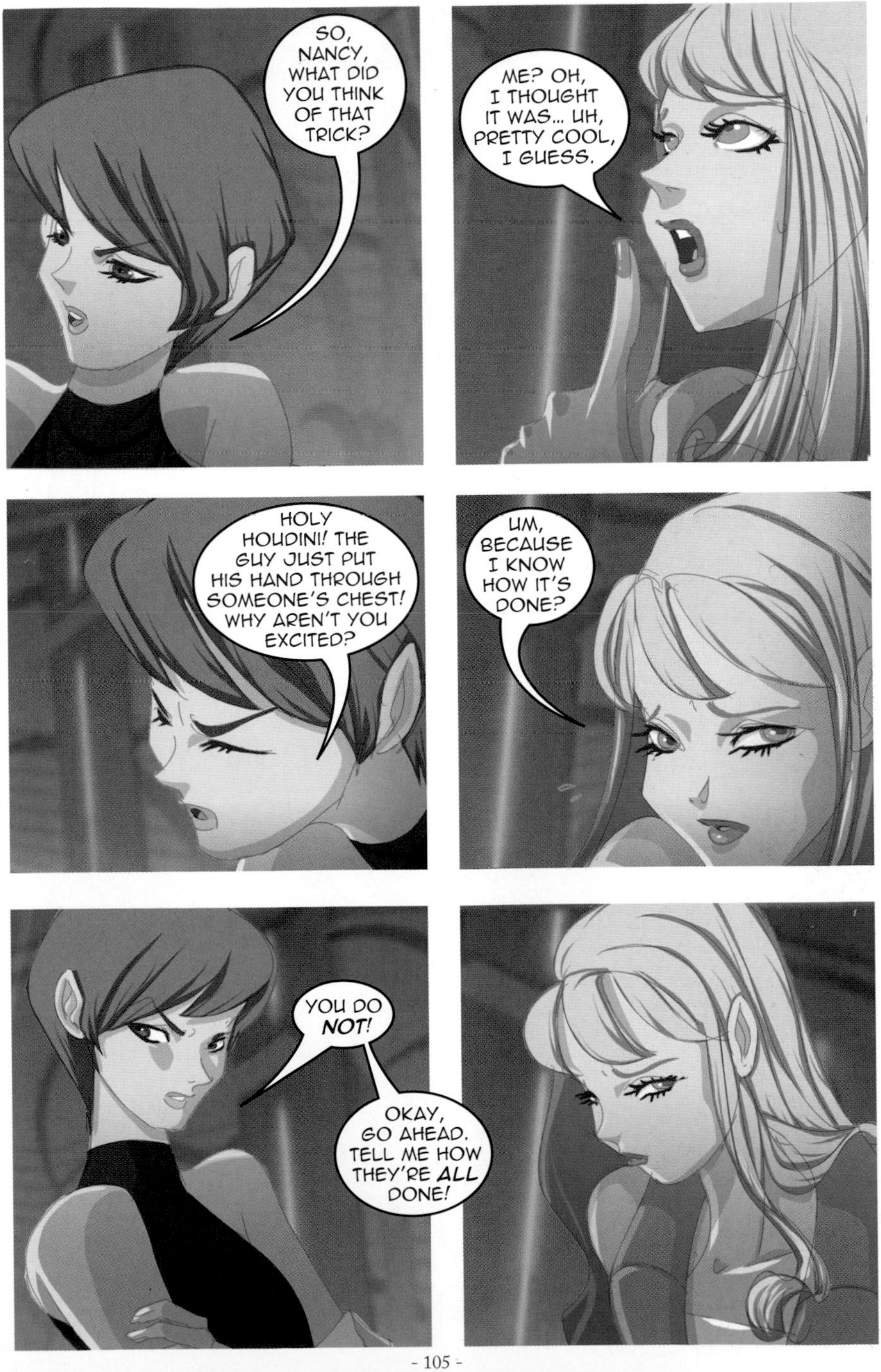
SO, NANCY, WHAT DID YOU THINK OF THAT TRICK?
ME? OH, I THOUGHT IT WAS... UH, PRETTY COOL, I GUESS.
HOLY HOUDINI! THE GUY JUST PUT HIS HAND THROUGH SOMEONE'S CHEST! WHY AREN'T YOU EXCITED?
UM, BECAUSE I KNOW HOW IT'S DONE?
YOU DO **NOT**!
OKAY, GO AHEAD. TELL ME HOW THEY'RE **ALL** DONE!

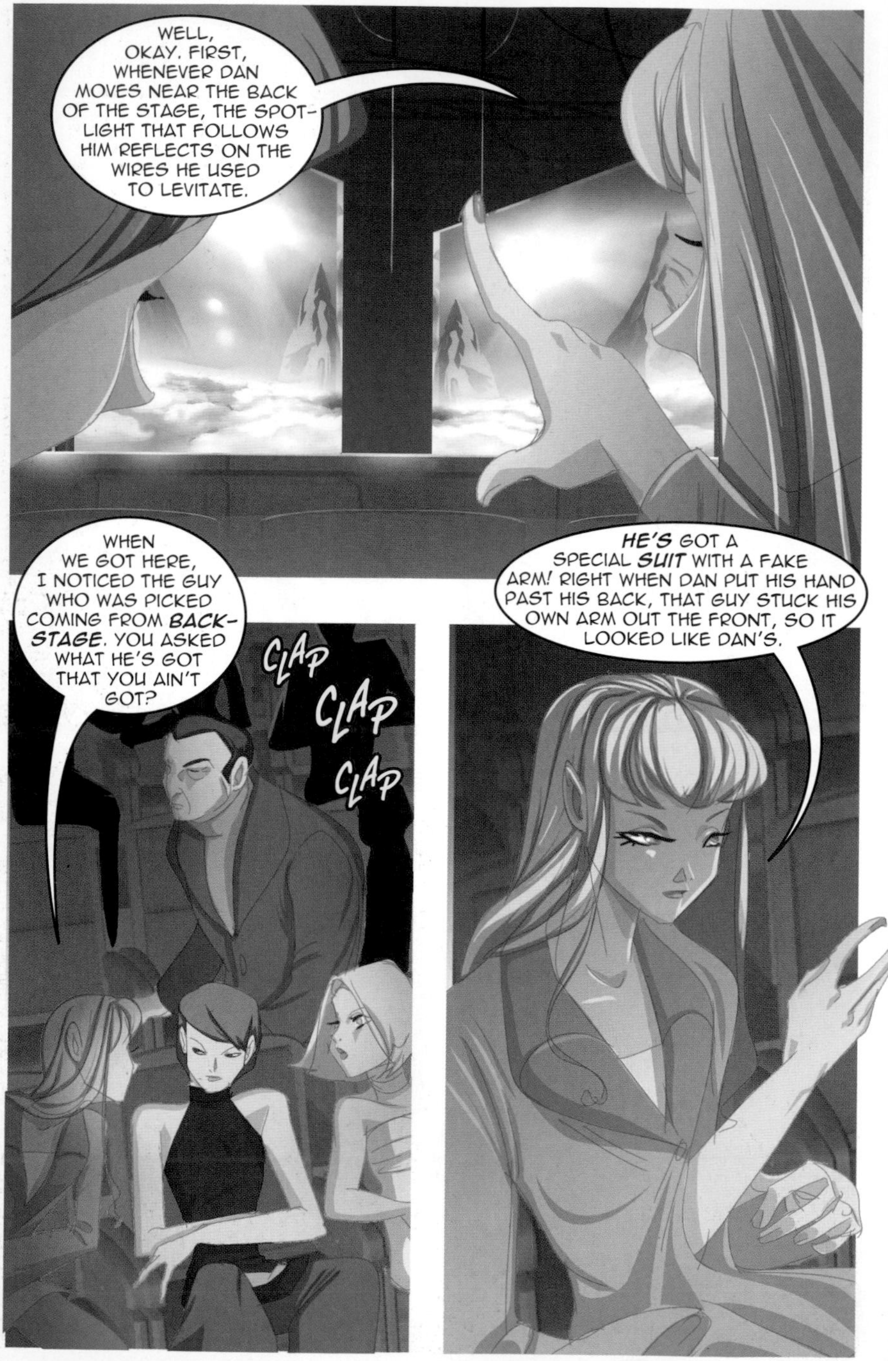
WELL, OKAY. FIRST, WHENEVER DAN MOVES NEAR THE BACK OF THE STAGE, THE SPOT-LIGHT THAT FOLLOWS HIM REFLECTS ON THE WIRES HE USED TO LEVITATE.
WHEN WE GOT HERE, I NOTICED THE GUY WHO WAS PICKED COMING FROM BACK-STAGE. YOU ASKED WHAT HE'S GOT THAT YOU AIN'T GOT?
CLAP
CLAP
CLAP
HE'S GOT A SPECIAL SUIT WITH A FAKE ARM! RIGHT WHEN DAN PUT HIS HAND PAST HIS BACK, THAT GUY STUCK HIS OWN ARM OUT THE FRONT, SO IT LOOKED LIKE DAN'S.

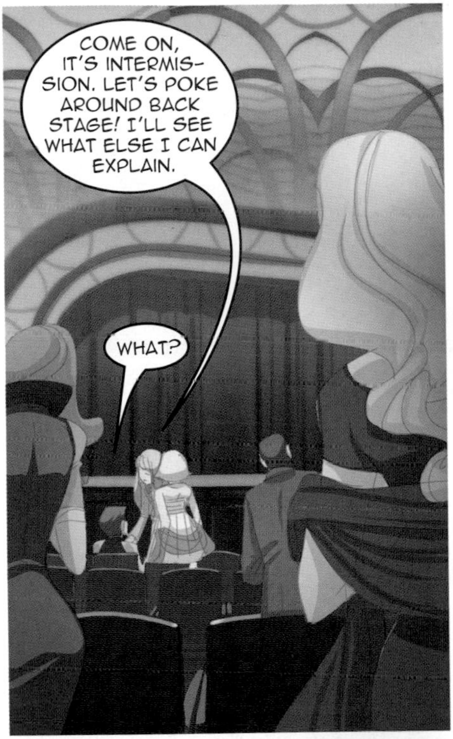
COME ON, IT'S INTERMIS-SION. LET'S POKE AROUND BACK STAGE! I'LL SEE WHAT ELSE I CAN EXPLAIN.
WHAT?

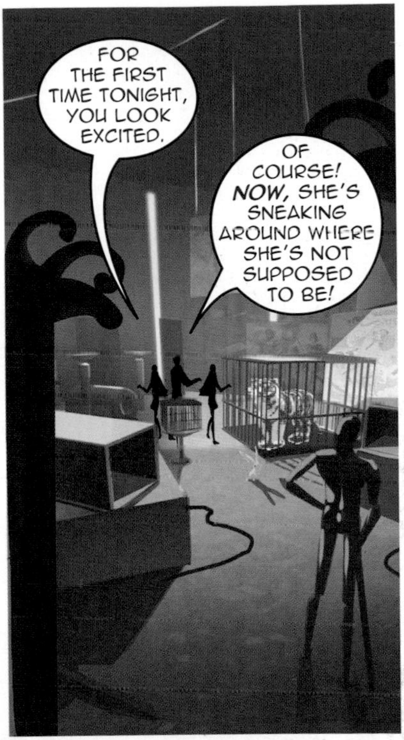
FOR THE FIRST TIME TONIGHT, YOU LOOK EXCITED.
OF COURSE! **NOW,** SHE'S SNEAKING AROUND WHERE SHE'S NOT SUPPOSED TO BE!

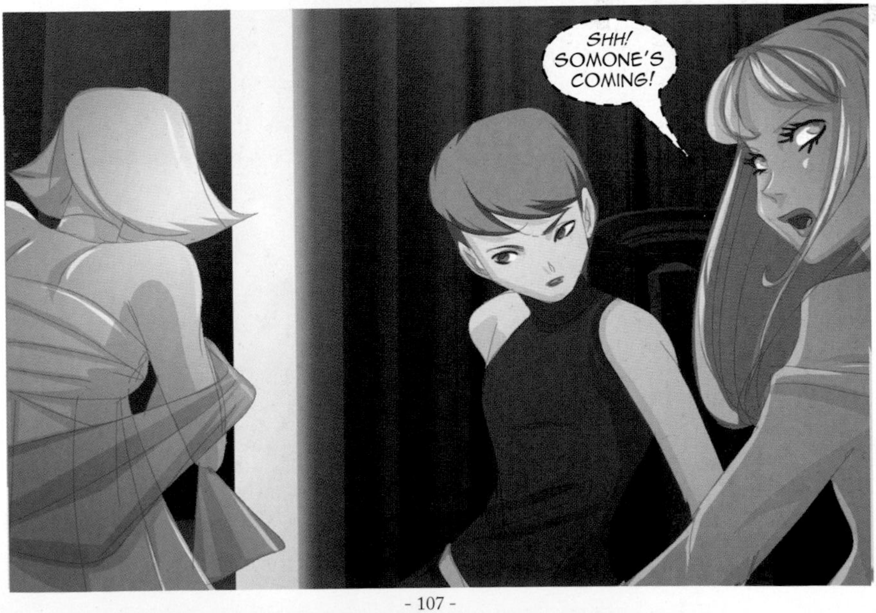
SHH! SOMONE'S COMING!

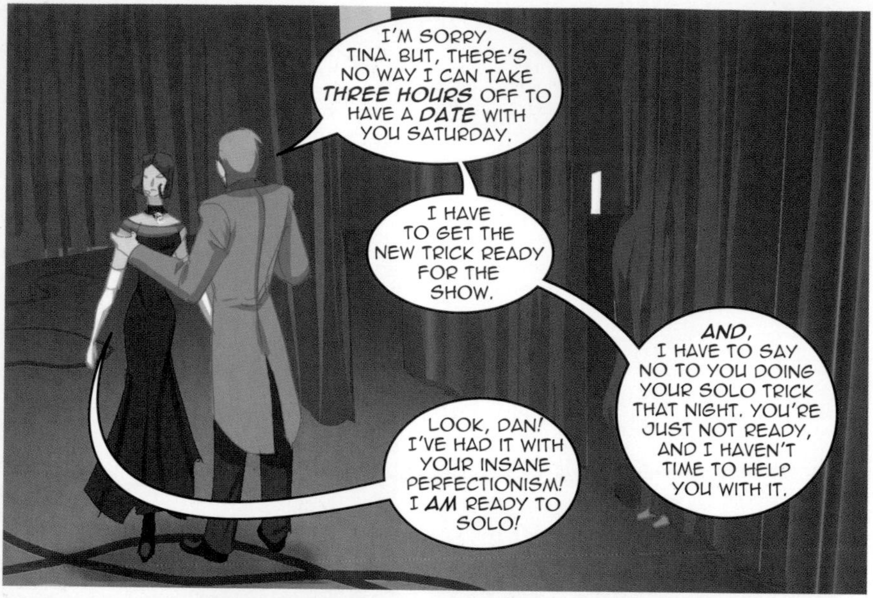
I'M SORRY, TINA. BUT, THERE'S NO WAY I CAN TAKE ***THREE HOURS*** OFF TO HAVE A ***DATE*** WITH YOU SATURDAY.
I HAVE TO GET THE NEW TRICK READY FOR THE SHOW.
AND, I HAVE TO SAY NO TO YOU DOING YOUR SOLO TRICK THAT NIGHT. YOU'RE JUST NOT READY, AND I HAVEN'T TIME TO HELP YOU WITH IT.
LOOK, DAN! I'VE HAD IT WITH YOUR INSANE PERFECTIONISM! I ***AM*** READY TO SOLO!

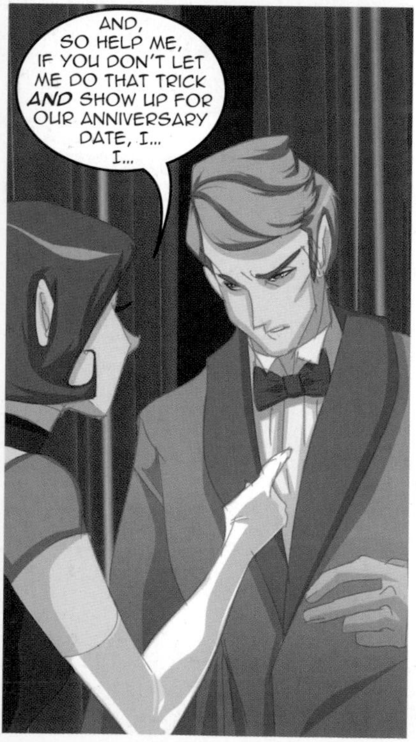
AND, SO HELP ME, IF YOU DON'T LET ME DO THAT TRICK ***AND*** SHOW UP FOR OUR ANNIVERSARY DATE, I... I...

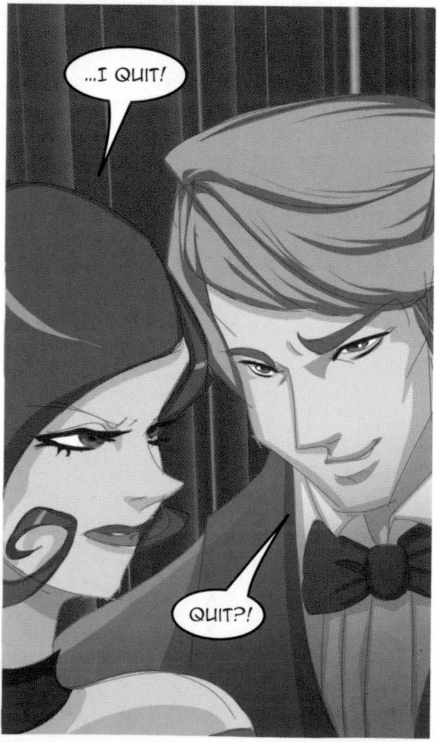
...I QUIT!
QUIT?!

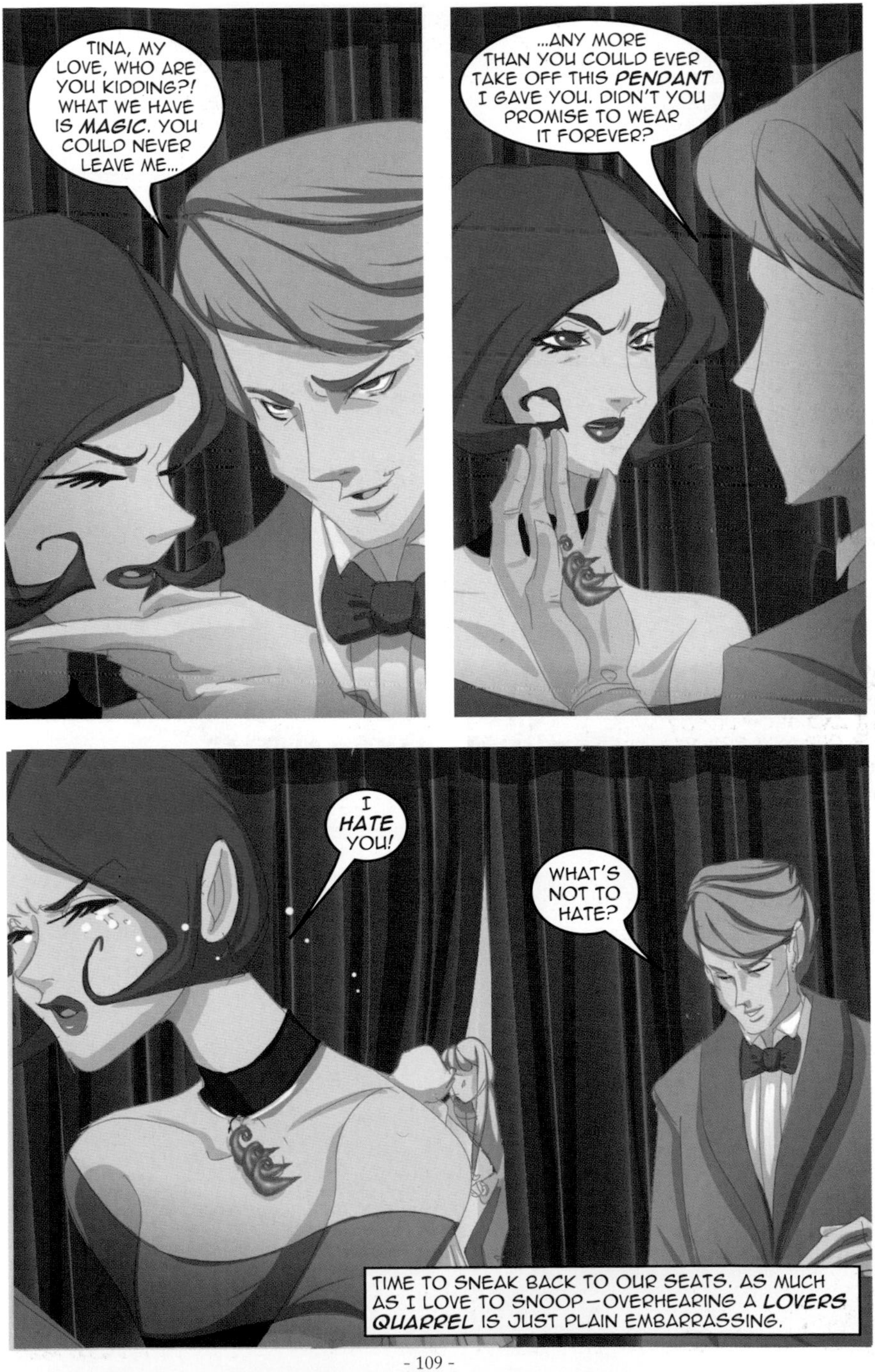
TINA, MY LOVE, WHO ARE YOU KIDDING?! WHAT WE HAVE IS MAGIC. YOU COULD NEVER LEAVE ME...
...ANY MORE THAN YOU COULD EVER TAKE OFF THIS PENDANT I GAVE YOU. DIDN'T YOU PROMISE TO WEAR IT FOREVER?
I HATE YOU!
WHAT'S NOT TO HATE?
TIME TO SNEAK BACK TO OUR SEATS. AS MUCH AS I LOVE TO SNOOP—OVERHEARING A LOVERS QUARREL IS JUST PLAIN EMBARRASSING.

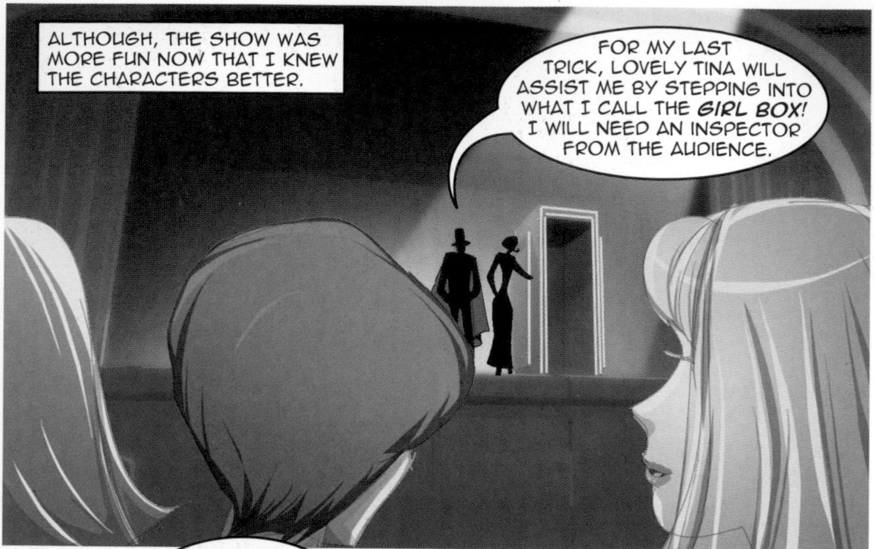
ALTHOUGH, THE SHOW WAS MORE FUN NOW THAT I KNEW THE CHARACTERS BETTER.
FOR MY LAST TRICK, LOVELY TINA WILL ASSIST ME BY STEPPING INTO WHAT I CALL THE *GIRL BOX*! I WILL NEED AN INSPECTOR FROM THE AUDIENCE.

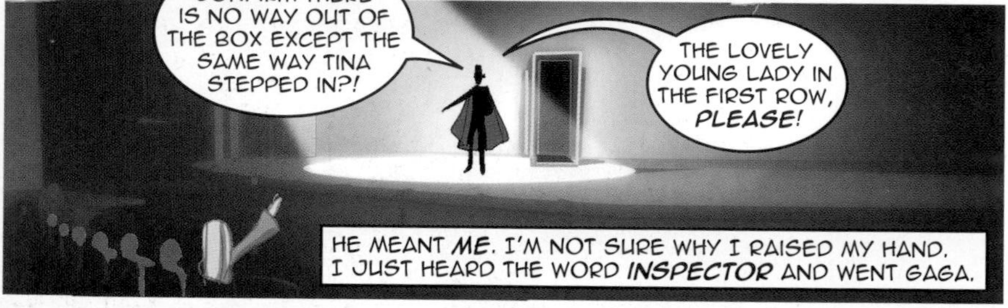
WHO WILL CONFIRM THERE IS NO WAY OUT OF THE BOX EXCEPT THE SAME WAY TINA STEPPED IN?!
THE LOVELY YOUNG LADY IN THE FIRST ROW, *PLEASE*!
HE MEANT *ME*. I'M NOT SURE WHY I RAISED MY HAND. I JUST HEARD THE WORD *INSPECTOR* AND WENT GAGA.

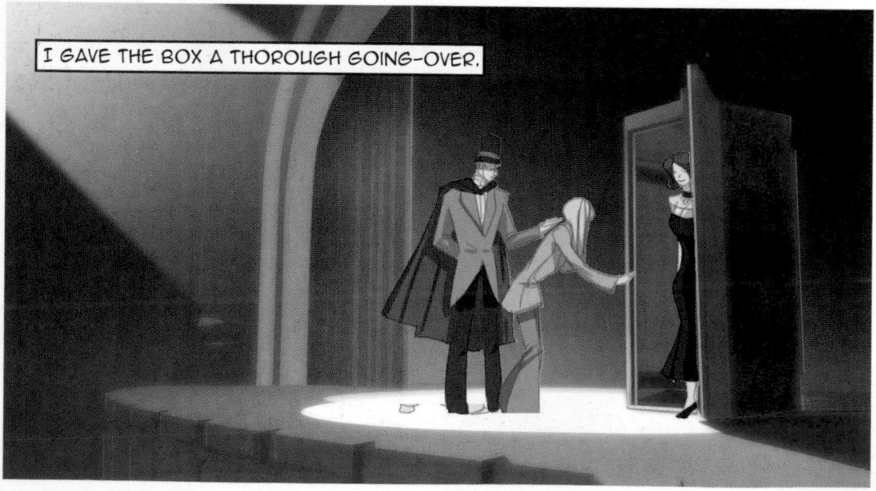
I GAVE THE BOX A THOROUGH GOING-OVER.

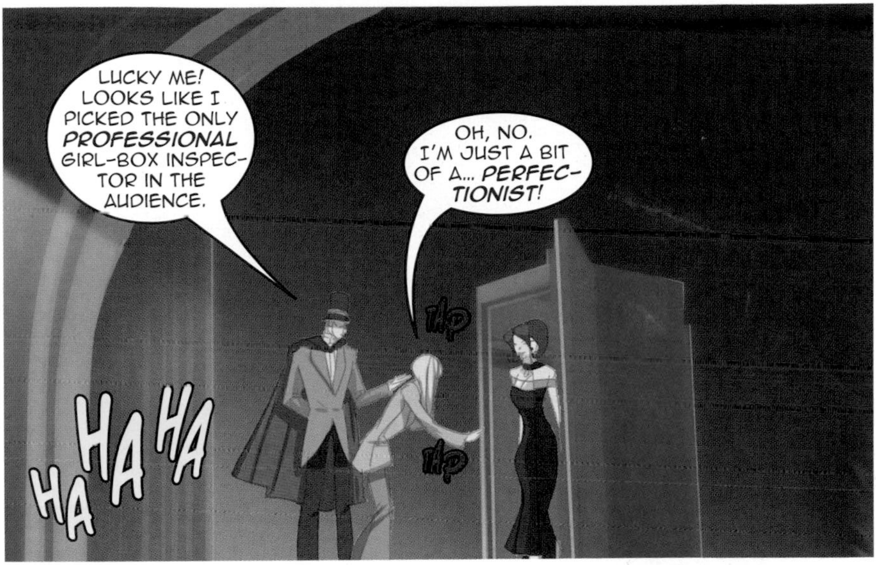
LUCKY ME! LOOKS LIKE I PICKED THE ONLY PROFESSIONAL GIRL-BOX INSPECTOR IN THE AUDIENCE.
OH, NO. I'M JUST A BIT OF A... PERFECTIONIST!
THP
THP
HA HA HA HA

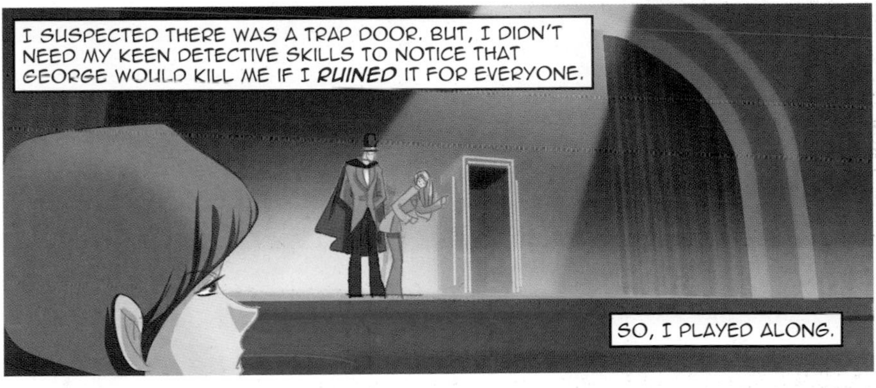
I SUSPECTED THERE WAS A TRAP DOOR. BUT, I DIDN'T NEED MY KEEN DETECTIVE SKILLS TO NOTICE THAT GEORGE WOULD KILL ME IF I RUINED IT FOR EVERYONE.
SO, I PLAYED ALONG.

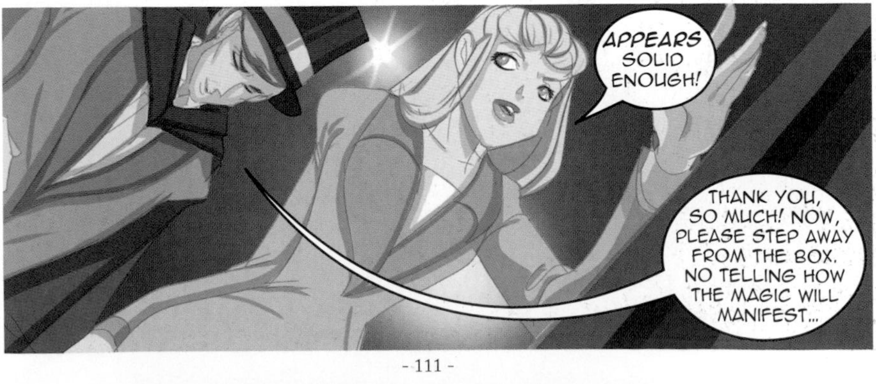
APPEARS SOLID ENOUGH!
THANK YOU, SO MUCH! NOW, PLEASE STEP AWAY FROM THE BOX. NO TELLING HOW THE MAGIC WILL MANIFEST...

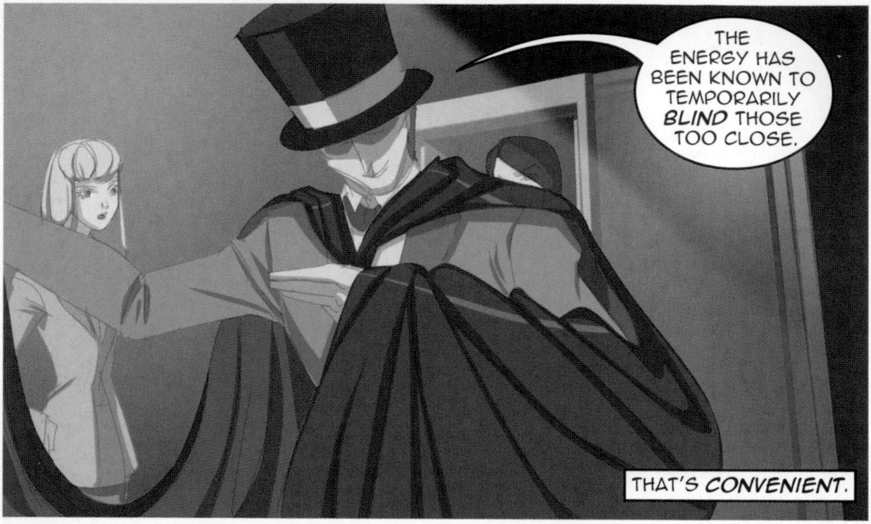
THE ENERGY HAS BEEN KNOWN TO TEMPORARILY BLIND THOSE TOO CLOSE.
THAT'S CONVENIENT.

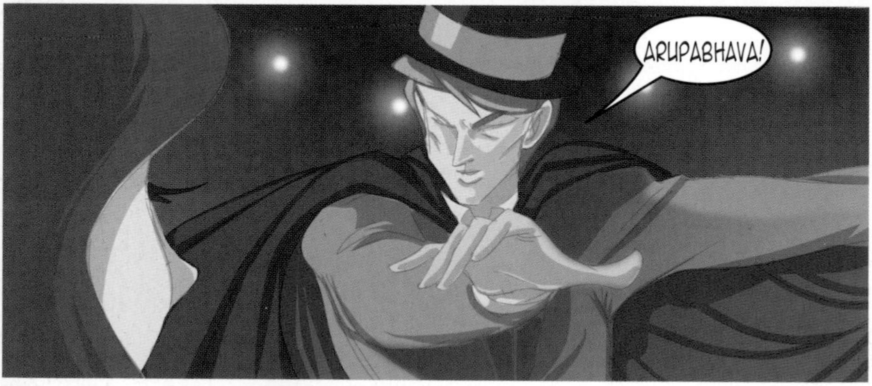
ARUPABHAVA!

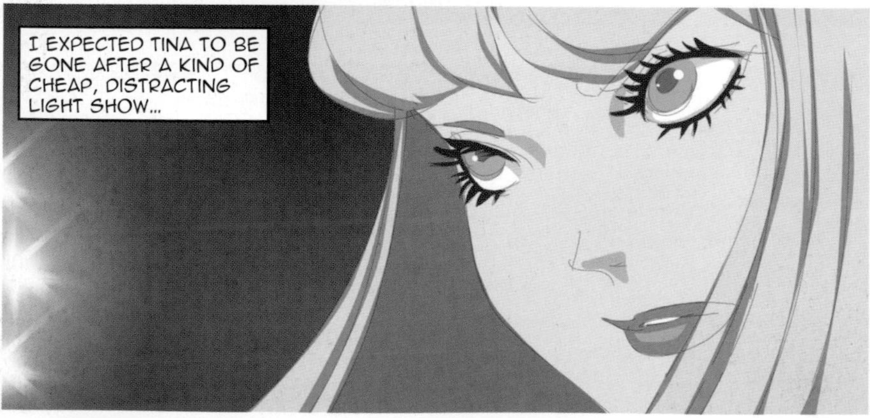
I EXPECTED TINA TO BE GONE AFTER A KIND OF CHEAP, DISTRACTING LIGHT SHOW...

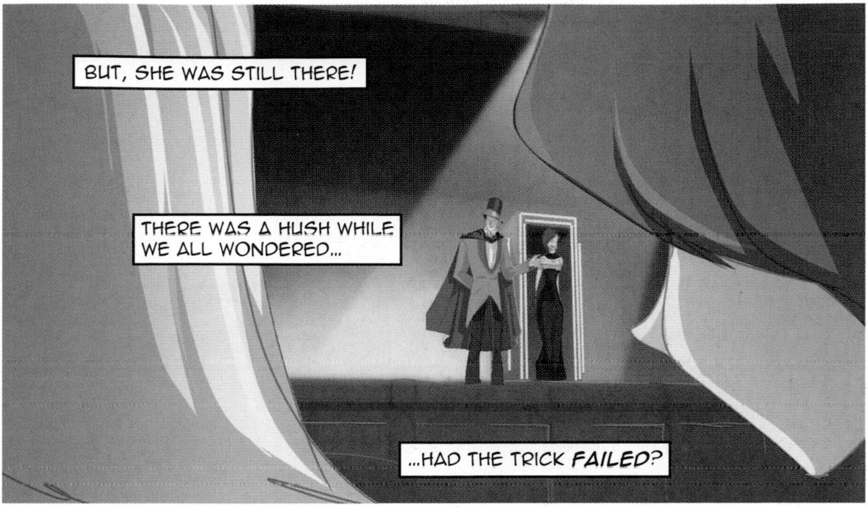
BUT, SHE WAS STILL THERE!
THERE WAS A HUSH WHILE WE ALL WONDERED...
...HAD THE TRICK **FAILED**?

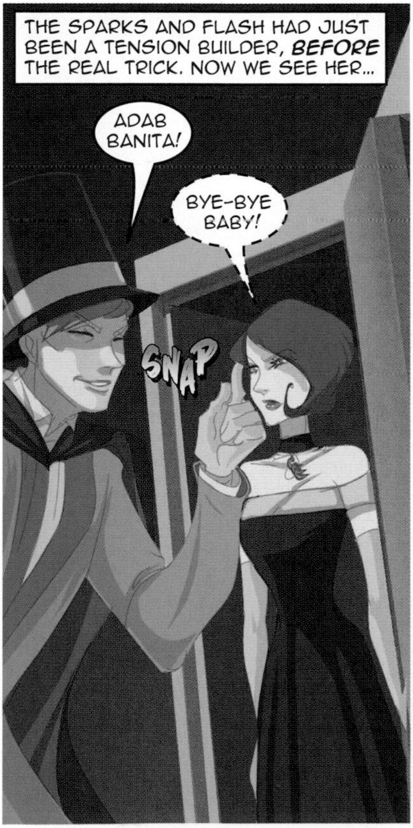
THE SPARKS AND FLASH HAD JUST BEEN A TENSION BUILDER, **BEFORE** THE REAL TRICK. NOW WE SEE HER...
ADAB BANITA!
BYE-BYE BABY!
SNAP

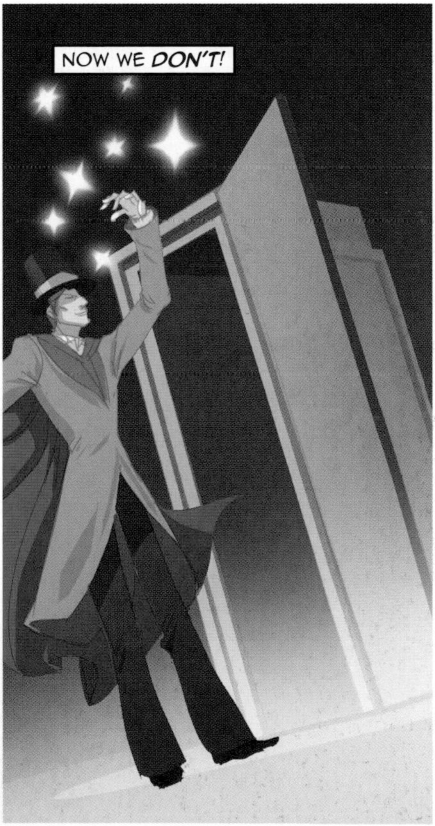
NOW WE **DON'T**!

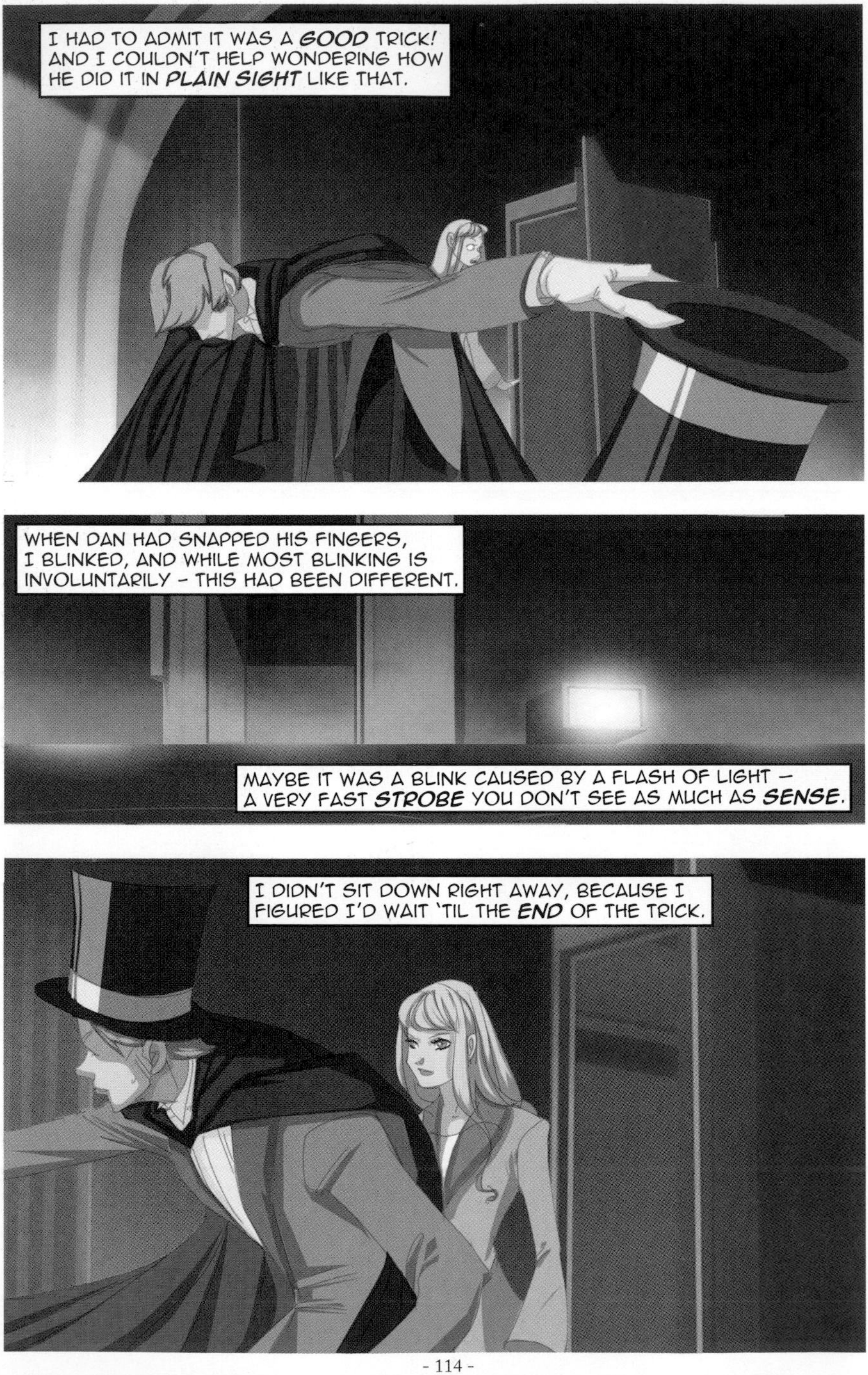
I HAD TO ADMIT IT WAS A ***GOOD*** TRICK! AND I COULDN'T HELP WONDERING HOW HE DID IT IN ***PLAIN SIGHT*** LIKE THAT.
WHEN DAN HAD SNAPPED HIS FINGERS, I BLINKED, AND WHILE MOST BLINKING IS INVOLUNTARILY – THIS HAD BEEN DIFFERENT.
MAYBE IT WAS A BLINK CAUSED BY A FLASH OF LIGHT – A VERY FAST ***STROBE*** YOU DON'T SEE AS MUCH AS ***SENSE***.
I DIDN'T SIT DOWN RIGHT AWAY, BECAUSE I FIGURED I'D WAIT 'TIL THE ***END*** OF THE TRICK.

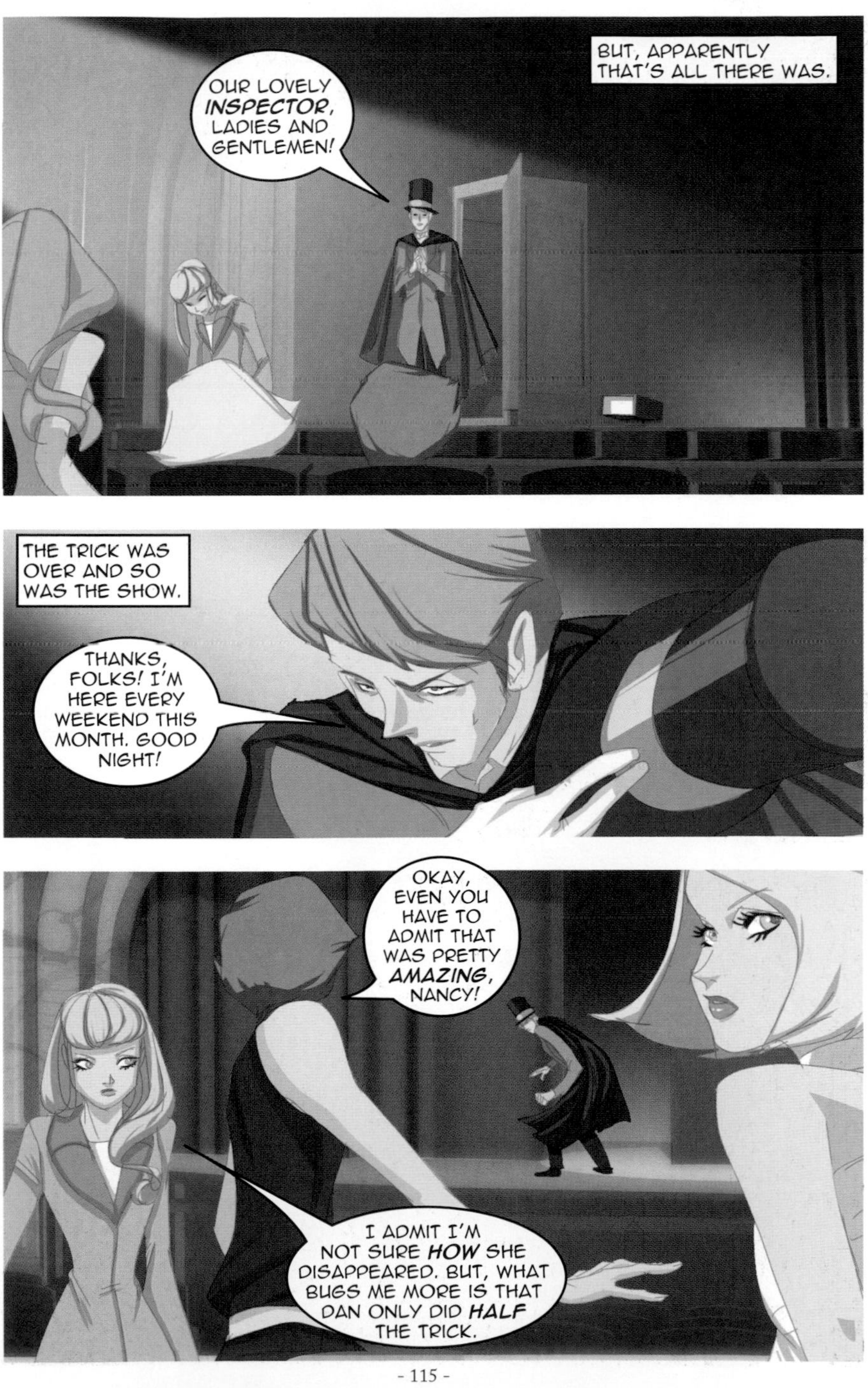
OUR LOVELY INSPECTOR, LADIES AND GENTLEMEN!
BUT, APPARENTLY THAT'S ALL THERE WAS.
THE TRICK WAS OVER AND SO WAS THE SHOW.
THANKS, FOLKS! I'M HERE EVERY WEEKEND THIS MONTH. GOOD NIGHT!
OKAY, EVEN YOU HAVE TO ADMIT THAT WAS PRETTY AMAZING, NANCY!
I ADMIT I'M NOT SURE HOW SHE DISAPPEARED. BUT, WHAT BUGS ME MORE IS THAT DAN ONLY DID HALF THE TRICK.

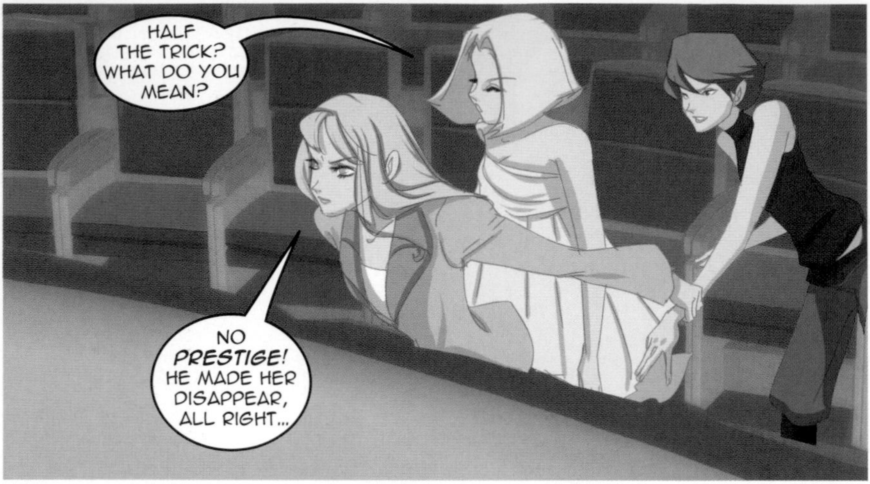
HALF THE TRICK? WHAT DO YOU MEAN?
NO *PRESTIGE!* HE MADE HER DISAPPEAR, ALL RIGHT...

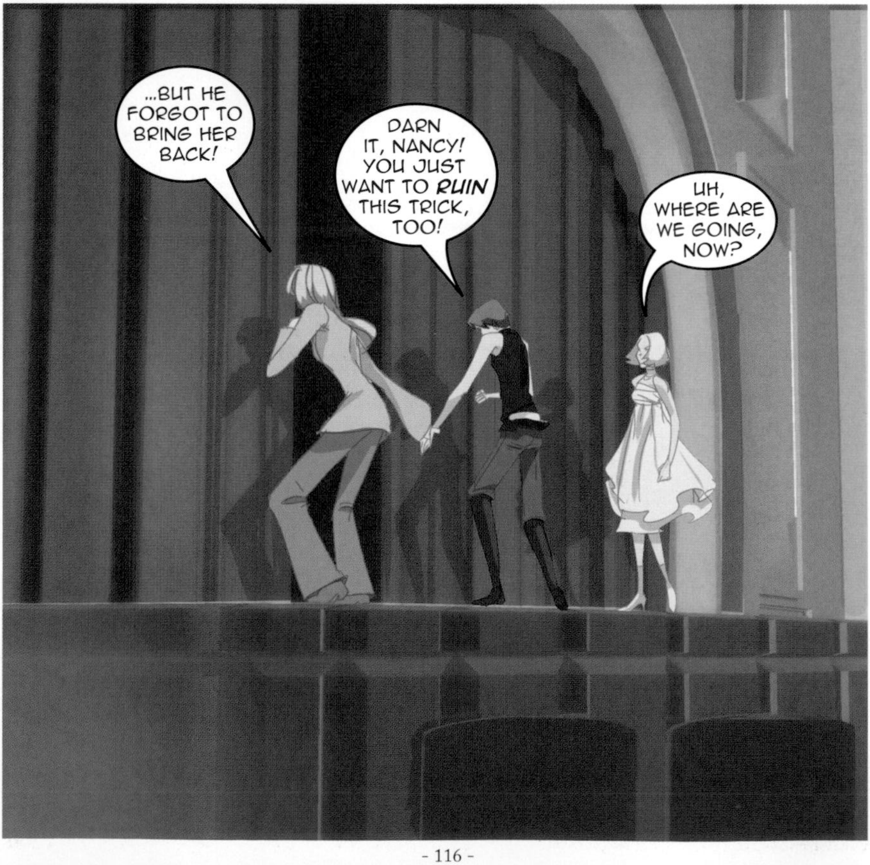
...BUT HE FORGOT TO BRING HER BACK!
DARN IT, NANCY! YOU JUST WANT TO *RUIN* THIS TRICK, TOO!
UH, WHERE ARE WE GOING, NOW?

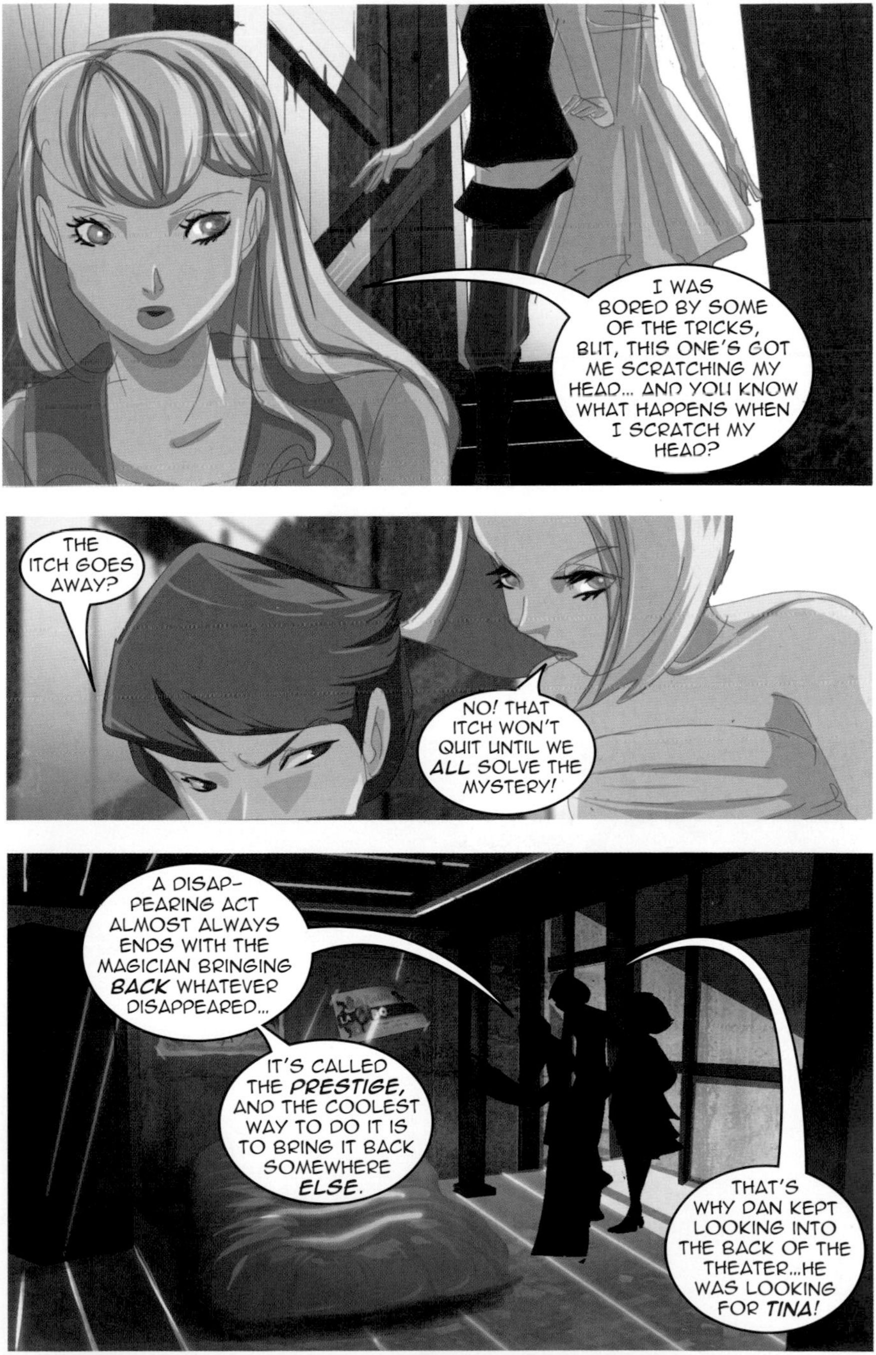
I WAS BORED BY SOME OF THE TRICKS, BUT, THIS ONE'S GOT ME SCRATCHING MY HEAD... AND YOU KNOW WHAT HAPPENS WHEN I SCRATCH MY HEAD?
THE ITCH GOES AWAY?
NO! THAT ITCH WON'T QUIT UNTIL WE ALL SOLVE THE MYSTERY!
A DISAP-PEARING ACT ALMOST ALWAYS ENDS WITH THE MAGICIAN BRINGING BACK WHATEVER DISAPPEARED...
IT'S CALLED THE PRESTIGE, AND THE COOLEST WAY TO DO IT IS TO BRING IT BACK SOMEWHERE ELSE.
THAT'S WHY DAN KEPT LOOKING INTO THE BACK OF THE THEATER...HE WAS LOOKING FOR TINA!

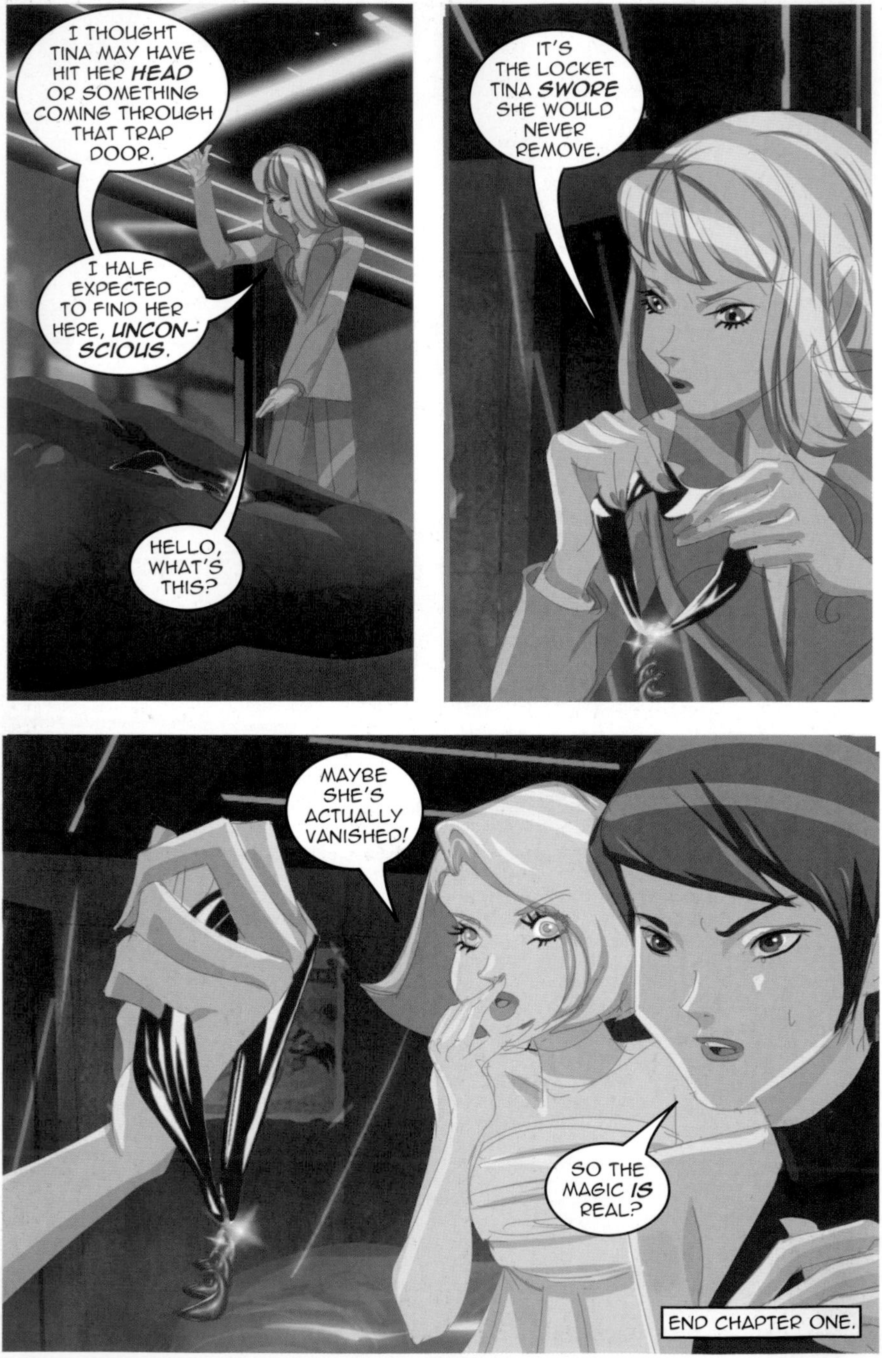
I THOUGHT TINA MAY HAVE HIT HER HEAD OR SOMETHING COMING THROUGH THAT TRAP DOOR.
I HALF EXPECTED TO FIND HER HERE, UNCON-SCIOUS.
HELLO, WHAT'S THIS?
IT'S THE LOCKET TINA SWORE SHE WOULD NEVER REMOVE.
MAYBE SHE'S ACTUALLY VANISHED!
SO THE MAGIC IS REAL?
END CHAPTER ONE.

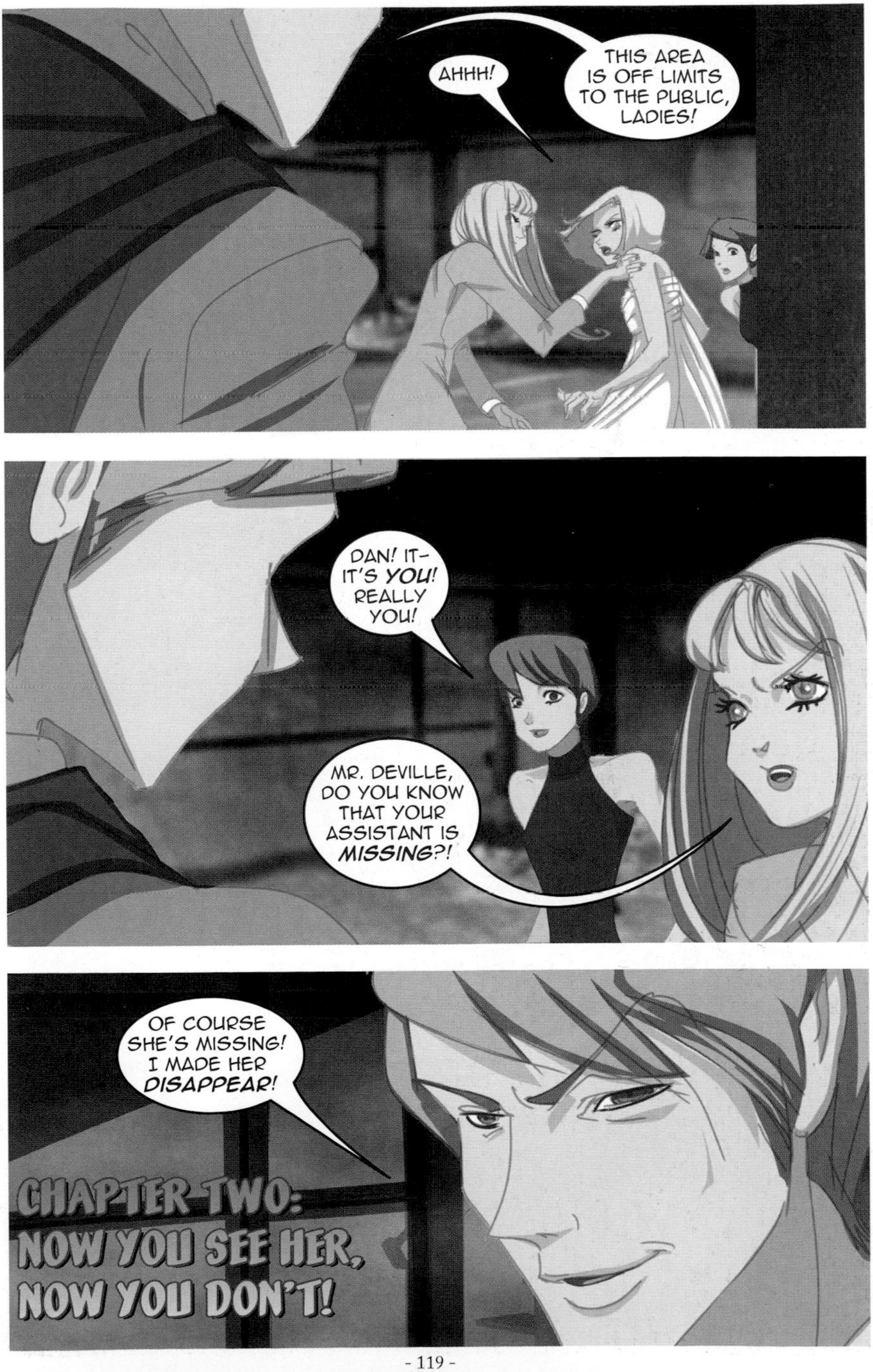
AHHH!
THIS AREA IS OFF LIMITS TO THE PUBLIC, LADIES!
DAN! IT-IT'S *YOU*! REALLY YOU!
MR. DEVILLE, DO YOU KNOW THAT YOUR ASSISTANT IS *MISSING*?!
OF COURSE SHE'S MISSING! I MADE HER *DISAPPEAR*!
CHAPTER TWO: NOW YOU SEE HER, NOW YOU DON'T!

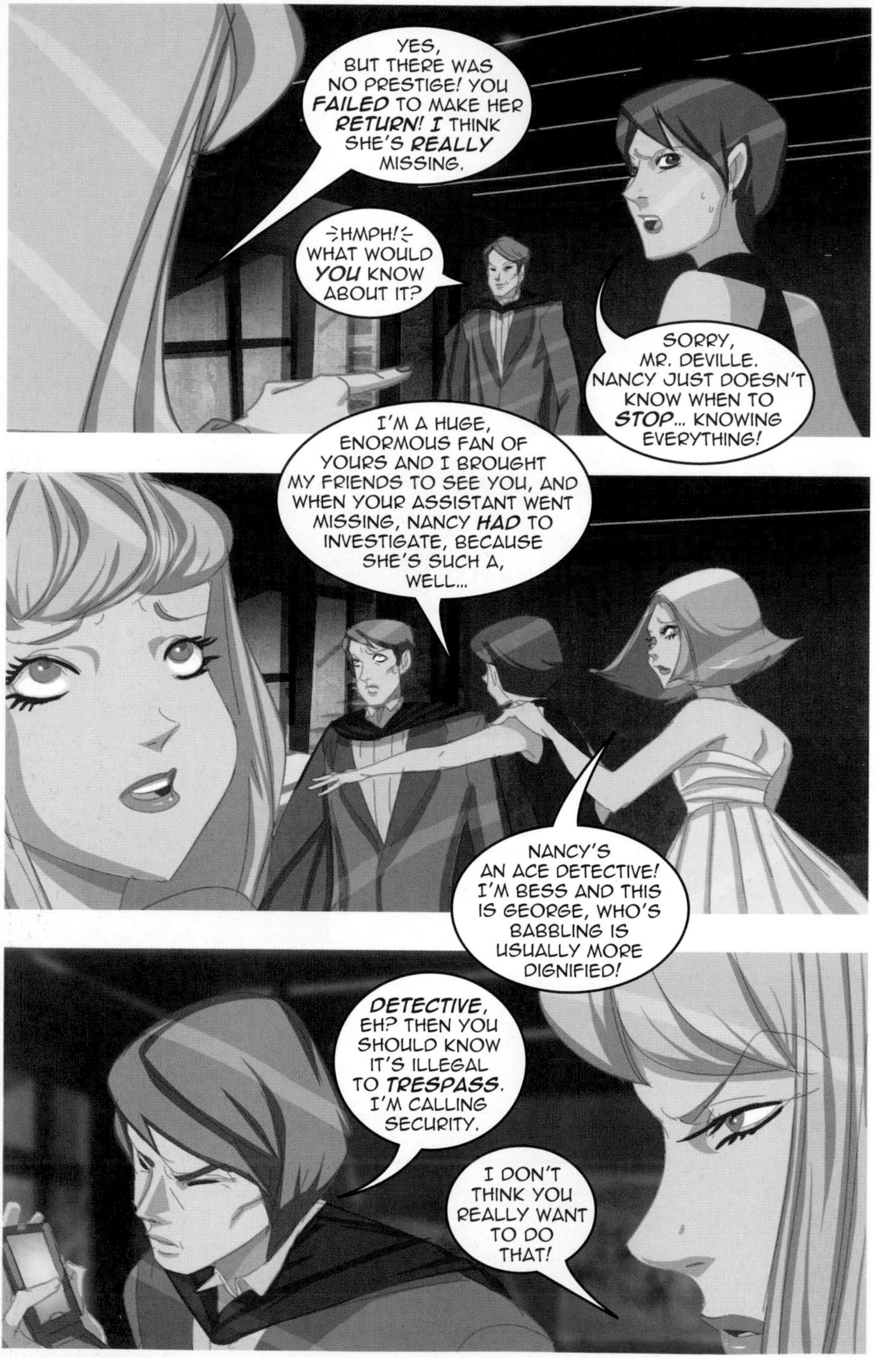
YES, BUT THERE WAS NO PRESTIGE! YOU FAILED TO MAKE HER RETURN! I THINK SHE'S REALLY MISSING.
HMPH! WHAT WOULD YOU KNOW ABOUT IT?
SORRY, MR. DEVILLE. NANCY JUST DOESN'T KNOW WHEN TO STOP... KNOWING EVERYTHING!
I'M A HUGE, ENORMOUS FAN OF YOURS AND I BROUGHT MY FRIENDS TO SEE YOU, AND WHEN YOUR ASSISTANT WENT MISSING, NANCY HAD TO INVESTIGATE, BECAUSE SHE'S SUCH A, WELL...
NANCY'S AN ACE DETECTIVE! I'M BESS AND THIS IS GEORGE, WHO'S BABBLING IS USUALLY MORE DIGNIFIED!
DETECTIVE, EH? THEN YOU SHOULD KNOW IT'S ILLEGAL TO TRESPASS. I'M CALLING SECURITY.
I DON'T THINK YOU REALLY WANT TO DO THAT!

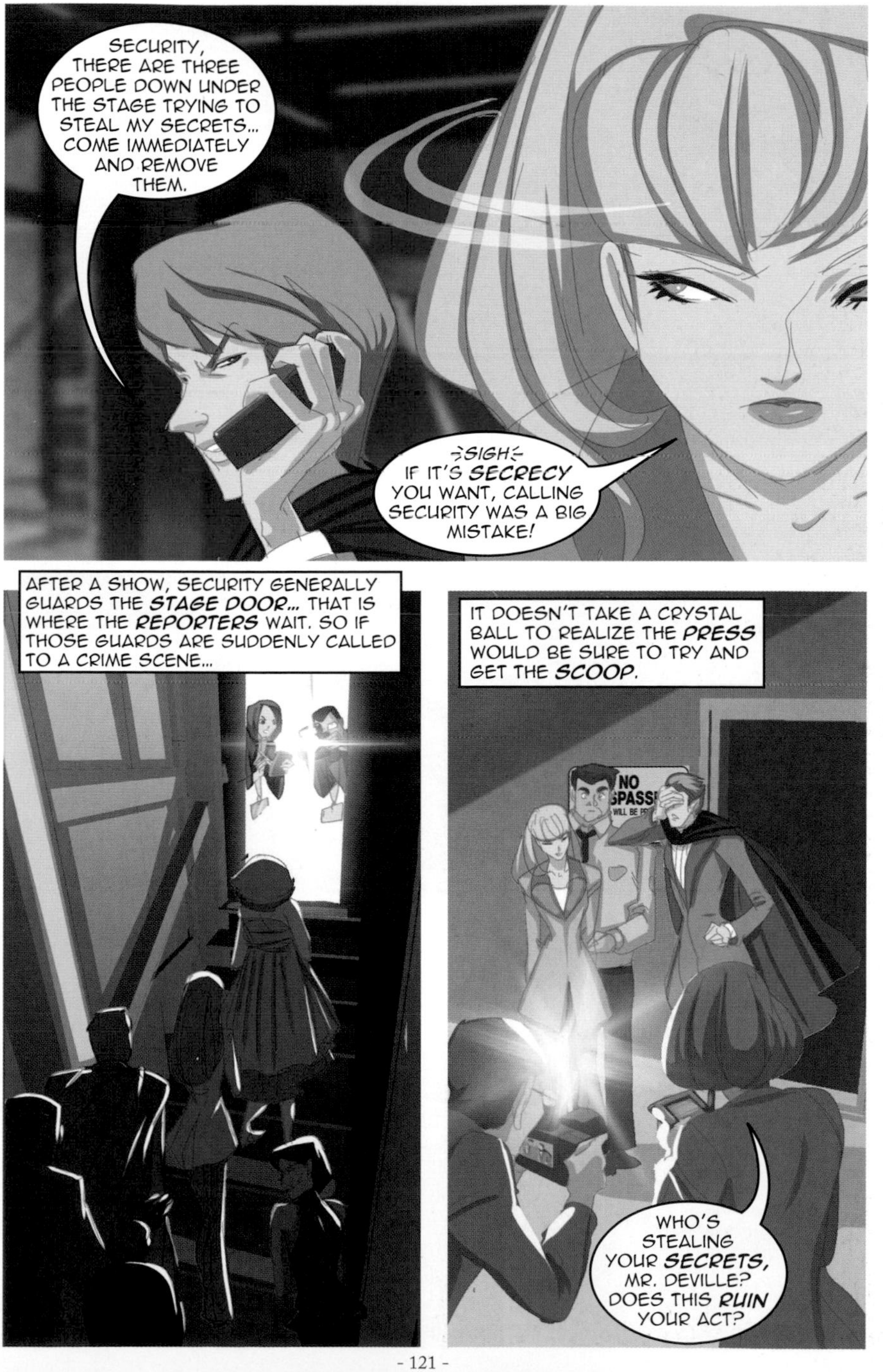
SECURITY, THERE ARE THREE PEOPLE DOWN UNDER THE STAGE TRYING TO STEAL MY SECRETS... COME IMMEDIATELY AND REMOVE THEM.
SIGH
IF IT'S SECRECY YOU WANT, CALLING SECURITY WAS A BIG MISTAKE!
AFTER A SHOW, SECURITY GENERALLY GUARDS THE STAGE DOOR... THAT IS WHERE THE REPORTERS WAIT. SO IF THOSE GUARDS ARE SUDDENLY CALLED TO A CRIME SCENE...
IT DOESN'T TAKE A CRYSTAL BALL TO REALIZE THE PRESS WOULD BE SURE TO TRY AND GET THE SCOOP.
NO
WHO'S STEALING YOUR SECRETS, MR. DEVILLE? DOES THIS RUIN YOUR ACT?

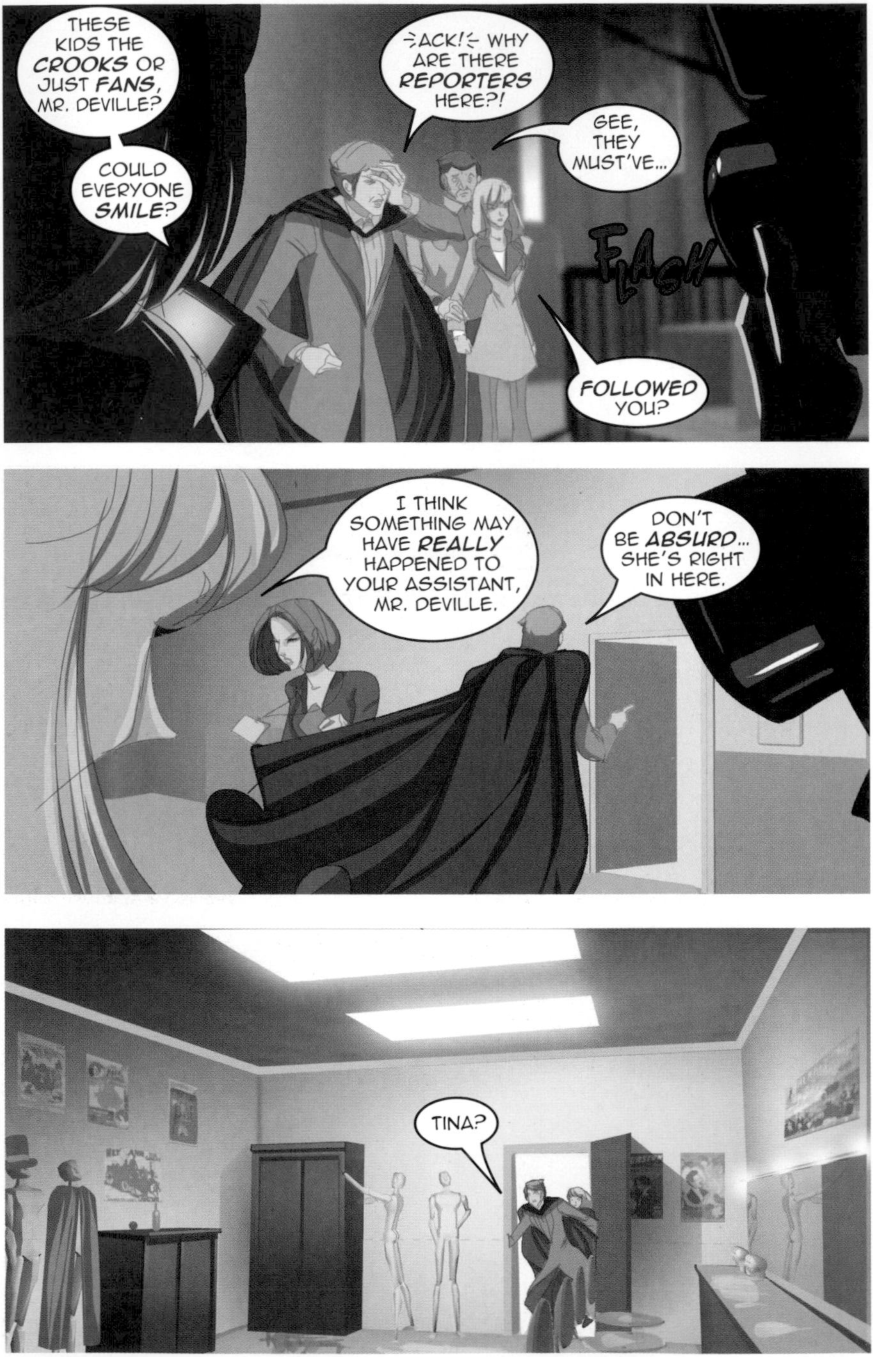
THESE KIDS THE CROOKS OR JUST FANS, MR. DEVILLE?
COULD EVERYONE SMILE?
⩦ACK!⩦ WHY ARE THERE REPORTERS HERE?!
GEE, THEY MUST'VE...
FLASH
FOLLOWED YOU?
I THINK SOMETHING MAY HAVE REALLY HAPPENED TO YOUR ASSISTANT, MR. DEVILLE.
DON'T BE ABSURD... SHE'S RIGHT IN HERE.
TINA?

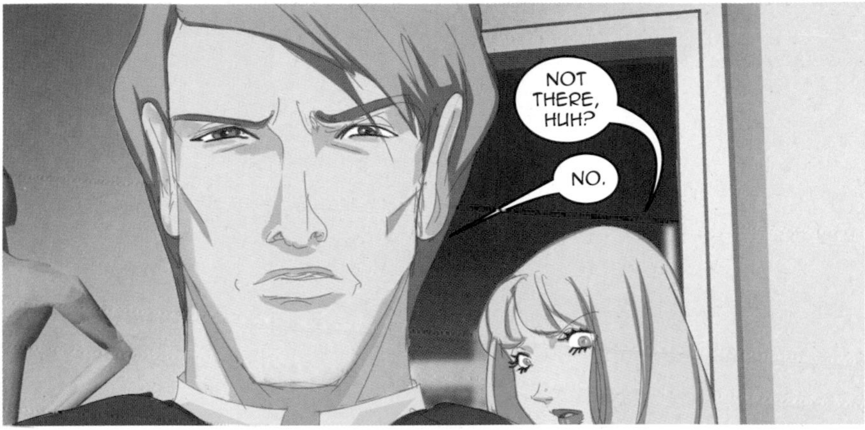
NOT THERE, HUH?
NO.

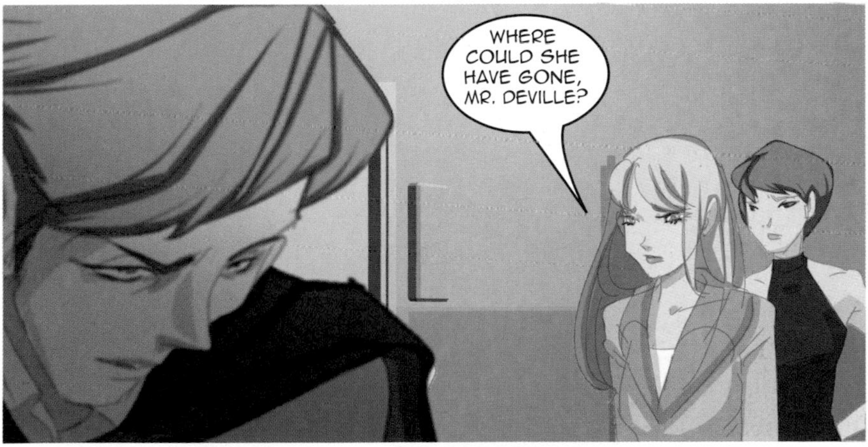
WHERE COULD SHE HAVE GONE, MR. DEVILLE?

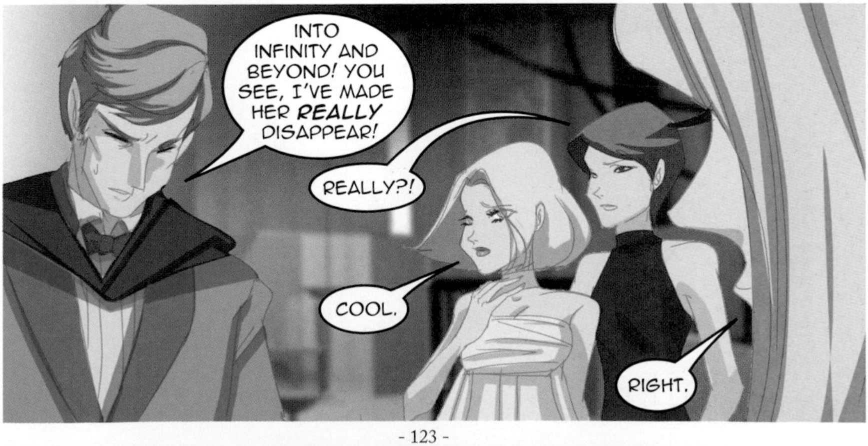
INTO INFINITY AND BEYOND! YOU SEE, I'VE MADE HER ***REALLY*** DISAPPEAR!
REALLY?!
COOL.
RIGHT.

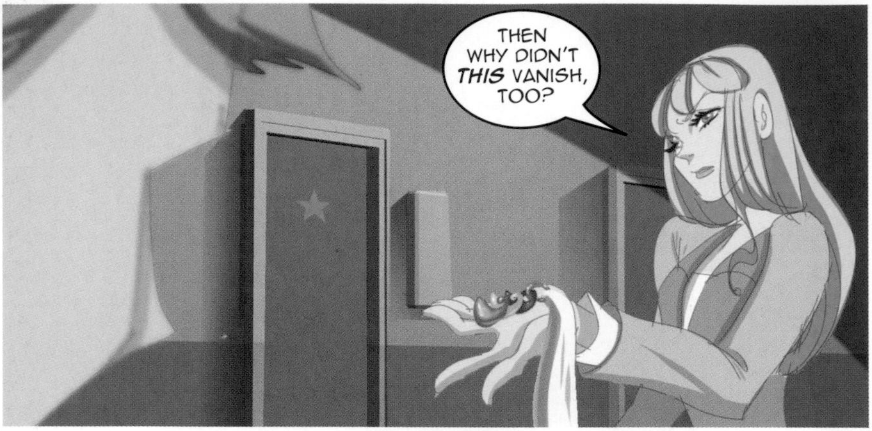
THEN WHY DIDN'T THIS VANISH, TOO?

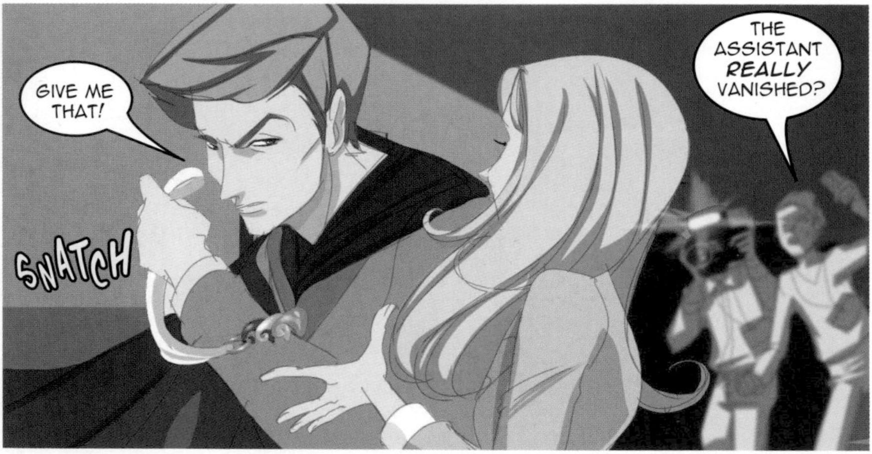
GIVE ME THAT!
SNATCH
THE ASSISTANT REALLY VANISHED?

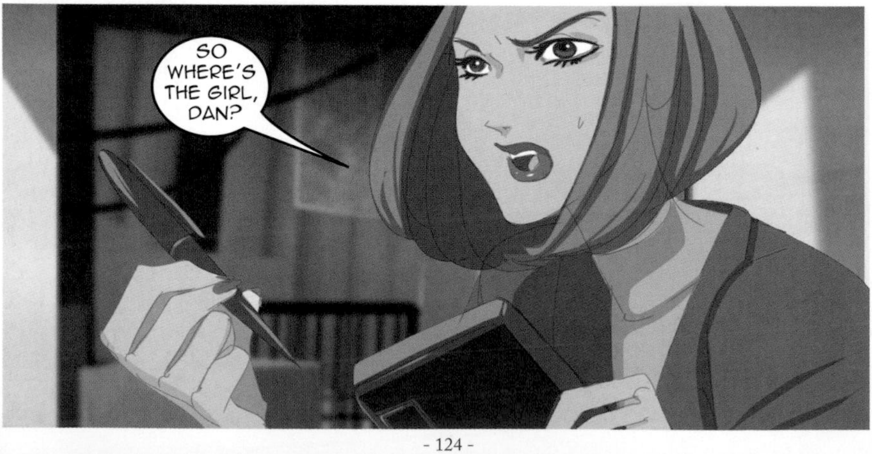
SO WHERE'S THE GIRL, DAN?

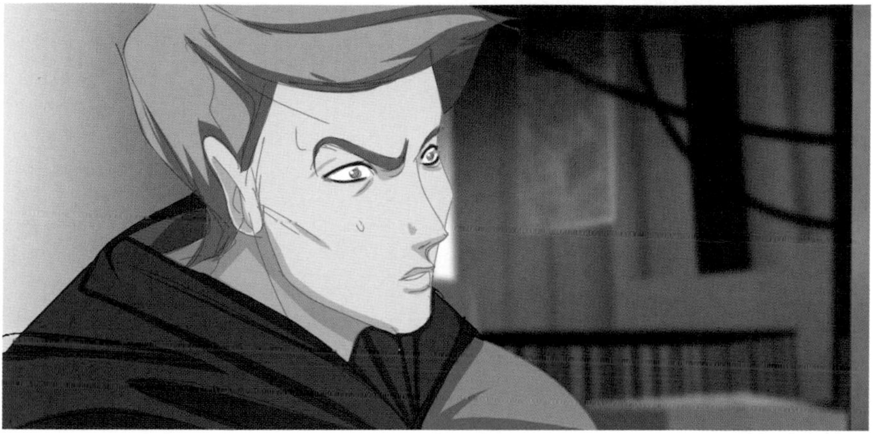

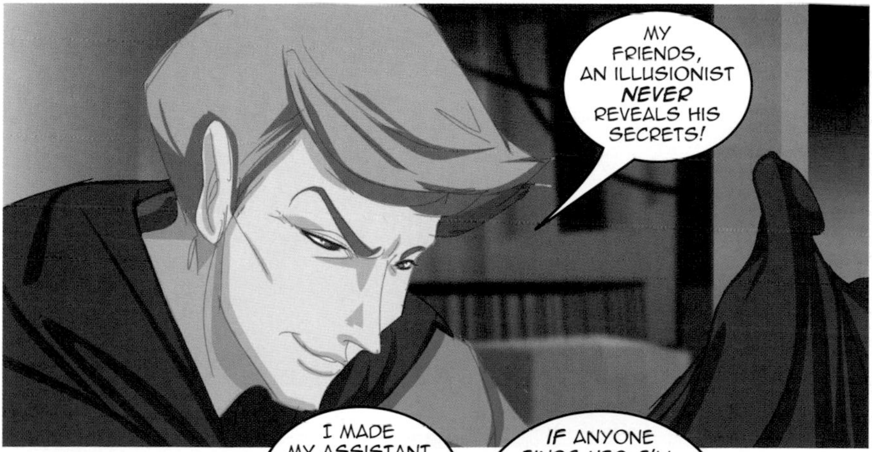

MY FRIENDS, AN ILLUSIONIST ***NEVER*** REVEALS HIS SECRETS!

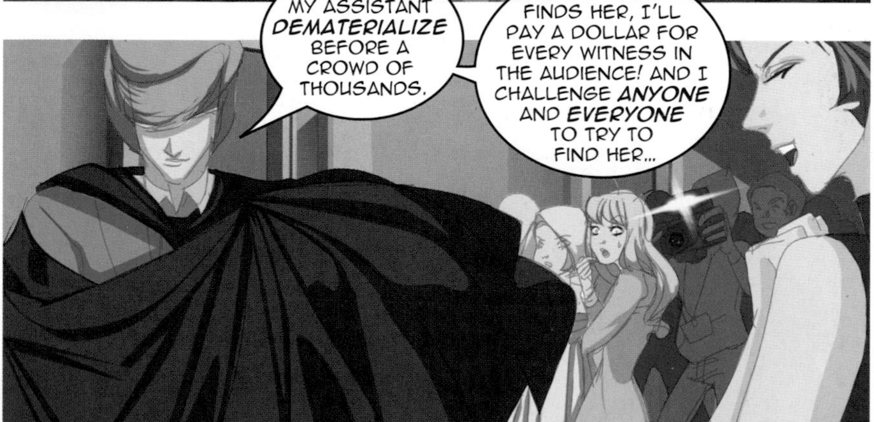

I MADE MY ASSISTANT ***DEMATERIALIZE*** BEFORE A CROWD OF THOUSANDS.
IF ANYONE FINDS HER, I'LL PAY A DOLLAR FOR EVERY WITNESS IN THE AUDIENCE! AND I CHALLENGE ***ANYONE*** AND ***EVERYONE*** TO TRY TO FIND HER...

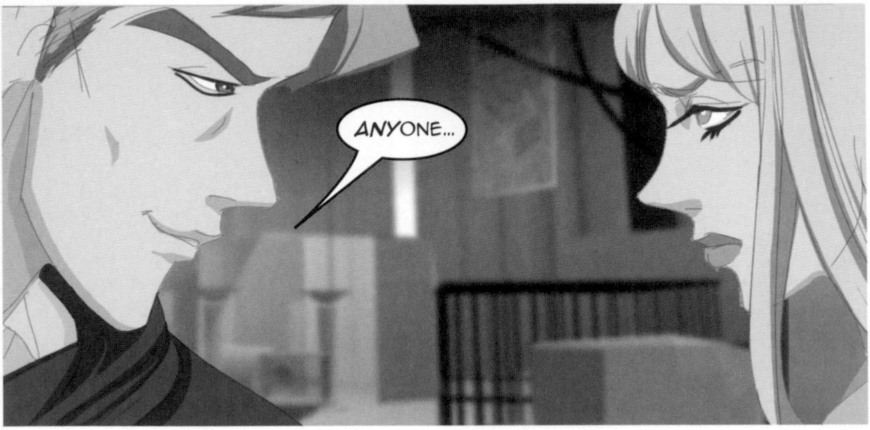
ANYONE...

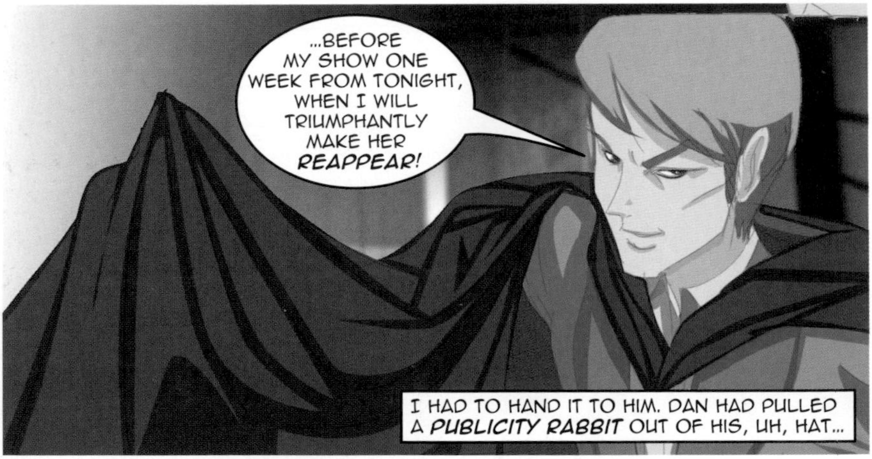
...BEFORE MY SHOW ONE WEEK FROM TONIGHT, WHEN I WILL TRIUMPHANTLY MAKE HER REAPPEAR!
I HAD TO HAND IT TO HIM. DAN HAD PULLED A PUBLICITY RABBIT OUT OF HIS, UH, HAT...

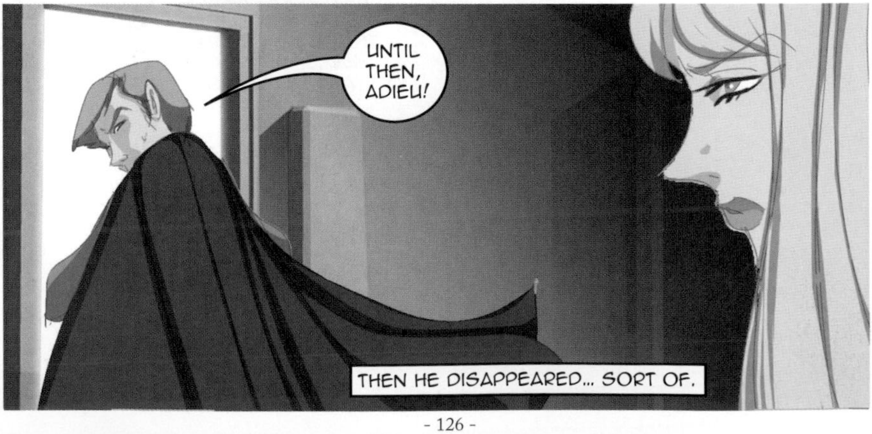
UNTIL THEN, ADIEU!
THEN HE DISAPPEARED... SORT OF.

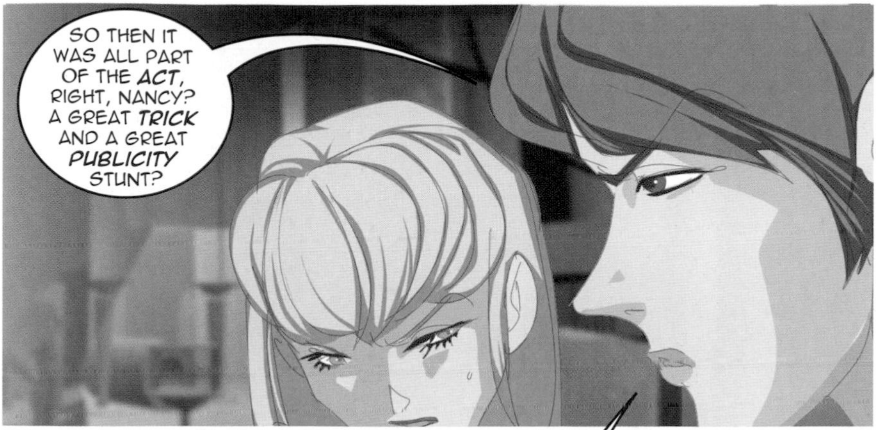
SO THEN IT WAS ALL PART OF THE *ACT*, RIGHT, NANCY? A GREAT *TRICK* AND A GREAT *PUBLICITY* STUNT?

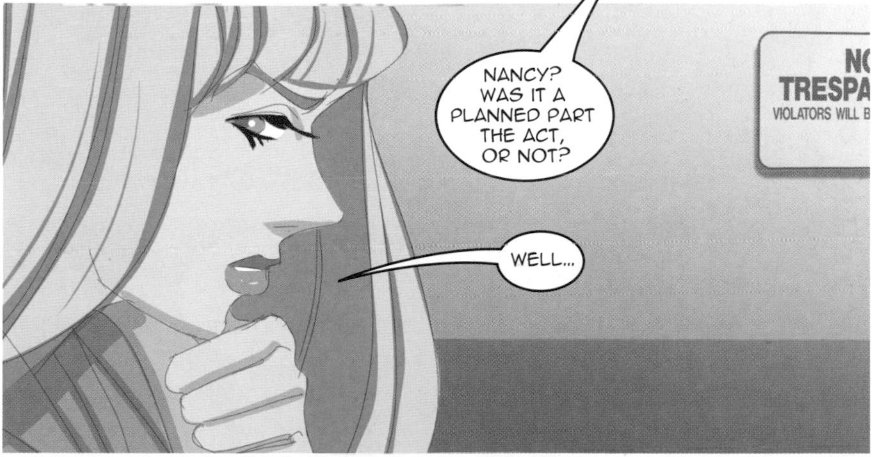
NANCY? WAS IT A PLANNED PART THE ACT, OR NOT?
WELL...

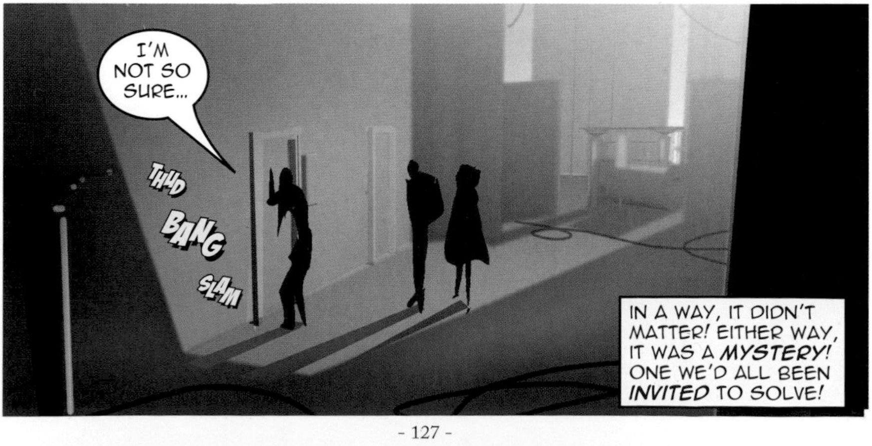
I'M NOT SO SURE...
THUD
BANG
SLAM
IN A WAY, IT DIDN'T MATTER! EITHER WAY, IT WAS A *MYSTERY!* ONE WE'D ALL BEEN *INVITED* TO SOLVE!

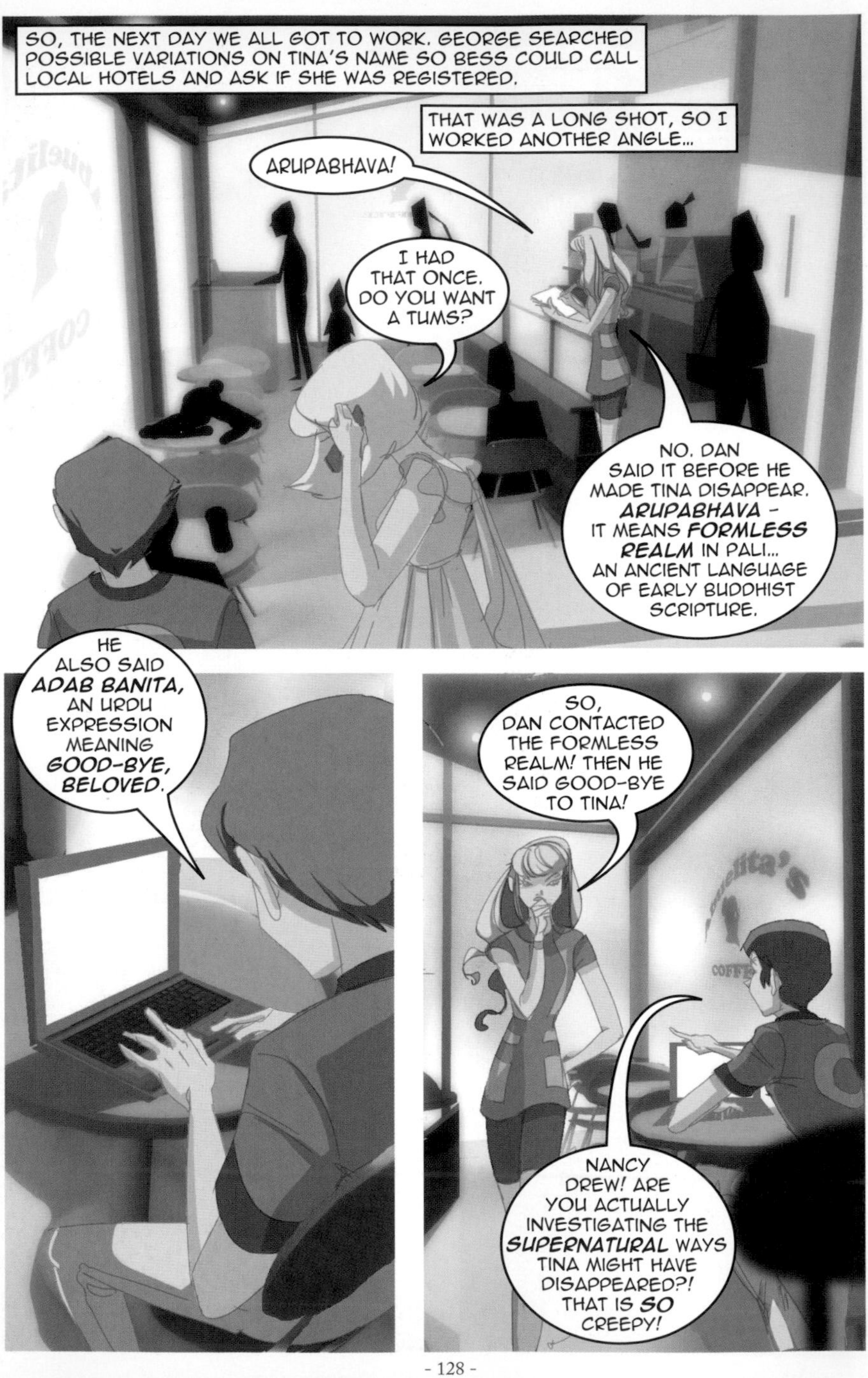
SO, THE NEXT DAY WE ALL GOT TO WORK. GEORGE SEARCHED POSSIBLE VARIATIONS ON TINA'S NAME SO BESS COULD CALL LOCAL HOTELS AND ASK IF SHE WAS REGISTERED.
THAT WAS A LONG SHOT, SO I WORKED ANOTHER ANGLE...
ARUPABHAVA!
I HAD THAT ONCE. DO YOU WANT A TUMS?
NO. DAN SAID IT BEFORE HE MADE TINA DISAPPEAR. ***ARUPABHAVA*** – IT MEANS ***FORMLESS REALM*** IN PALI... AN ANCIENT LANGUAGE OF EARLY BUDDHIST SCRIPTURE.
HE ALSO SAID ***ADAB BANITA,*** AN URDU EXPRESSION MEANING ***GOOD-BYE, BELOVED.***
SO, DAN CONTACTED THE FORMLESS REALM! THEN HE SAID GOOD-BYE TO TINA!
NANCY DREW! ARE YOU ACTUALLY INVESTIGATING THE ***SUPERNATURAL*** WAYS TINA MIGHT HAVE DISAPPEARED?! THAT IS ***SO*** CREEPY!

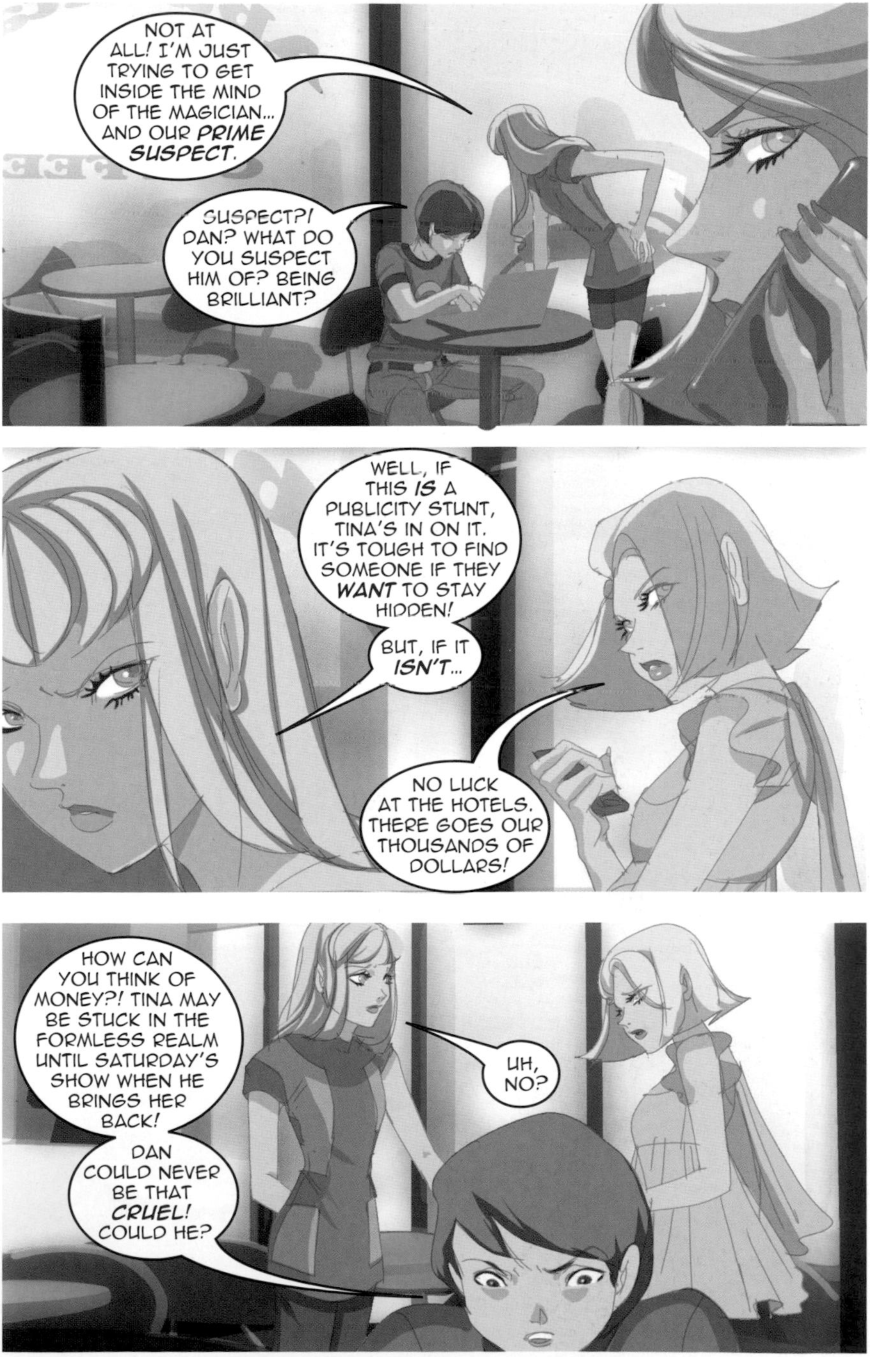
NOT AT ALL! I'M JUST TRYING TO GET INSIDE THE MIND OF THE MAGICIAN... AND OUR PRIME SUSPECT.
SUSPECT?! DAN? WHAT DO YOU SUSPECT HIM OF? BEING BRILLIANT?
WELL, IF THIS IS A PUBLICITY STUNT, TINA'S IN ON IT. IT'S TOUGH TO FIND SOMEONE IF THEY WANT TO STAY HIDDEN!
BUT, IF IT ISN'T...
NO LUCK AT THE HOTELS. THERE GOES OUR THOUSANDS OF DOLLARS!
HOW CAN YOU THINK OF MONEY?! TINA MAY BE STUCK IN THE FORMLESS REALM UNTIL SATURDAY'S SHOW WHEN HE BRINGS HER BACK!
DAN COULD NEVER BE THAT CRUEL! COULD HE?
UH, NO?

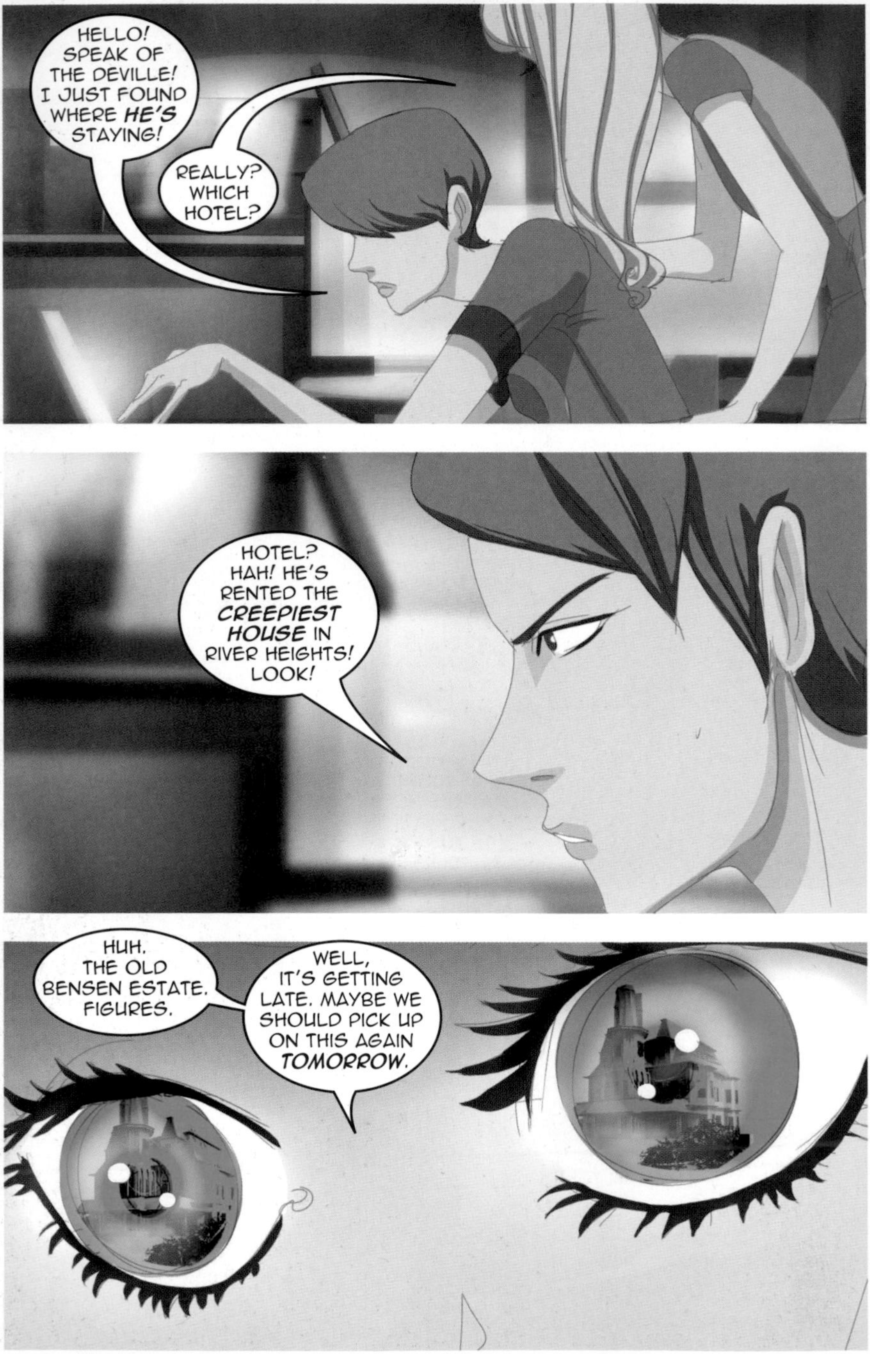
HELLO! SPEAK OF THE DEVILLE! I JUST FOUND WHERE **HE'S** STAYING!
REALLY? WHICH HOTEL?
HOTEL? HAH! HE'S RENTED THE **CREEPIEST HOUSE** IN RIVER HEIGHTS! LOOK!
HUH. THE OLD BENSEN ESTATE. FIGURES.
WELL, IT'S GETTING LATE. MAYBE WE SHOULD PICK UP ON THIS AGAIN **TOMORROW**.

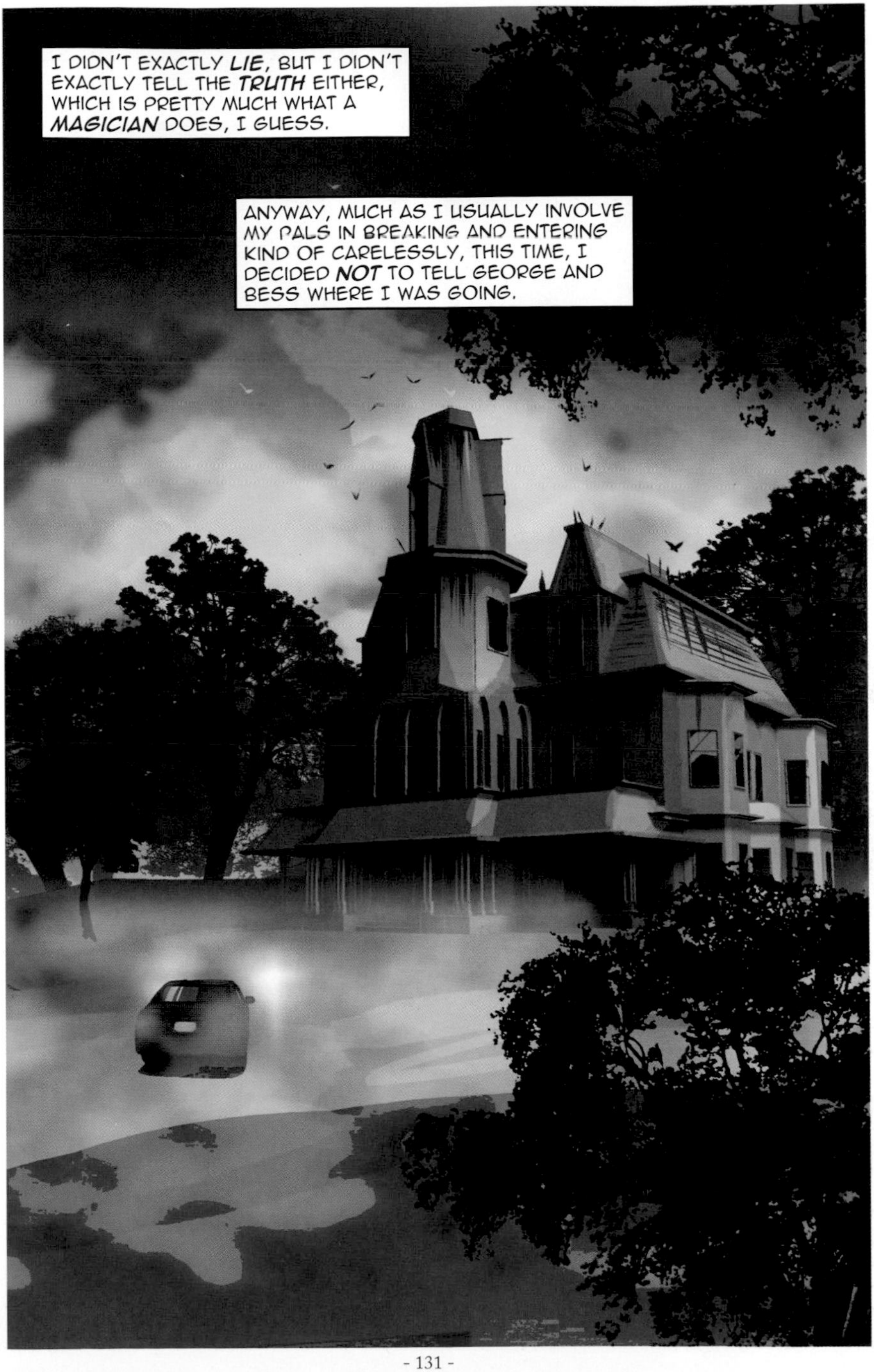
I DIDN'T EXACTLY LIE, BUT I DIDN'T EXACTLY TELL THE TRUTH EITHER, WHICH IS PRETTY MUCH WHAT A MAGICIAN DOES, I GUESS.
ANYWAY, MUCH AS I USUALLY INVOLVE MY PALS IN BREAKING AND ENTERING KIND OF CARELESSLY, THIS TIME, I DECIDED NOT TO TELL GEORGE AND BESS WHERE I WAS GOING.

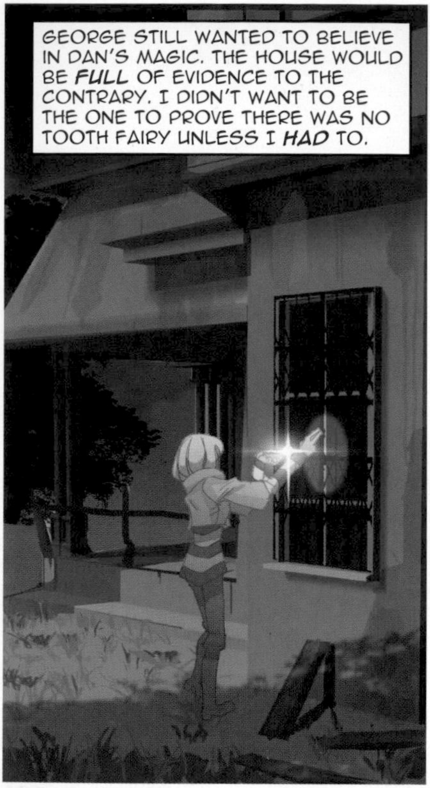
GEORGE STILL WANTED TO BELIEVE IN DAN'S MAGIC. THE HOUSE WOULD BE FULL OF EVIDENCE TO THE CONTRARY. I DIDN'T WANT TO BE THE ONE TO PROVE THERE WAS NO TOOTH FAIRY UNLESS I HAD TO.

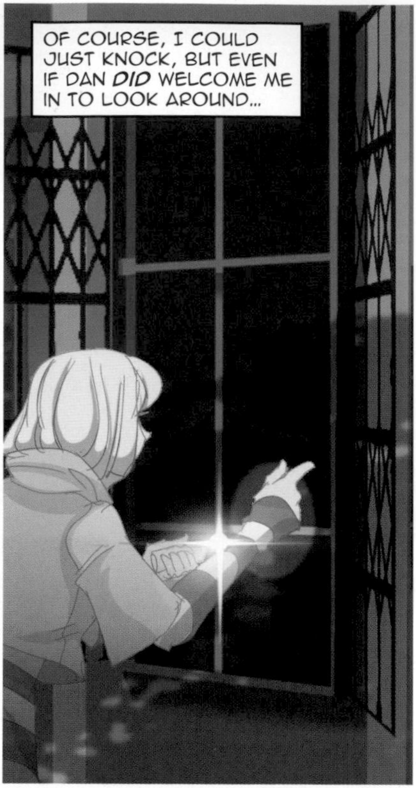
OF COURSE, I COULD JUST KNOCK, BUT EVEN IF DAN DID WELCOME ME IN TO LOOK AROUND...

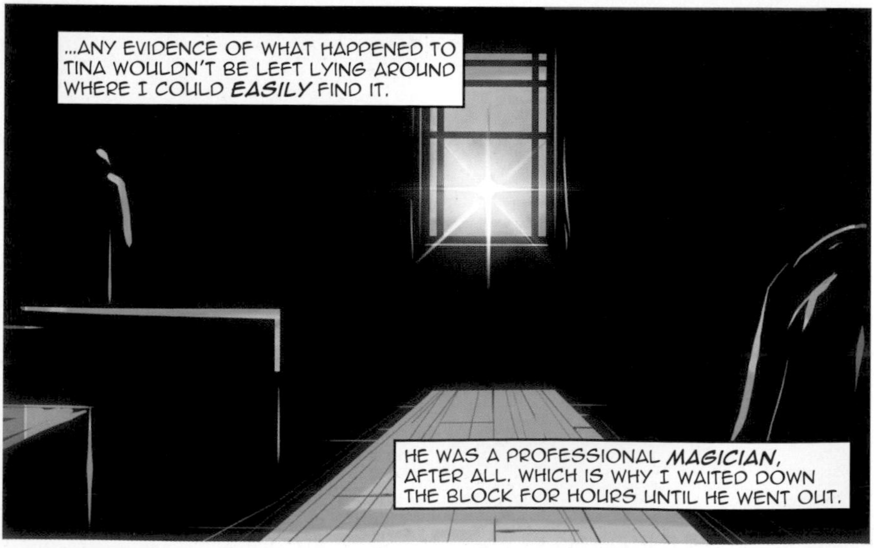
...ANY EVIDENCE OF WHAT HAPPENED TO TINA WOULDN'T BE LEFT LYING AROUND WHERE I COULD EASILY FIND IT.
HE WAS A PROFESSIONAL MAGICIAN, AFTER ALL. WHICH IS WHY I WAITED DOWN THE BLOCK FOR HOURS UNTIL HE WENT OUT.

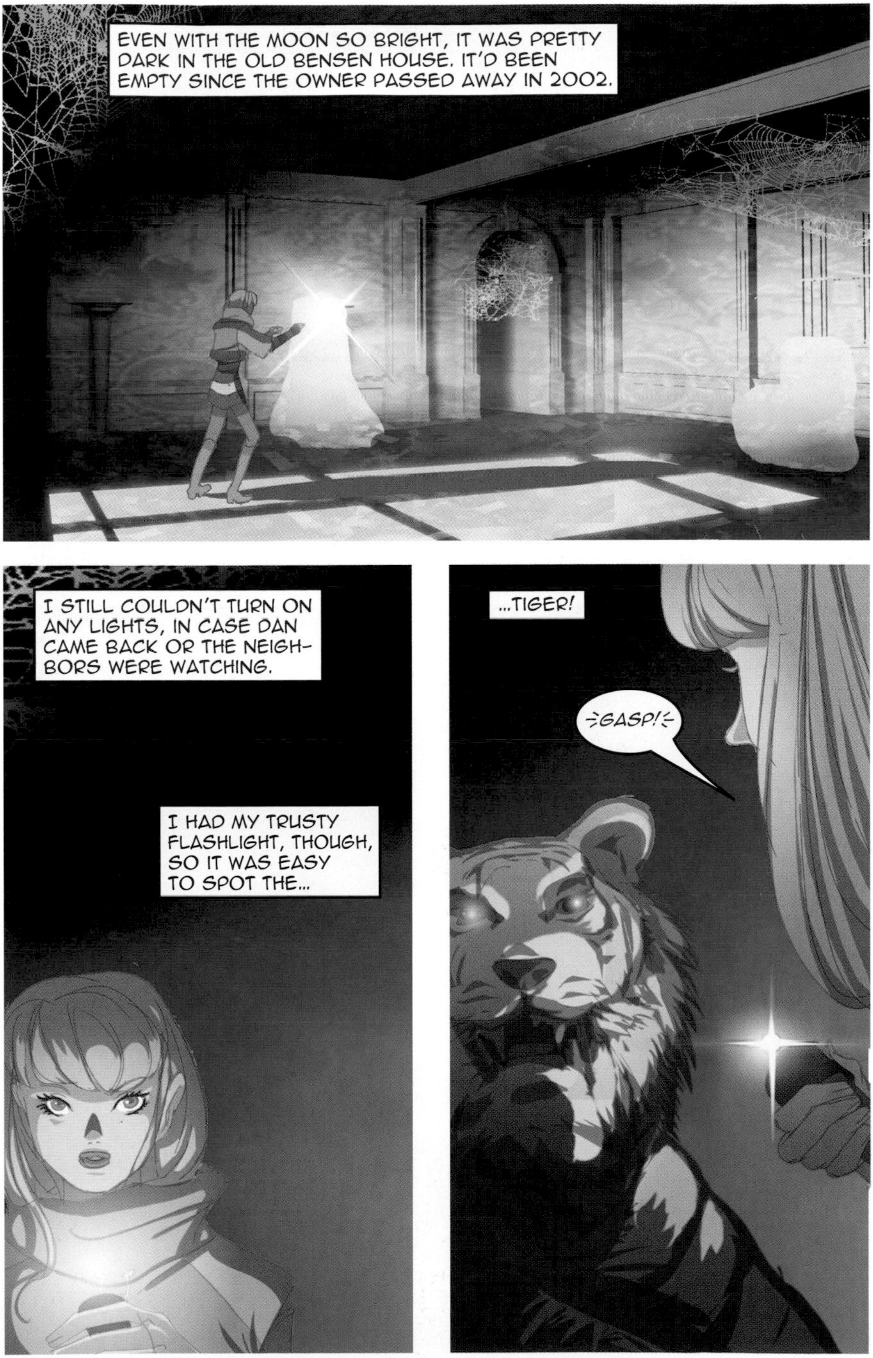
EVEN WITH THE MOON SO BRIGHT, IT WAS PRETTY DARK IN THE OLD BENSEN HOUSE. IT'D BEEN EMPTY SINCE THE OWNER PASSED AWAY IN 2002.
I STILL COULDN'T TURN ON ANY LIGHTS, IN CASE DAN CAME BACK OR THE NEIGHBORS WERE WATCHING.
I HAD MY TRUSTY FLASHLIGHT, THOUGH, SO IT WAS EASY TO SPOT THE...
...TIGER!
GASP!

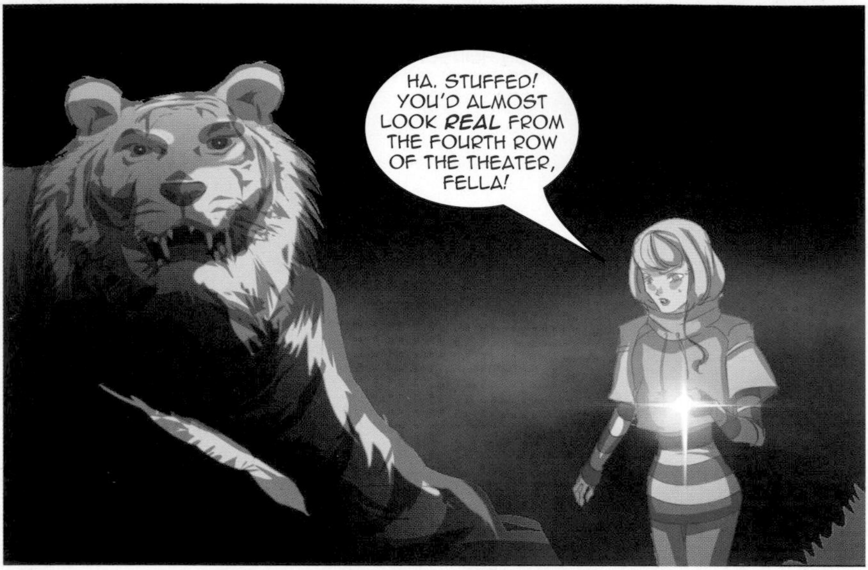
HA. STUFFED! YOU'D ALMOST LOOK REAL FROM THE FOURTH ROW OF THE THEATER, FELLA!

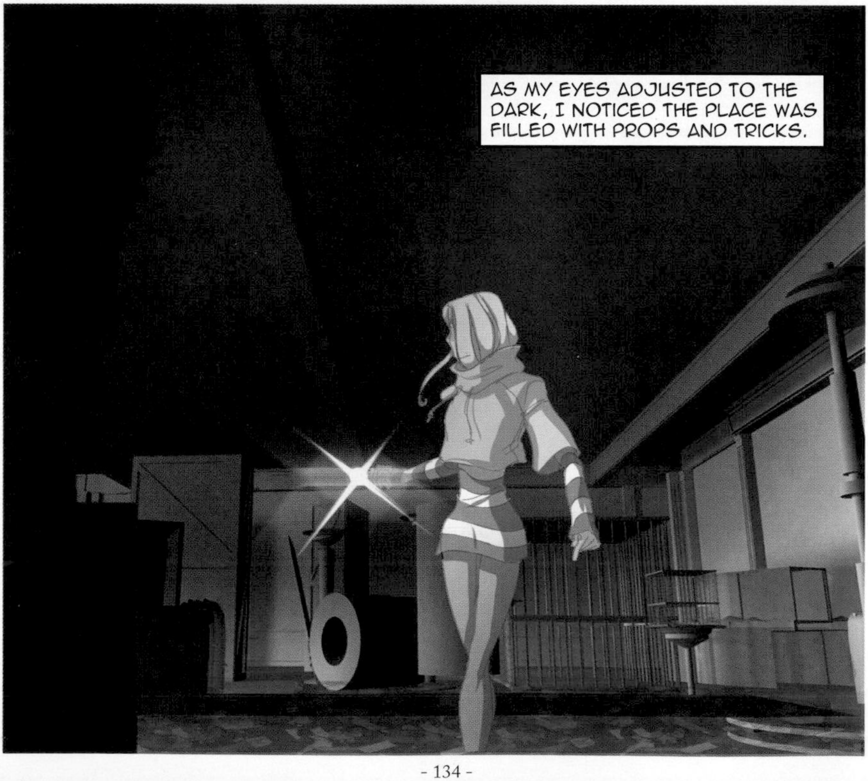
AS MY EYES ADJUSTED TO THE DARK, I NOTICED THE PLACE WAS FILLED WITH PROPS AND TRICKS.

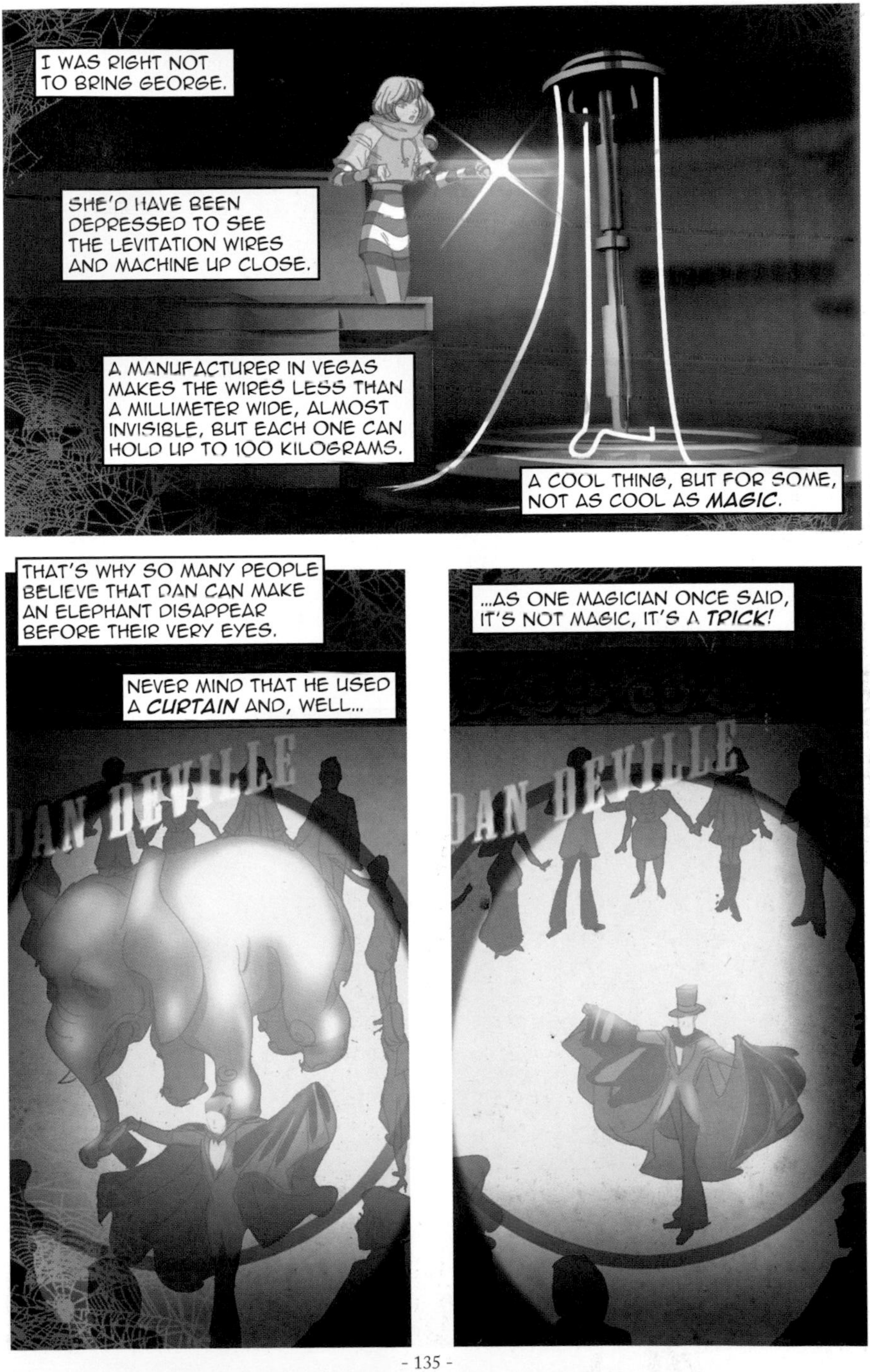
I WAS RIGHT NOT TO BRING GEORGE.
SHE'D HAVE BEEN DEPRESSED TO SEE THE LEVITATION WIRES AND MACHINE UP CLOSE.
A MANUFACTURER IN VEGAS MAKES THE WIRES LESS THAN A MILLIMETER WIDE, ALMOST INVISIBLE, BUT EACH ONE CAN HOLD UP TO 100 KILOGRAMS.
A COOL THING, BUT FOR SOME, NOT AS COOL AS *MAGIC*.
THAT'S WHY SO MANY PEOPLE BELIEVE THAT DAN CAN MAKE AN ELEPHANT DISAPPEAR BEFORE THEIR VERY EYES.
NEVER MIND THAT HE USED A *CURTAIN* AND, WELL...
DAN DEVILLE
...AS ONE MAGICIAN ONCE SAID, IT'S NOT MAGIC, IT'S A *TRICK*!
DAN DEVILLE

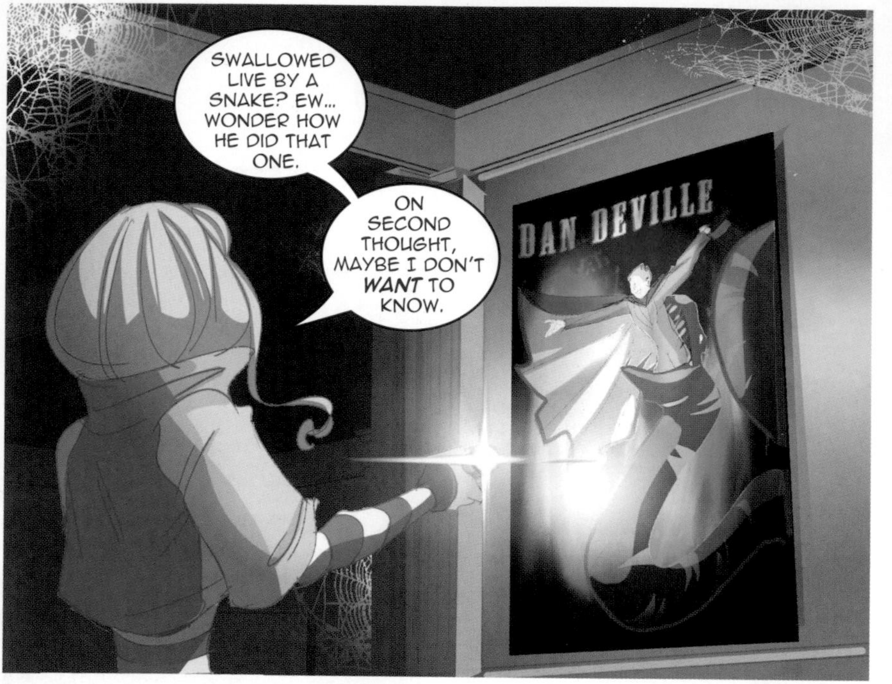
SWALLOWED LIVE BY A SNAKE? EW... WONDER HOW HE DID THAT ONE.
ON SECOND THOUGHT, MAYBE I DON'T *WANT* TO KNOW.
DAN DEVILLE

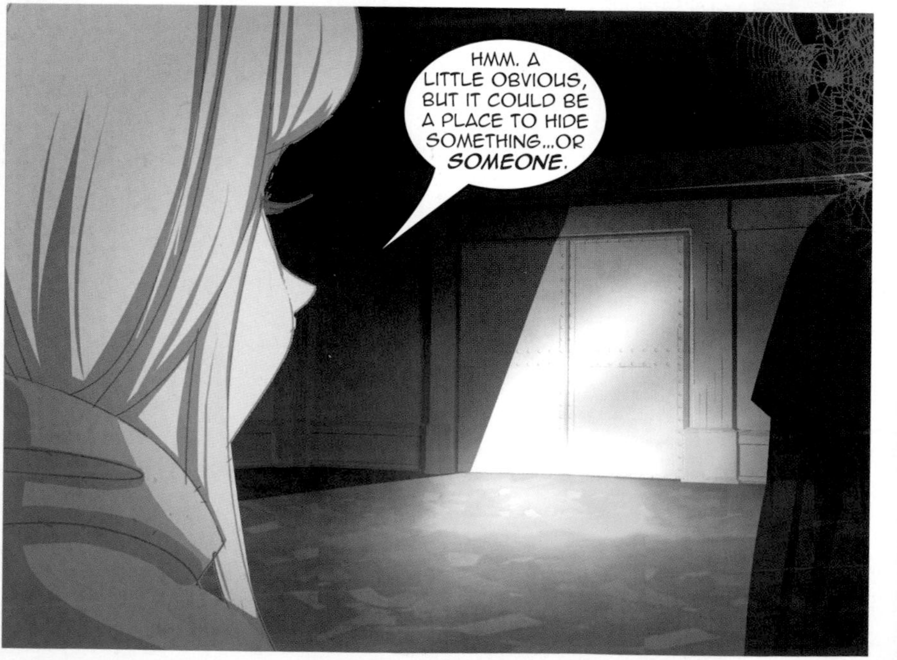
HMM. A LITTLE OBVIOUS, BUT IT COULD BE A PLACE TO HIDE SOMETHING...OR *SOMEONE*.

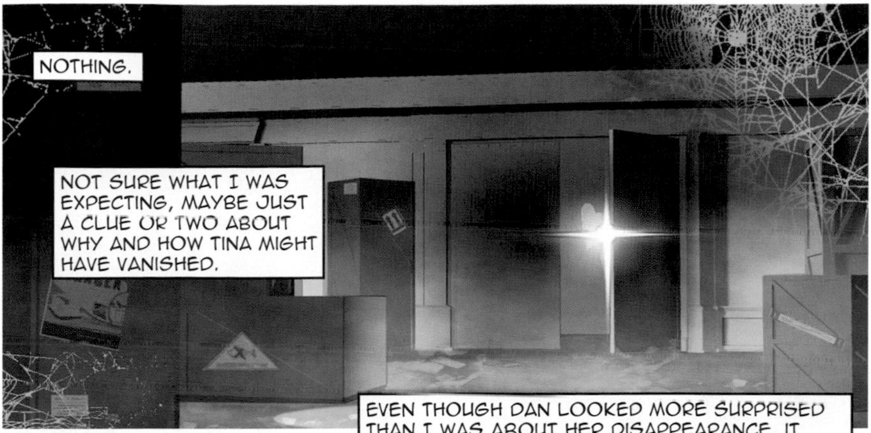
NOTHING.
NOT SURE WHAT I WAS EXPECTING, MAYBE JUST A CLUE OR TWO ABOUT WHY AND HOW TINA MIGHT HAVE VANISHED.
EVEN THOUGH DAN LOOKED MORE SURPRISED THAN I WAS ABOUT HER DISAPPEARANCE, IT *COULD* HAVE BEEN AN ACT. HE MAKES A PRETTY GOOD LIVING FOOLING PEOPLE.

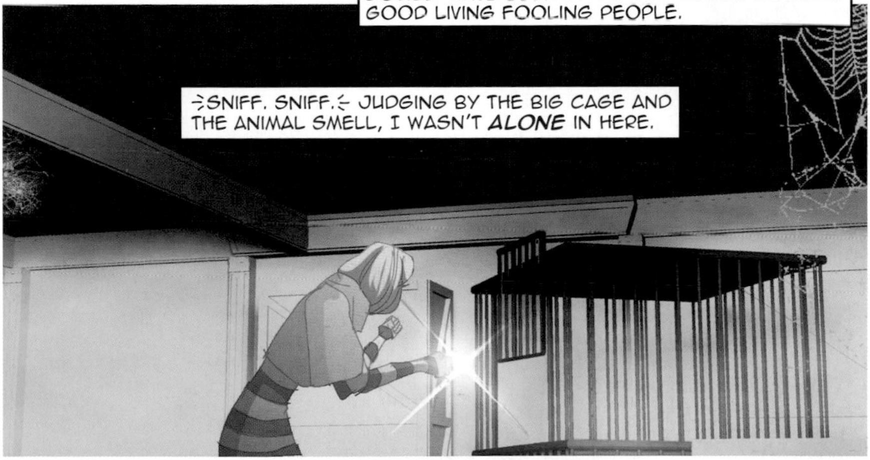
⇒SNIFF. SNIFF.⇐ JUDGING BY THE BIG CAGE AND THE ANIMAL SMELL, I WASN'T ***ALONE*** IN HERE.

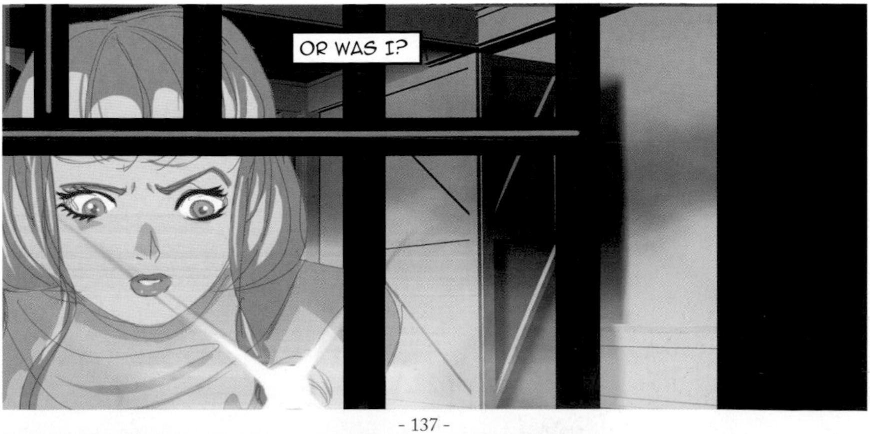
OR WAS I?

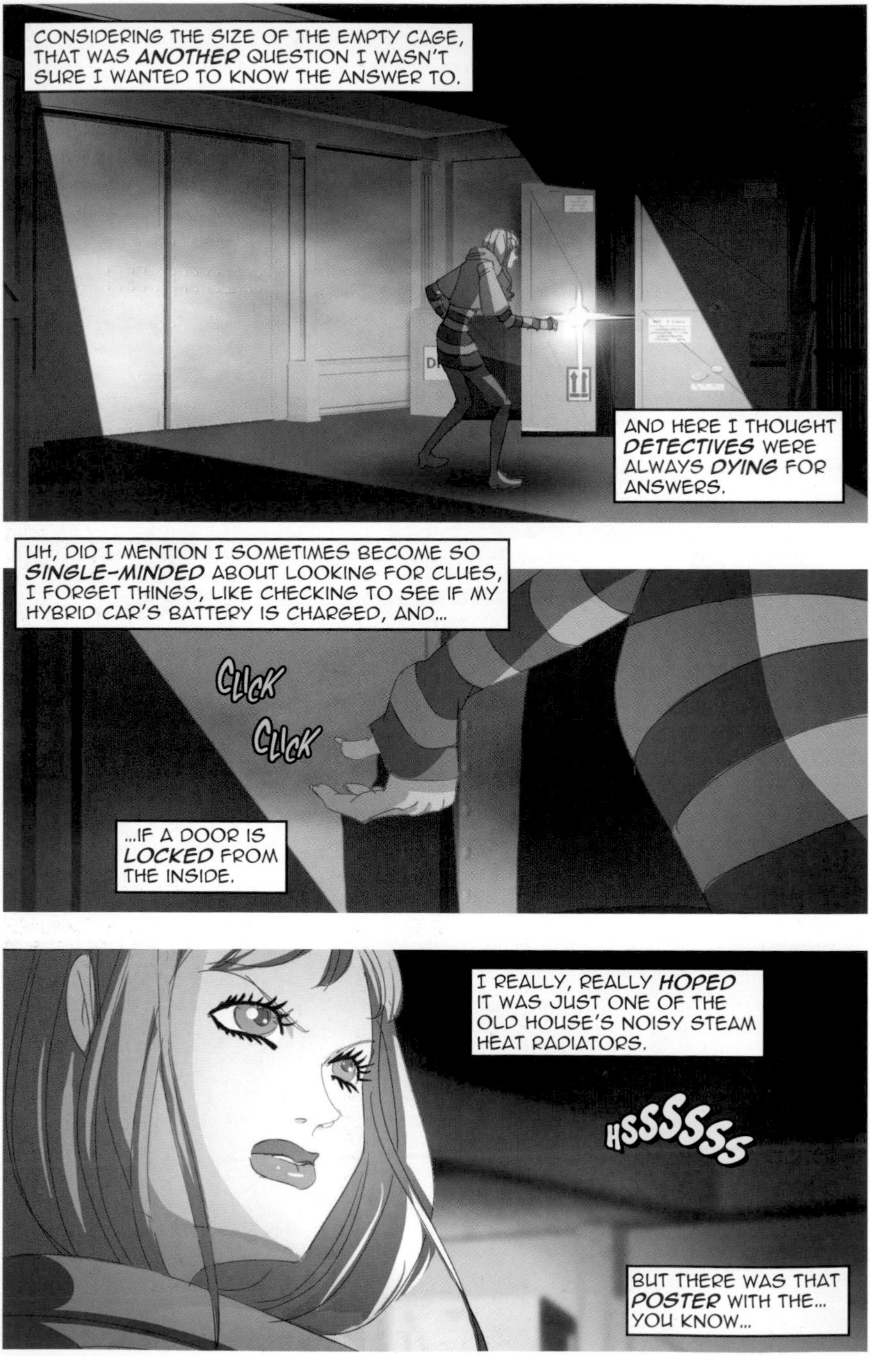
CONSIDERING THE SIZE OF THE EMPTY CAGE, THAT WAS ANOTHER QUESTION I WASN'T SURE I WANTED TO KNOW THE ANSWER TO.
AND HERE I THOUGHT DETECTIVES WERE ALWAYS DYING FOR ANSWERS.
UH, DID I MENTION I SOMETIMES BECOME SO SINGLE-MINDED ABOUT LOOKING FOR CLUES, I FORGET THINGS, LIKE CHECKING TO SEE IF MY HYBRID CAR'S BATTERY IS CHARGED, AND...
CLICK
CLICK
...IF A DOOR IS LOCKED FROM THE INSIDE.
I REALLY, REALLY HOPED IT WAS JUST ONE OF THE OLD HOUSE'S NOISY STEAM HEAT RADIATORS.
HSSSSSS
BUT THERE WAS THAT POSTER WITH THE... YOU KNOW...

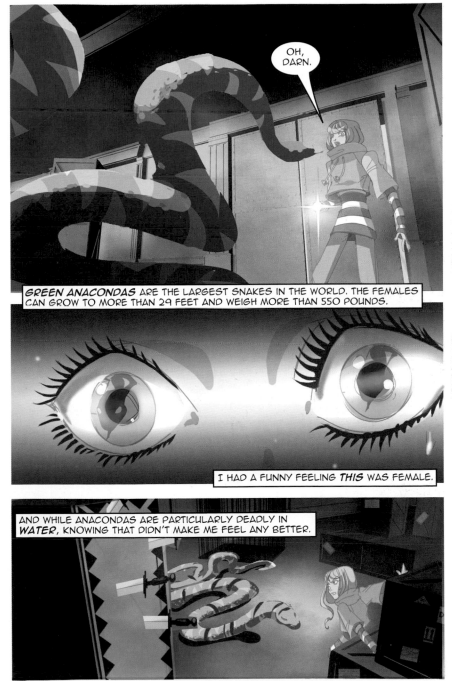

GREEN ANACONDAS ARE THE LARGEST SNAKES IN THE WORLD. THE FEMALES CAN GROW TO MORE THAN 29 FEET AND WEIGH MORE THAN 550 POUNDS.

I HAD A FUNNY FEELING *THIS* WAS FEMALE.

AND WHILE ANACONDAS ARE PARTICULARLY DEADLY IN *WATER*, KNOWING THAT DIDN'T MAKE ME FEEL ANY BETTER.

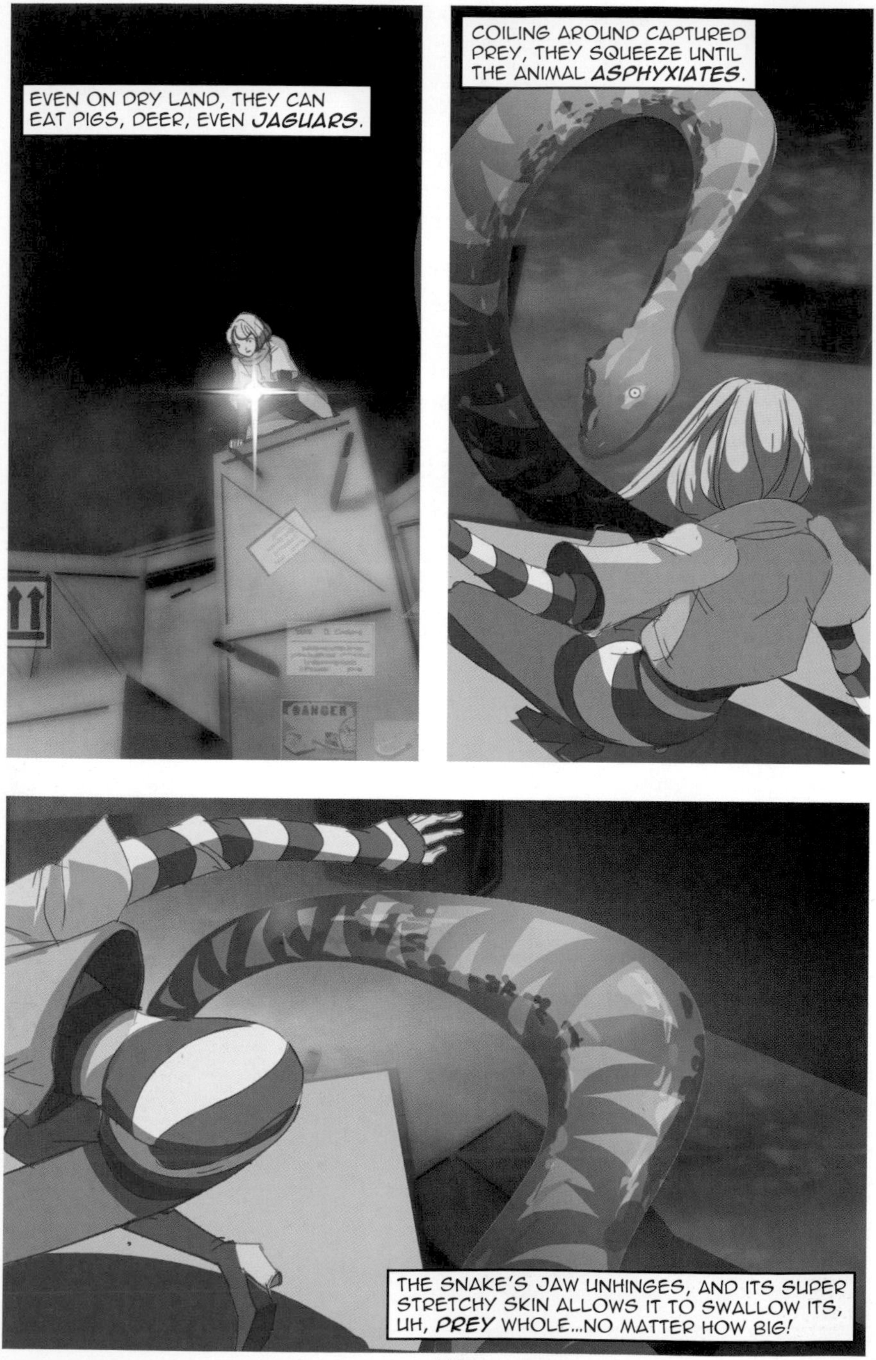
EVEN ON DRY LAND, THEY CAN EAT PIGS, DEER, EVEN *JAGUARS*.
COILING AROUND CAPTURED PREY, THEY SQUEEZE UNTIL THE ANIMAL *ASPHYXIATES*.
DANGER
THE SNAKE'S JAW UNHINGES, AND ITS SUPER STRETCHY SKIN ALLOWS IT TO SWALLOW ITS, UH, *PREY* WHOLE...NO MATTER HOW BIG!

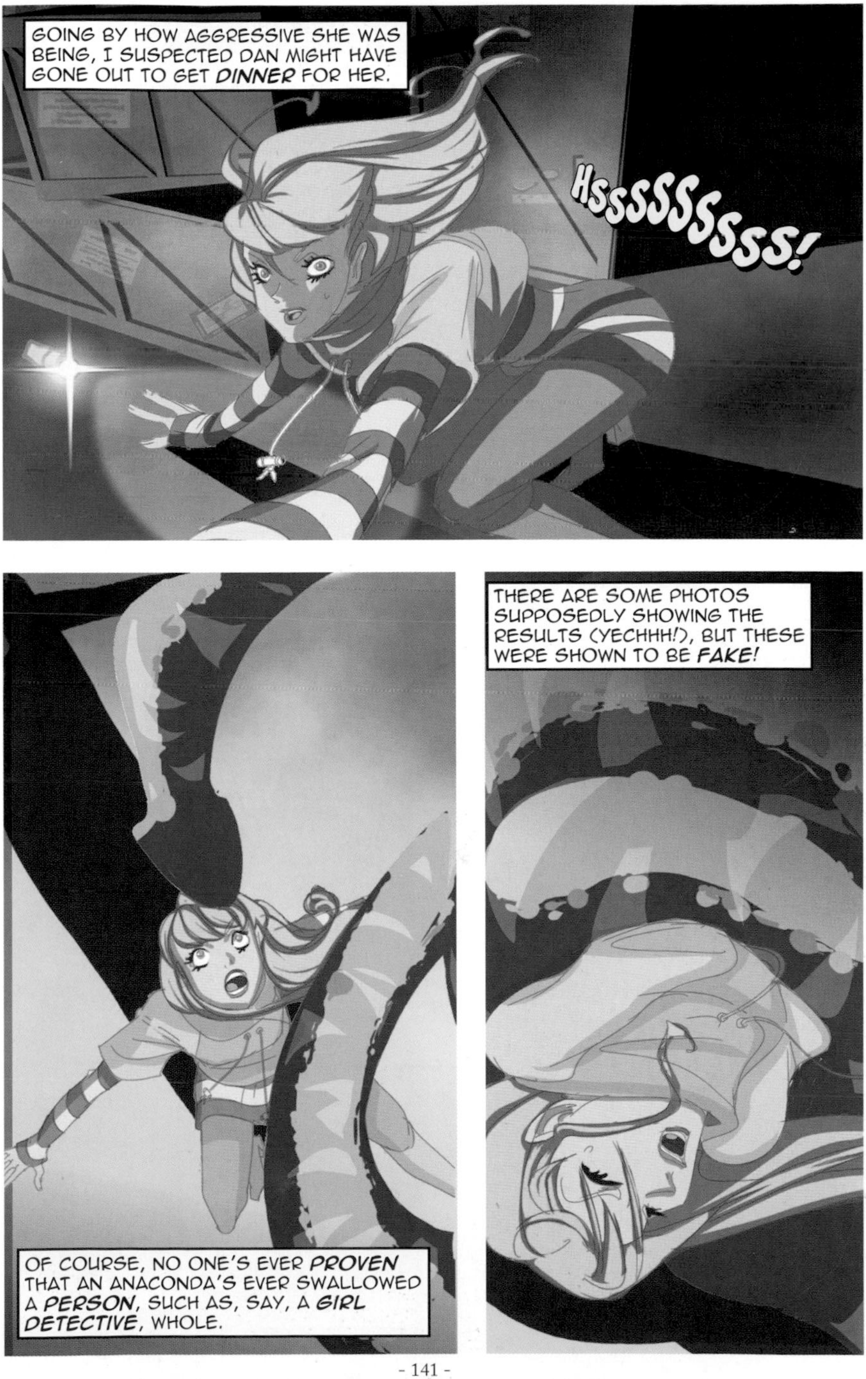
GOING BY HOW AGGRESSIVE SHE WAS BEING, I SUSPECTED DAN MIGHT HAVE GONE OUT TO GET *DINNER* FOR HER.
HsssSSSSsss!
OF COURSE, NO ONE'S EVER *PROVEN* THAT AN ANACONDA'S EVER SWALLOWED A *PERSON*, SUCH AS, SAY, A *GIRL DETECTIVE*, WHOLE.
THERE ARE SOME PHOTOS SUPPOSEDLY SHOWING THE RESULTS (YECHHH!), BUT THESE WERE SHOWN TO BE *FAKE!*

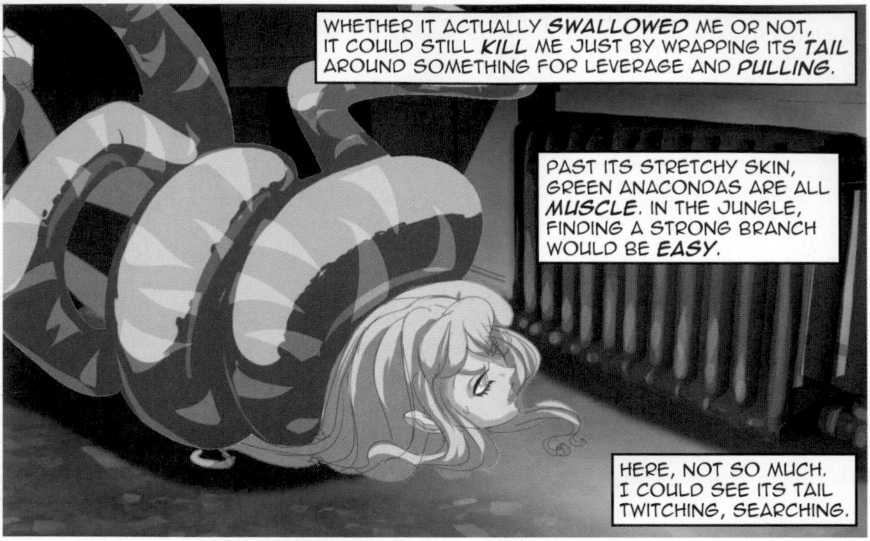
WHETHER IT ACTUALLY SWALLOWED ME OR NOT, IT COULD STILL KILL ME JUST BY WRAPPING ITS TAIL AROUND SOMETHING FOR LEVERAGE AND PULLING.
PAST ITS STRETCHY SKIN, GREEN ANACONDAS ARE ALL MUSCLE. IN THE JUNGLE, FINDING A STRONG BRANCH WOULD BE EASY.
HERE, NOT SO MUCH. I COULD SEE ITS TAIL TWITCHING, SEARCHING.

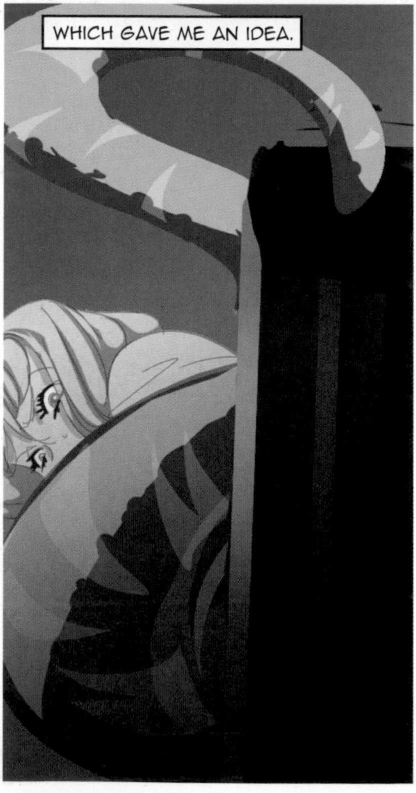
WHICH GAVE ME AN IDEA.

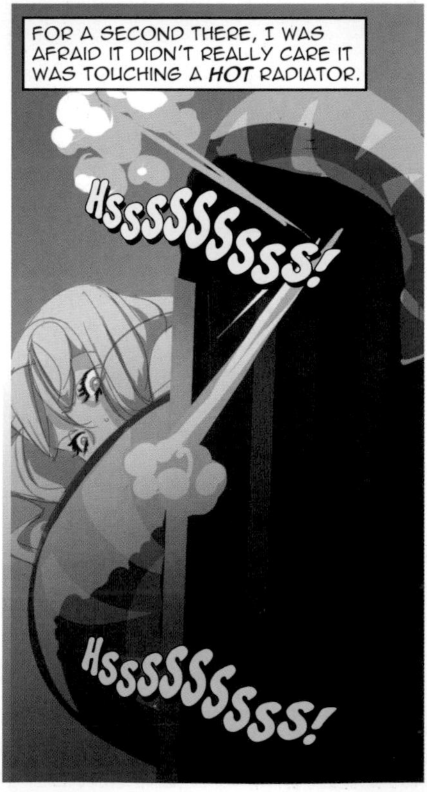
FOR A SECOND THERE, I WAS AFRAID IT DIDN'T REALLY CARE IT WAS TOUCHING A HOT RADIATOR.
HsssSSSSsss!
HsssSSSSsss!

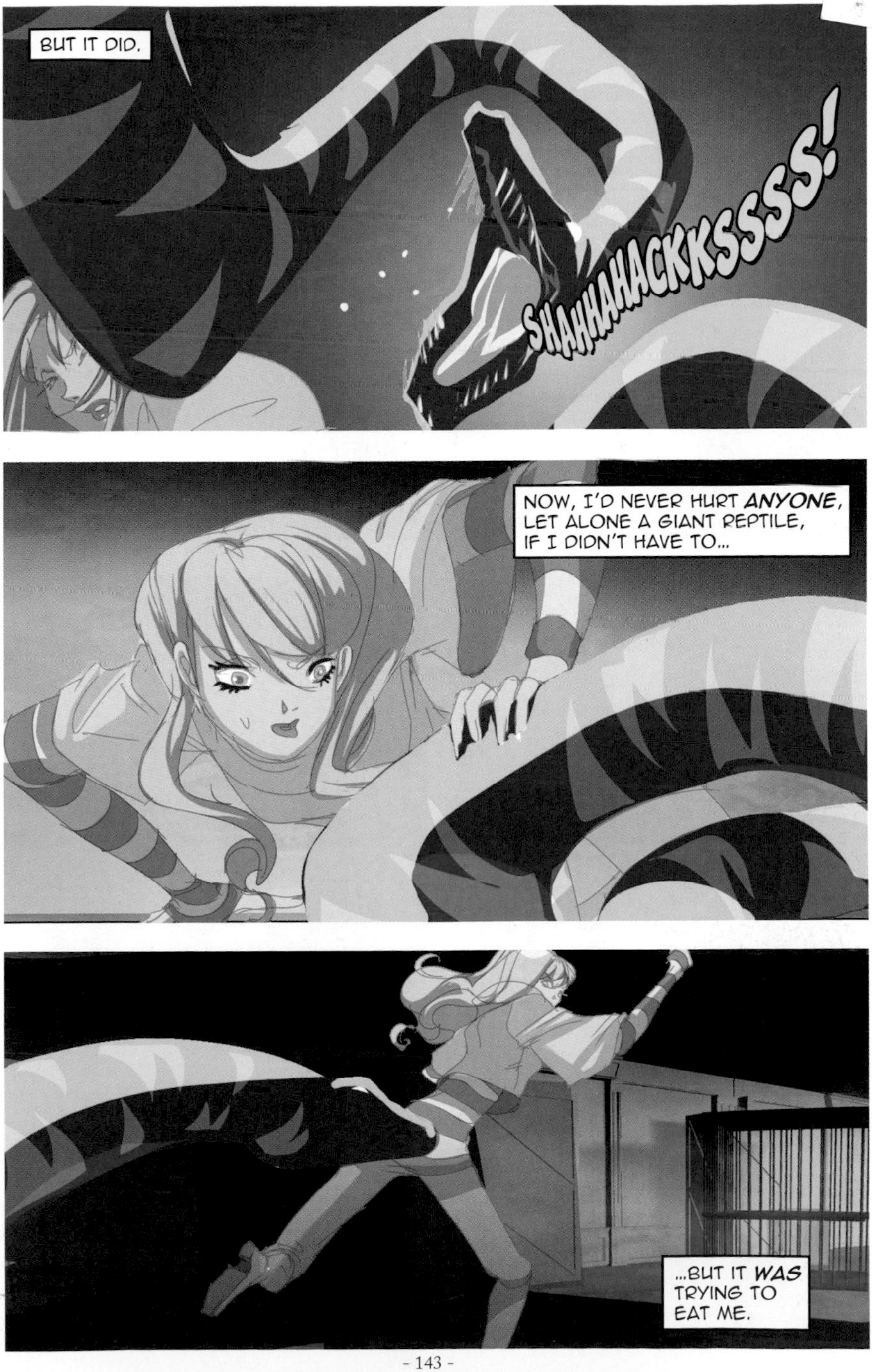
BUT IT DID.
SHAHHAHACKKSSSS!
NOW, I'D NEVER HURT ANYONE, LET ALONE A GIANT REPTILE, IF I DIDN'T HAVE TO...
...BUT IT WAS TRYING TO EAT ME.

MS. ANA CONDA PROBABLY WOULDN'T BE HAPPY ABOUT SEEING ME IN HER *HOME*, BUT I FIGURED IF THE BARS COULD KEEP HER *IN*, THEY COULD ALSO KEEP HER *OUT*!

CLINK!

BRRP

BRRP

MY CELL PHONE'S RINGING! I CAN GET *HELP*!

OH, NO! I MUST HAVE *DROPPED* IT OUTSIDE THE CAGE!

BRRP

BRRP

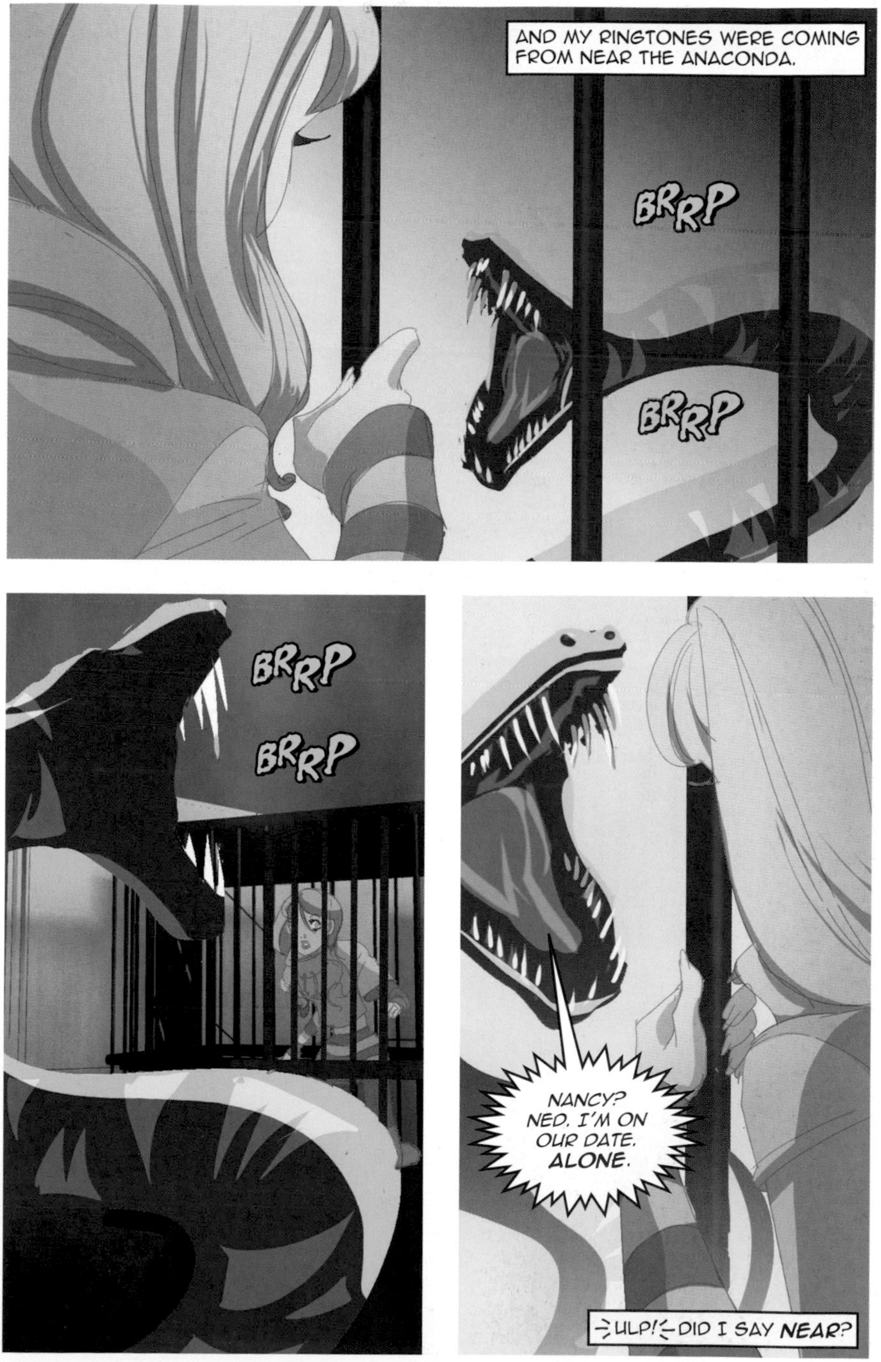

AND MY RINGTONES WERE COMING FROM NEAR THE ANACONDA.
BRRP
BRRP
BRRP
BRRP
NANCY? NED. I'M ON OUR DATE. **ALONE**.
–ULP!– DID I SAY **NEAR**?

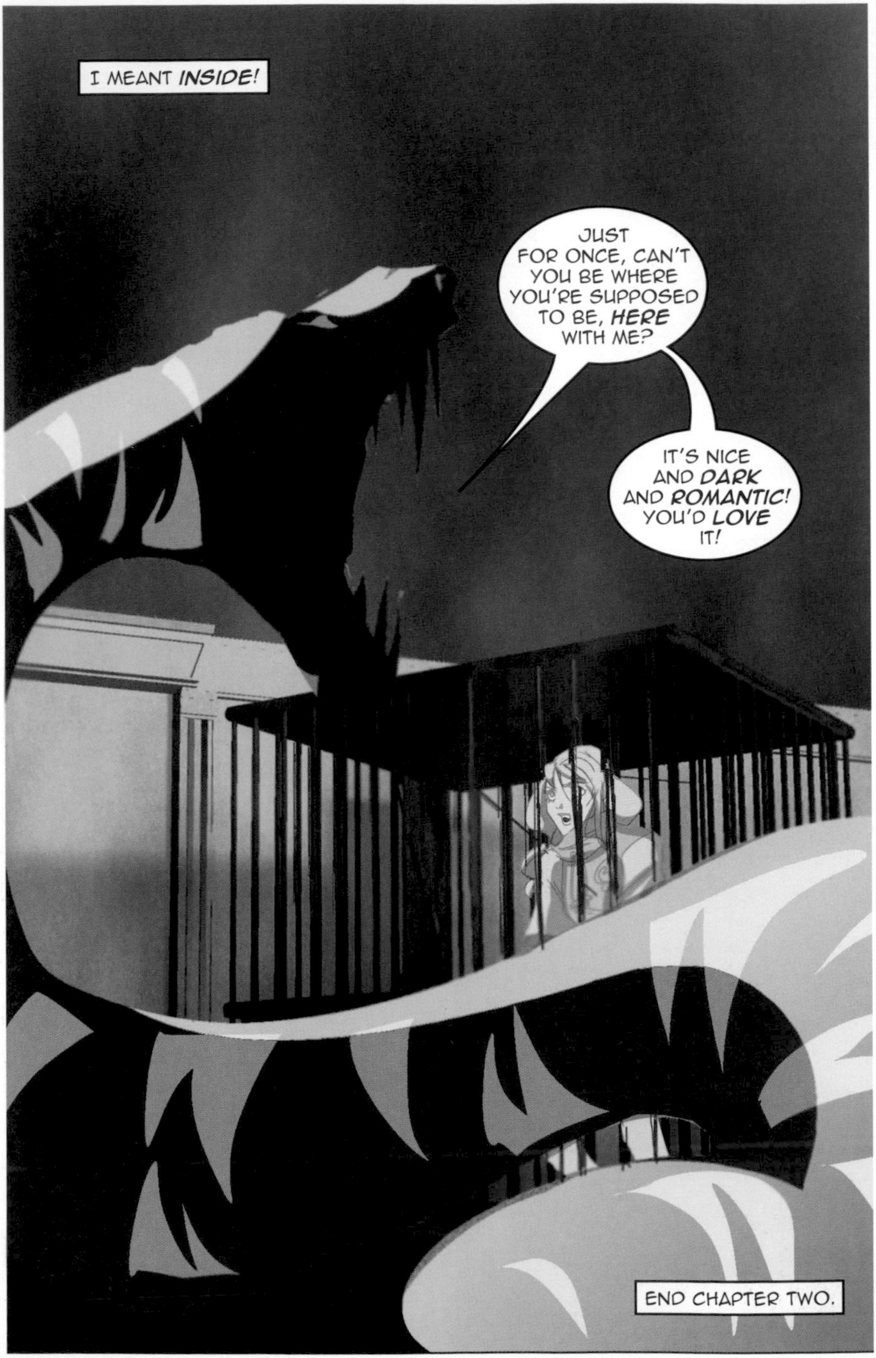
I MEANT *INSIDE!*
JUST FOR ONCE, CAN'T YOU BE WHERE YOU'RE SUPPOSED TO BE, *HERE* WITH ME?
IT'S NICE AND *DARK* AND *ROMANTIC!* YOU'D *LOVE* IT!
END CHAPTER TWO.

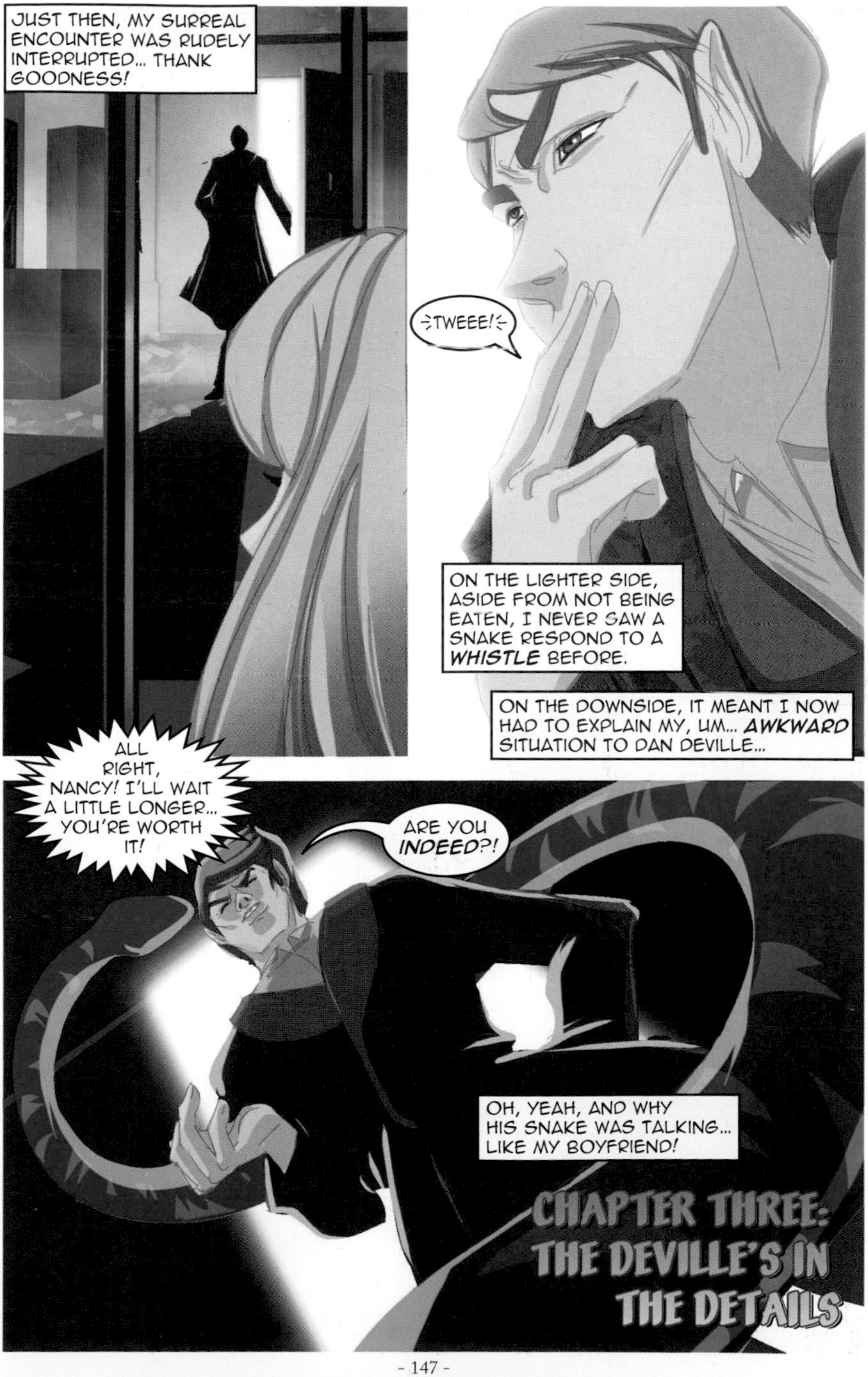
JUST THEN, MY SURREAL ENCOUNTER WAS RUDELY INTERRUPTED... THANK GOODNESS!
TWEEE!
ON THE LIGHTER SIDE, ASIDE FROM NOT BEING EATEN, I NEVER SAW A SNAKE RESPOND TO A *WHISTLE* BEFORE.
ON THE DOWNSIDE, IT MEANT I NOW HAD TO EXPLAIN MY, UM... *AWKWARD* SITUATION TO DAN DEVILLE...
ALL RIGHT, NANCY! I'LL WAIT A LITTLE LONGER... YOU'RE WORTH IT!
ARE YOU *INDEED*?!
OH, YEAH, AND WHY HIS SNAKE WAS TALKING... LIKE MY BOYFRIEND!
CHAPTER THREE: THE DEVILLE'S IN THE DETAILS

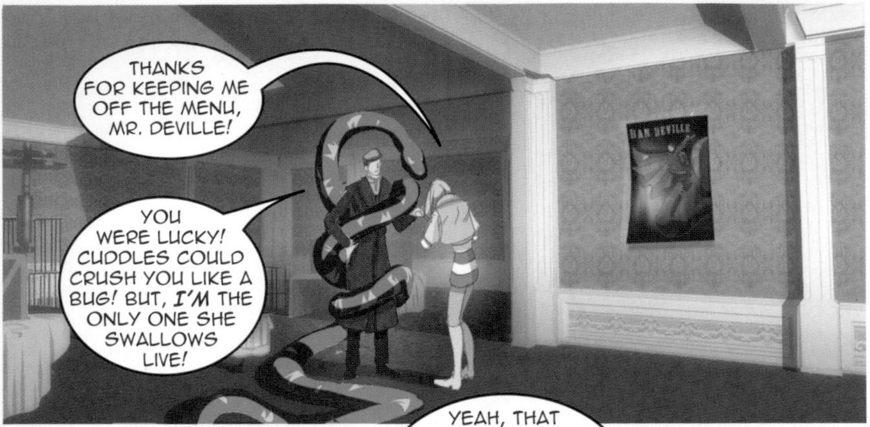
THANKS FOR KEEPING ME OFF THE MENU, MR. DEVILLE!
YOU WERE LUCKY! CUDDLES COULD CRUSH YOU LIKE A BUG! BUT, *I'M* THE ONLY ONE SHE SWALLOWS LIVE!
DAN DEVILLE

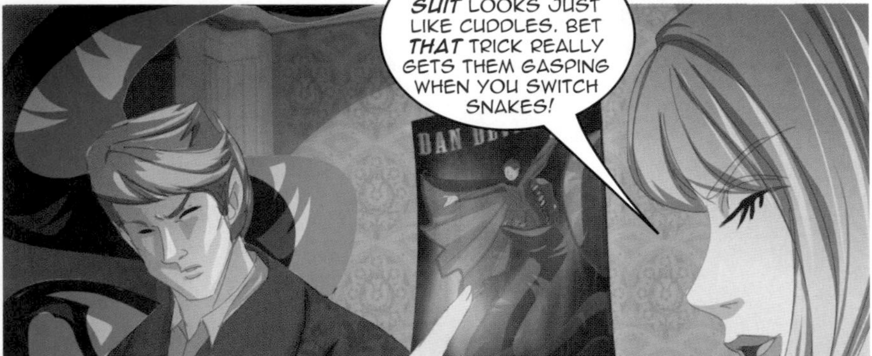
YEAH, THAT ***RUBBER SNAKE SUIT*** LOOKS JUST LIKE CUDDLES. BET ***THAT*** TRICK REALLY GETS THEM GASPING WHEN YOU SWITCH SNAKES!

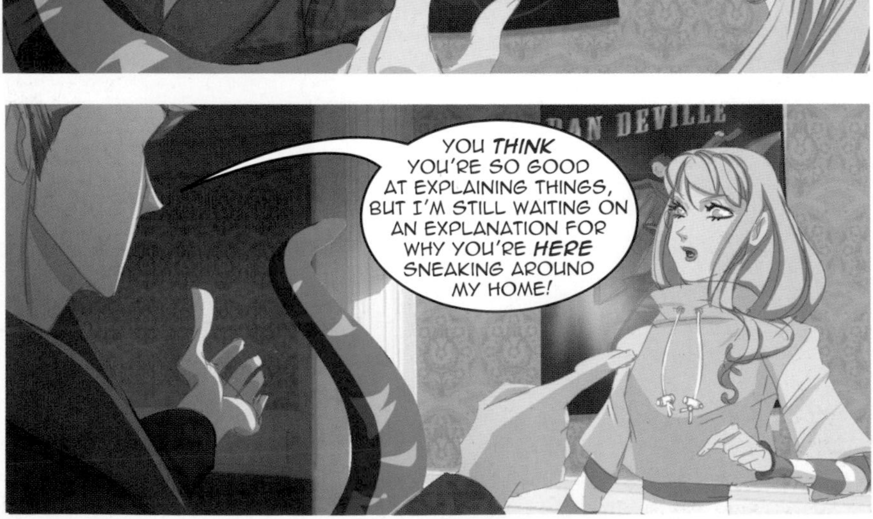
DAN DEVILLE
YOU ***THINK*** YOU'RE SO GOOD AT EXPLAINING THINGS, BUT I'M STILL WAITING ON AN EXPLANATION FOR WHY YOU'RE ***HERE*** SNEAKING AROUND MY HOME!

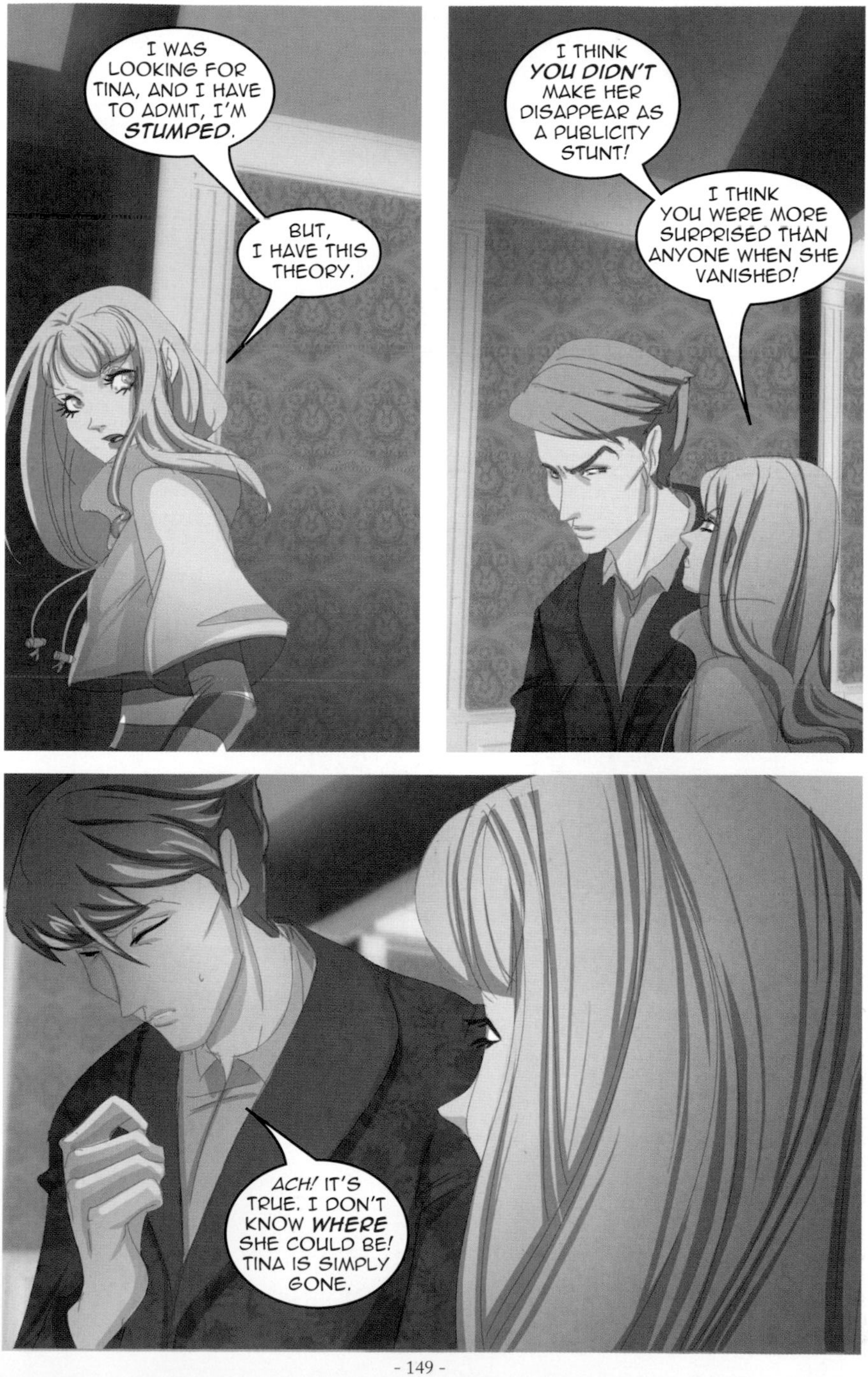
I WAS LOOKING FOR TINA, AND I HAVE TO ADMIT, I'M **STUMPED**.
BUT, I HAVE THIS THEORY.
I THINK **YOU DIDN'T** MAKE HER DISAPPEAR AS A PUBLICITY STUNT!
I THINK YOU WERE MORE SURPRISED THAN ANYONE WHEN SHE VANISHED!
ACH! IT'S TRUE. I DON'T KNOW **WHERE** SHE COULD BE! TINA IS SIMPLY GONE.

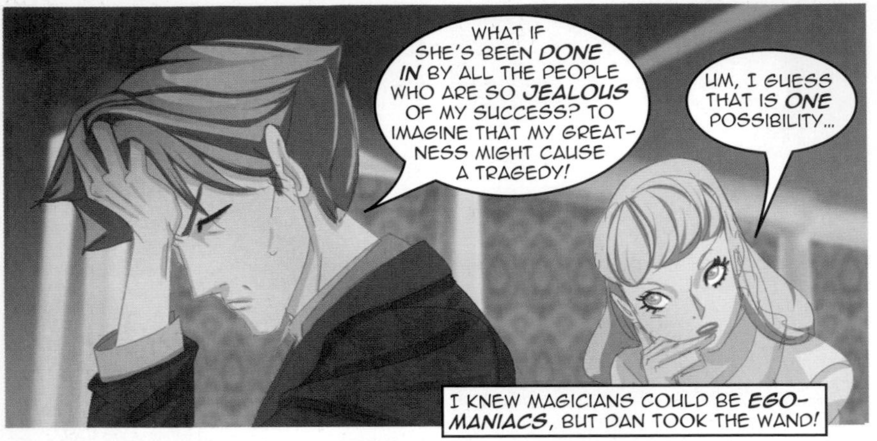
WHAT IF SHE'S BEEN *DONE IN* BY ALL THE PEOPLE WHO ARE SO *JEALOUS* OF MY SUCCESS? TO IMAGINE THAT MY GREAT-NESS MIGHT CAUSE A TRAGEDY!
UM, I GUESS THAT IS *ONE* POSSIBILITY...
I KNEW MAGICIANS COULD BE *EGO-MANIACS*, BUT DAN TOOK THE WAND!

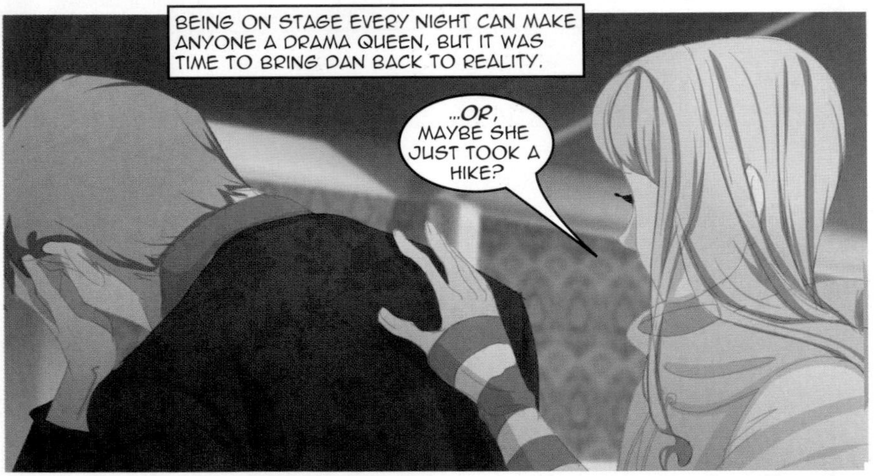
BEING ON STAGE EVERY NIGHT CAN MAKE ANYONE A DRAMA QUEEN, BUT IT WAS TIME TO BRING DAN BACK TO REALITY.
...*OR*, MAYBE SHE JUST TOOK A HIKE?

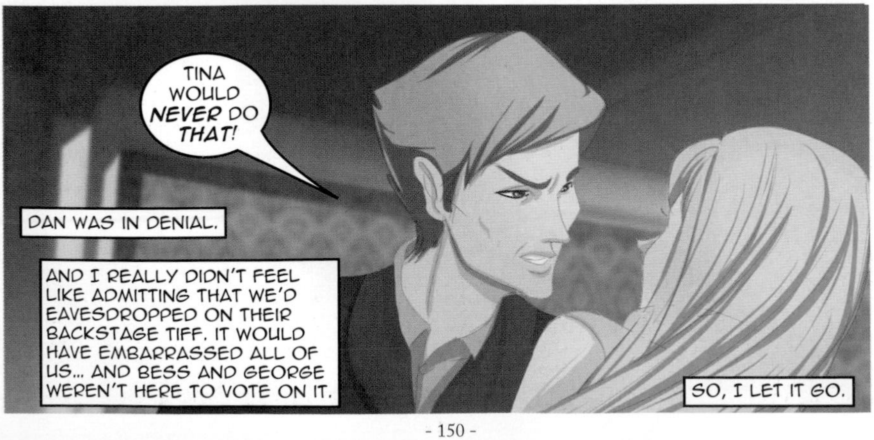
TINA WOULD *NEVER* DO *THAT*!
DAN WAS IN DENIAL.
AND I REALLY DIDN'T FEEL LIKE ADMITTING THAT WE'D EAVESDROPPED ON THEIR BACKSTAGE TIFF. IT WOULD HAVE EMBARRASSED ALL OF US... AND BESS AND GEORGE WEREN'T HERE TO VOTE ON IT.
SO, I LET IT GO.

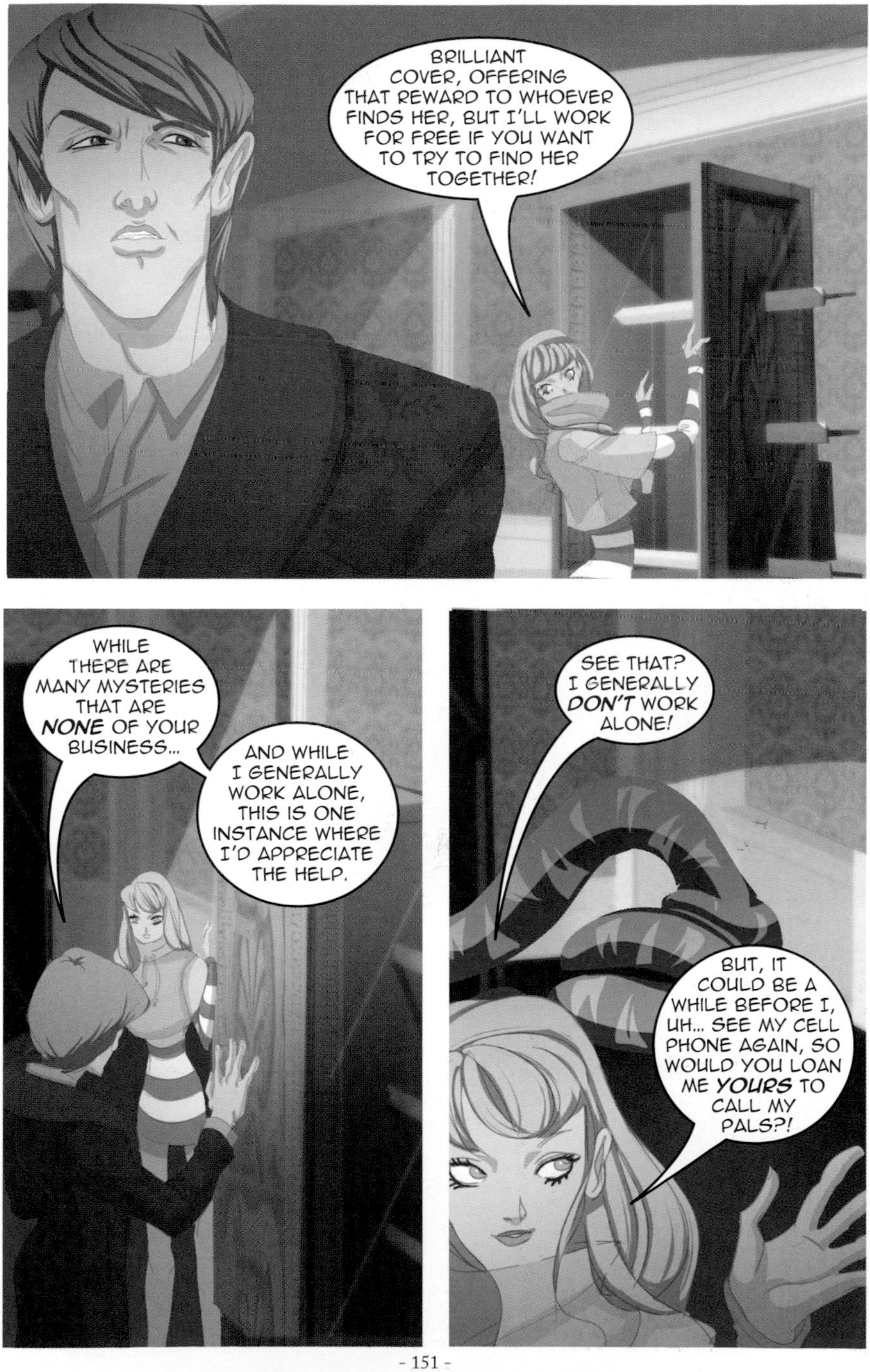

BRILLIANT COVER, OFFERING THAT REWARD TO WHOEVER FINDS HER, BUT I'LL WORK FOR FREE IF YOU WANT TO TRY TO FIND HER TOGETHER!
WHILE THERE ARE MANY MYSTERIES THAT ARE *NONE* OF YOUR BUSINESS...
AND WHILE I GENERALLY WORK ALONE, THIS IS ONE INSTANCE WHERE I'D APPRECIATE THE HELP.
SEE THAT? I GENERALLY *DON'T* WORK ALONE!
BUT, IT COULD BE A WHILE BEFORE I, UH... SEE MY CELL PHONE AGAIN, SO WOULD YOU LOAN ME *YOURS* TO CALL MY PALS?!

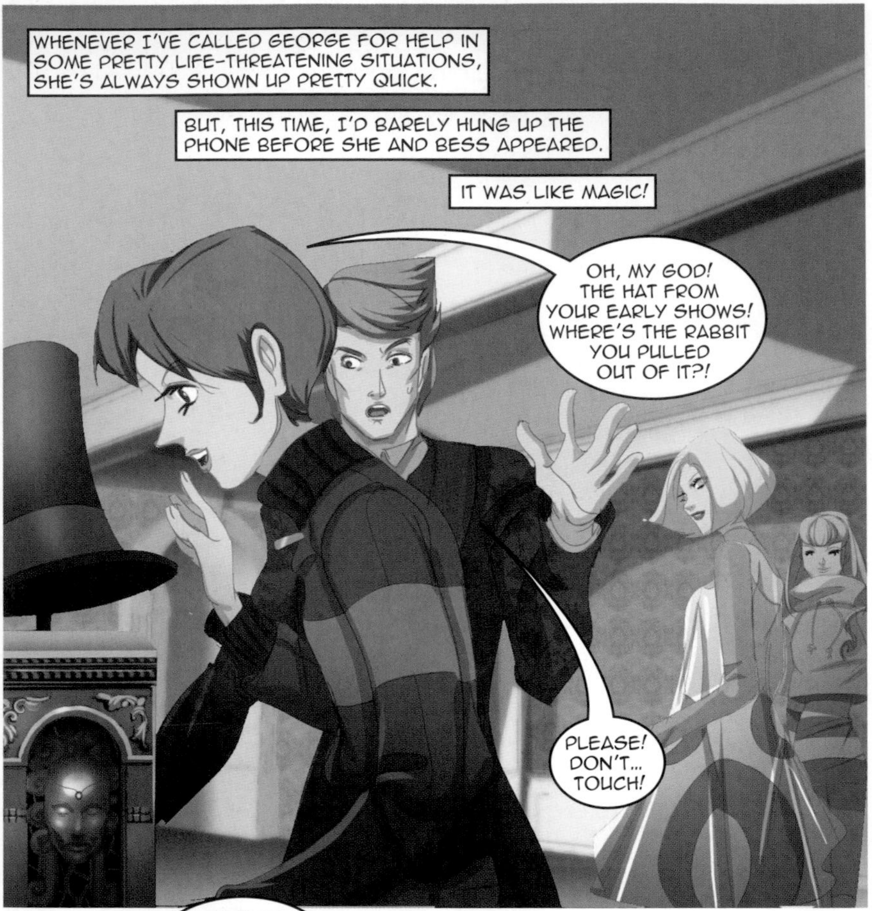
WHENEVER I'VE CALLED GEORGE FOR HELP IN SOME PRETTY LIFE-THREATENING SITUATIONS, SHE'S ALWAYS SHOWN UP PRETTY QUICK.
BUT, THIS TIME, I'D BARELY HUNG UP THE PHONE BEFORE SHE AND BESS APPEARED.
IT WAS LIKE MAGIC!
OH, MY GOD! THE HAT FROM YOUR EARLY SHOWS! WHERE'S THE RABBIT YOU PULLED OUT OF IT?!
PLEASE! DON'T... TOUCH!

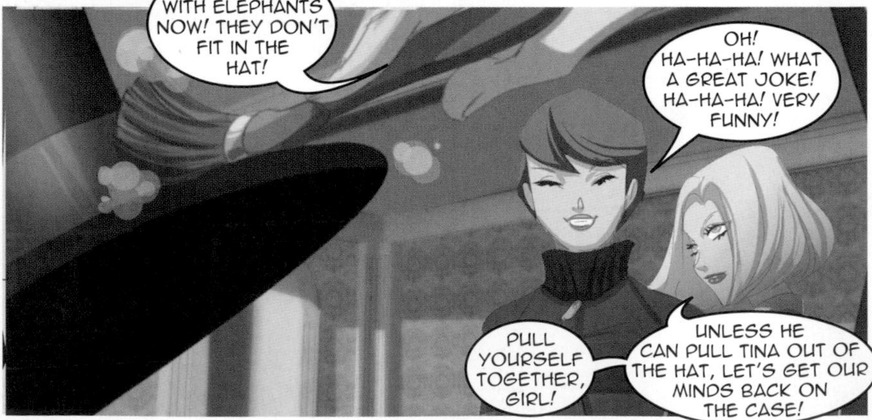
I WORK WITH ELEPHANTS NOW! THEY DON'T FIT IN THE HAT!
OH! HA-HA-HA! WHAT A GREAT JOKE! HA-HA-HA! VERY FUNNY!
PULL YOURSELF TOGETHER, GIRL!
UNLESS HE CAN PULL TINA OUT OF THE HAT, LET'S GET OUR MINDS BACK ON THE CASE!

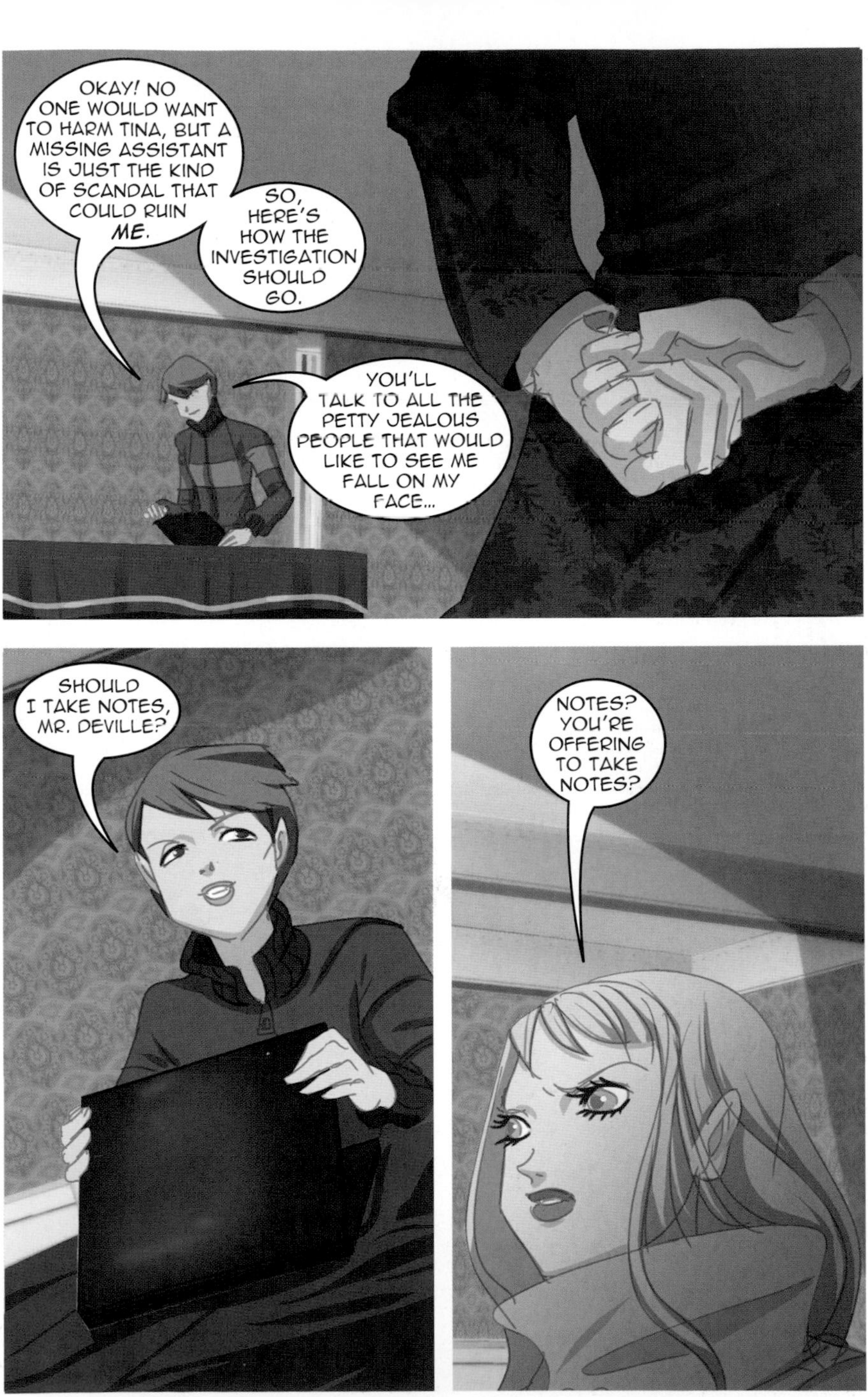
OKAY! NO ONE WOULD WANT TO HARM TINA, BUT A MISSING ASSISTANT IS JUST THE KIND OF SCANDAL THAT COULD RUIN ME.
SO, HERE'S HOW THE INVESTIGATION SHOULD GO.
YOU'LL TALK TO ALL THE PETTY JEALOUS PEOPLE THAT WOULD LIKE TO SEE ME FALL ON MY FACE...
SHOULD I TAKE NOTES, MR. DEVILLE?
NOTES? YOU'RE OFFERING TO TAKE NOTES?

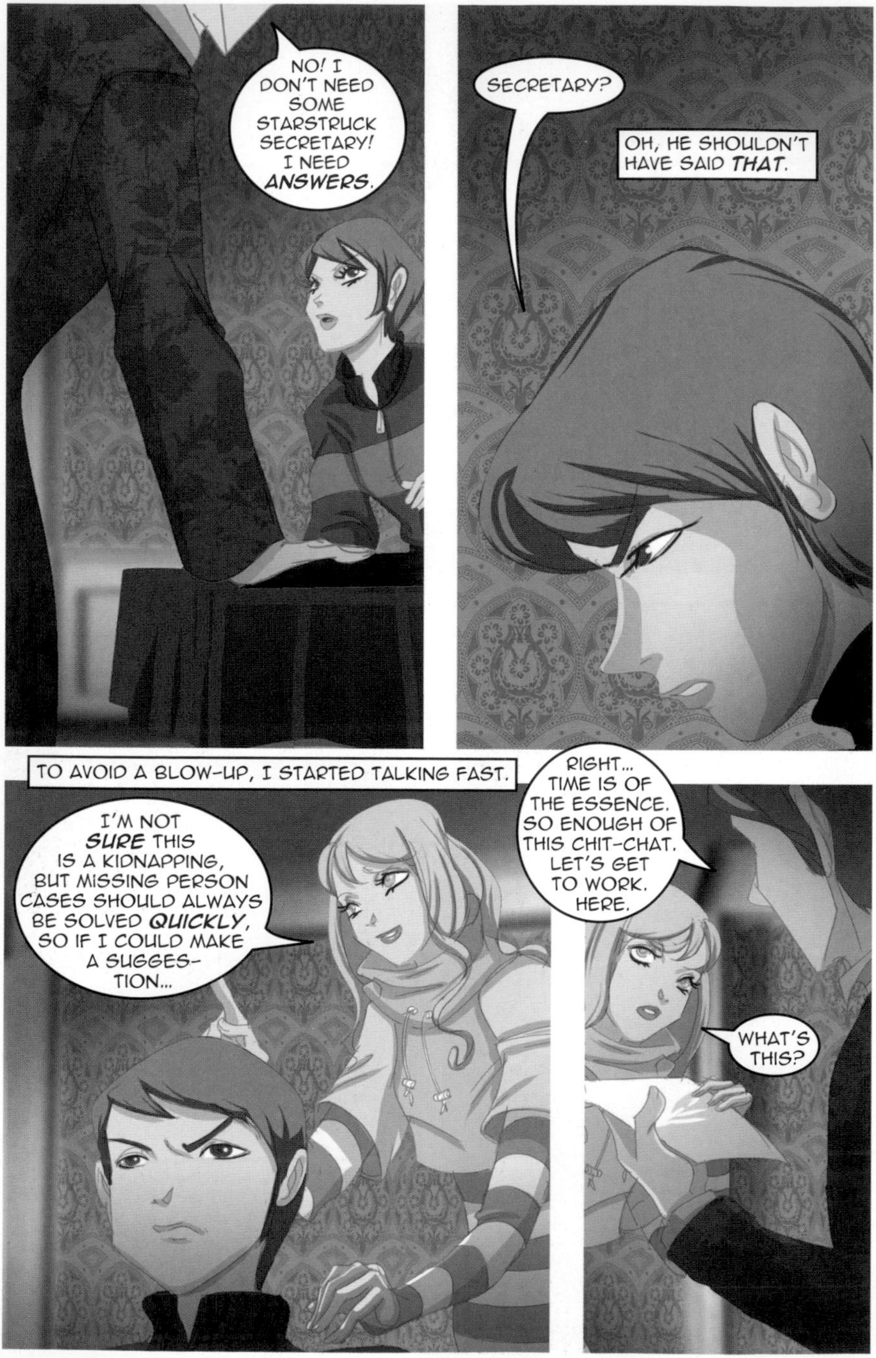
NO! I DON'T NEED SOME STARSTRUCK SECRETARY! I NEED ANSWERS.
SECRETARY?
OH, HE SHOULDN'T HAVE SAID THAT.
TO AVOID A BLOW-UP, I STARTED TALKING FAST.
I'M NOT SURE THIS IS A KIDNAPPING, BUT MISSING PERSON CASES SHOULD ALWAYS BE SOLVED QUICKLY, SO IF I COULD MAKE A SUGGES-TION...
RIGHT... TIME IS OF THE ESSENCE. SO ENOUGH OF THIS CHIT-CHAT. LET'S GET TO WORK. HERE.
WHAT'S THIS?

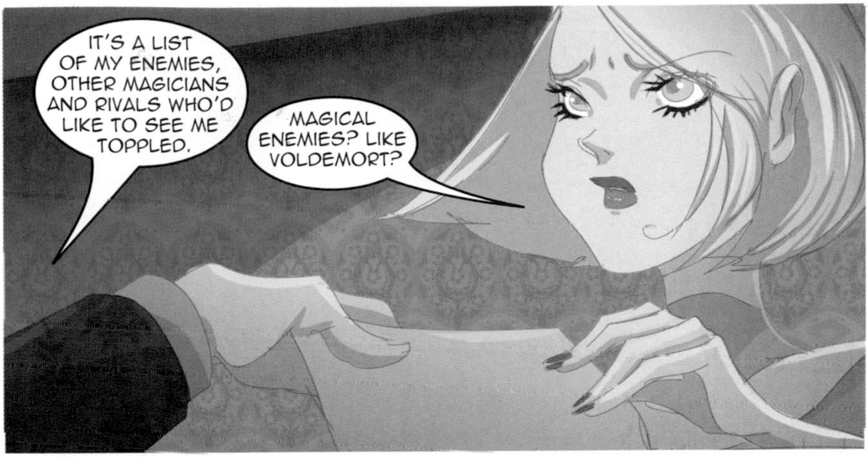
IT'S A LIST OF MY ENEMIES, OTHER MAGICIANS AND RIVALS WHO'D LIKE TO SEE ME TOPPLED.
MAGICAL ENEMIES? LIKE VOLDEMORT?

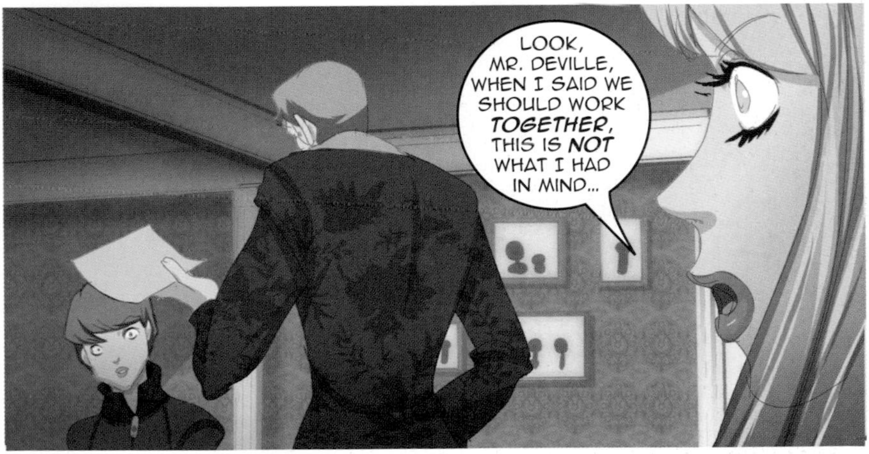
LOOK, MR. DEVILLE, WHEN I SAID WE SHOULD WORK *TOGETHER*, THIS IS *NOT* WHAT I HAD IN MIND...

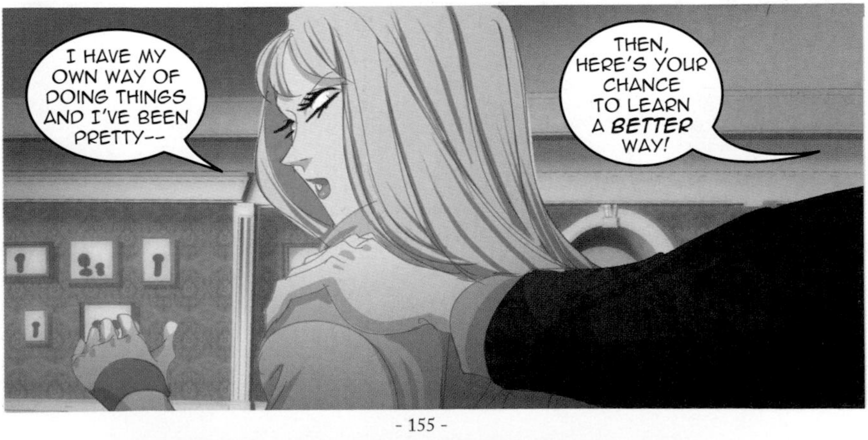
I HAVE MY OWN WAY OF DOING THINGS AND I'VE BEEN PRETTY--
THEN, HERE'S YOUR CHANCE TO LEARN A *BETTER* WAY!

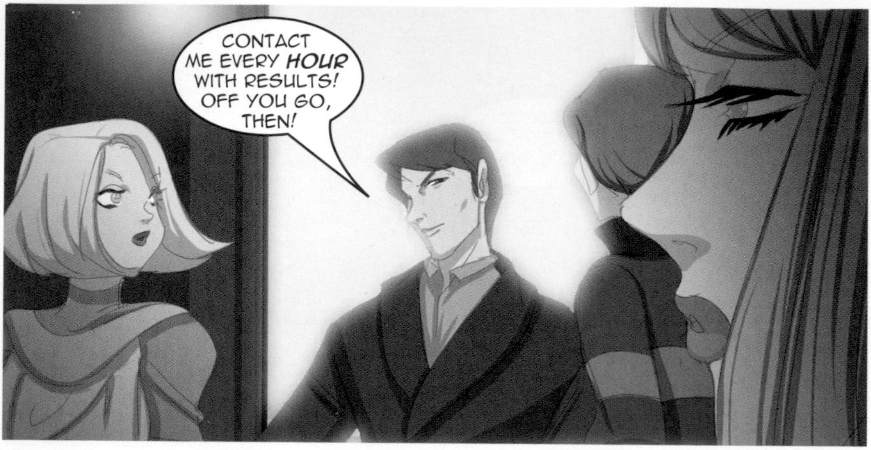
CONTACT ME EVERY HOUR WITH RESULTS! OFF YOU GO, THEN!

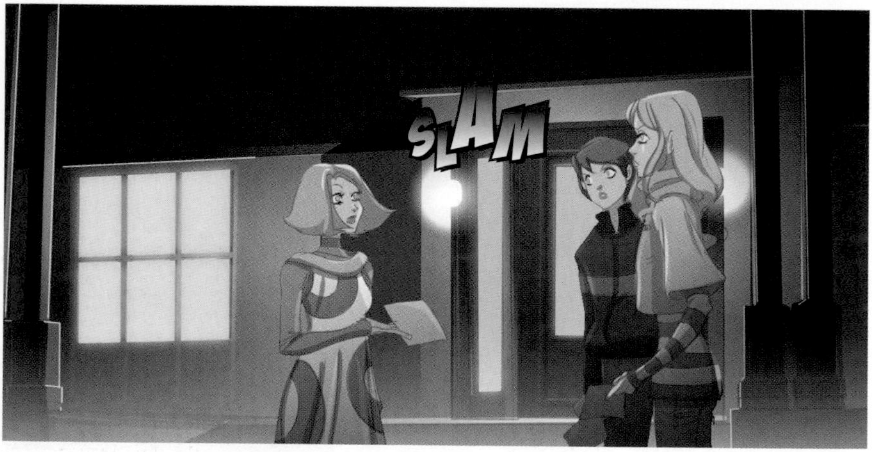
SLAM

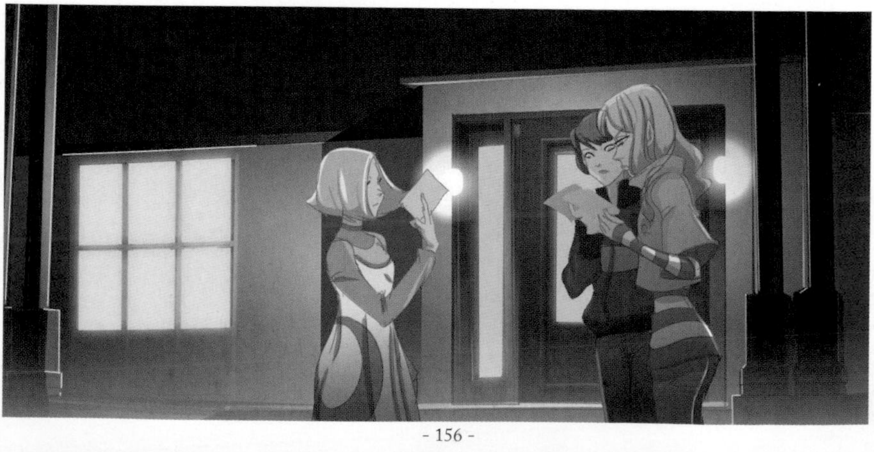

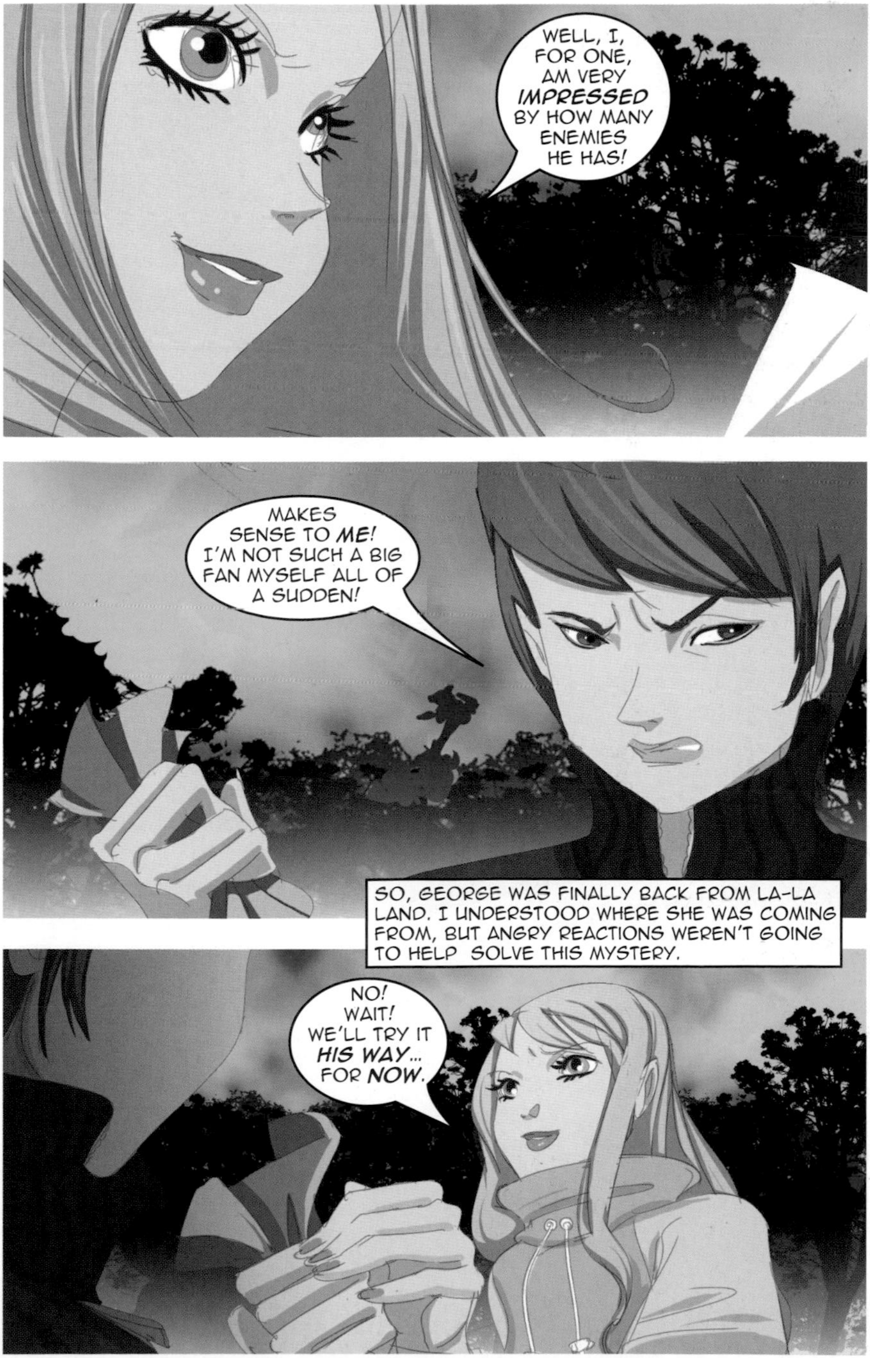
WELL, I, FOR ONE, AM VERY *IMPRESSED* BY HOW MANY ENEMIES HE HAS!
MAKES SENSE TO *ME*! I'M NOT SUCH A BIG FAN MYSELF ALL OF A SUDDEN!
SO, GEORGE WAS FINALLY BACK FROM LA-LA LAND. I UNDERSTOOD WHERE SHE WAS COMING FROM, BUT ANGRY REACTIONS WEREN'T GOING TO HELP SOLVE THIS MYSTERY.
NO! WAIT! WE'LL TRY IT *HIS WAY*... FOR *NOW*.

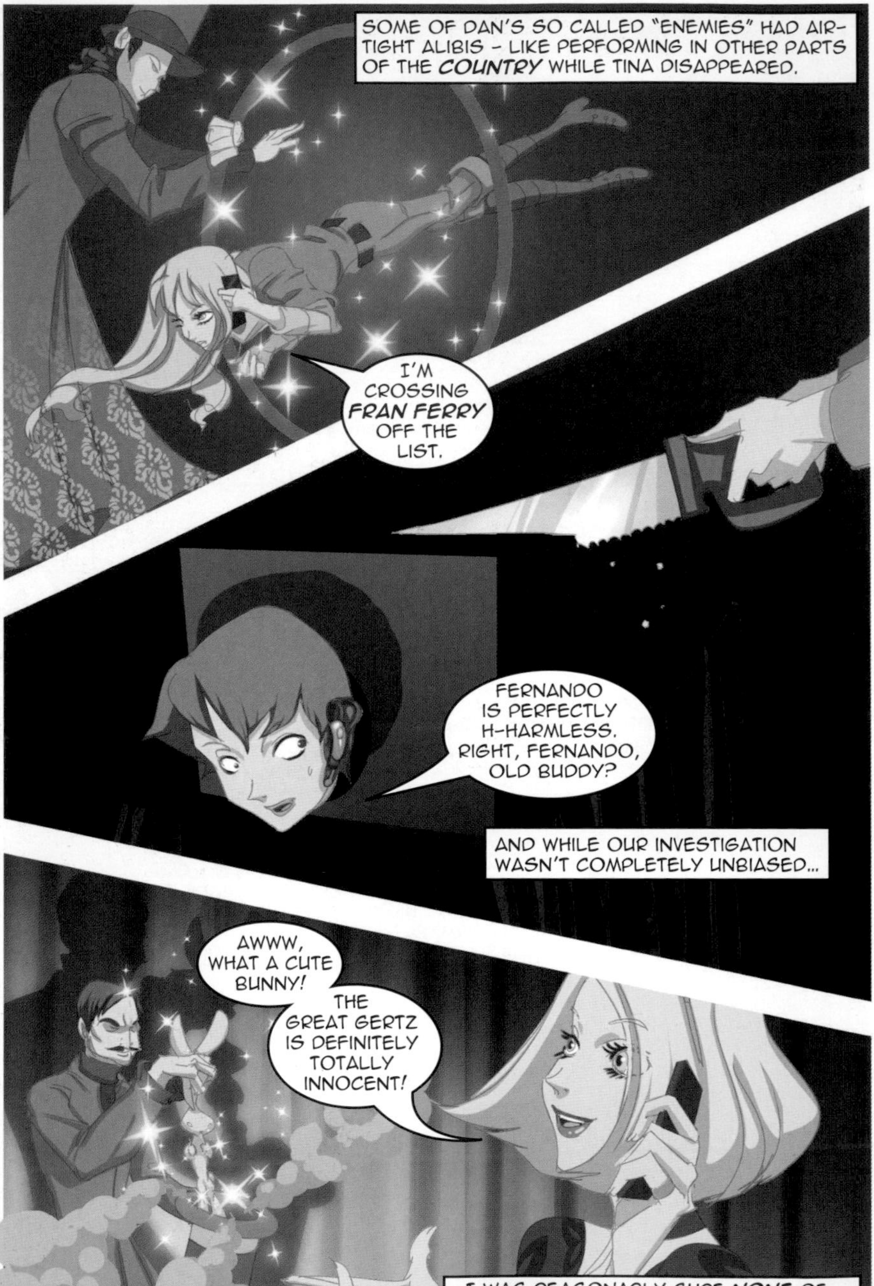
SOME OF DAN'S SO CALLED "ENEMIES" HAD AIR-TIGHT ALIBIS - LIKE PERFORMING IN OTHER PARTS OF THE *COUNTRY* WHILE TINA DISAPPEARED.
I'M CROSSING *FRAN FERRY* OFF THE LIST.
FERNANDO IS PERFECTLY H-HARMLESS. RIGHT, FERNANDO, OLD BUDDY?
AND WHILE OUR INVESTIGATION WASN'T COMPLETELY UNBIASED...
AWWW, WHAT A CUTE BUNNY!
THE GREAT GERTZ IS DEFINITELY TOTALLY INNOCENT!
...I WAS REASONABLY SURE *NONE* OF THE MAGICIANS WE VISITED WERE NEARLY AS OBSESSED WITH DAN AS DAN WAS!

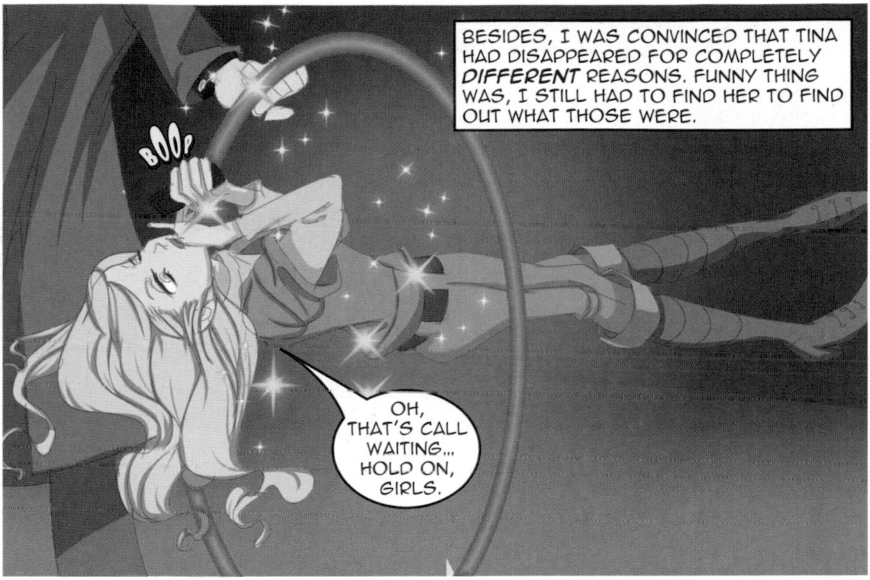
BESIDES, I WAS CONVINCED THAT TINA HAD DISAPPEARED FOR COMPLETELY **DIFFERENT** REASONS. FUNNY THING WAS, I STILL HAD TO FIND HER TO FIND OUT WHAT THOSE WERE.
BOOP
OH, THAT'S CALL WAITING... HOLD ON, GIRLS.

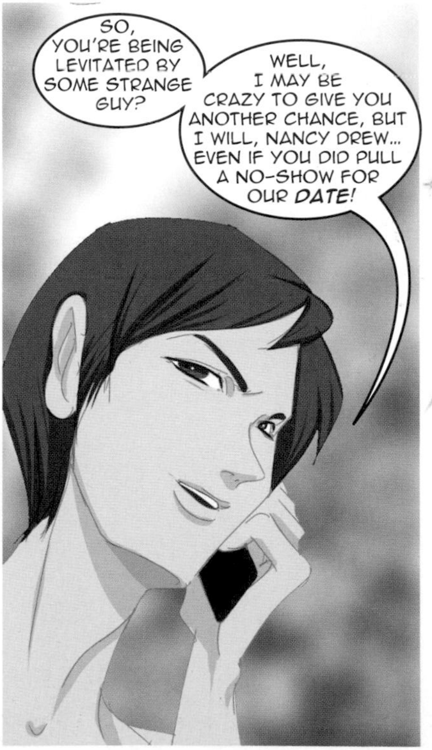
SO, YOU'RE BEING LEVITATED BY SOME STRANGE GUY?
WELL, I MAY BE CRAZY TO GIVE YOU ANOTHER CHANCE, BUT I WILL, NANCY DREW... EVEN IF YOU DID PULL A NO-SHOW FOR OUR **DATE**!

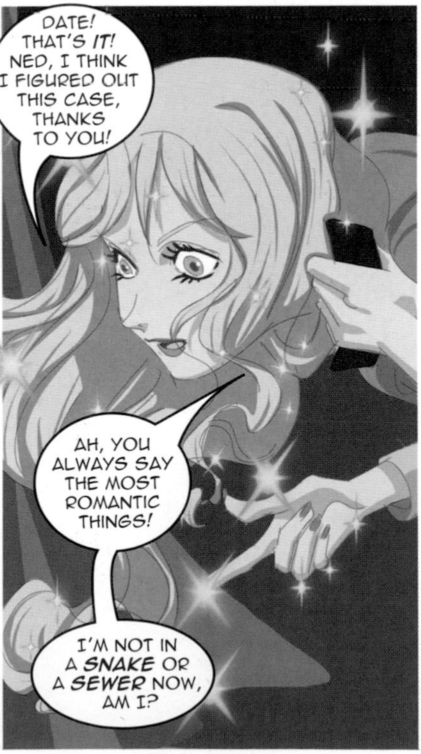
DATE! THAT'S *IT*! NED, I THINK I FIGURED OUT THIS CASE, THANKS TO YOU!
AH, YOU ALWAYS SAY THE MOST ROMANTIC THINGS!
I'M NOT IN A **SNAKE** OR A **SEWER** NOW, AM I?

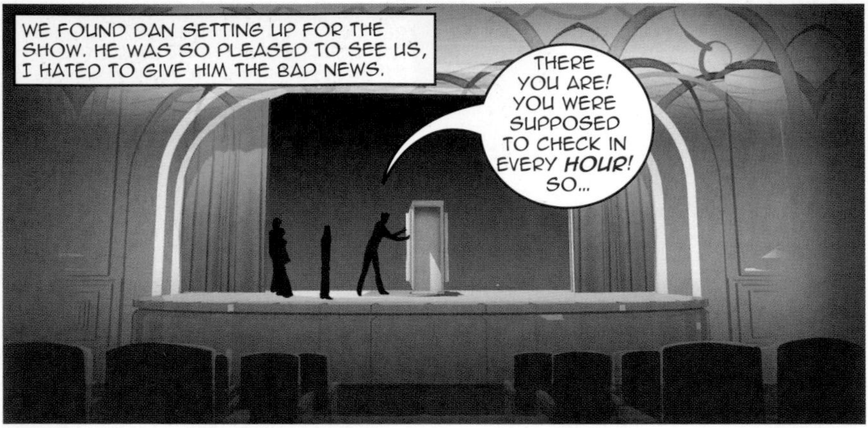
WE FOUND DAN SETTING UP FOR THE SHOW. HE WAS SO PLEASED TO SEE US, I HATED TO GIVE HIM THE BAD NEWS.
THERE YOU ARE! YOU WERE SUPPOSED TO CHECK IN EVERY HOUR! SO...

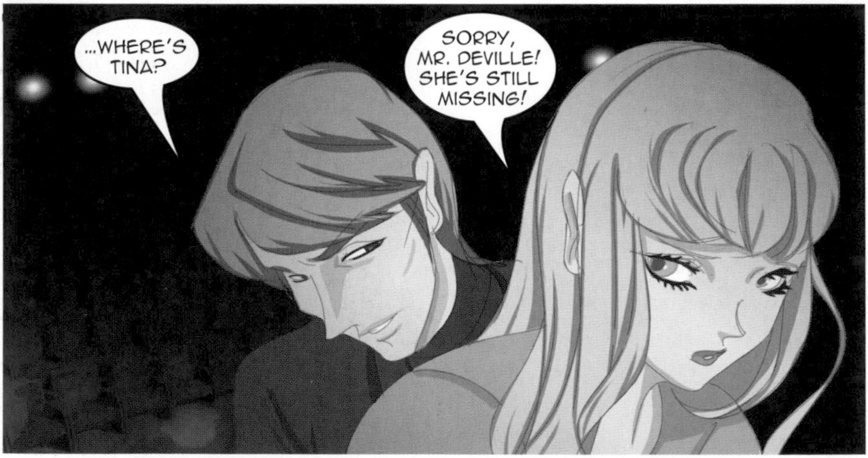
...WHERE'S TINA?
SORRY, MR. DEVILLE! SHE'S STILL MISSING!

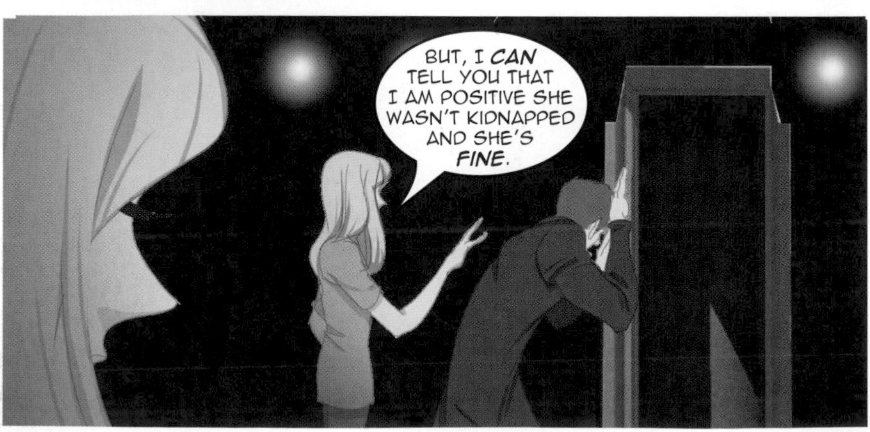
BUT, I CAN TELL YOU THAT I AM POSITIVE SHE WASN'T KIDNAPPED AND SHE'S FINE.

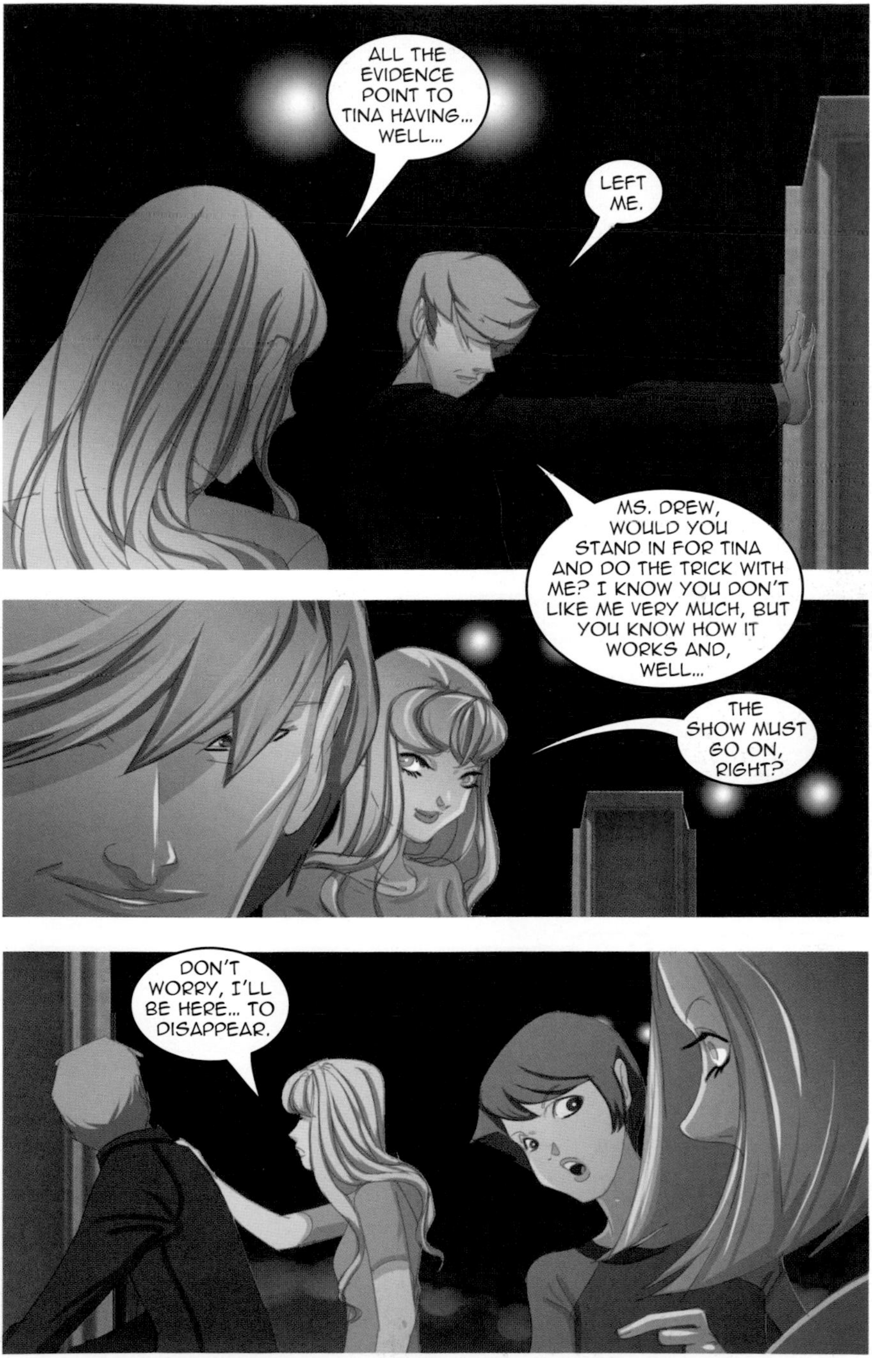

ALL THE EVIDENCE POINT TO TINA HAVING... WELL...
LEFT ME.
MS. DREW, WOULD YOU STAND IN FOR TINA AND DO THE TRICK WITH ME? I KNOW YOU DON'T LIKE ME VERY MUCH, BUT YOU KNOW HOW IT WORKS AND, WELL...
THE SHOW MUST GO ON, RIGHT?
DON'T WORRY, I'LL BE HERE... TO DISAPPEAR.

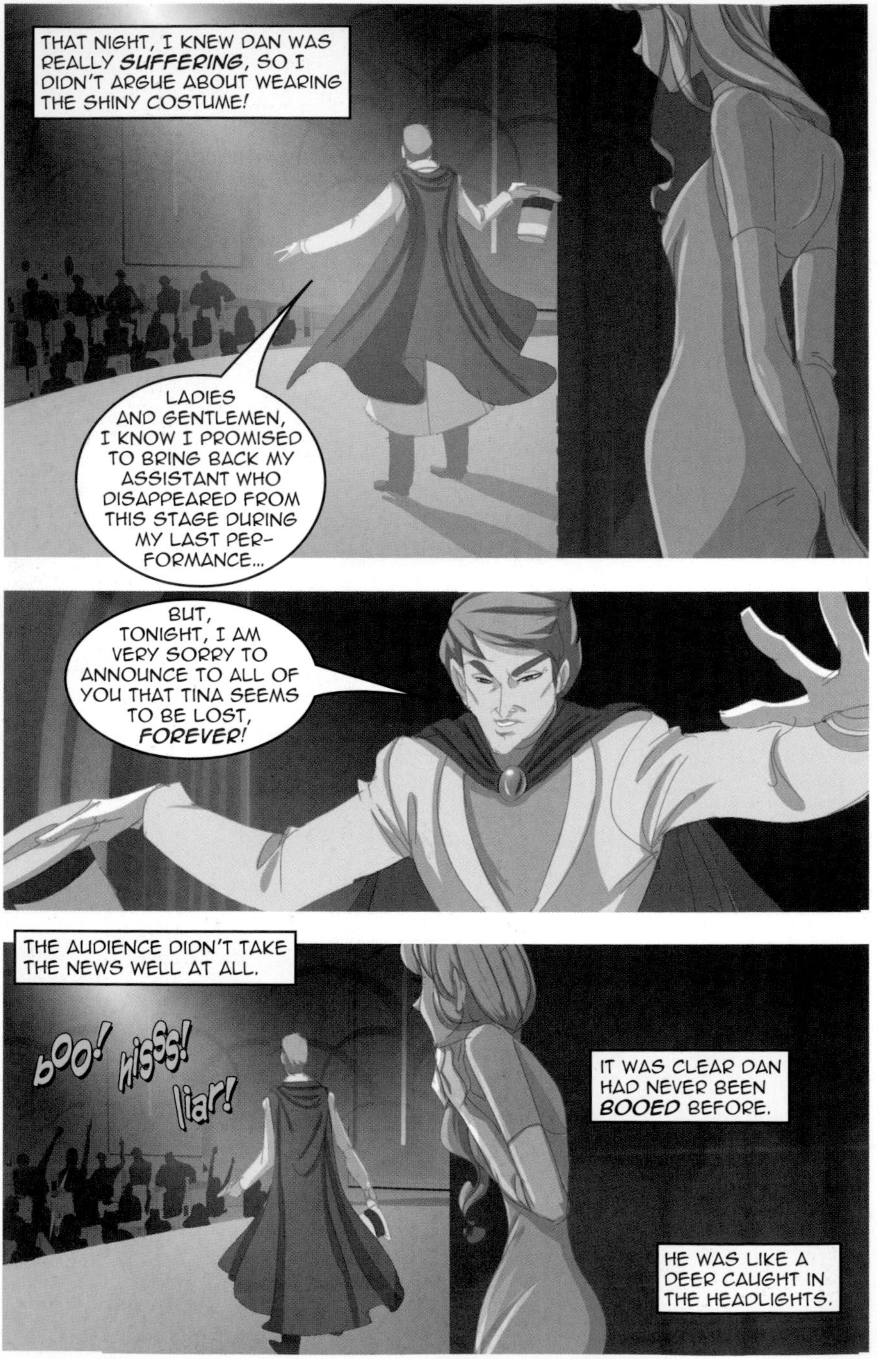
THAT NIGHT, I KNEW DAN WAS REALLY **SUFFERING**, SO I DIDN'T ARGUE ABOUT WEARING THE SHINY COSTUME!
LADIES AND GENTLEMEN, I KNOW I PROMISED TO BRING BACK MY ASSISTANT WHO DISAPPEARED FROM THIS STAGE DURING MY LAST PER-FORMANCE...
BUT, TONIGHT, I AM VERY SORRY TO ANNOUNCE TO ALL OF YOU THAT TINA SEEMS TO BE LOST, **FOREVER**!
THE AUDIENCE DIDN'T TAKE THE NEWS WELL AT ALL.
bOO! hiSSS! liar!
IT WAS CLEAR DAN HAD NEVER BEEN **BOOED** BEFORE.
HE WAS LIKE A DEER CAUGHT IN THE HEADLIGHTS.

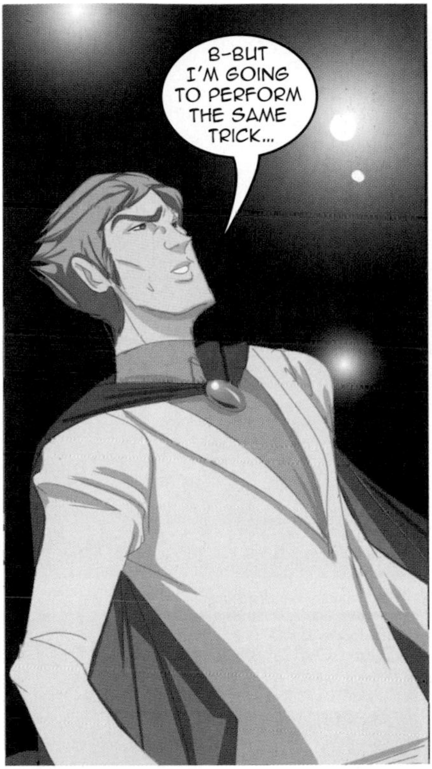
B-BUT I'M GOING TO PERFORM THE SAME TRICK...

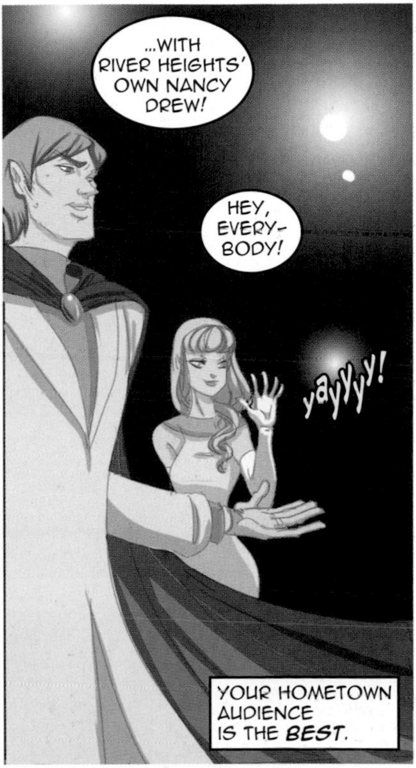
...WITH RIVER HEIGHTS' OWN NANCY DREW!
HEY, EVERY-BODY!
yayyyy!
YOUR HOMETOWN AUDIENCE IS THE *BEST*.

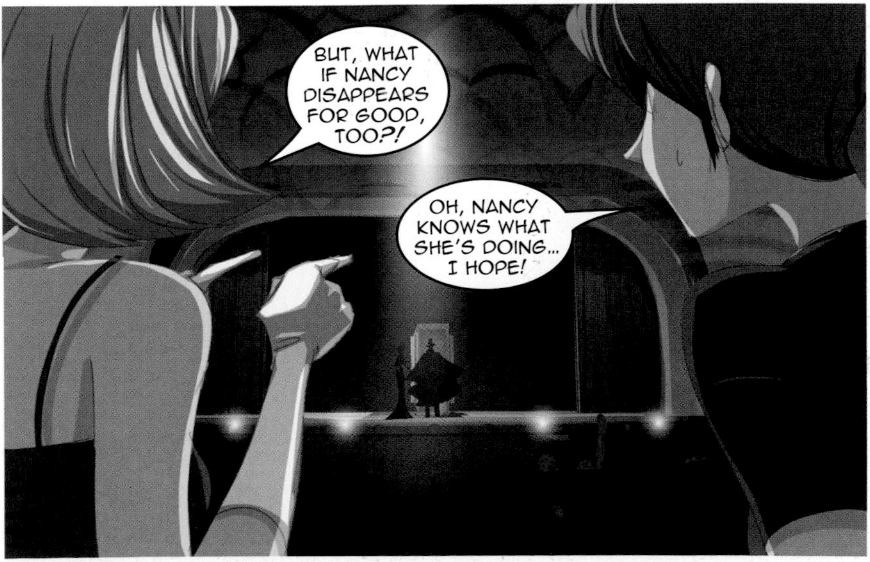
BUT, WHAT IF NANCY DISAPPEARS FOR GOOD, TOO?!
OH, NANCY KNOWS WHAT SHE'S DOING... I HOPE!

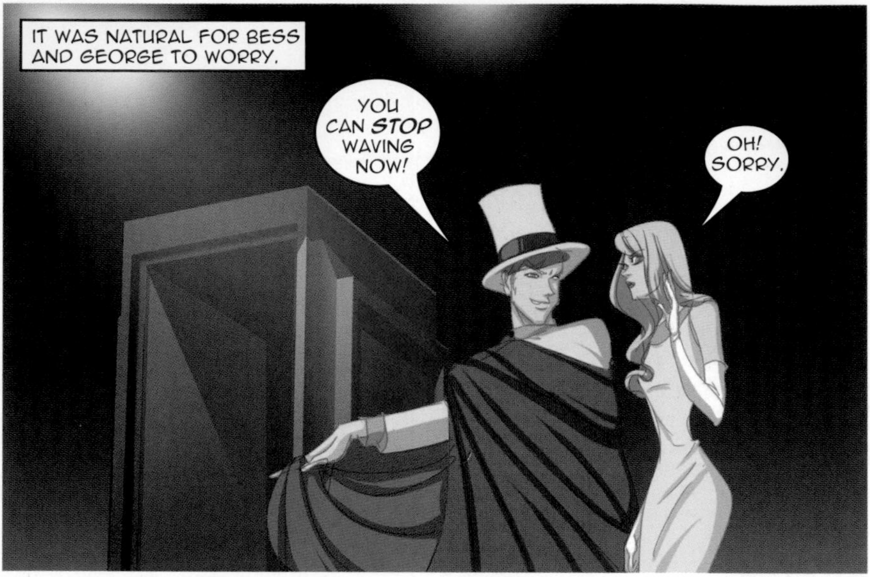
IT WAS NATURAL FOR BESS AND GEORGE TO WORRY.
YOU CAN **STOP** WAVING NOW!
OH! SORRY.

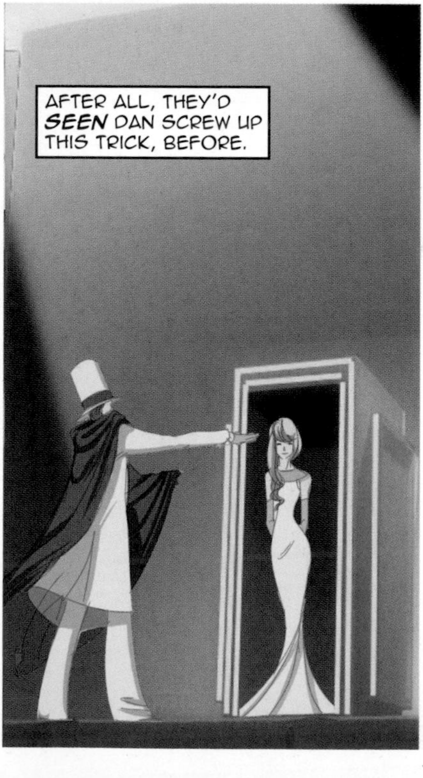
AFTER ALL, THEY'D **SEEN** DAN SCREW UP THIS TRICK, BEFORE.

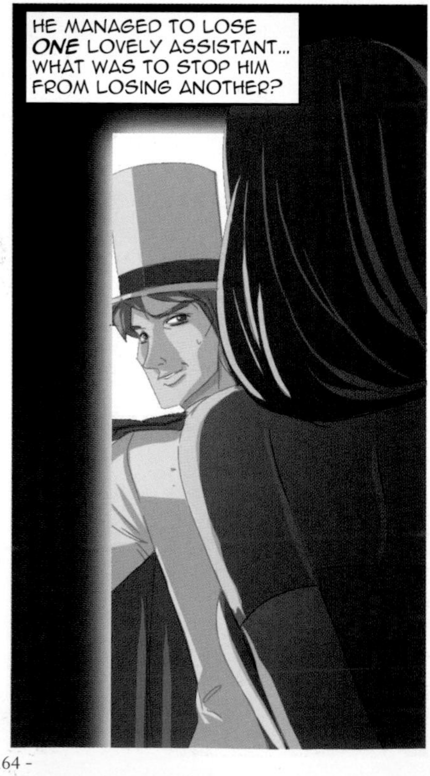
HE MANAGED TO LOSE **ONE** LOVELY ASSISTANT... WHAT WAS TO STOP HIM FROM LOSING ANOTHER?

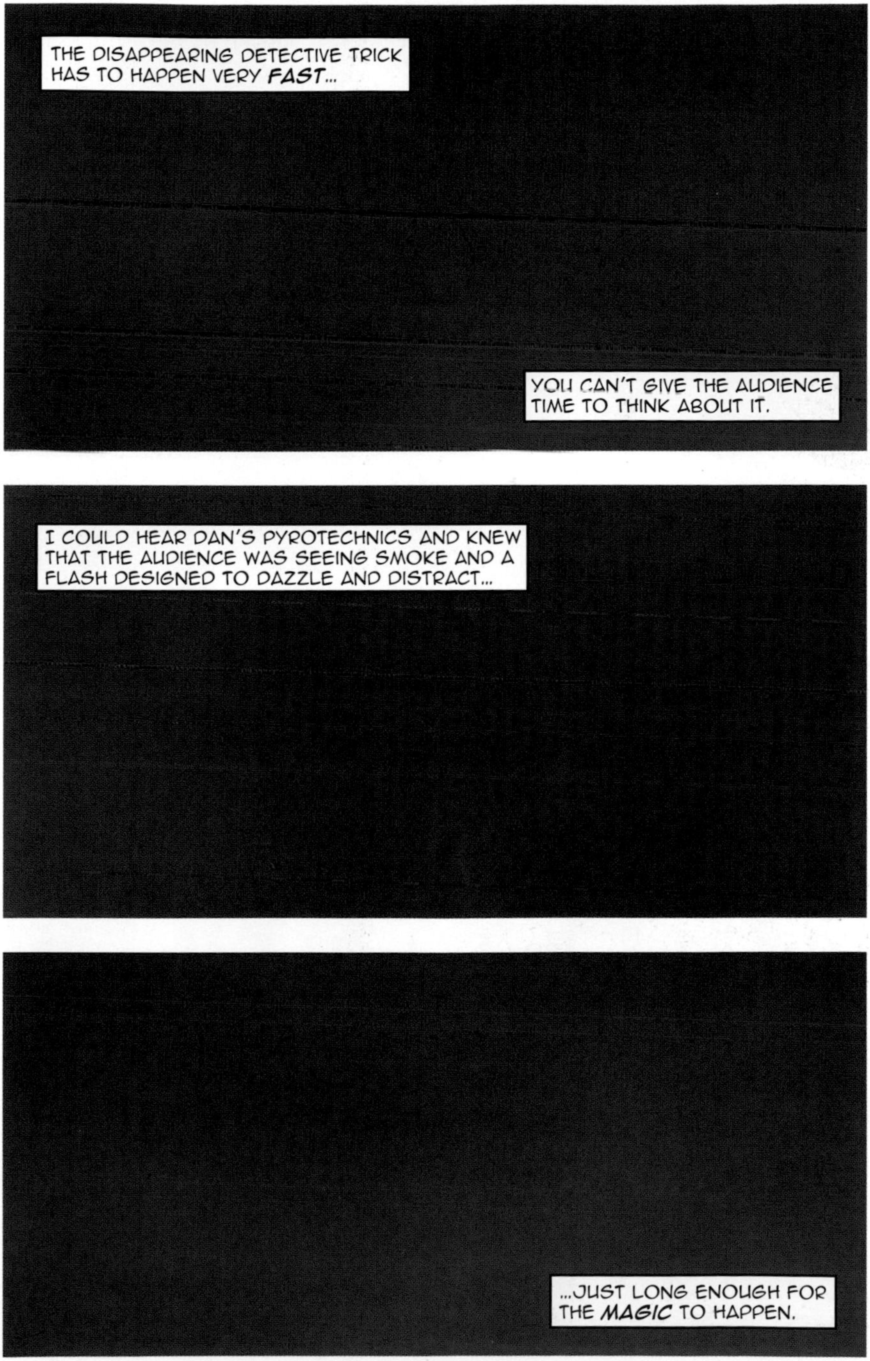
THE DISAPPEARING DETECTIVE TRICK HAS TO HAPPEN VERY FAST...
YOU CAN'T GIVE THE AUDIENCE TIME TO THINK ABOUT IT.
I COULD HEAR DAN'S PYROTECHNICS AND KNEW THAT THE AUDIENCE WAS SEEING SMOKE AND A FLASH DESIGNED TO DAZZLE AND DISTRACT...
...JUST LONG ENOUGH FOR THE MAGIC TO HAPPEN.

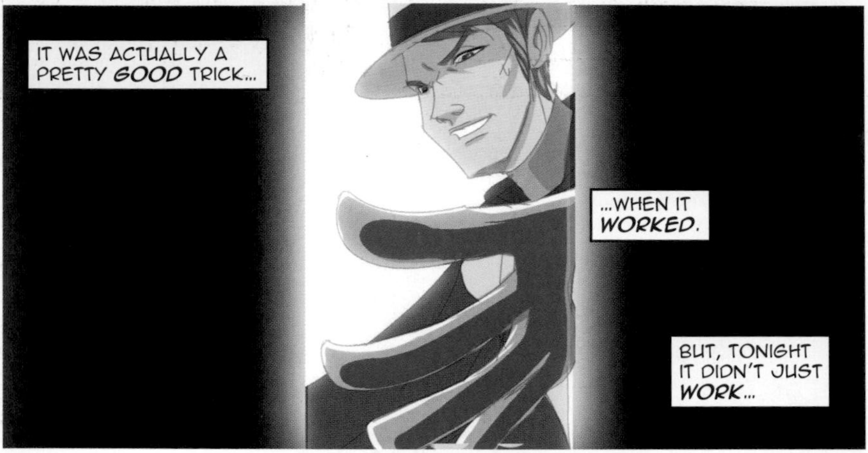
IT WAS ACTUALLY A PRETTY GOOD TRICK...
...WHEN IT WORKED.
BUT, TONIGHT IT DIDN'T JUST WORK...

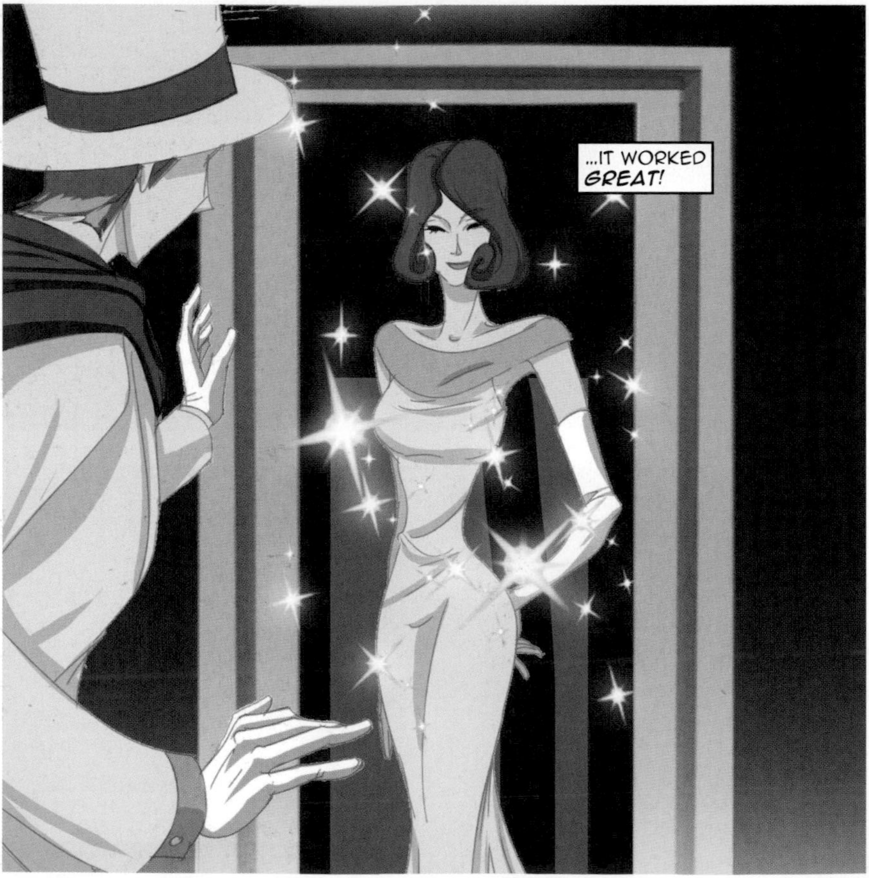
...IT WORKED GREAT!

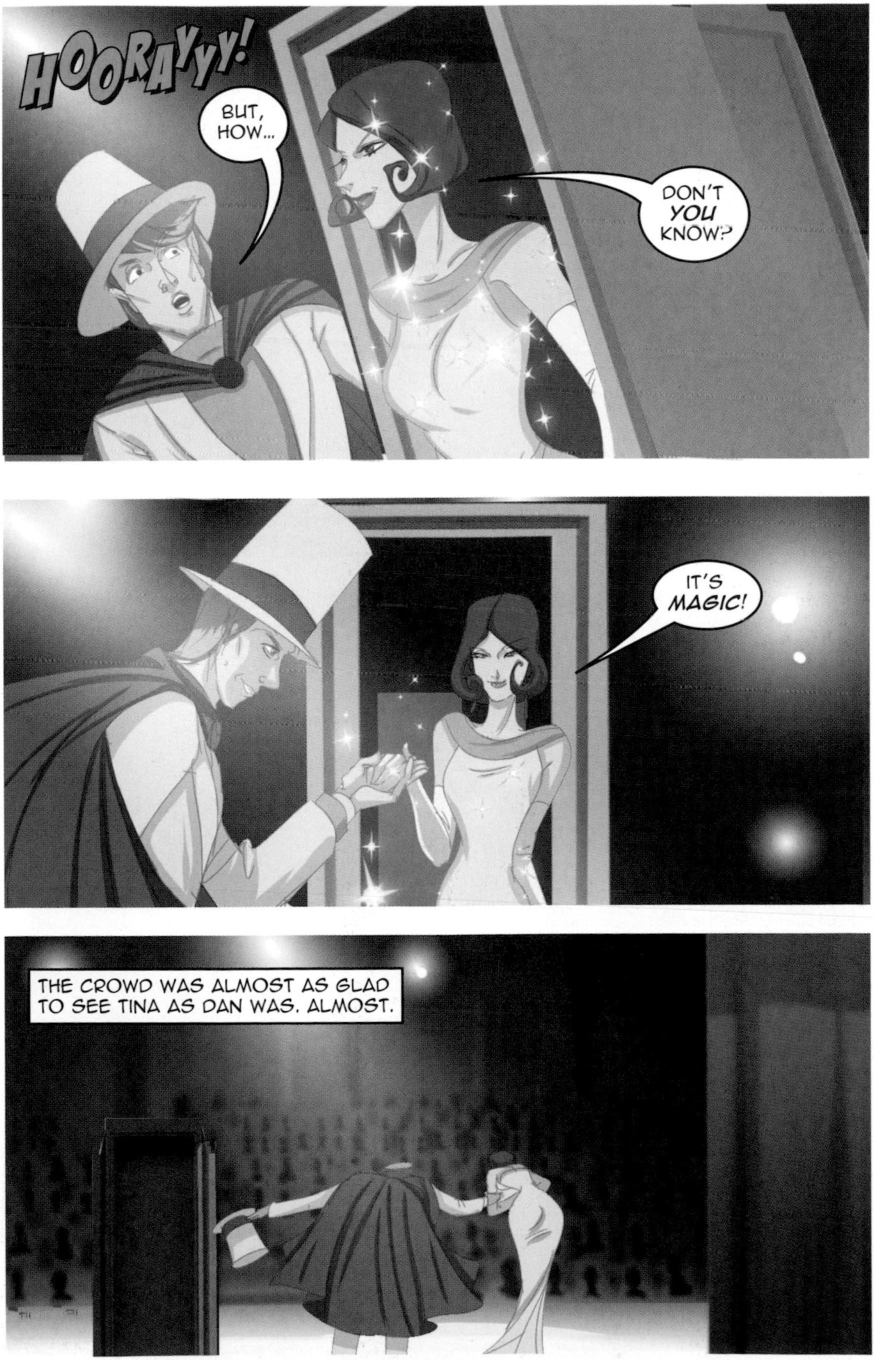
HOORAYYY!
BUT, HOW...
DON'T YOU KNOW?
IT'S MAGIC!
THE CROWD WAS ALMOST AS GLAD TO SEE TINA AS DAN WAS. ALMOST.

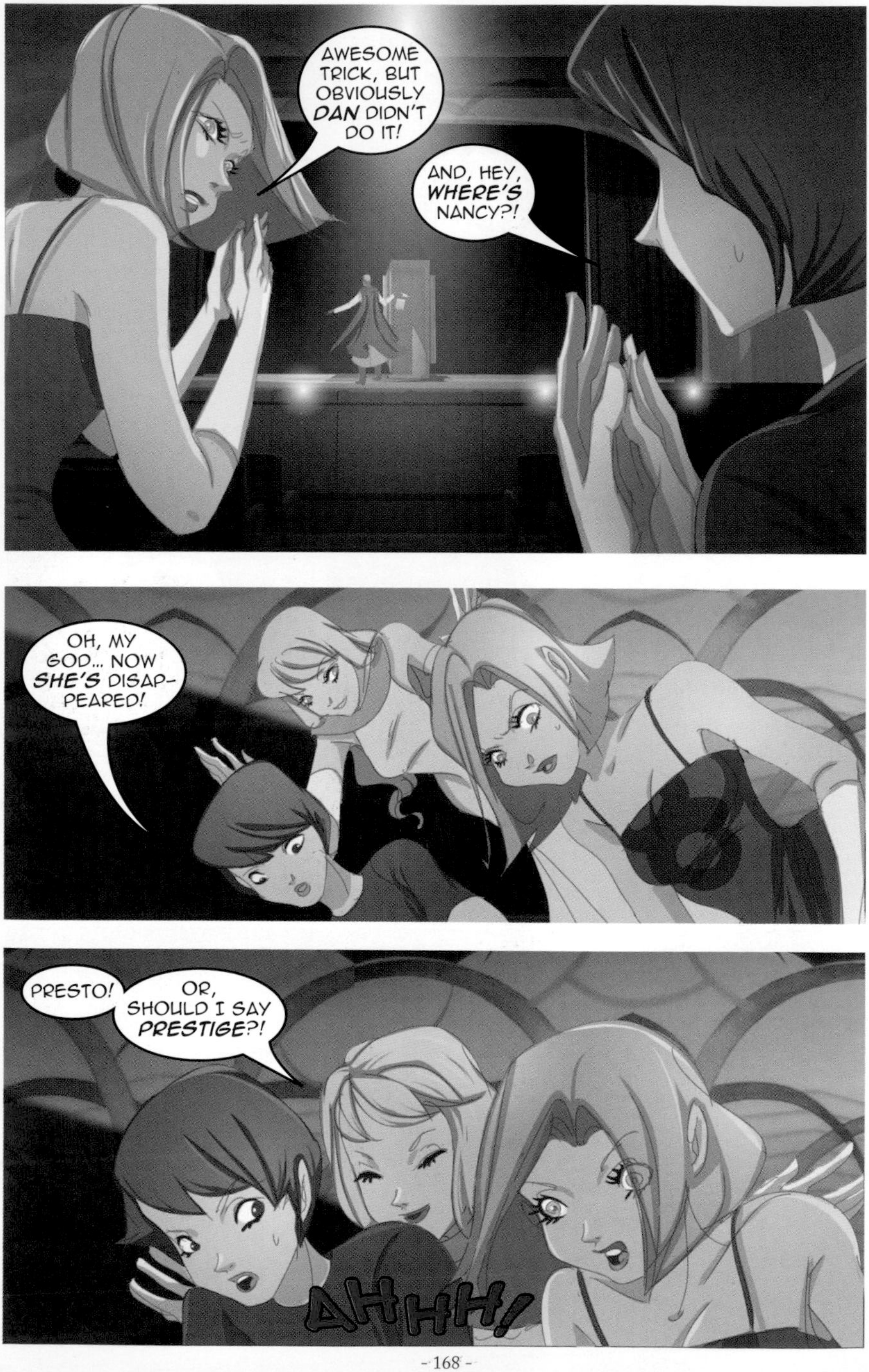
AWESOME TRICK, BUT OBVIOUSLY DAN DIDN'T DO IT!
AND, HEY, WHERE'S NANCY?!
OH, MY GOD... NOW SHE'S DISAPPEARED!
PRESTO!
OR, SHOULD I SAY PRESTIGE?!
AHHH!

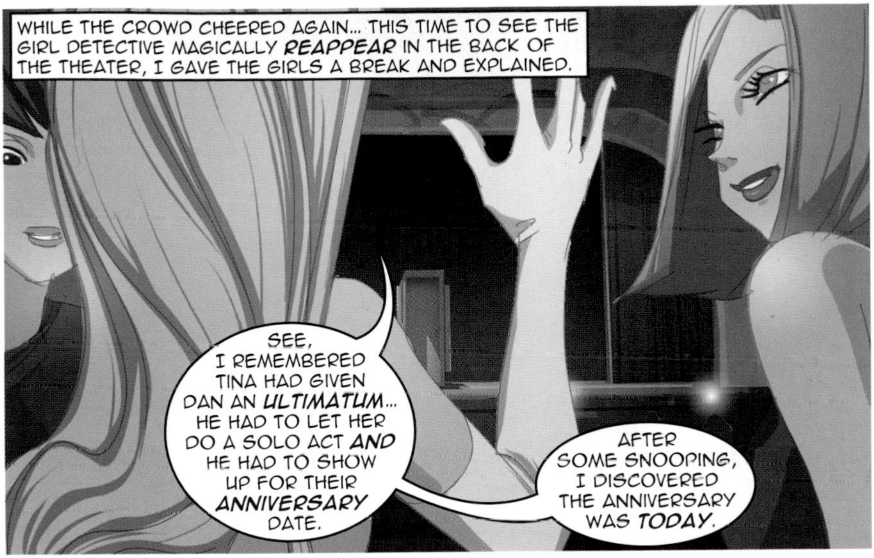
WHILE THE CROWD CHEERED AGAIN... THIS TIME TO SEE THE GIRL DETECTIVE MAGICALLY *REAPPEAR* IN THE BACK OF THE THEATER, I GAVE THE GIRLS A BREAK AND EXPLAINED.
SEE, I REMEMBERED TINA HAD GIVEN DAN AN *ULTIMATUM*... HE HAD TO LET HER DO A SOLO ACT *AND* HE HAD TO SHOW UP FOR THEIR *ANNIVERSARY* DATE.
AFTER SOME SNOOPING, I DISCOVERED THE ANNIVERSARY WAS *TODAY*.

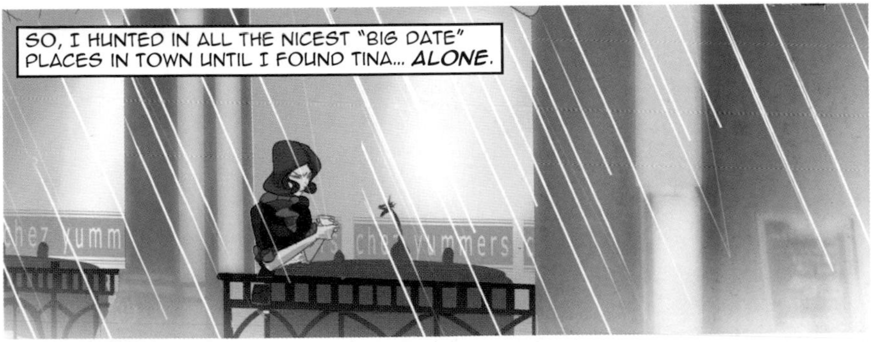
SO, I HUNTED IN ALL THE NICEST "BIG DATE" PLACES IN TOWN UNTIL I FOUND TINA... *ALONE*.

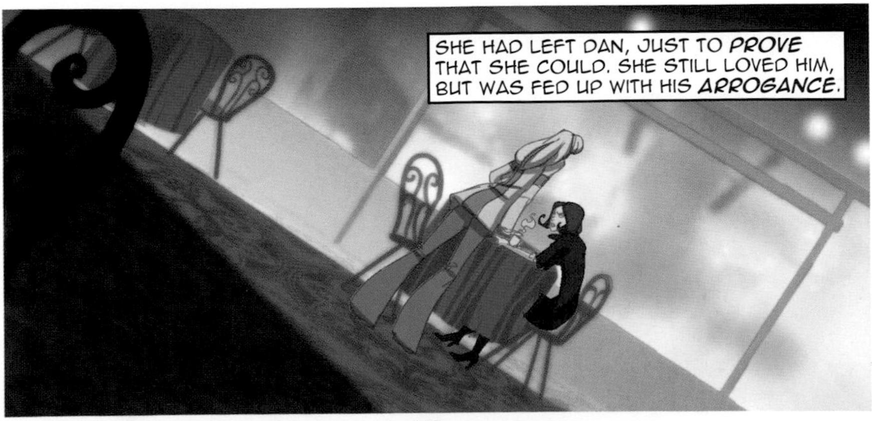
SHE HAD LEFT DAN, JUST TO *PROVE* THAT SHE COULD. SHE STILL LOVED HIM, BUT WAS FED UP WITH HIS *ARROGANCE*.

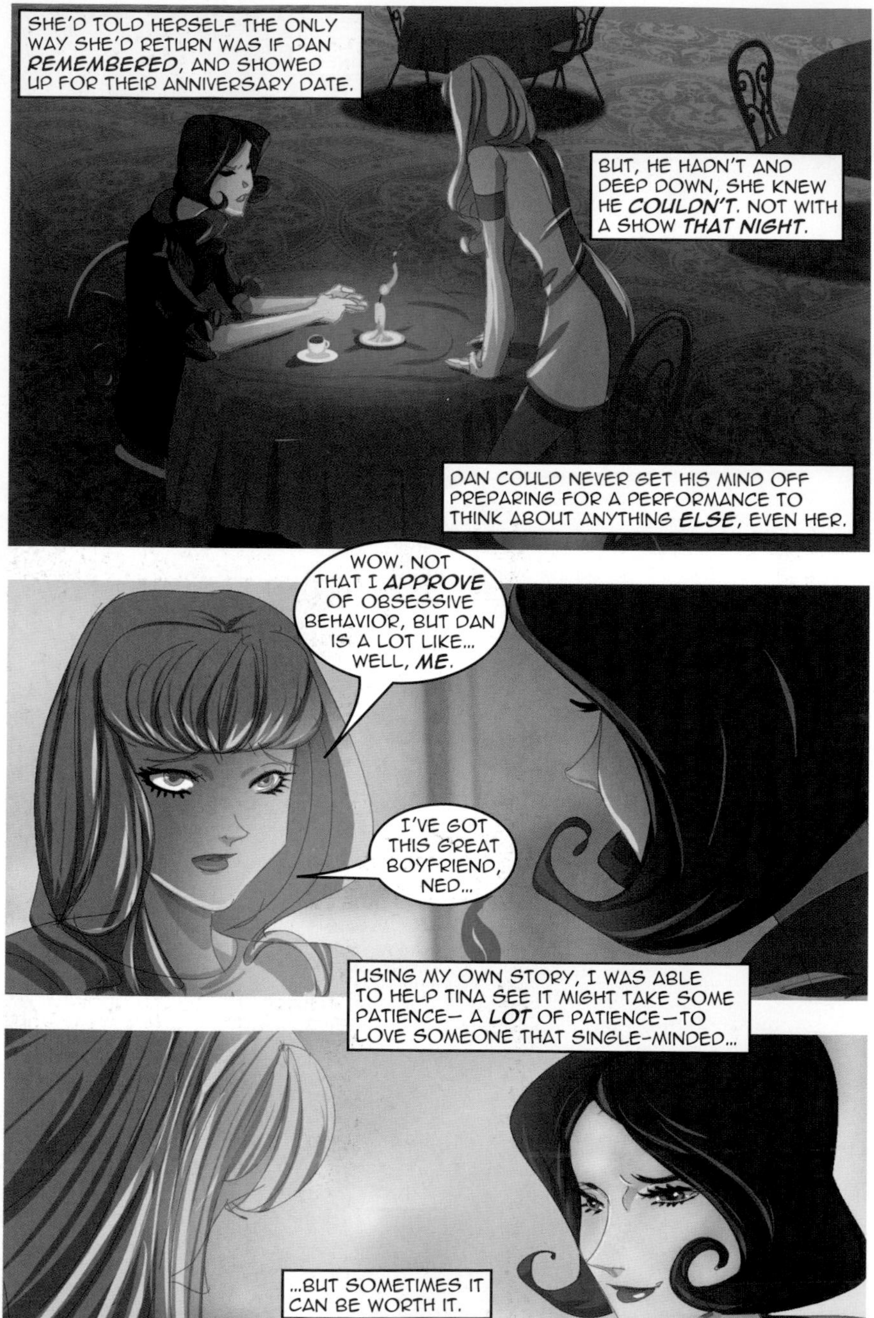

SHE'D TOLD HERSELF THE ONLY WAY SHE'D RETURN WAS IF DAN *REMEMBERED*, AND SHOWED UP FOR THEIR ANNIVERSARY DATE.
BUT, HE HADN'T AND DEEP DOWN, SHE KNEW HE *COULDN'T*. NOT WITH A SHOW *THAT NIGHT*.
DAN COULD NEVER GET HIS MIND OFF PREPARING FOR A PERFORMANCE TO THINK ABOUT ANYTHING *ELSE*, EVEN HER.
WOW. NOT THAT I *APPROVE* OF OBSESSIVE BEHAVIOR, BUT DAN IS A LOT LIKE... WELL, *ME*.
I'VE GOT THIS GREAT BOYFRIEND, NED...
USING MY OWN STORY, I WAS ABLE TO HELP TINA SEE IT MIGHT TAKE SOME PATIENCE— A *LOT* OF PATIENCE—TO LOVE SOMEONE THAT SINGLE-MINDED...
...BUT SOMETIMES IT CAN BE WORTH IT.

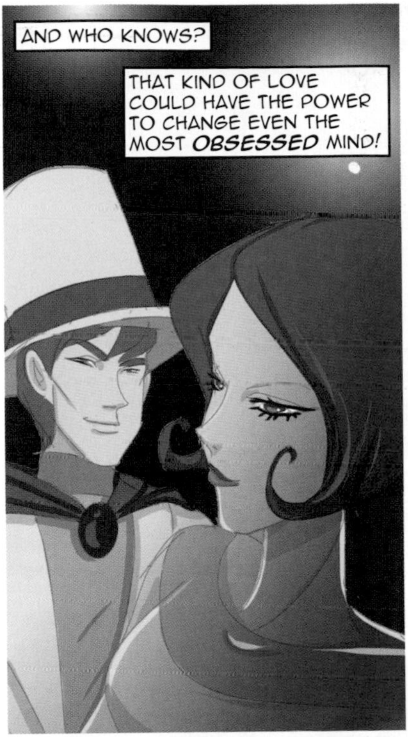
AND WHO KNOWS?
THAT KIND OF LOVE COULD HAVE THE POWER TO CHANGE EVEN THE MOST OBSESSED MIND!

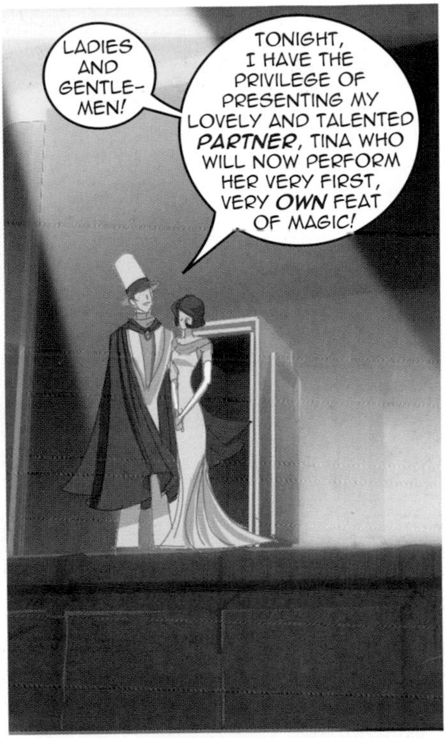
LADIES AND GENTLE-MEN!
TONIGHT, I HAVE THE PRIVILEGE OF PRESENTING MY LOVELY AND TALENTED PARTNER, TINA WHO WILL NOW PERFORM HER VERY FIRST, VERY OWN FEAT OF MAGIC!

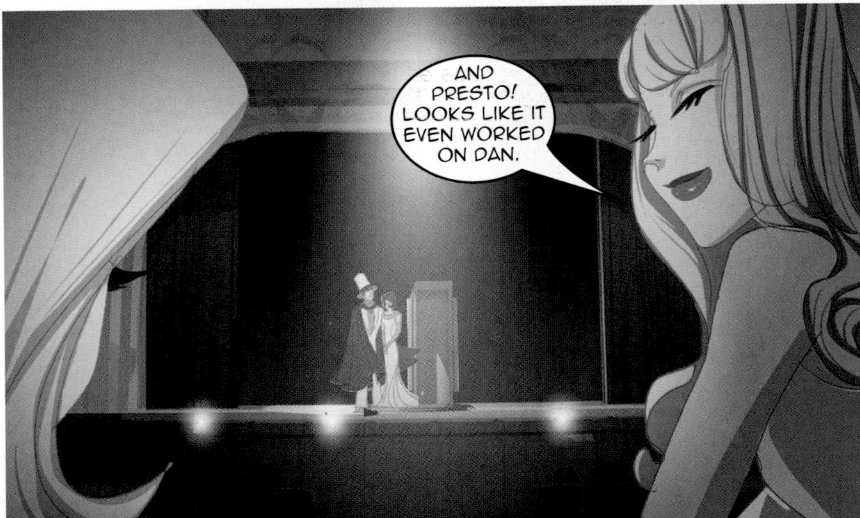
AND PRESTO! LOOKS LIKE IT EVEN WORKED ON DAN.

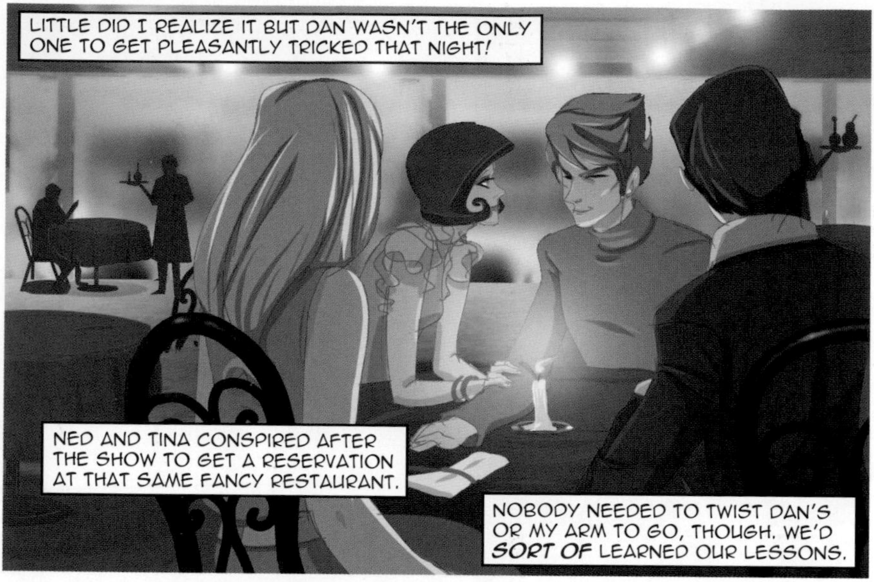
LITTLE DID I REALIZE IT BUT DAN WASN'T THE ONLY ONE TO GET PLEASANTLY TRICKED THAT NIGHT!
NED AND TINA CONSPIRED AFTER THE SHOW TO GET A RESERVATION AT THAT SAME FANCY RESTAURANT.
NOBODY NEEDED TO TWIST DAN'S OR MY ARM TO GO, THOUGH. WE'D SORT OF LEARNED OUR LESSONS.

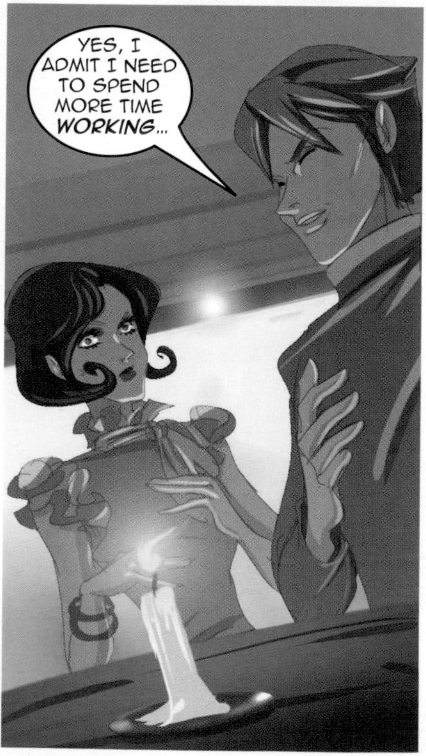
YES, I ADMIT I NEED TO SPEND MORE TIME WORKING...

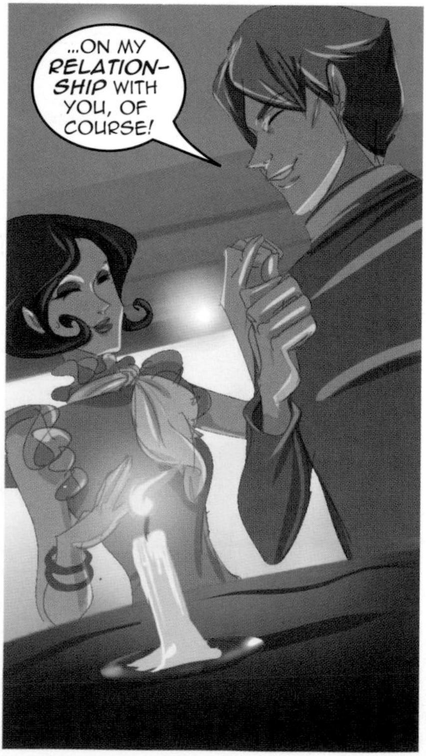
...ON MY RELATIONSHIP WITH YOU, OF COURSE!

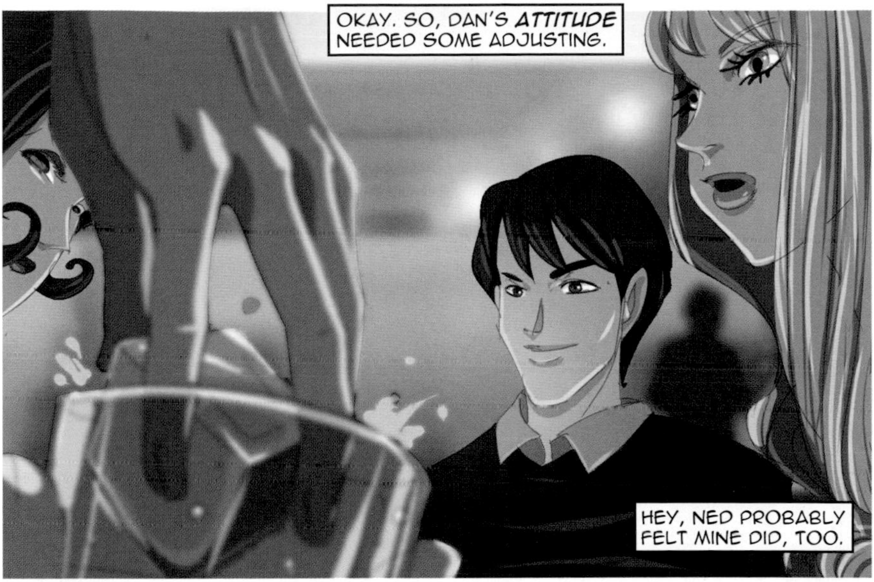
OKAY. SO, DAN'S *ATTITUDE* NEEDED SOME ADJUSTING.
HEY, NED PROBABLY FELT MINE DID, TOO.

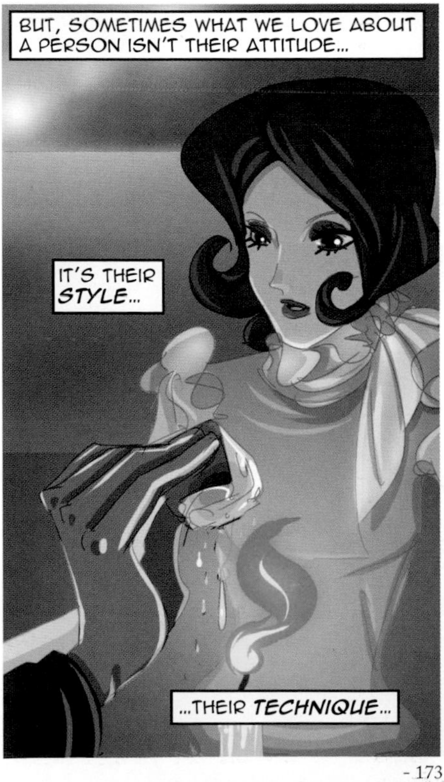
BUT, SOMETIMES WHAT WE LOVE ABOUT A PERSON ISN'T THEIR ATTITUDE...
IT'S THEIR *STYLE*...
...THEIR *TECHNIQUE*...

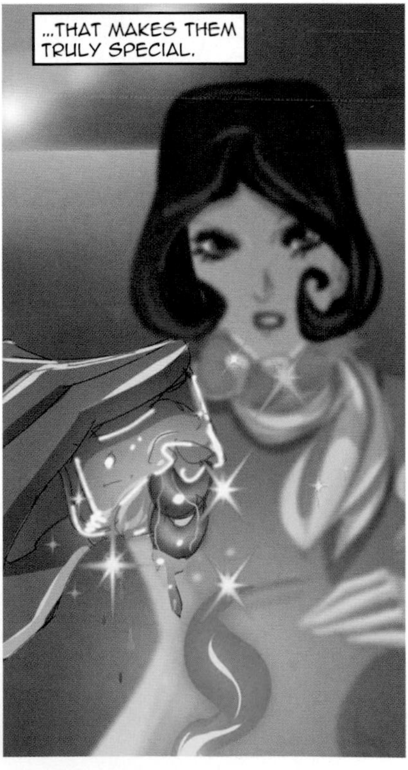
...THAT MAKES THEM TRULY SPECIAL.

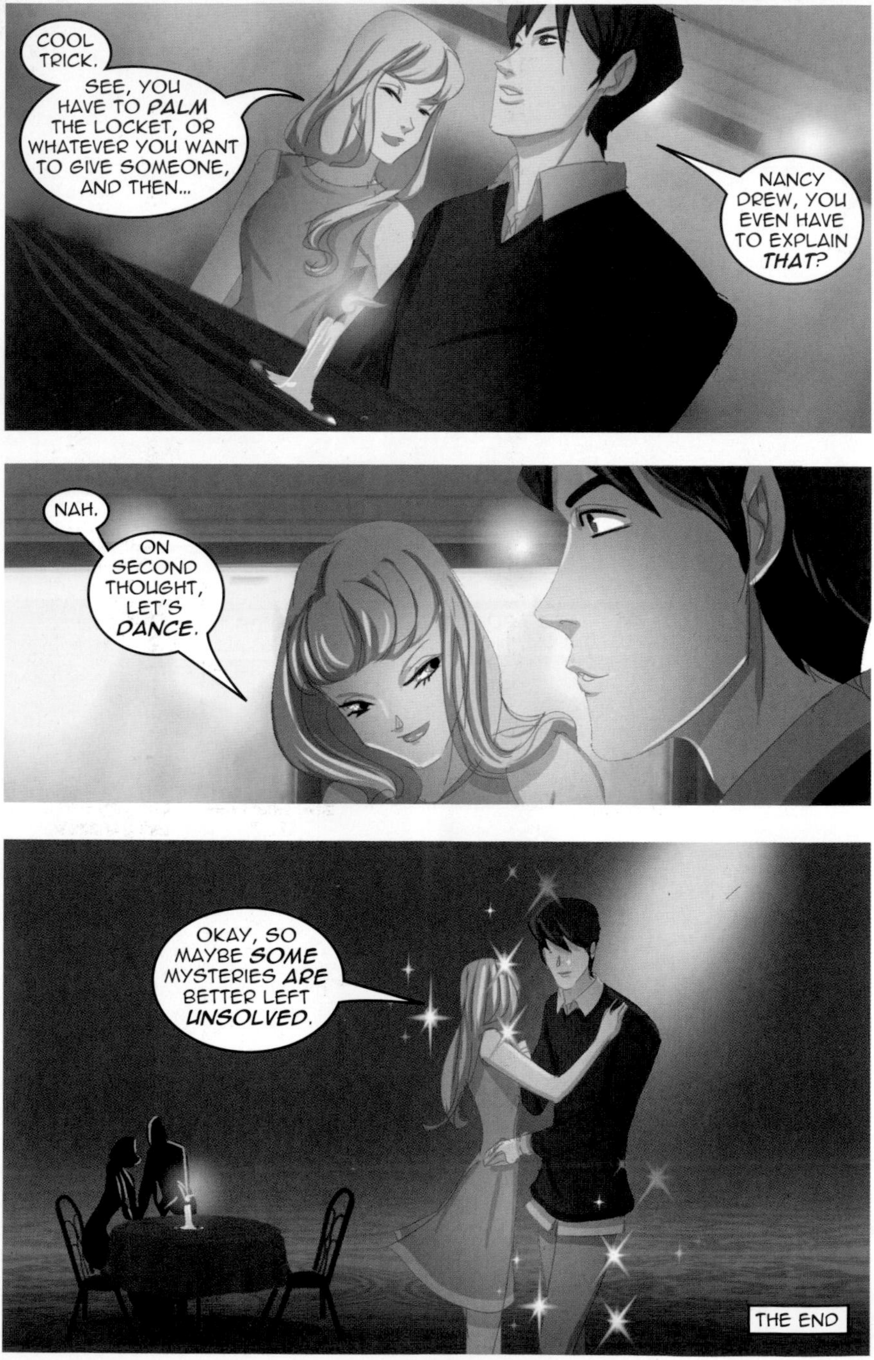
COOL TRICK.
SEE, YOU HAVE TO PALM THE LOCKET, OR WHATEVER YOU WANT TO GIVE SOMEONE, AND THEN...
NANCY DREW, YOU EVEN HAVE TO EXPLAIN THAT?
NAH.
ON SECOND THOUGHT, LET'S DANCE.
OKAY, SO MAYBE SOME MYSTERIES ARE BETTER LEFT UNSOLVED.
THE END

NANCY DREW GRAPHIC NOVELS AVAILABLE FROM PAPERCUTZ

#19 "Cliffhanger"

#12 "Dress Reversal"

#13 "Doggone Town"

#14 "Sleight of Dan"

#15 "Tiger Counter"

#16 "What Goes Up..."

#17 "Night of the Living Chatchke"

#18 "City Under the Basement"

#20 "High School Musical Mystery" 1

#21 "High School Musical Mystery" 2

The New Case Files #1 "Vampire Slayer" Part 1

The New Case Files #2 "Vampire Slayer" Part 2

NANCY DREW graphic novels are available at booksellers everywhere.

NANCY DREW AND THE CLUE CREW graphic novels are $7.99 each in paperback, and $11.99 in hardcover, except #1, which is $6.99 in paperback, $10.99 in hardcover. NANCY DREW GIRL DETECTIVE graphic novels are $7.95 each in paperback and $12.95 each in hardcover. except #20 and 21, $8.99PB/$13.99HC. NANCY DREW THE NEW CASE FILES are $6.99PB/$10.99HC. You may also order online at papercutz.com. Or call 1-800-886-1223, Monday through Friday, 9 – 5 EST. MC, Visa, and AmEx accepted. To order by mail, please add $4.00 for postage and handling for first book ordered, $1.00 for each additional book and make check payable to NBM Publishing. Send to: Papercutz, 160 Broadway, Suite 700, East Wing, New York, NY 10038.

NANCY DREW GIRL DETECTIVE graphic novels are also available digitally wherever e-books are sold.

papercutz.com

Available on the iPad
App Store

Nancy Drew: Ghost of Thornton Hall

Some Families Keep Deadly Secrets!

Jessalyn Thornton's fateful sleepover at the abandoned Thornton estate was supposed to be a pre-wedding celebration, but the fun ended when she disappeared. While her family searches for clues, others refuse to speak about the estate's dark past. Did something supernatural happen to Jessalyn, or is someone in Thornton Hall holding something besides family secrets?

EVERYONE
E | Mild Violence
ESRB CONTENT RATING   www.esrb.org

Copyright © 2014 Her Interactive, Inc. HER INTERACTIVE, the HER INTERACTIVE logo and DARE TO PLAY are trademarks of Her Interactive, Inc. NANCY DREW is a registered trademark of Simon & Schuster, Inc. Licensed by permission of Simon & Schuster, Inc. Other brands or product names are trademarks of their respective holders.